Chronicles
of the
HEdge

A Novel

Jeff Ovall

Xulon Press
344 Maple Ave. West, #302
Vienna, VA 22180
703-691-7595
XulonPress.com

All views expressed are solely the individual author's and do not reflect the position of any governmental agency or department.

All Scripture quotations, unless otherwise indicated, are taken from the Holy Bible; New International Version (NIV). Copyright 1973, 1978, 1984 by International Bible Society.

To Arthur and Lucille Ovall.
Thanks for being great parents. Love you both!

Acknowledgements

As with any major endeavor in life, writing a book is rarely a solo venture. Thanks so much to the many friends and relatives who offered their encouragement and advice throughout this project; especially my two cheerleaders from Toledo, Cindy and Mom.

Thanks, Debra, for your prayers and support, and for being my closest confidant. "So she became his wife, and he loved her." Gen 24:67

To Justyn and Skylar, thank you for understanding the many times when Dad had to plant himself at the keyboard instead of hanging out with you. You are both blessings from God.

And to Tim, it hasn't been the same at the bus stop since you left. Thanks for your friendship and advice. You really made a difference.

"Behold, the days are coming," says the Lord God,
"That I will send a famine on the land,
Not a famine of bread,
Nor a thirst for water,
But of hearing the words of the Lord"

Amos 8:11 (NKJV)

Prologue

Approaching the eve of the third millennium, there was great anticipation for the future of mankind. Optimism flourished, humanity teetered on the edge of the old order, ready to explode into the new.

Slowly, however, the darker side of human nature once again manifested itself. The quest for power became paramount to all else; territorial politics and class battles became the cry of the day. Dreams of the perfect world began to fade.

These struggles saw many groups fall from the political landscape. As with the early Church, those professing a Christian faith became outcasts. Under heavy persecution, they were forced to practice their faith in secret underground enclaves. Their persecutors were determined to finish the Christian genocide that had begun over two thousand years ago.

Humanity's Edge (HEdge) is the reigning world government. Ten consortium members representing every sector of the globe make up the HEdge Council, the supreme authority of the land. Forty Sector Chiefs were tendered appointments to oversee the world's finances; appointments only the HEdge Council could terminate.

Living under the shadows of this godless regime, Christians risk their lives daily as they struggle to share the gospel of Jesus Christ. And as the war rages, God's people don't falter, but instead rise to the occasion in a mighty way.

So the struggle continues; the evils of the world seducing the souls of the many, while God's remnant battles against all odds to bring salvation to a lost and dying world.

Chapter

1

The intersection of Christopher Street and McDougal was always a heavily trafficked corner. It sat in the heart of one of Manhattan's many popular tourist spots. More subdued than the blazing hundred-story neon outlined buildings of the Times Square area, it enjoyed a relaxed atmosphere of quaint ethnic restaurants, pubs, and novelty shops. Thousands of people from every niche of society merged on this corner daily, and amazingly, even with its maelstrom of human activity, life managed to quietly coalesce from one day into the next without so much as a back page story.

Today, however, would be different.

Seated at an end table near the window of one of the corner's busy restaurants, John Rex sipped his coffee while keeping a vigil on the sidewalk outside. A medium sized man in his late thirties; John was blessed with a sharp mind and a healthy trim body.

The round table he was seated at was barely large enough to support his coffee and lunch plate. He stretched while glancing at the neon wall clock. Time was moving at a tediously slow pace. He took another sip. He was on his second cup, considering a third.

He was excited at the prospect of meeting his childhood friend, Andrew, after so many years. John reflected back to when he left New

York City as a young boy with his mother, moving to California. His parents had divorced, and not wanting to remain in the same town as her husband, his mother accepted a job offer clear across the country. The relocation was harsh on the family. His older brother was forced to stay with his father, while John was swept across country with mom. With his family in ruins, John was also forced to leave his very best friend, Andrew, behind. The memories ached.

But now, for the first time since pulling away from the curb in front of his childhood home decades ago, waiving goodbye to his dad, his brother, and his best friend, John was about to meet Andrew again. He could hardly wait.

He was also looking forward to meeting Keeyon, a close friend of Andrew's. Like Andrew, Keeyon was a missionary in the Eastern United States Sector. John held them both in the highest regard, along with all the other missionaries that served in this treacherous region. Though HEdge military forces were a power to be reckoned with all across the globe, the Eastern U.S. Sector Forces were especially ruthless. They trampled Christianity with a determination only Satan himself could appreciate.

John ran his fingers through his dense beard. Since most of the photographs circulating through HEdge showed him with a younger, clean-shaven face, the beard was a necessity. Some of the composite drawings came close, but not enough to distinguish him from millions of other men with beards. His wife, Melody, thought the whiskers gave him a boyish cuteness and was quietly tickled that he finally let it grow out.

Melody was a loving woman who had survived many close calls and near disasters while sharing her faith alongside her husband. She never left his side or his convictions. Caring for their eleven-year-old son, Matthew, prevented her from accompanying John on many of his missionary trips. But she would always keep him in her prayers.

The Western U.S. Sector's underground Christian network provided abundant support for her and Matthew during her husband's absences. The network had millions of Christians spanning the sector from the central United States to the west coast; a network in which her husband was consummately involved.

Unfortunately, Melody and Matthew could not accompany John on this trip. He wanted to bring them along, especially to meet Andrew, but the dangers inherent in the Eastern U.S. Sector made that impossible. Combing his fingers through his beard, he sat immersed in deep thought. Gone only two days and he already missed them so much. "I'll bring them next time to meet Andrew," he sighed; unaware he was making a commitment he would never be able to keep.

Almost before he finished his thought, two familiar shapes appeared across the street. The pair came from around the corner, stopped in front of the corner pub and stood talking to one another.

The bustling crowds kept passing in front blocking John's view of them. He could see that one was a tall dark skinned man with short hair, the other was thinner built, light skinned with medium length brown hair. An excitement welled up inside. "Andrew and Keeyon?"

The dark skinned man stepped in front of the other, blocking John's view of him. Finally, John decided he had had enough. The anticipation was too much. He got up from the table, swiped his debit card through the scanner near the front door, and stepped outside.

Leaving the shaded protection of the cafe, the dizzying hot rays of the early afternoon sun beat down on him. Starting across the street, he laid his hand over his brows to avert the sun. He was halfway across when the darker gentleman stepped aside, allowing John a clear view of the other man. Much to his joy, he was indeed his old friend, Andrew.

Andrew saw him at the same instant. Both men's faces lit up. John speeded his pace. Andrew motioned something to Keeyon while starting toward the street. The two men merged as John stepped over the curb.

Andrew's face aglow, he held out is hand. John took it while asking in his childhood slang, "How's it going, big head?" That was it. Andrew laughed as he pulled John into a full embrace. John returned the hug with every bit as much enthusiasm.

Feeling somewhat like a third wheel, Keeyon stood with his hands dangling in his pockets, looking beyond his friends to the rush of tourists behind them.

The Village Pub was as busy as ever. A minimum of four bartenders was necessary to properly serve the raucous crowds meandering in and out. It was a favorite watering hole for local residents and tourists alike.

Herb Duncan, one of its bartenders, was on his way to deliver two foaming mugs to a young couple seated near the window. The obese and unkempt bartender abruptly dropped the mugs on their table while demanding payment in full. His only hint of a business-like courtesy was a half grunt, half thanks, as the young man gingerly placed a debit card into his waiting palm.

On his way back to the counter, Herb decided a breath of fresh air was in order. He would return the customer's card afterward. He yelled above the crowd's roar to inform another bartender that he was going outside for a minute. "Longest minute in history," he mused.

Entering the doorway, he elbowed an inbound customer and threw his belly into a few others as he pummeled his way through the swinging door. "Watch it, punk!" he threatened as one of the customers objected.

Once outside, he sucked in a deep breath. The stench he was forced to inhale daily inside the pub nearly drove him mad. He hated the place and he detested the tourists, always asking for directions or complaining about something. He couldn't remember the last time they left him a tip worth talking about. Cheap lowlifes! If he could, he would send every one of them back home in a box.

Feeling a need to vent, he began cursing every tourist in sight, quietly swearing at each, especially the happy ones. How dare they enjoy themselves on this miserable day in this miserable city. He hated them all.

Scanning the entire corner, he was nearly finished when he noticed an especially disturbing sight, two men shaking hands then hugging each other. They seemed deliriously happy. Whatever the occasion, Herb knew they weren't pretending; he could see tears streaming down their faces. They were probably long lost relatives, maybe brothers who haven't seen each other in years. He hated watching them. The only brother he had was a drunken bum who only showed up on holidays for a free meal.

These two were really beginning to annoy him. Didn't they have anywhere else to flaunt their stupid emotions? He watched one of them turn to a black man and embrace him too. As he stared contemptuously at the three men, something occurred to him. The men looked familiar, something about them. He knew them from somewhere. The brown haired man looked especially familiar. *But why?*

Maybe he had served them a drink? No, that wasn't it. Something else. But what was it?

Then it struck him. "You've got to be kidding me!" he gasped excitedly. "Is that John Rex? No, can't be. Yeah, that's him, cept he's got a beard! And the black guy, that's Keeyon Webster! And the other guy's Andrew Hoyte! This is unbelievable!"

Ducking back inside, he rushed over to call the police.

Herb Duncan considered himself a fair man, someone who would do just about anything for anyone. In fact, he thought of himself as probably the nicest guy he knew. But even he had his limits, and Christianity was certainly it. He despised Christians; he loathed them, the intolerant beasts! And here was a wonderful opportunity to get rid of three of them all at once!

He couldn't believe his luck. Not even two weeks ago HEdge Forces had circulated pictures through the neighborhood of some of the most wanted criminals in the Sector, and today, right outside his pub, stood three of the worst!

"Maybe this isn't such a bad day after all." Herb chuckled as he dialed the six-digit Christian Hot-line number. "Not a bad day at all."

Unaware of the excitement their presence had aroused, the happy trio of Keeyon, Andrew, and John, departed around the corner on their way to a relaxed and comfortable locale, where they could engage in a good meal and some good conversation, discussing old times along with new.

Chapter

2

The attention of every straining face within the crammed New York State Auditorium was focused on the front stage. The fortunate ones stirred in their seats, twitching their eyes back and forth, being teased by any hint of activity from up front, while the remaining thousands, having arrived too late to be seated in the enormous auditorium, stood anxiously in the isles, waiting eagerly to hear this man of global importance speak to them of worldly issues, and how those issues would affect their lives.

Centered at the forefront of the acoustically engineered auditorium was a massive, brightly glossed, wooden stage. The stage covered an area half the size of a football field. It was adorned from one end to the other with large beige, tulip-shaped vases. Each vase stood two foot tall with bright flower bouquets stretching another foot. Vivid colors were splashed throughout the floral arrangements, bringing an exuberant glow to the stage.

The cordless ultra-sensitive microphone clicked with nervous electricity as it patiently sat, center stage, mounted on a six-foot metallic stand, as though pleading for someone to lift it and show the world what it could do.

Outside the enormous building, beyond the lavender draped walls of the air-conditioned auditorium, stood thousands more restless citizens waiting in the sweltering heat of the afternoon sun. Each begging for some movement in the endless lines, wishing hopelessly for a chance to pass beyond the police barricades and through the majestic doors of the auditorium, to listen to Samuel Treppin speak.

Back inside, a steady hum of excitement rippled through the audience. Waves of anxious sighs followed any sudden noises escaping from the front. A low rumble of determined cheers began reverberating from the rear of the auditorium, spreading quickly until finally, like an out of control virus, the entire hall erupted into a wild chorus of thundering applause. The very walls of the building seemed to throb from the roars of the overcharged crowds.

Behind the massive stage curtains, out of sight from the delirious audience, over-wrought stagehands were quickly arranging musical instruments for the second time in the last sixty minutes. Mr. Benjamin Gordon and Mr. Thomas Jerome ordered the musicians back on stage since the Sector Chief had not yet arrived.

As the stagehands were running this way and that, Mr. Jerome gave Mr. Gordon a frantic, desperate stare. Clutching the hairs on both sides of his head, he turned towards the screaming audience, then back to Mr. Gordon. "Where is he? How could a guy that travels with an army of security guards suddenly disappear? Why haven't we heard from him, Ben? What in blazes are we going to do?"

Beyond perplexed, Mr. Jerome was outright distressed. Leaning against the wall, he swung his open palm into it, then yelped from the predictable pain it brought.

"Ben!" he exclaimed while vigorously shaking his hand. "These people are getting unglued! If Treppin doesn't show up soon they're liable to turn this place upside down! We've got to tell them something. Anything! What about saying Treppin's sick? The band can play for a couple more hours while everyone clears out. The crowd won't be happy, but at least they won't be building up more steam!"

"Talk to me, Ben!" he pleaded. "What are we going to do?"

Benjamin Gordon stood noncommittal in deep thought. Long furrows etched across his mahogany face highlighting the many challenging years he's managed the complex. His arms were crossed, resting on his small but developed potbelly. Raising his left hand, he began rubbing his chin in a slow methodical motion.

This had to be the biggest turnout in the fifteen years he's managed the place. All the old attendance records were being shattered, and the numbers would be even more staggering if you included the thousands still outside clamoring to get in.

He tried to recall the last time any Sector Chief gave a public speech on HEdge policy rather than simply stating the policy and letting politicians relay it to the public. At least five years, he thought, and Treppin gave that speech too.

"Amazing," Mr. Gordon pondered aloud, "as important as Treppin's people said this speech was, you'd think he would have arrived by now."

He realized most of the other Sector Chiefs wouldn't have given this crowd a second thought. "Let them wait," would have been their attitude. But Treppin was different; he was more considerate than that. Mr. Gordon recalled some of the occasions he had observed Treppin mingling with common folk, like the time he showed up unannounced in a congested shopping center with his security guards in tow. The guards were clearly upset with the whole affair, scanning the crowds for threatening shoppers, while Treppin openly enjoyed himself, squeezing through the crowds, shaking hands and sharing small talk. Several people fainted from the excitement of having a Sector Chief in their midst, while others rushed to get a closer look.

No, Gordon concluded, Treppin wasn't like the other Sector Chiefs; at least he didn't used to be. Not unless the seven years on the job has finally gotten to his head.

"I hope not," he sighed inwardly.

Benjamin considered the scenario. How dumb could he have been letting Treppin's people convince him to allow general admission for an event this big? But they were adamant. They said Treppin wanted the affair to be like a friendly town hall meeting. They insisted general admission was the best way to go. Less hassles so more people would show up.

"Ha!" he blew out a laugh. The idea of general admission for a headliner like Samuel Treppin suddenly struck him as morbidly funny. How could he have been so blind?

They had to handle this situation with extreme caution. He realized the dangerous waters into which he and Mr. Jerome were treading. Sector Chiefs were only a position below the HEdge Council and therefore had to be treated delicately. The wrong move, the wrong decision, could well cost them their jobs, if not more.

Loosening his stoic demeanor, Ben pulled a handkerchief from his shirt pocket and wiped the moisture from his forehead. He turned towards the audience and took a deep breath. His stomach was burning from an ulcer he'd been fighting the last few months, which made the whole matter even more unbearable. But he had to deal with it nonetheless, and the first order of business was to set Thomas Jerome straight. He didn't like what he was hearing from his long time partner.

"So tell me, Tom," he began, "do you really want to go out there and tell thousands of exasperated people that their honorable Mr. Treppin won't be gracing them with his presence today, because he's sick? Do you really want to tell them that, only to have Mr. Treppin and his entourage arrive five minutes later? And then do you want to face Treppin himself, and explain how you felt the crowds were getting a little too antsy so you sent them all home packing?" He paused to let the thought sink in.

"Tom, this is no time to fall apart. We have to control this situation, not let it control us! We've done everything we possibly can up to this point; security is on riot alert, local HEdge forces have been put on notice, and we're sending the band out again to keep the crowds occupied. For right now, that's all we can do!"

Ben raised both hands in the direction of the screaming audience. "Can you hear those people? About half of them have been waiting in that horrid line for well over twenty-four hours! Some for over two days, who knows how long the rest of those nuts have been waiting. And you want to just send them on their merry way? As though this were some kind of rained out picnic or something?"

He began pacing in a circle. Thomas followed behind, step for step.

"And then there's Treppin," Benjamin continued, "do you really want to face him with that story? I don't think so."

Benjamin increased his pace. Unable to keep up, Thomas found a safe haven outside the circle and remained there, watching and listening.

"Just consider what our options are, Tom. Better yet, consider what they aren't! Because I don't really see any right now, other than what we're doing. If we close the place down, we risk a riot. Worse yet, our necks would be on the block for Treppin's people! No, Tom, forget that option. Just forget it. It won't work. Not yet anyway."

Mr. Gordon stopped his traipsing for a second. "Tom, we have no choice but to stall. Whatever it takes to get from now to the time Treppin walks through those doors, or we get word from his camp of other intentions; one or the other. But until then, we have to stay on course; keep the band playing and keep security on alert."

He grabbed Thomas by the shoulders. "Face it, Tom, we have a fifty-fifty chance of coming out of this with our heads still intact. We have to ride this one out, buddy. We have to."

Thomas shook his head in weary resolve. Ben was right, as usual. He always had a way of setting the facts in their proper order, even if that order wasn't to your liking.

"Yeah, okay," Thomas muttered, his shoulders drooping. "But I hope he gets here quick."

"He has to," Ben agreed. "He has to."

With the debate over, Benjamin Gordon and Thomas Jerome walked despondently back to their own offices and got on their respective videophones to contact security. Both demanded an update on exterior and interior crowd control. Both dreading what the replies would eventually be, and both ending the discussion with the same desperate plea, "Oh, and by the way, has anyone heard from Samuel Treppin yet?"

Chapter

3

Standing in front of the metal reinforced door, the tall pallid man reached under his collar for the thin necklace that hung loosely around his neck. Pulling the necklace over his head, a small link in the chain caught a lock of his stringy dark hair. The man let out a deranged curse as he finished pulling the chain over. Eyeing it quickly, he grabbed the small plastic disk fastened to it and pressed it over a circular scanner mounted beside the door. He held it there for barely a second, and then removed it. The large door immediately began rising into the grooved opening in the ceiling, until a second had passed, and it was gone.

Confronting the tall man from the inside of the doorway was a stocky female HEdge security guard. She was standing erect, poised for resistance, both arms lifted slightly from her sides, her holster gleaming with an automatic weapon slicked for easy access. Behind her stood another guard, only male, taller and meaner, but more at ease.

The male guard recognized at once the shallow dark eyes and colorless features of the man standing in the doorway. He discreetly tapped the female on her back. Looking up to the tall man, he politely rendered a greeting. "Good afternoon, Mr. Banchard. Can we help you with anything, sir?"

Without acknowledging the guard's welcome or offer of assistance, Roderick Banchard entered the passageway, brushing past the female guard without so much as a glance. The male guard carefully stepped aside to allow him clear passage, fully understanding the man's inaudible reply, "Shut up and get out of my way. If I need any help I'll ask for it."

Banchard's black-leather shoes squeaked as they made contact with the marble floor in the lobby. Upon reaching the elevators, the squeaks were replaced with a harsh thudding as Roderick pounded the elevator call-button.

Within seconds the elevator arrived. Its doors flew open for the pallid man, and then closed again with him as the sole passenger.

Inside, he grunted, "Fifty-nine." An animated female voice responded softly, "Floor fifty-nine," as the elevator began its smooth assent up the long shaft.

As he stood gripping the waist-high bronze rail circling the inside of the elevator, Roderick's mind raced over the events of the last thirty minutes.

First, a call came in from the 19th precinct in lower Manhattan. A bartender claimed to have spotted John Rex, Andrew Hoyte and Keeyon Webster outside his pub in old Greenwich Village.

Then a second call; Benjamin Gordon requesting HEdge troop support at the New York State Auditorium. Apparently the crowds were getting edgy waiting for Treppin. Gordon was afraid they might tear the place apart if he doesn't show up soon. Normally Roderick would have deferred the request to the New York police department. But it was customary for HEdge Forces to assist anytime a high-ranking HEdge official was involved; and a Sector Chief certainly qualified as that.

Roderick was actually happy for the request. He had a score to settle with Benjamin Gordon anyway. After receiving several reports of secret Christian gatherings inside the auditorium, with Gordon constantly denying any knowledge of them, Roderick had almost given up on the issue. But he never stopped being suspicious. He was convinced they were happening, and that Gordon knew. In fact, some of the reports even mentioned him by name as a key organizer.

And now Gordon is asking for HEdge troop support? Not a problem!

Roderick grinned. He would be happy to oblige Gordon in his time of need. Of course other matters had to be taken into consideration as well, such as the potential danger the auditorium posed to society with all its alleged illegal activities. But that little matter would be easily remedied. Gordon would understand. Roderick snickered.

Before leaving his office Roderick ordered half his New York based HEdge Forces on standby alert ready to mobilize on a moment's notice. Which he intended to give once he reached the Eastern U.S. Sector HEdge Command and discussed the issue with Samuel Treppin; if Treppin was still there.

"But John Rex, Andrew Hoyte, and Keeyon Webster, together! Now that was exciting news!" A wicked grin consumed his face.

"Imagine that," he reveled, "John Rex, right in our own back yard!"

HEdge intelligence reported he was coming east. And now he has finally arrived! An excited quiver rushed through Roderick as he considered what the next few hours could unfold: First Benjamin Gordon shut down for good; then Rex, Hoyte, and Webster, captured!

"This is too much!" he thrilled.

Fully enjoying himself, he burst into a high-pitched giggle. "Too much! Just too much!" The giggling got louder.

Suddenly the elevator stopped and the doors flew open. Standing in the lobby were three grim security guards, as surprised as he, watching him giggle to himself.

Slightly embarrassed, Roderick pulled himself together as he exited the elevator and trounced past the guards. Caught in the awkward moment, the three guards looked around as if they had suddenly misplaced something.

Roderick treaded down the spacious hallway, paying no attention to the pastel murals on the walls or the mahogany-framed portraits of the HEdge Council staring out at him. His mind was preoccupied.

His right hand balled into a fist as he contemplated his upcoming meeting with the Sector Chief. A growing rage began swelling inside, growing stronger and meaner with each step. He knew Treppin would object to using HEdge troops to go after the three Christians. "An extravagant waste of manpower better left to the local police," he would say.

Roderick raged as he considered his dilemma. Samuel Treppin's main problem was that he didn't understand the real issues at hand. He wastes too much time spewing out philosophies of a utopian one-world society, where mankind's adversities will be overcome by our inherent good nature.

Of course Treppin was right to a certain degree. Global interdependence was the key to a one-world society. His gross oversight however, was this supposed good nature he accuses everyone of having.

Roderick smirked at the thought. He knew differently. Contrary to the well wishes of Samuel Treppin, humanity is afoul with evil. Brimming with every sort of devilish delight imaginable; and Roderick could imagine quite a bit.

He continued down the hall carrying his contentious smirk with him. He was quite aware of the other side of human nature; the side that Treppin and people of his ilk refused to see: the evil side.

Yes, that was the real issue at hand, the evil side, and how best to nurture it. Other issues were just window dressing, obstacles to blur the vision of curious souls.

The ten members of the HEdge Council understood the simplicity of it. He was sure the other Sector Chiefs understood as well. But Treppin was a different story. He was a square peg in a round hole. All this good-nature stuff was out of place.

Chapter

4

Reaching the end of the hallway, Banchard rounded the corner and walked a few steps toward the large glass doors. The Sector Chief's petite secretary, Ms. Jennifer Bajon, was on the other side, sitting smartly at her desk rifling through a large manila folder. An attractive woman in her mid-thirties with no serious relationships in the wings, she was always a focal point for Roderick on his weekly visits.

Beyond the secretary, Roderick saw two men, one sitting on the lengthy olive-green sofa, and the other pacing nervously in front.

The two men were Treppin's favorite Advisors out of a team of eleven assigned to him by the HEdge Council. The Advisors served as the Sector Chief's eyes and ears to societal trends and attitudes. They advised the Sector Chief on nearly every action he was about to take, well before he took it.

Distracted from her folder, Ms. Bajon looked up to see Banchard entering. She tensed at the sight of him. As usual, he walked to the edge of her desk, hovering for a few seconds, overpowering the air with his stench cologne.

Like most people, she found the man intimidating. She sensed an aura of power about him, a deceitful power that could drive good men to perform horrendous deeds. She didn't like this man, but was afraid of him. Somehow, she knew to be afraid of him.

"Good afternoon, Mr. Banchard," she managed with a certain uneasiness. "Can I help you with anything?"

Roderick attempted a smile but failed miserably, succeeding only with a sneer. "Hello, Jennifer. You're looking as lovely as ever. I trust everything is well?"

Ms. Bajon felt an eerie sensation crawl over her skin. She wanted to rub her arms but was afraid he would notice her repulsion. Instead, she put on a face.

"Thank you, actually today is a little hectic. Mr. Treppin isn't feeling well, and I'm worried he's still going to attempt to give his speech at the State Auditorium."

"Not feeling well?" Roderick did all he could to sound sincere. "I'm sorry to hear that. Nothing serious I hope."

A few feet away, the stout, scholarly looking HEdge Advisor that was pacing back and forth, suddenly stopped. Taking notice of Roderick, he bolted towards him. "Roderick! Have you been informed that your troops may be needed at the auditorium?"

Reluctantly breaking his gaze from Ms. Bajon's light brown eyes, Roderick turned to the Advisor and answered smugly, "Yes, I have, as a matter of fact." He grinded, "That's one of the reasons I'm here."

Mr. Lester Ellis, the thinner, balding HEdge Advisor, nearly leaped from the sofa when he saw Roderick.

"Mr. Banchard, how many men are you going to need? Where are they now? Can they make it to the auditorium in the next fifteen minutes?"

Roderick was seething. These imbeciles have finally lost their minds! They haven't been this jittery since the HEdge Council made an impromptu visit to the Sector Chief's office a year ago.

"Wait a minute!" he burst while turning to Lester. "Before you guys mug me, why don't you try giving me some information? Like, is Mr. Treppin going to give his speech or not! And if not, why hasn't it been called off!" He paused. "Can either of you relax long enough to tell me exactly what is going on around here!"

Lester was in no mood to tangle with the Chief of Eastern U.S. Sector HEdge Forces. Gregory can handle this one. He retreated back to the couch and sat down.

Gregory resumed his anxious pacing. He detested Roderick, but like it or not, Banchard controlled the entire Eastern U.S. Sector HEdge Forces. To do battle with such a person could be considered foolhardy, if not outright stupid.

"Roderick, we have a problem," Gregory finally began. "Mr. Treppin will more than likely not be making his speech at the auditorium this afternoon. I'm afraid he's very ill." Gregory flashed a tired look over to Lester.

"However, Mr. Treppin still desires to make the speech regardless of his present condition. We have staunchly advised him not to do so. And at this moment he is in his office debating whether to heed our advice."

Roderick was loaded with questions. What exactly was wrong with Treppin that his Advisors were urging him not to go on? Do they realize how many people are waiting! Have they forgotten about all the global networks geared up to broadcast the speech?

Roderick was losing patience. If Treppin wants to go on, let him!

Suddenly a loud thud came from the closed door of the Sector Chief's private office, then another, followed by a burst of laughter. A second later the door flew open as the solid, bulky frame of the forty-five year old Samuel Treppin walked, or rather, stumbled out.

"Hellooooo, Roderick . . . you fiendish fellow," Treppin slurred as he waved a near-empty bottle of vintage 1956 Chablieau Blanc wine through the air.

"Roderick, let me share a few stories with you, may I? Come over and sit with me."

Treppin crisscrossed his path to the couch. Once reaching it, he let gravity take over as his body flopped clumsily to a sitting position next to Lester Ellis.

His mouth gaping open, Samuel exhaled into his Advisor's face. "Lester, how have you been, my good friend? And your family? Tell your wife 'Hi' for me, would you? I really like her. She's a good woman, Lester."

Attempting to avoid Samuel's powerful breath, Lester turned aside slightly. "Thank you, sir. I will."

Suppressing a chuckle, Jennifer covered her mouth with the manila folder, then hastily got up and excused herself. Before any heads could turn, she was out the door.

Roderick glared at Gregory, who instantly raised his eyebrows and shoulders as if to say, "Don't blame me. I didn't give him any."

Treppin resumed. "Roderick, my beastly friend, as I was saying, Greg and Lester here insist that I renege on my commitment to give a speech at the, the, what's the name of that place, Lester?" he asked while looking over to Gregory.

"Uh um," Lester cleared his throat. "The New York State Auditorium, sir."

"Ah yes, the auditorium." Treppin abruptly stopped. He put his hand to his mouth as if to hide a burp. "Oh dear, I'm really not feeling well, gentlemen. I've got some pills in my desk." His face went pale as he stood and sloppily ran back to his private office, bumping into the door on his way out.

Once Samuel was beyond earshot, Roderick pounced over to Gregory. Scowling down at him, he fumed. "How could you let Treppin get plastered right before a major speech? You call yourself an Advisor! Where was your advice today! I'll have your job for this you little weasel!"

Gregory was thrown aback by Roderick's harsh words. At first, draped in fear; he was afraid of what this diabolical rogue was capable of. But then, just as quickly, a venomous anger surged to the surface. As dangerous as Roderick Banchard was, he could be controlled. And Gregory knew exactly how to do it.

"Keep your comments to yourself, Banchard!" he roared back. "Who are you to come in here and threaten me! You have no right, or authority! I don't care about your position; you only have as much power as Treppin gives you! And don't even think I can't bend his ear enough to realize he'd be better off without your lame existence!"

Roderick was flush with hatred. Gregory White was a spineless snake who hid behind Samuel Treppin's coattails. Left on his own, he wouldn't last a week in this jungle. But standing behind Treppin, he could accomplish nearly anything he wished.

The two men have faced off many times in the past but this is the first time Gregory had the guts to say what they both knew: as long as Samuel Treppin considered him one of his most valued Advisors, Roderick was in no position to wage a political war against him.

Catching himself before reaching for Gregory's throat, Roderick turned around and brought his left hand to his chin, considering his next move.

This is not over, Roderick swore to himself. *Gregory White will get his due someday. The sooner the better.*

But for right now, there was no alternative but to settle for a stale-mate.

Shortly, Roderick turned back, and in a much less hostile voice, began backpedaling. "This is ridiculous, Gregory. Here we are being petty with each other while multitudes are waiting to hear from the Sector Chief. What do you say we drop this little disagreement and get on with the business at hand. Namely, what to do about Treppin's speech?" Roderick finished with the charm of a beaten snake.

Gregory was still poised for blood. Winning a confrontation with Roderick always felt good, and he was more than ready to go a second round, though it didn't seem necessary. Seeing how quickly Roderick recoiled when put on the defensive told him that. Releasing a sigh, he nodded. The short battle was over. He won. Now there were more immediate concerns that needed their attention.

"There's only one thing we can do," Roderick urged. "Cancel Treppin's speech."

The two Advisors nodded. This was exactly what they wanted to hear. With a third party in agreement, maybe Samuel would listen to reason.

Roderick finished, "There's no way around it. The HEdge Council will have us stuffed and mounted if we let him go on like that."

Gregory nodded in agreement. "Now all we have to do is convince the boss. Want to give it a try, Roderick? We've been over it a dozen times with him." Surrendering the discussion, Gregory walked to the sofa and plopped down.

Staring over the heads of the two Advisors, into the Sector Chief's private office, Roderick was pleasantly surprised at what he saw.

"Gregory, Lester, trust me," he grinned. "Mr. Treppin will not be going to the New York State Auditorium today. You have my word on that."

Glimpsing coolly over to one another, the two shared their doubts. How could Roderick be so sure?

"Look behind you, gentlemen," Roderick ordered, reading the disbelief on their faces.

The two turned to scan Treppin's office. As they did, they noticed a lump in the center of his desk, and suddenly Gregory realized the reason for Roderick's confidence. The lump was Treppin! He was out cold!

They faced each other; all three relieved.

Seeing a way to capitalize on the situation, Roderick pulled his chair closer to the two Advisors and leaned forward, waiting for their complete attention.

Finally, he spoke. "Listen. There's something neither of you know about. And it's hot. Really hot! Just thirty minutes ago a member of my staff received a call from some bartender in lower Manhattan. He claims to have spotted John Rex, Andrew Hoyte and Keeyon Webster, right outside his pub!"

Roderick watched their expressions.

Gregory was first to react. "John Rex is here? In New York?" He looked over to Lester to share in the marvel. But Lester responded trivially, "We've been expecting Rex to come east for quite some time, so I'm not entirely surprised. Though finding him with Hoyte and Webster is quite an eyeful. Are you sure this bartender knew what he was talking about?"

Leaning closer, Roderick asked with a terse edge, "Have we been distributing thousands of photographs of these men over the past few months for nothing, Lester? Because if you feel we have, I suggest you advise Mr. Treppin to stop wasting his money on silly pictures and spend it on more worthy causes."

Lester pressed back into the cushions. "No, Roderick, I didn't mean to insinuate we've been wasting money. In fact, I'm sure your information is quite accurate. I just felt a need to offer that insight."

"Thank you for your confidence, Lester," Roderick quipped as he straightened back in his chair. Looking over to Gregory, then briefly to

Lester, he zeroed in on his primary objective.

"Now, with this hot tidbit of news, I propose we use a portion of our HEdge Forces to capture these three men while they're within our grasp."

A moment of nervous silence passed. Gregory cleared his throat before speaking. "Roderick, you know Mr. Treppin's feelings on this matter. He has stated time and again, he does not want us flaunting our troops around town beating up on Christians anymore. Makes us look bad. Besides, that's a job for the city police."

Roderick was afraid this was coming. He didn't like working with the police. He knew his HEdge Forces - he knew how they worked - he controlled how they were trained - and most importantly, he trusted them. The city police had public relations to deal with, citizen's complaints and the like. His Forces had no such concerns. They answered only to senior HEdge officials, no one else. If something happened that might draw a leery eye, his Forces would know what to do. He wasn't so sure the city police would.

Hesitating, Gregory realized he had struck a nerve.

"Besides Roderick, we'll need our people to quell the riot that might break out at the auditorium." A brief pause. "I know we can't tell you what to do with your troops. We haven't the authority. Only Mr. Treppin and the HEdge Council can do that. However, if you disregard Mr. Treppin's stated concerns on this matter, I'm afraid I'll have no choice but to make him aware of your decision once he recovers. I'm sorry, but there is no other way."

Gregory was finished, and glad for it. He had no energy left. If Roderick wanted to argue the case, he would argue alone.

Roderick glared with contempt. The day had started out so promising; he actually thought he had a chance at convincing Treppin to release HEdge troops to go after the three Christians, and was utterly confident once Treppin was out of the way it wouldn't be a problem getting his Advisors to agree. But who would have guessed this snake would have the gall to defy him! Roderick considered how long he would have to wait before taking Gregory White out of business. *Not long*, he promised. *Not long at all.*

He conceded. The city police would have to do.

"Okay, I'll get the NYPD. But if those three get away, you and I will revisit this discussion. Do you understand me?"

"Fine," Gregory agreed, happy to be done with the matter.

"One last thing," Roderick interjected. "You have to declare a news blackout. No pictures or stories can leave that auditorium once the riot hits. Because when it does, it's going to be nasty, and we don't need the world watching HEdge Forces cleaning up a mess created by a Sector Chief. Wouldn't look well for HEdge, or Mr. Treppin."

Gregory was in total agreement though he was skeptical of Roderick's intentions. Intuition told him that the news blackout would be for more than simply protecting someone's image. In fact, he suspected image had nothing to do with it. Rather, he figured the charade of loyalty was just a vehicle for giving his troops free reign to squelch the riot any way they saw fit. He'd seen it too many times with Roderick. But that was no concern of his.

"Agreed," Gregory said without a hint of compassion for the thousands of lives his decision may have just condemned.

With all three in agreement, Gregory motioned for Roderick and Lester to follow him into the Sector Chief's office. Leading them to Treppin's desk, he gently nudged Samuel aside to access the control panel on top. He lightly tapped one circle on the panel, then another. Instantly, two videophones rotated out from the walls in the rear corners of the office.

He motioned Roderick to the videophone on the right while he and Lester went to the other.

A few moments later all the necessary arrangements were made and the meeting was over. Roderick was first to leave. No farewells were extended or received. Shortly after, Jennifer Bajon returned. Gregory quickly filled her in on the events, and then asked her to contact security to have someone cleanup Mr. Treppin's office and tuck him in for the night.

With that completed, he and Lester departed the office. Both were hopeful Roderick would catch the three Christians. Neither was comforted from the afternoon's discussion, and neither liked the expression on Banchard's face as he left. Granted, Roderick had no authority over them, but nonetheless, they knew how things worked. And more importantly, they knew how he worked.

Gregory second-guessed himself for a moment. Did he really think Roderick would no longer be a threat? He wasn't so sure.

Chapter

$$5$$

Dexter Jones returned the six-inch videocomm to its cradle on the press box wall. Nudging his cameraman, Tim Dopler, he said in an uneasy tone, "Tim, we have to leave."

Turning towards Dexter, Tim stopped fidgeting with the equipment. "Huh? What'd you say?"

"We have to leave," he answered vaguely.

Looking up from the roll of cable he was unwinding, Tim pressed, "What do you mean, Treppin hasn't even shown up yet!"

"That was Lombard calling from the truck," Dexter explained. "She said the office just received orders from HEdge Command. She said HEdge is shutting us down. They've declared a news blackout on the auditorium."

Tim nearly tripped over a cable at that.

"A news blackout! What do you mean, news blackout?"

"Just what I said. HEdge has declared a news blackout. Lombard said the studio wants us back immediately."

"You're serious?" Tim asked unbelievingly. "I've never heard of a news blackout right before a Sector Chief's speech."

"I know, it's pretty strange isn't it? Lombard didn't like it either. All she could say for sure was that HEdge declared a blackout, and we're supposed to pack up and get outta here as soon as possible. That's it."

Through the corners of their eyes, they both noticed a sudden flurry of activity in the press box. Pandemonium had struck. Hundreds of news people were simultaneously stripping down their recording gear, loading them into hard-shell protective cases and stacking them near the elevators and escalators. Everyone was rushing, as if a single authority had commandeered the entire press box and ordered everyone out at once.

Sensing the urgency of the moment, Tim quickly started gathering his equipment. But Dexter continued standing as he observed the sudden chaos around him. "I guess we weren't the only ones to get the call."

Tim was on his knees rolling several cables onto one disk.

Placing one hand on his hip, the other in his pants pocket, Dexter considered his next statement.

"Tim, I'm not going."

"Say what? What do you mean, you're not going?"

Exasperated, Dexter answered, "Do you have a hearing impediment, Tim? I said I'm not going! Pretty self-explanatory isn't it?"

"Yeah, it explains you're going nuts! Now, please clarify . . . what do you mean, you're not going?"

Dexter searched for the words to describe the gut feeling that hit him the moment Lombard told him of the news blackout. It was as if every nerve in his body was screaming out for him to stay. Being raised in one of the toughest neighborhoods in upstate New Jersey, he learned long ago to trust his instincts. They carried him this far, he saw no reason to discount them now.

"Something's happening here, Tim."

"Yeah, I'll say. You're going bananas, that's what's happening!" Tim continued rolling cable and sorting the recording instruments as quickly as he could.

"Don't ask me why, but I have this odd feeling, like a premonition. Something important is about to happen, and whatever it is, I need to see it. I need to record it."

Completely dumbfounded, Tim stopped wrapping the cable and stood.

"Dex, don't you see what's happening? The place is a madhouse! Look at everyone. They're all leaving. And by the looks of things, I'd say they're in quite a hurry, too! So let's quit jaw jacking and get packed up, okay?"

"Listen, Tim," Dexter intoned, "you can go, just leave one of the recorders behind. I'll tape what I can. And I promise, when I get back to the studio you'll be first to see it. All right? What do you say?"

Tim couldn't believe this. Not another person in the press box was standing still. Everyone was running around, packing and lugging, everyone that is, except he and Dexter.

He tried to fathom what could possibly be going through Dexter's mind. If HEdge called for a news blackout, it didn't matter whether Dexter recorded anything or not, he wouldn't be able to broadcast it anyways. So why risk your neck sticking around here?

Taking one step closer to Dexter, he stood face to face. "I'm not sure you have a grasp of what's happening here, guy. Has it occurred to you that we don't really have much say in the matter? Don't you kind of think since HEdge called the blackout, and everyone else seems to have gotten the same word, that we're not supposed to be here? That they don't want us here?"

Dexter gazed at Tim. He was correct. Dexter knew that staying behind was not a sensible, much less, logical action. In fact, he was sure it would be considered a violation of some HEdge regulation. If caught, he knew he'd have a sorry time explaining himself. But that, he realized, was the key. He must not get caught.

He knew Tim couldn't understand, and that was all right. He didn't completely understand it himself. One step at a time, he figured. The reasoning would come later; he hoped. The only thing that mattered right now, was to make sure one recorder be left behind.

Tim almost refused his companion. The answer was on the tip of his tongue, ready to be hurled out, but just before uttering his answer, he withdrew it. The determination in Dexter's eyes and the intensity in his voice said it all. There was no way he could talk him out of this. And, unfortunately, there was no way Tim was going to leave without him.

The fact was, Dexter was more than simply a working companion; he was a real friend, and a dependable one. Over the many years they have known each other, Dexter had been more support to him than his own family. He felt closer to Dexter than he did his own kin. He couldn't leave him now. Not in this mess. If anything happened, the guilt would ride him longer than he cared to think.

"Okay, Dex, you idiot. I'll leave a recorder behind. But on one condition . . . I stay with it. I'm not going to trust you with one of these jewels. Darn things cost more than you and I make in a year!"

Dexter was stunned. He didn't expect this.

"Thanks, Tim, but really, all I need is a recorder, you can go, just leave the recorder behind. This is my idea, and to be honest, there is a certain element of danger to this. You shouldn't have to risk it just because I am."

"Don't flatter yourself, pretty boy. I'm doing this for myself too. This whole thing stinks. It doesn't add up. First, Treppin is more than an hour late, the crowds are going berserk, then we hear about a news blackout, and Treppin still isn't here. Something smells real bad, Dex. I just want to see it through."

The press box was nearly empty. Everyone had vacated except a few news people still scrambling to get their gear onto the elevator. Dexter realized they had to move fast. Plans had to be made if they were going to stay behind.

"Thanks, buddy," Dexter finally accepted the offer. "I really appreciate it. But remember, you don't have to. If you change your mind, you can go anytime, okay?"

Without answering, Tim took Dexter's outstretched hand in his, and shook it. "No prob," Tim smiled. "I'm with you."

"Thanks again, friend."

Starting with the business at hand, Dexter said, "We've got to get everything packed except one recorder, then take it all down to the truck. I'll tell Lombard we're riding back with some cronies from the press box. Then we'll run back up here. There's no telling how much time we've got, so let's move!"

Fortunately, Tim had already accomplished the majority of the packing. The rest was finished in a matter of seconds. They lugged their gear to the elevator, and were gone.

Sitting in a corner of the now-empty press box, beneath a complementary juice and wine table, was a fully charged recorder, planted by Dexter and Tim, to remain hidden until their return.

Chapter

6

"**A** news blackout? Who ordered a news blackout? HEdge Command? The entire press box is evacuating? This can't be happening! I know, I know, I heard you!"

Benjamin Gordon slammed the videophone receiver down on his desk. He couldn't believe what he had just heard. Worst-case scenario had dropped squarely into his lap.

He ran out of his office and headed down the hall to Jerome's office. Reaching his partner's door, he heard Thomas' voice rising to a quivering scream, stating almost word for word what he had just shouted into his videophone. As he opened the door, he saw the receiver drop from Thomas' extended palm and bounce off the floor.

Thomas looked up to where Benjamin was standing in the doorway. In a weak, surrendering voice, he mumbled, "He's not coming. A blackout can only mean one thing, he's not coming." Thomas began to laugh, loud and full. He slapped his hands firmly onto the desk while his body heaved with boisterous laughter, nearly choking himself.

But then, as quickly as it started, the laughter stopped. Thomas Jerome was spent. Slouching over his desk, he stared absently to the floor. Only his heavy breathing continued.

Seeing Thomas' nearly collapsed state, Benjamin gently approached and laid a friendly hand on his shoulder. Leaning over to make eye-contact, Benjamin compassionately said, "It's all right, Tom, we'll work this thing through, believe me, it'll be all right."

Thomas heard every word, but ignored them. His concern for the raucous crowds was a thing of the past. The only conscious thought that remained was finding a way out—literally. He knew Benjamin wouldn't let him just walk away at a time like this. So he would have to do it on the sly.

Benjamin turned to see two security guards standing in the doorway gawking at them. They looked lost. Their immaturity and lack of experience in the security field was evident from their expressions.

Benjamin shouted, "Get over here and help, will you?"

The guards jumped, almost colliding as they shot through the doorway. Before Benjamin turned completely back to Thomas, the two were at his side.

Turning to the guard on his left, he said, "You stay here. Call medical and have someone come up right away. Don't take your eyes off him, do you hear me?"

The young security guard nervously answered, "Yes sir. I'll stay right here."

"And you're going to call medical, right?" Benjamin pressed.

"Yes sir, that's right. I'll call medical right away, sir."

He pointed to the other guard. "You come with me. We need to get this crowd under control." He leaped up and ran out the door.

Once in the hall, Benjamin asked the guard, "Where's Henderson?"

Susan Henderson was the auditorium's Chief of Security. She was a tough, older woman who had been working security in the auditorium since it was built twenty years ago. She started as a door guard, and progressed up the ranks until being assigned security chief. Her competence was above reproach, her dedication beyond question. She was the fiber that held the five hundred strong security force together.

"Last I saw her, she was directing the guards at the front gates."

"Call her," Benjamin ordered.

The guard pulled the miniature transceiver from his belt and lifted it to his mouth. "Captain Henderson, this is Sergeant Duram with Mr.

Gordon. Come in please."

The Sergeant held the transceiver to his mouth for a few seconds waiting for a response.

"Call her again," Benjamin ordered.

"Captain Henderson, come in please. This is Sergeant Duram with Mr. Gordon. Come in, please."

"Sergeant, Captain here, what's up?"

Benjamin yanked the transceiver from the Sergeant's hand.

"Captain, what's it looking like out there?"

Immediately recognizing Benjamin's voice, she answered, "It's rough going, Ben. The crowds are too big. They're breaking up fast, trying to squeeze through the gates. I've got over a hundred of my biggest men at the gates right now, and they're busier than ever! Any news inside?"

"We've got trouble, Susan, big trouble. Have you gotten word of the news blackout?"

"News blackout? What are you talking about?"

Benjamin sighed.

"HEdge Command declared a news blackout on the auditorium. Still no official word, but my guess is, Treppin won't be making it today."

Silence.

"Ben, this is unbelievable. Are they sending help? We're going to need it. These people are already on the edge. Once they hear they've wasted hours in line for nothing, I'm afraid of what might happen."

"Troops are on the way, Susan."

"Good!" She paused. "Ben, you have to go on stage and announce Treppin's not going to make it. These people have to know now before things get any worse, if it's not already too late. Can you do that, Ben?"

"Sure," Benjamin scoffed. "I've been wanting some stage time anyway."

"Okay, Ben. Give me about fifteen minutes to spread the news outside. By then, hopefully, I'll have the exterior crowds starting on their way, and then you can pass the word inside.

"By the way, Ben, what are you going to say about Treppin?"

He thought a second. There was only one thing he could say.

"Tell them he's sick, can't make it, and will reschedule."

"Sounds good, Ben. Remember, the crowd is tense enough, so keep your cool. If you sound nervous or worried, they'll pick it up in a heartbeat and it'll spread like wildfire. Next you'll have a stampede on your hands. So sound calm." She added, "Get the rear sections cleared out first. I'll have security play ushers. Good luck!"

"Thanks, Susan. We'll have to share a cocktail after this is over."

"You know I don't drink, Ben. But I'll be happy to join you for a soda. See you then."

Ben handed the transceiver back to Sergeant Duram, and then motioned for him to follow as he ran down the hall towards the backstage.

While running, Benjamin heard Captain Henderson's voice sounding out from the Sergeant's transceiver, bringing her security force up to date on the news-blackout and directing numbers of them to form up in the rear of the auditorium to usher the audience out as needed.

Ben admired the calmness and directness in her voice. He could imagine the nervous reception the guards must be giving this latest message. They were going to earn their pay today.

Thomas Jerome glanced over to the nervous security guard sitting in the chair next to him. The guard just finished calling medical; they were on their way.

Noticing Thomas staring at him, the surprised guard asked, "Mr. Jerome, are you feeling better, sir?"

"Just fine, Sergeant thanks for asking." Taking a deep breath. "Guess I lost my cool a little bit. I don't know what came over me, but I'm feeling much better now." Pausing casually. "I need to pay a visit to the men's room . . . Mother Nature is calling. I'll be back in a few minutes."

"Sir, are you sure you're all right? Would you like me to go with you, just in case?"

"Thanks," he chuckled, "but some things are meant to be done alone. Keep guard over my office, will you? I'll be back in fifteen minutes."

"Y-Yes, sir." The guard didn't like this. Something didn't feel right. But what else could he do? Resigned to his position, he sat and worried, hoping his intuition was wrong.

Thomas closed the door on his way out. Then, hesitating for a moment, he turned decidedly to the right—the opposite direction of the restrooms. In less than fifteen minutes he was at the backstage exit of the auditorium, nonchalantly opening the door and taking a deep breath of fresh air. Then, without so much as a glance over his shoulder, he stepped outside, relieved.

When the medical personnel arrived at his office a minute later, the guard informed them that Thomas should be back from the restroom shortly. So they waited while watching the clock. After fifteen minutes and still no sign of him, they became suspicious. Jumping to their feet, they ran from the office to scout him out in the halls and restrooms, but he was nowhere to be found. Thomas Jerome was gone.

Benjamin reached the backstage with Sergeant Duram at his side. Hidden from the audience, he stood behind the stage curtain motioning to the musicians to lower their tempo and volume. The entertainers understood, and shortly the music was playing at a moderate rhythm, calm and tranquil.

Taking the Sergeant's transceiver again, he hooked it onto his belt and took a deep breath as he headed out on stage. Finally at the center of the enormous platform, the bandleader graciously stepped aside from the microphone, giving Benjamin due honors. Thanking him as he took the microphone, Benjamin gazed out over the audience—and froze.

Standing backstage passively listening to the roar of the crowds was one thing, but to all of a sudden be thrown center stage, and to see first hand the masses jammed into the monstrously large auditorium, with all those thousands of faces staring directly up at you, was quite another. Benjamin found himself in an unexpected state of shock. He opened his mouth to speak, but nothing came out.

As if on queue, small pockets of restlessness erupted throughout the massive auditorium. Benjamin looked out in icy terror as he watched the audience slowly begin to unravel.

A familiar sound suddenly blurted from his side, startling him.

"Ben, do it!" He heard Susan's stern voice coming over the transceiver on his belt.

Beyond his visual range, in one of the many exits, Susan Henderson stood, watching him on the large two story video screens mounted on each side of the stage. She immediately understood his predicament.

"Do it!" she commanded a second time.

The familiar voice shook him from his daze. Pulling himself together, he began his announcement. "Ladies and gentlemen, may I please have your attention."

His voice boomed out across the auditorium.

"Ladies and gentlemen, may I have your attention."

This time the crowds seemed to settle a little. He seized the opportunity.

"Hello, I'm Benjamin Gordon, manager of the New York State Auditorium. I'm very glad you all had a chance to come out and join us today. However, I'm afraid I have the unenviable task of making the following announcement."

Swallowing hard, he continued. "Our Sector Chief, Mr. Samuel Treppin, has come down with a sudden illness. As a result, he is unable to join us today. He extends his sincere thanks to all of you for coming out to see him, and he deeply apologizes for not being able to be here with you."

A mild roar erupted. Benjamin quickly added, "As soon as Mr. Treppin's presentation can be rescheduled, we'll announce it through all the networks. I assure you, everyone will be offered another chance to see him, at no cost. You have my word."

The roar gradually died down.

So far, so good, Benjamin considered. A milder reaction than he had expected.

He continued, "Therefore, on behalf of the New York State Auditorium, may I extend my heartiest thanks to all of you for being such a perfectly mannered audience. I want to personally thank you for your patience, and wish you a safe trip home.

"Now if you please, while the musicians continue to play, would the ladies and gentlemen in the rear sections of the auditorium, kindly and slowly find your exits. Security guards will help direct you to the doors.

"Ladies and gentlemen in the balconies, please begin your way down to the main level exits. Everyone in the forward sections of the auditorium please remain seated until your rows have been cleared for leaving."

He repeated the instructions several times as the crowds began filtering out. With the situation seeming to be under control, he made his final statement. "The musicians will continue to perform until everyone has had a chance to depart. So please, relax and enjoy the music until your section has been signaled to leave. Again, thank you very, very much for your patience. Have a wonderful day and a safe trip home."

Benjamin turned towards the musicians and gave them a full bow then started back towards the stage curtain. He felt pretty good. The announcement went well, at least as well as one could expect. Aside from the short outburst right after he announced the Sector Chief wasn't making it, the crowd seemed surprisingly tame.

As Benjamin reached the stage curtain, Sergeant Duram's hand was outstretched to congratulate him. Benjamin shook it along with a dozen other people milling around to compliment him. Modestly receiving their praise and good will, Benjamin's mind remained on the audience and how smoothly their exodus was going.

After several minutes with no obvious signs of unrest, Benjamin felt satisfied all was well. But as he unclipped the transceiver from his belt to return it to Sergeant Duram, his sense of well being vanished as he heard Susan Henderson's alarmed voice blare out from it.

"Ben! Benjamin, can you hear me?" Her voice was desperate; her words were quick and excited.

"Susan, I hear you. What's wrong?"

"Ben, they're here! HEdge is here, but they're not helping, Ben! The crowds started to leave, everything was fine, the crowds inside started clearing out, but when HEdge showed up, things started getting out of control. The crowds were overwhelming the troops, and before you knew it, HEdge started firing at everyone! I don't know how to stop them! They're shooting! Ben, everyone's going crazy!"

In the background Ben heard shouts and screams. He could hear Susan being knocked around as she talked. He thought he heard a low, angry voice ordering her to turn off her transceiver.

"Susan, are you all right?" he asked urgently. "Can you come inside?"

Her voice came over the transceiver one last time with a loud, painful scream, "Ben . . . help!" Then Benjamin's transceiver went dead. Susan's voice was replaced with silence.

He looked pleadingly down to the transceiver, as if begging it to come to life. "Susan? Susan? Are you all right? Can you hear me? Susan!"

Suddenly an uproar sounded from the other side of the stage curtain diverting his attention. He ran to see what was making the ruckus. Just as he reached the curtain, the musicians plowed past, shouting as they ran, warning everyone to get out right away!

Not heeding their advice, he rushed beyond the curtain and onto the stage, then stopped in shock, horrified at what he saw. The auditorium was in complete mayhem. People were jammed up against every exit, fighting and shoving to get out of the doors, while at the same time thousands seemed to be pressing on the outside, insanely trying to force their way in.

Benjamin watched in dread as people ran from one blocked exit to another, as in large herds, trampling everything and everyone in their path. He could see collisions as several herds rammed into each other trying to get to opposite exits.

Those huddling at the doors pushing to get out were forced down, falling over as the doors smashed open with the crowds outside barreling in, stampeding over them.

Then with utter disbelief, Benjamin heard gunfire echoing into the auditorium, followed by thousands of HEdge soldiers mounting their attack on the unarmed civilians scrambling everywhere, running for their lives.

Benjamin ran to center stage, snapped the microphone from its stand, then shouted into it with all his might.

"What are you doing? Stop shooting! Stop!" Suddenly Benjamin toppled down. A bullet found its way into his right kneecap causing him to crumple over and fall hard to the floor. The microphone flew from his hand, landing with a bounce and a thump half way across the stage.

Struggling to retrieve it, Benjamin crawled along the stage, ignoring the pain burning in his right leg. He was almost within reach of the microphone; just another couple inches and he would have it. But then, the determination of his heroic efforts were dashed, as another, more accurate bullet struck him in the temporal lobe on the left side of his head. The force of the bullet knocked him over on his back, lifeless, his arms outstretched; the static microphone at his fingertips. Benjamin Gordon was dead.

The massacre continued for nearly twenty minutes, after which every civilian inside was either dead or close to it. Fatigued, the soldiers finally lowered their guns. Apart from the soldiers' weary movements and some isolated cries from the dying, the room was silent. A morbid calm blanketed the auditorium.

Chapter

$$\overline{\underline{7}}$$

Colonel Dirk Reynolds studied the gory battle zone outside the auditorium as he marched slowly through the front gates. His posture was strikingly erect, his face hard and cold. The two-inch triangular HEdge logo sparkled from his starched blue uniform shirt. The only disruption to his near perfect symmetrical appearance was the HEdge revolver jutting from his side.

A large assemblage of officers followed behind, scanning the grounds, admiring the finished product of their skillful troops.

The entourage of officers paraded past dozens of soldiers who were working tirelessly to clear a path for them; dragging and pushing corpses aside, lifting bodies of men and women, tossing them out of the way. Even with all their efforts, the Colonel was forced at times to lift his long sinewy legs over a fallen victim.

After several minutes of inspecting the human debris scattered outside the auditorium, Reynolds and his flock headed inside. They entered through the main lobby, continuing ambitiously through the lounge area, all the while indulging their senses with the lurid images around them.

The Colonel was finally standing outside the auditorium's main hall. A junior officer respectfully held one of the few remaining hinged doors open for him. The Colonel approached. Hesitating briefly, he looked around to examine the ghastly images in the lobby. With a simple nod, indicating his satisfaction, he stepped through.

He walked twenty paces before stopping. The magnitude of the auditorium was breathtaking in itself, but the added assortment of bodies sprawled everywhere made the scene even more surrealistic. He was impressed.

Finally, he turned to his officers and congratulated them on a job well done. Society would benefit much from the sweat of their hard labor. Then he saw it. A bright light flickered from a window in one of the press box sections high above. It wasn't a light so much as a bright reflection. He strained upwards to see what had caused it. The press box was too high for him to see well, but he continued gazing anyway, swearing he'd seen something.

The assembled officers caught on to his concern as they began staring up as well. Eventually one of them thought he saw the reflection too, but wasn't sure until it flickered at a different angle. Then he was sure he had it. Excitedly raising his arm, he pointed while exhorting his fellow officers to look where he was staring.

Just then, two strangers bolted up inside the press box, partially exposing themselves to the officers and soldiers below. One of them appeared to be carrying something under his arm as he followed the other dashing out the press box exit.

The Colonel and his men were stunned. Who were they? Where did they come from? What were they doing up there?

Reynolds' chest heaved, "Get them, you imbeciles!" he screamed, "And any recorders they have!" Rambling on, he cursed his officers for their oversight. But before he could finish, the main level had completely cleared as everyone made their way to the elevators and stairwells chasing after the two men. No one wanted to be the last in his sights when he finished his tirade.

Dexter and Tim spurted through the press box exit. Dexter hugged the recorder under his arm as he ran. Exasperated, Tim asked, "Did you see that? Can you believe those guys?"

Dexter answered impatiently, "We'll talk about it later, right now we've got to get out of here, and fast! What's the quickest way out?"

"You're asking me? This is only the third time I've been in this place. I thought you were the expert here!"

"Great," Dexter groaned while sprinting down the hallway. The elevators and escalators were out of the question. Their only hope was in the stairwells, if he could just find some. After another fifty feet, he spotted one. Pushing the lock release, the door flew open as they raced through, hustling down the stairs.

Gripping the handrails, they leaped several stairs at a time, whipping around the corners of each stairwell landing. Dexter clung onto the recorder with one hand, doing his best to grab the handrails with the other. He knew it would be a miracle if they got all the way from the sixth floor to the main level without HEdge troops catching them. But that was their only hope, and so far the miracle was holding out. They had already passed two levels and were now on the fourth floor.

Dexter began getting a false sense of security when he suddenly heard the rumbling of hundreds of soldiers stomping up the stairs towards them. Their hearts sank as they heard the soldiers' angry battle cries penetrating the air.

Dexter and Tim were between floors and weren't sure if they could beat the soldiers to the next level without being seen, but they had no choice, their momentum was too strong to stop. So they continued as fast as they could, daring to reach the third level first.

The battle cries were getting louder and the third level was still a long flight down. They speeded recklessly, leaping over far too many steps with each single bound, risking broken necks if either should lose their balance.

Finally reaching the third level, they hurried through the stairwell door and quickly closed it, being careful to be as quiet as possible.

Just as the door shut, they felt vibrations under their feet as the soldiers thundered past on the other side, continuing their rapid ascent up the stairs.

Realizing they weren't discovered, they started down the hallway, relieved for the moment.

The hall was lined with accounting offices on both sides. They checked for unlocked doors as they ran just in case they might need somewhere to duck into fast. But every door was locked.

Rushing down the hall, they suddenly came upon a flood of soldiers staring them down from the opposite end. They skidded to a stop. A moment of awkward silence passed, as both parties were surprised at the sudden turn of events. Finally, the lead officer lifted his gun and fired off a shot, missing Tim by a hair.

Dexter spotted a stairwell immediately to their left. As Tim began raising his arms in surrender, Dexter jerked him by the back of his shirt, pulling him in. Once again they were in flight down the stairs, but this time leaping over even more steps at a time, almost clearing half the flight, touching down only a few times.

They heard the door above flung open as soldiers raced into the stairwell in quick pursuit. Worsening the situation, they heard more soldiers running up the stairwell from below. There was only one way they could make it to the second level without getting caught; they had to leap over the rails and land by the stairwell door at least fifteen feet below. But if they missed, they'd fall to their deaths to the ground floor. Not a pleasant thought.

Hardly pausing to consider it, Dexter leaped first, still lugging the recorder tight under his arm as he flew through the air. He landed right beside the second level door. Tim followed, barely making the landing. Dexter reached out to grab him as he teetered on the edge of the stairwell. Regaining his balance, he and Dexter hurried through the doorway, beating the HEdge soldiers only by seconds.

Dexter led the way down the second level corridor, running along the wall as the stairwell door behind smashed open with HEdge soldiers storming through.

Finally at an opening in the wall that led to the first tier balcony, Dexter spun around it and ran down the many rows of vinyl seats. At the bottom, he glimpsed over the rail to see how far below the main level was.

Staring down the sixteen-foot drop, his mouth hung open. But there was no time to think. He slung the recorder strap over his shoulder and climbed the rail. Looking up to find Tim, he was surprised to see him already hanging, ready to drop. A bullet flew over their heads, motivating them to let go.

Releasing their grips, they fell the distance to the seats below, tumbling as they hit. Tim yelped with pain. He hurt something, but it wasn't his legs because he was up and running almost as quickly as Dexter.

Fortunately, with all the soldiers ordered to the upper levels, there was no one left on the ground floor to stop them except the Colonel, who was madly running at them from the opposite side of the auditorium. Furious, he aimed his revolver, firing feverishly at them. A few wild shots bounced off the walls. One came within a foot of Dexter.

Tim and Dexter sped through the lounge and main lobby areas until finally reaching the front entrance. They stopped at the open doors just before going outside, where they saw hundreds of soldiers removing bloodied corpses littered over the grounds.

The sight petrified Tim. Dexter nudged him to continue walking, whispering for him to try to act normal.

Gathering their wits, they walked out together, stepping through the large center doors of the auditorium, acting as though they belonged. Trying to act calm, they improvised a conversation about how well the soldiers had performed.

A soldier working nearby stopped and glanced suspiciously over to them. Scared, Tim forced a smile while wishing him a good day. The soldier responded with an even grimmer stare as he wiped his bloodied hands onto his already red-splotched shirt. Almost losing it, Tim quickly turned away, trying his best to remain calm.

Dexter suppressed his fright pretty well. In fact, fright was the last thing on his mind. Looking out over the many piles of corpses, he began to feel sick. He tried to understand how human beings could inflict such needless suffering onto one another. He read of such atrocities throughout the ages, but who would have believed it was still possible today, with the almighty HEdge in control?

He almost broke into laughter. Civilization had once again been duped. We thought we finally had it right, we thought we found the key, the answer, and it was HEdge. HEdge was the final cure for all of humanity's ailments.

Dexter could hardly keep from laughing. "What went wrong this time," he moaned.

Hugging the recorder, he considered what was on the disk. Other people would want to see this, he was sure of it.

At the front gate, they were finally past all the soldiers when they heard a commotion stirring back at the auditorium doors. They had been discovered. They heard the soldiers yelling for them, ordering them to stop.

A bullet flew past, grazing Dexter's left arm. They started running full stride again. In seconds they were out of the gates and into the large parking lot surrounding the auditorium. Another bullet flew past.

They were doomed and they both knew it. The parking lot was much too large to clear before the bullets got them or the soldier's trucks eventually caught up.

Dexter could hear Tim's heavy breathing. He felt sad for his good friend. If only Tim had left when he had the chance. Then he wouldn't be caught up in this mess. He could see that Tim was struggling to keep pace. *Thanks for being such a good friend*, Dexter thought to his partner. *I love ya, buddy.*

So this would be their fate, to be killed in a parking lot. Not a fitting end, Dexter considered, especially after all they had been through. Better to have died inside. At least he wouldn't have had to see the devastation outside as well.

They continued running.

From behind they heard a vehicle racing up to them, revving its engine. No surprise. Won't be long now.

They heard a horn blowing from the vehicle. Dexter turned to his right expecting to dodge another bullet, but was surprised to see it wasn't a HEdge truck after all; it was their studio truck. And Lombard was hunched behind the wheel, motioning them to jump inside.

Lombard pressed the door release, allowing the sliding door to open. Running full stride, Dexter threw himself into the moving truck while holding the recorder as tightly as he could. Tim leaped in as soon as Dexter was out of the way.

Seeing the two men were safely inside, Lombard pressed the accelerator to the floor and sped out of the parking lot.

"Lombard, I love you!" Dexter shouted. "How did you know we needed you?"

"I knew you guys were up to something when I unloaded only two of the three recorders we brought with us. But I never expected to find you dingbats out here dodging bullets! What was going on back there?"

"You wouldn't believe us if we told you," Dexter answered. "We've got it all on film though. Wait till you see it! It'll knock your socks off!"

Tim laid on his back, groaning quietly. Dexter laid his hand over Tim's arm to comfort him. "Tim's hurting real bad. We need to get him to medical quick."

A few minutes later Lombard was pulling into the underground parking lot of HRS studios. She drove to the main entranceway and stopped.

"I'll let you out here so you can get Tim up to the clinic."

She added, "You don't look so good either, Dex. Look at your left arm."

He raised his arm. Blood was trickling down, leaving a long red streak on his sleeve. But he wasn't concerned. He leaned over to help Tim out of the truck.

"Have the Doc check you both, okay?" Chris implored.

"Don't sweat it," Dexter assured her. "Thanks again. You were great back there."

"No problem, Dex. I'll see you as soon as I park, okay." She smiled.

Dexter winked at her as he wrapped his right arm around Tim to help him into the building.

Shifting the truck into reverse, Lombard spun it around and parked. In a few minutes she was back with her friends inside the HRS health clinic.

Lieutenant Baumgartner, the senior HEdge officer at the front gates, spread his arms out wide, motioning to his soldiers to hold their fire. The truck was gone, but that was all right. He saw the bold letters stenciled on its back. The letters read, "HRS." He knew all about HRS studios.

It would be easy to track down the truck. The two men and their driver might take a little bit longer but he was sure he would have them by nightfall.

Reynolds was still inside cursing his soldiers when the Lieutenant delivered his welcome news. Only slightly appeased, the Colonel ordered him to gather a dozen soldiers to take with him to HRS studios to apprehend the two men, their recorder, and the disk, especially the disk. That was his primary concern. The two men were secondary. In fact, he finally told the Lieutenant to do as he pleased with the men, but he wanted the disk.

Popping a sharp salute, Baumgartner immediately went about picking a dozen soldiers to take with him. Soon, they were departing in two mid-size HEdge trucks en route to HRS studios.

Reynolds remained behind. There was more work to be done and he wasn't leaving anything to chance. Mr. Banchard had given him explicit orders what to do once the riot was over. Now it was time to carry out those orders.

He instructed his officers to have their men stack all the human remains against the auditorium. Once finished, he ordered the entire building to be set ablaze.

Fifty minutes later, as Colonel Reynolds and his cavalcade of Hedge vehicles were cruising a few blocks from the auditorium, he noticed a sudden flash off his windows. With a smile, he twisted in his seat to see the volcano of flames shooting up from where the New York State Auditorium stood. After watching for a few minutes, he relaxed back into his soft leather seat and smirked. "Banchard wanted an inferno, well he got one. Another job well done."

Banchard would find some way to express his gratitude for this latest of deeds. Reynolds sat comfortably back in his seat, arrogantly wondering what that reward might be.

Chapter

$$\overline{8}$$

John Rex, Andrew Hoyte, and Keeyon Webster walked three blocks up Christopher Street then turned right on Eighth, joking and sharing stories along the way.

Eighth Street was typical old Greenwich Village. Rows of red brick, two-level novelty shops lined the street for several blocks up. Tall leafy trees planted over the years by city workers to give it a rural flavor shaded the sidewalks intermittently.

The three men paid little attention to the intricate window displays beckoning them to enter and purchase goods. Not interested in shopping, their sights were on dinner, at least Andrew and Keeyon's were. John had just finished lunch, but no matter, Andrew was leading this parade and John was happy to be a part of it.

A block and a half up, Andrew spotted a quaint little restaurant, the front of which seemed barely large enough to support a picture window. A rustic wooden sign that read, Welcome Cafe, hung above the doorframe.

Andrew motioned that this place should do fine for calming their appetites. He held the door as John and Keeyon entered. Only a few brief steps inside the narrow entranceway and they saw it grow into a spacious dining hall packed with busy tables.

A cheerful waiter sporting a bushy mustache and neatly trimmed black hair led them to the rear to one of the few available tables. The place was bustling with business. *Another misperception*, John considered with delight. The restaurant's exterior would have suggested desperately little business. But now, he could see well over a hundred customers enjoying an afternoon meal. Only a short while in New York and he was already mesmerized by its subtle surprises. *This is going to be fun*, he admitted. *If only Melody and Matthew could have made the trip.*

With each of them finally seated at the table, the waiter took their orders and left for the kitchen.

Settling down, the three men began discussing personal matters, family lives, marriages, and children. Keeyon and John spoke of their joys and challenges of marriage, while Andrew offered entertaining tales of living in New York City.

The discussion was interrupted as the waiter returned with their meals.

"Care to say grace, John?" Andrew asked.

"Be honored."

After praying, the three men proceeded to devour their meals, making small talk between bites.

Finishing first, John laid his fork down, guzzled the last of his soda, and sat for a minute. "You know what?" he finally broke in. "I never have gotten the whole story of how you two met. I've heard it was in prison. Is that true?"

Keeyon and Andrew shared a chuckle before answering. Finally, Keeyon said, "Yes, John, it was in jail. We were both arrested for sharing the Gospel on campus; same campus too, just different dormitories. Didn't know each other at the time, but when we met in jail we knew right away our meeting was divinely appointed.

"Incredible how God works, isn't it?" Andrew intoned. "Both of us witnessing on the same campus, yet not knowing each other until God brought us together. Ever since then, we've been ministering together; a preaching team for God."

John gleamed, "Amen, brother."

After another minute, Keeyon leaned forward. In a serious tone, he uttered, "We thought times were hard then, John, but they've only gotten worse. We've been forced to keep an even lower profile."

His jaw tightening, John asked, "Banchard again? So he's not letting up a bit, is he?"

"No, John, not at all," Andrew affirmed. "Banchard is seriously out to get us; but not just us. He wants the whole network shut down. He seems insanely driven to do battle against God's Church. How a man of his caliber reached such a high position in HEdge is a chilling thought."

Leaning back in his chair, Keeyon added, "The battle line has been drawn. He's made it very clear our days are numbered. The man means to do us real harm."

"And he wants you, John. Real bad," Andrew said. "Our sources tell us that Banchard is worried sick you're going to expand your network into his sector. He's seen what the network accomplished out west, and believe me, he doesn't want you here."

John listened intently to every word, realizing the threat Banchard posed.

After a few minutes more, Andrew shifted the subject, asking, "Say, how's your brother doing, John? Have you talked to him lately? With his position in HEdge, he could sure help us."

"Yes, he could," John answered with a drawn face. "But we haven't talked in years. We can't. If we did, I would be arrested and who knows what would happen to him. He certainly could help, but he's not the same kid we grew up with, Andrew. I wish he was, I really do."

Andrew and Keeyon could hear the sadness in his voice. They were acutely aware of the irony surrounding the two brothers' lives.

Neither knew what to say to comfort their good friend. The subject obviously pricked an open wound, bringing a moment of awkward silence to the table.

Breaking the ice, Keeyon started up about how eager he was to see the west coast network expand east. John agreed as he shared some news from the western side of the continent. Soon, the three men were engaged in discussions on how to better serve the Lord by combining their resources, with the ultimate goal of linking every underground Christian community across the globe.

And so the details of the conversation started to unfold, with each man providing their own piece to the large puzzle, hunkering in for what could be a lengthy discussion.

Chapter

$$9$$

The four doors of the van opened simultaneously. Six men leaped out, each wearing the symbolic silver HEdge logo on their blue uniform shirts.

Another van screeched to a halt only a few feet from where the first had stopped. Six more men scrambled out. Soon, more than a dozen vehicles littered the intersection of Christopher and McDougal; most of them NYPD cruisers hauling police to the site.

Unloading from the cruisers, the officers began throwing barricades up. In no time, they had every intersection within a four-block radius closed off to road traffic. The only exception being the many cruisers that continued pulling up on both sides of the street to unload more officers.

Scores of pedestrians stopped to watch. As they loitered on the sidewalks their numbers multiplied until people were literally on each other's heels, choking off any movement on the walkways. The police began squeezing them into even tighter quarters pushing them back off the street and out of the area.

Many in the crowd were getting hostile toward the police, shouting curses, venting their anger for the sudden inconvenience thrust on them. But the police were ready. As the first object was hurled from the crowds, the police fired a shot over their heads, a sure warning; reminding everyone just who was in charge.

A few pedestrians continued taunting the police, but unless they got close enough to be a threat, they were ignored. The majority flowed quietly and obediently through the barricades .

Half way up the road were fifty or so police captains standing behind a circle of HEdge officers. In front of them stood one tall, lanky man. He held everyone's attention as his dark sullen eye's scanned their faces. Every man present knew of Roderick Banchard, and none of them were especially comfortable with being in his company.

His tight pale skin seemed to pull at the bones as he began screaming. "Where is the Village Pub? I want to see Herb Duncan, now!" Roderick was fuming. Here he was with a quarter of the New York City Police Department and not one had a clue as to why they were here. Never mind the fact they were ordered on scene only minutes earlier, with no time for mission briefings or the like. That was their problem, not his.

A few officers standing on the outer rim of the cluster rushed down the street to where the Village Pub was located. The first officer shoved his way through the many pedestrians gawking from the doorway. Once inside, he shouted for Herb Duncan.

"Yeah, what d'ya want him for?" Herb answered from behind the counter.

The officer hustled over to the bar. Twenty other officers were now inside the pub with him.

"Are you Herb Duncan?"

"Why do you want to know?" Herb muttered as if he had better things to do.

The officer reached over the counter, grabbed Herb by his dirty shirt and yanked him up to the edge.

"If you're Herb Duncan, Mr. Banchard wants to talk to you now. And I mean now!"

Oops, what's going on here? Better play along.

In a more congenial tone, Herb asked, "Who's Roderick Banchard?"

"He's our boss, creep. And he could be the difference between a good and a bad day. Believe me, you don't want him to give you a bad day. Now, if I have to ask one more time if you're Herb Duncan, I'm just going to shoot you and be done with the matter. You got that?" He was reaching down to his holster as he tugged on Herb's shirt. The other officers were already behind the bar, ready to lift the sloppy galoot over if necessary.

"Okay, I'm Herb Duncan. What does this Mr. Banchard want me for?"

Without a word, the officers behind the bar lifted Herb onto the counter and shoved him to the other side. Herb was caught completely off guard, he rolled helplessly over the top of the bar and splashed down on a couple bar stools before slamming to the floor. He cursed as he tried to lift himself up. The officer on the other side pulled him up and heaved him out the door. The others quickly shuffled behind, helping him along his way.

As they got nearer to the center of the intersection, they could hear Banchard continuing his tirade performance in front of the many nervous captains unfortunate enough to have duty today.

As quickly as they could, they pushed Herb through the clogged circle into the center, until he was face to face with his interrogator, Roderick Banchard.

Roderick stopped his rantings as he took notice of the filthy slob thrown before him. He snickered while grinning at Herb. Stepping closer, he surveyed him up and down. Herb was petrified. He didn't know what this was all about, and he didn't recognize the man who was hawking over him, but he was smart enough to realize he was in way over his head.

His knees began shaking beneath his baggy pants. He held his hands together over his extended potbelly. He couldn't look this tall man in the eyes. When he did, he felt as though his soul was being pierced, which was odd since Herb never considered himself as having a soul.

The police officer that tugged Herb from the pub, introduced him to Roderick.

"So you're Herb Duncan?" Roderick asked while holding a fixed gaze on him. "Tell me, are you the one who reported seeing John Rex, Andrew Hoyte and Keeyon Webster?"

So that's what this is all about, Herb thought to himself, a little more at ease. These guys came to catch those three Christians. Well, it's about time. Must have been at least an hour since he made the call. He was starting to wonder if they were ever going to show up. But all these cops? Why so many? You'd think a war was being fought.

"Yeah, I'm Herb Duncan. And I made the call. I thought . . ."

"I'm not concerned with what you thought, just tell me where they are! Which way did they go when you last saw them?"

The ease that temporarily soothed Herb, evaporated instantly. He felt his knees begin to weaken again. To be truthful, he had no idea which direction they had gone. When he returned from making his call, they had already left. But something intuitively told Herb he would be better off picking a direction, any direction, than to admit he didn't know.

He nervously pointed south in the direction of Eighth and Seventh streets.

"Sir, the last I saw, they were headed down that way."

Roderick peered into Herb's eyes as if excavating for more information. But he didn't have time to prod further. Too much time had already been wasted!

He turned towards the nearest Hedge officer and ordered him to lock Duncan up until the three Christians were found. He then ordered another officer to distribute the pictures of Rex, Hoyte, and Webster. "Everyone! Get a copy! I want these men found! Especially Rex. Go and find me Rex!"

Taking a handful of pictures, each captain ran back to their squads to pass them out, eager to get the search for the three fugitives underway.

Andrew, Keeyon and John held each other's hands while their heads were bowed in prayer. The network was growing, and now they would tie the east with the west, increasing their resources to serve God. John would get his programmers to download all their inside-HEdge information, all their Bible printing outlets, their overseas liaisons and other valuable resources to help the east coast network grow.

The three men ended their conversation with a unanimous, "Amen!"

Pulling a picture of Melody and Matthew from his wallet, John handed it over to Andrew.

"I've been waiting to give this to you. It's only a few months old. Melody said she doesn't like her hairstyle, but I told her it looks beautiful. Matthew looks great too, doesn't he?"

Andrew and Keeyon looked the picture over. After browsing a minute, Andrew said, "Matt's a fine looking young man, John. Doesn't want to stop growing, does he? And Melody is as lovely as ever. What's she see in you?" he chuckled.

"Yeah, what's up with that?" Keeyon teased along, smiling.

"Now, now, boys, jealousy is a sin," John corrected.

"On point as always," Andrew laughed.

Just then, a young man burst through the front door of the restaurant, gasping for air. *Can't be more than seventeen*, John considered.

Rushing past the waiter, who cast him a worried look, the young man stopped in the center of the dining room.

Breathing heavily, he spoke in short sentences.

"The police are headed this way! Banchard is only two blocks up. They're looking for you, Mr. Rex."

He directed the comment to the back table where John, Andrew and Keeyon were sitting.

"He's got the police combing the neighborhood. They're showing everyone your picture . . . and some people are pointing here . . . saying they saw you come in. Banchard is hot and he's at the head of the pack!"

Andrew and Keeyon jumped up.

"Everyone stay calm," Andrew instructed as he scanned the room.

"Dave, Ed, and William, you guys sit at this table. Enrico and Camille, move to Dave's table and spread out so it looks like you belong.

"We planned for this folks, unfortunately the plan has to be activated. You are all a blessing. May God keep you safe."

Keeyon pointed towards the young man that delivered the message.

"Jose, do you know if any police saw you come in here?"

"I don't think so. I came up the back alley and swung around the front."

"Come with us," Keeyon ordered. "Just in case."

John was taking this all in. He was dumbfounded. All this time he thought they were in a secular environment surrounded by strangers, when in fact; he's been with God's people all along!

It was all making sense now. He understood why no one had entered since the three of them had come in. Come to think of it, he hasn't seen anyone leave either. Amazing! This whole thing was planned. Everyone here is a Christian! The restaurant is a front!

Andrew turned to John, "Follow me, my friend. We haven't much time."

Dazed, John got up to move. He faced everyone in the dining room, and with deep emotion, said, "God bless you all, and thank you very much."

Not a person in the room spoke; they didn't have to. Respect, honor, and love beamed from their faces. John didn't want to leave them; he wanted to stay.

Keeyon tugged at his shirt. "It's time to leave, my friend. They know their roles. This was their choice."

John reluctantly turned as he followed Keeyon through the kitchen door behind Andrew and Jose.

Continuing through a second doorway, they rushed over to a set of stairs leading to a supply room in the basement. All four were on the stairs heading down when they heard the front doors of the restaurant slam open.

Moving fast, Andrew led them into a dark corner in the basement. Large sacks of flour, oats, and sawdust were leaning against the wall. Andrew heaved a large sack of flour aside, and then shoved another over. Now all that remained was a dark empty corner, at least that's how it appeared to John. Hurrying by, Andrew leaned over, grabbed a handle and lifted a heavy plate off the floor. It opened on a hinge.

Andrew directed Jose and John to go in first. They hurried in. Loud footsteps pounded above, heading through the kitchen. Keeyon jumped through, with Andrew following. Before closing the hatch, Andrew maneuvered a large sack of oats against it to fall over the plate once it closed, hopefully concealing it.

Jose was in the lead. The three men followed, stepping carefully down a wooden flight of stairs, grappling onto a shaky wooden banister as they went. The only illumination was a narrow beam provided by a simple flashlight Keeyon was holding.

The floor beneath felt hard and cold; the room was musty and damp. John felt a sudden chill sneak into his clothes.

As Keeyon aimed the flashlight ahead, John could see a concrete wall with a large gaping hole in its center. Beyond the hole, he could see the flashlight's beam reflecting off shiny strips of metal along the ground.

Suddenly, he heard an intense roar coming towards them, getting louder and fiercer until everyone had to cover their ears. The source of the deafening noise was approaching fast. A bright light suddenly consumed the entire space. Then seemingly out of nowhere, a monstrous, blaring subway train speeded past, whipping the wind up all around. In seconds it was gone. The men were once again bathed in darkness.

Andrew led the small contingent through the gaping hole and across the train-tracks, then headed down the long dark tunnel. In fifteen minutes they were back out in the sunlight, well beyond the reach of Roderick Banchard and his HEdge Forces.

Chapter

10

The front doors of the Welcome Cafe burst open seconds after Andrew led his small group into the basement. Police officers scuttled in, trampling through the center of the dining room, swinging their loaded rifles freely as they went.

Every patron stopped their conversations and took immediate notice of the sudden bombardment of officers. The first group ran straight to the kitchen, then split up with some continuing up the stairs, others scurrying into the basement. The rest crammed into the dining room taking a stand in any vacant space they could find.

Suddenly, the officer nearest the front door shouted, "Attention!"

At that word every police officer in the room snapped to a sharp, erect stance, throwing their rifles down to their sides and pulling their legs together, some clicking their heals.

The dining room took on a nervous air as everyone became silent and still.

From outside, heavy determined footsteps could be heard making their way through the entrance. Every patron's focus was on those steps. The officers poised forward but their eyes strained sideways toward the door. Everyone knew the source of those footsteps, and everyone, including the officers, felt the tension rise as the author of those steps entered the room.

Roderick Banchard walked into the dining room. The officers nearest him stepped discreetly aside to clear his path. He continued his slow gait, not uttering a single word, his eyes bouncing from table to table. He was hunting for a familiar face he had seen only in pictures, but one he was sure to recognize the second he saw it, beard or no beard.

Taking his time, he spent an inordinate amount screening the faces at some tables, while skimming quickly over others. Walking slowly down the center isle, he continued his intense search, actively scanning from one person to the next. The patrons could do little more than return his stare, albeit in a shortened version.

Roderick was almost through the entire room, yet no John Rex. None of the faces looked vaguely familiar, not a one. A lump formed in his throat as the thought of losing Rex seeped into his mind, the victory slowly creeping away.

"Where is he? C'mon, show yourself, Rex!" he muttered angrily to anyone that could hear.

Roderick wanted this man. He was determined not to let him infect the eastern sector the way he did out west. He knew all too well what Rex had accomplished out there, infiltrating their troops, rumored to have converted thousands of HEdge soldiers to the Christian faith.

A rage smoldered inside. Could Rex have gotten away so quickly?

"Anyone in the kitchen?" he barked to an officer standing at the rear.

"No sir. Every cook and waiter has been accounted for, sir." He pointed to the line of men and women along the wall dressed in white aprons splattered with cooking stains. "That's all of them, sir."

Not satisfied, Roderick bantered, "Is there anyone else in the building? Upstairs, downstairs, anywhere?"

"No sir. We've checked everywhere on all three levels. This is all we have, sir."

Turning to the nearest officer, Roderick demanded, "Give me a picture of Rex!"

Yanking the photo from the officer's hand, Roderick addressed everyone in the room.

"This is the man we're searching for. His name is John Rex. We've been told he came in here within the past hour. I want to know where he is! Who can tell me?"

No answers. Only blank stares.

He handed the photo to a person seated at a table nearest him. Turning back to his officer, he snapped his fingers for the other photographs. In a moment Roderick had an armful of pictures of Andrew Hoyte, Keeyon Webster, and more of Rex. He held some of them up for all to see.

"These two men have been seen with Rex. All three are considered armed and very dangerous. I need to know if anyone has seen them!"

He instructed his officers to pass them around. The patrons scanned the photos, pretending to study each before handing them on. But no one admitted to seeing any of the three men in question.

Pacing the center isle as the pictures were being circulated, Roderick's rage was growing. "I was told these men entered this establishment during the last sixty minutes. It's inconceivable that no one has seen them! I want to know where they are, and I want to know NOW!"

He was losing his patience with these people. Everyone in the room held the same empty stare; as if they had no idea what he was talking about.

How could that be? It didn't make any sense!

Roderick continued his pacing, glancing up at faces, and then looking back to the floor. These people had to know something. They had to!

At the rear of the dining room he spotted a small photograph on the floor. Bending over to pick it up, he noticed something odd about it; for some reason it struck him as familiar, but for the life of him couldn't figure out why. It was a picture of a woman and a young boy. He certainly didn't know either of them. He turned the picture over and saw two names written on the back: Melody, Matthew.

A man sitting at the table nearest Roderick, volunteered, "That's my wife and son. I must've dropped it when you guys came in."

Roderick was about to hand the photograph over, but changed his mind. For no apparent reason, he asked, "What's your wife's name?"

Dave Saunders was doing all he could to remain calm. He knew the picture belonged to Mr. Rex. He caught a glimpse of it just before Roderick picked it up. But what was his wife's name? He knew it began with an M. M something. Margaret? Madaline? Meigon. Close, but not quite. Melody! That's it!

"Melody, sir," Dave said as he reached for the photograph.

Roderick didn't like this. Something wasn't right. He held onto it.

"What's your son's name?"

Perspiration was forming above his brow. Dave could feel the tension building in the room. Time seemed to pause as everyone waited for his answer. He could sense the silent prayers of his friends.

Please, God, give me the answer, the right name, please.

Looking up to the deranged man, he answered, "Matthew."

Roderick heard something in his voice, something other than his answer: a lack of confidence? Worry?

"Where do you live?"

"Long Island, sir. My friends and I came into the city to enjoy a nice meal and see a few sights."

"What's your name?"

"Dave Saunders, sir."

"Let me see your identification."

Pulling his wallet from his back pocket, Dave removed his fake HEdge Citizen ID Card, and handed it over. Roderick examined it for a few seconds, and then gave it back. Then ignored him as he handed the photograph of Melody and Matthew to an officer behind him.

"Have this scanned on the Data Network right away. I want a digital parity made of both the woman and the boy."

Probably a useless endeavor, but something inside, a sixth sense perhaps, insisted he have the picture analyzed. It would take only a few minutes. The picture would be fed into a digital scanner mounted inside one of the HEdge vehicles. The information would be sent via microwave to the Central Intelligence Data Bank in mid-Manhattan, and fully analyzed there.

The photograph would be digitally recomposed. Every curve, every minute facial detail, the exact iris colors and textures would be instantaneously scanned and paired up digitally with every photo-record on file in the HEdge World Data Bank.

The complete process would take no more than ten minutes. Then the matter would be resolved, and the picture discarded. Dave Saunders would be minus one family photo. A small matter to ease Roderick's curiosity.

"I'll ask again. Has anyone seen these three men? They are considered extremely dangerous and need to be apprehended before anyone gets hurt."

Blank faces! Everywhere, blank faces! Roderick was fuming. He had wasted enough time with these idiots while Rex was somewhere out there hiding.

He motioned towards the door as he screamed to the officers, "Get out of here! Rex is somewhere in the neighborhood! I want him found!"

Every officer in the room jumped at his command, dodging through the isles and racing out the door with Roderick on their tail.

After the last officer was gone, Dave Saunders blew out a healthy sigh of relief.

Fifteen minutes later, the officer that had taken the photograph to be analyzed was leaning over a printer, excitedly reading the computer's analysis as it came out. When it finished, he ripped it off and rushed out the door, hollering for a police contingent to follow. Fifty officers immediately came up behind.

Pulling a videocom from his pocket as he ran, the officer called for Banchard, using the Urgent Signal to get priority over any other calls.

Roderick looked furious as he came on the screen.

Continuing to run, the officer exclaimed, "Sir, that photograph we had analyzed . . . the woman's name is Melody Brown, her son's name is Matthew Brown, and their address is 1625 Old Orchard Village, Alameda, California. Sir, the man in that restaurant said he lived on Long Island. He lied. We have no record of a Dave Saunders on Long Island.

"Intelligence has received reports that Rex's wife and son might be named Melody and Matthew. No one knows for certain, but this evidence could support that conclusion!"

Suddenly Roderick understood the familiarity of the picture; the boy's face. His eyes. They were Rex's! A spitting image of John Rex! Why hadn't it occur to him before? That could only mean Rex was there after all! And everyone in the restaurant was covering for him! Everyone! How could that be?

"Has the western sector been notified?" Roderick shouted.

"Yes, sir. The report was automatically forwarded to the western sector headquarters. They have troops on their way to the address right now."

Roderick snickered, "Not bad. Get your troops to the restaurant right away! We'll be there in four minutes!"

"Yes, sir. I'm only a block away now. I've got a squad with me. We'll take the place by force if we have to! No one will get away!"

The Welcome Cafe was surrounded in a matter of seconds. Taking thirty officers with him, the lead officer charged through the front door. As he reached the dining room, he stopped and stood in shock. The place was deserted! Not a person was there! Not one!

"This isn't going to go well with Banchard," he moaned. Not well at all.

Just then, Roderick stormed through the cluster of officers at the door, ranting and raving in all his glory, shouting epithets to everyone, promising the restaurant's patrons they would pay for wasting his time and covering for Rex.

As Roderick finally made it through the congested passageway, he stopped. His jaw dropped as he looked into the vacant space. Assuming a wild, insane glare, he scanned the room. Finally, he looked over to his officer. "Where did they go? We've only been gone for a few minutes!"

The officer was afraid to answer. What could he say? No one knew where they had gone. Police were standing guard in the front and back of the building. There was no way they could have escaped that quickly without being seen. No way!

Roderick spotted something sitting on a table near the wall. As he walked over, he recognized it. "A Bible? They left a Bible! They were all Christians after all! The restaurant was a front!"

He was furious. They escaped! Every last one of them! And to make matters worse, they mocked him by leaving a Bible! Of all things, a Bible!

Swinging his right leg with every ounce of hateful energy he could muster, Roderick kicked the bottom center of the table. As his foot struck, the table flew in the air breaking in the middle with both halves flying in opposite directions. The Bible flew across the room as if it had wings. It hit one of the officers in the chest and fell to the floor. The officer anxiously brushed his jacket where the Bible had struck.

Roderick threatened the lead officer that if he could not find where they had escaped to, his meager existence on this planet would be cut short. Rampaging out the door, Roderick cursed every officer in his path. Their incompetence overwhelmed him. Nothing more than worthless scum! If only he had his HEdge Forces, then everything would have been different! "Samuel Treppin is to blame for this, along with his two goons, White and Ellis. They will pay for this! Each one of them!"

Between rantings, a soothing thought came to him, "Mrs. Rex and little Rex, Melody and Matthew Brown?"

He had to consider this latest development. He was sure it could fit nicely into his plans. Yes, nicely indeed.

Chapter

11

Lieutenant Benson stood leaning against the front door of the HEdge utility truck, his hands tucked loosely inside his trouser pockets as he chewed on a long blade of grass. His legs were crossed, one lying atop the other.

He stood, as if in a trance, watching the bright flames dance and skip across the late afternoon sky, their reflections prancing back and forth on the lens of his wire-rimmed glasses. He was mesmerized by their beauty and elegance, dipping this way, then that, gracefully leaping around a corner, daintily licking through a blown-out window.

And their songs! Their magnificent songs! The high sopranos screamed from the crumbling rooftops of what use to be the New York State Auditorium, reaching out to any trained ear that could appreciate their erratic melodies. Low baritones moved in as voluminous waves of flames gutted entire sections of the building. Loud tenors fluctuated in and out as chunks of the auditorium were consumed in the wild blaze; a chorus of voices rambling throughout the enormous building.

Better than a free concert in the park, the Lieutenant grinned, his eyes glued to the crumbling inferno.

Benson was in charge of the one hundred and seventy soldier HEdge platoon left behind to oversee the final demise of the New York State

Auditorium. He had soldiers posted at equal intervals around the building, keeping a safe distance from the flames. If any pedestrians dared come near, they were shooed away immediately. If they resisted, they were to become part of the bonfire.

Each soldier diligently held their post while anxiously waiting for the Lieutenant's orders to clear out and go home.

But he was in no hurry. In fact, the last thing on his mind was going home. After all, what was there to go home to? His family was gone . . . his wife, his son . . . both gone.

But what grieved Thomas Benson the most was that he had warned them not to go to the auditorium. He told his wife there would be too many people there. Everyone wanted to see Samuel Treppin. The place would be a madhouse; the crowds would be uncontrollable. He had warned her, but she wouldn't listen.

Since he was on duty with the New York branch of the Eastern Sector HEdge Forces, he had to be available in case HEdge called him in. Consequently, he couldn't go to the auditorium with his family, so his wife and son went without him; even after his strong urgings not to.

How ironic that he would be called to help with crowd-control at of all places, the New York State Auditorium! To add to the irony, in one of the largest buildings in New York, to find himself only yards from where his wife and son were struggling through the crowds, in the exact situation he had warned them about!

But this was no time to play told-you-so. He recalled his wife's relieved smile when she looked over and saw him standing with his soldiers. He could see that his wife and son were hard-pressed trying to move anywhere in the jammed shoulder-to-shoulder crowd. He remembered reaching to her, to pull her and his son to safety. If they were just a little closer he would have had them. Just a little closer.

But then, everything broke loose.

He remembered hearing a gunshot. Then a second, and a third. Wasn't sure where they came from or who fired them, which wasn't important at the moment. All that really mattered was the affect they had on the troops around him. Like a rubber band stretched to its limit then snapping apart, likewise the strained nerves of his soldiers had snapped at the sound of the gunshots and immediately assumed full combat status.

Before he knew it, a flurry of gunfire had started going off all around him. Shocked, he watched his soldiers ferociously shooting, unloading their ammo into the terrified audience. He had ordered them to stop but it was too late, a firestorm had begun and no one was listening to anyone.

He recalled turning back to his wife and son just as they took their first hit, then second. Before he could say or do anything, they were down under the now-stampeding crowd.

It was more than he could take. Something inside him had snapped at that point. A mental distinction between reality and fantasy had meshed, and then vanished altogether. He was no longer Lieutenant Thomas Benson, but a raving maniac bent on avenging his family's death.

He remembered pulling his rifle up and firing, shooting with even more savagery than his soldiers. Squinting and drooling, he repeatedly aimed then shot, until it became obvious the process was too slow, so he put the rifle on automatic and began sending barrages of gunfire into the frenzied crowds.

The last thing he remembered was chasing people through the corridors of the auditorium, hunting them down, and shooting. He blanked out after that.

Dropping the blade of grass from his mouth, he fell to his knees, and wept. He had warned them not to go. They should have listened, if only they had listened. Heavy tears poured from his eyes. How could they have gone? How?

A few soldiers nearby noticed him, but remained silent, letting him purge his emotions without interruption.

After some time, Benson stood back up, retrieved a hanky from his pocket and wiped his face dry. He returned to his previous stance, leaning against the truck, admiring the flames. They were all that mattered anymore. They were beautiful.

All of a sudden he could see his wife, her lovely curved figure dancing in them, moving seductively through the glowing stalks. She was waving to him, calling for him to join her. Then he saw his son, Brandon, calling out from his mother's side. "Dad, Dad, come in. Dad, we miss you."

Another tear dropped as he listened to the impassioned calls from his wife and son. He loved them so much. He seldom went anywhere without them, except today of course. The one time they really needed him . . . and he wasn't there.

"Dad, Dad, come in, Dad. I miss you, Dad!"

Benson was drowning in guilt. After failing them once, he was determined not to do it again. He began walking towards the burning building, eager to hug his wife and son, to tell them how sorry he was for not being there for them.

Taking a few more steps, a soldier called to him.

"Lieutenant. Lieutenant Benson. Are you all right, sir?"

The soldier distracted him for a moment. He stopped and turned.

"All right?" Benson asked himself. "All right!" Then he began to laugh. *Was he all right*? He wondered crazily. *Was he all right*! He laughed hard.

The soldier stood straight-faced realizing whatever was going on in his boss' mind was serious stuff.

Finally, Benson stopped his laughing. "Son, I'm fine. You'll have to excuse me. I was just getting a little caught up in the flames."

He looked back to the burning building. He couldn't see his wife or son anymore. They were gone, both of them. Gone.

Wiping a few lingering tears from his eyes, he took in a deep breath, and then addressed the soldier with his old concerned and caring tone.

"I'm fine, Sarge, thanks for asking. We'll be out of here in another fifteen minutes or so."

The soldier seemed to accept his comments without question. "Yes, sir." Then offered, "Let me know if you need anything, okay, sir?"

"Thanks, Sarge. Will do."

Benson turned towards the flames again. His mind wandered. His life, as he knew it, was over. He had no desire to start planning another future. His family was gone, and with them, a large part of himself. A much larger part than he ever would have guessed. All that remained now was an empty shell, flesh and bones, with no purpose, no reason, and no hope.

Only one thought seemed even remotely worth his efforts anymore.

And if he followed through with the logical actions required by that thought, he knew his life would be brought to an abrupt end, which actually made the idea even more appealing. Yes, the thought was definitely worth pursuing.

The thought smoldering through his disturbed mind was, revenge. Revenge for the catastrophe heaped needlessly upon his family. Revenge for the lonely nights he would be doomed to live from here on.

"Yes, that would be a worthy cause," he decided. "Revenge." The last remaining purpose to his now useless life would be to find the individual responsible for the death of his family, and then to take revenge on that individual.

But whom would he blame? Not his men. He would never know who actually fired the bullets that killed his family. No, that would be impossible. It had to be someone else, someone responsible for putting them into this predicament in the first place.

The only person that came to mind was his Colonel. He's the one that ordered the troops here. He was the man in charge of this mess. Yes, he was responsible for his wife and son's death, and now, he would be the one to pay the price for those deaths.

Benson immediately went about planning his superior's assassination. It would be an easy task. Just a simple visit to his office, a few kind words, and then he would take out his revolver, pull the trigger, and "BOOM!" the job would be finished. Nothing complicated.

Of course Benson knew what the consequences of that action would be. But that was fine too. He had no reason to live any longer. Better to join his wife and son in the flames.

"Sergeant," Benson ordered. "Time to gather the troops. Let's go home."

The Sergeant still noticed a strange tone to his boss' voice, something strangely off. To be honest, he suspected his boss had just gone over the edge. He had no psychological training to support his hunch. He couldn't prove it. But he was sure of it nonetheless. And he wondered what it was that had pushed his boss over. Lieutenant Benson was his favorite platoon leader since signing up with HEdge Forces eight years ago, and he hated seeing him like this.

"What a lousy day," the Sergeant grumbled as he began collecting his troops. "What a lousy day."

Chapter

12

The swinging metal doors to the HRS Studio infirmary flew open as Ted Ferguson charged through, his thick bulky frame lunging into the health clinic, grunting angrily as he searched for the three news people whom he had assigned to cover the Sector Chief's speech at the auditorium. His thinning gray hair tossed in the breeze as he dashed around the corner. Stomping towards the outpatient treatment rooms, he disregarded the medical receptionist who stood to offer her assistance.

Dexter Jones and Chris Lombard sat quietly in the corner of the small outpatient treatment room watching Doctor Omri treat Tim Dopler's right shoulder. Lying calmly on the cushioned table in the center of the room, Tim waited for the Doctor's prognosis. Just then, the door of the treatment room burst open.

The three reporters were amazed to see their boss, the Chief Editor of HRS Studios, barge in. Mr. Ferguson was panting savagely as he pulled the long stogy from between his teeth. Seeing their boss' face, they knew right away they were in trouble.

"Oh brother," Chris said under her breath.

"Pardon me? Do you have a problem?" Ferguson scowled at her.

"No sir," Chris answered, immediately regretting her careless remark.

"Good, because I'm not leaving until I learn what in blazes the three of you have been up to?"

Marching right over to Dexter, who was still seated, Ferguson pressed his stubby index finger down into his chest.

"You! You were in charge! You were ordered to leave the auditorium. You got the message, didn't you?" he asked as he looked over to Chris Lombard.

"Yes sir," Dexter answered, "I got the message. I don't exactly know how to explain this, but . . ."

Ferguson's face was on fire. "You don't know how to explain what? You got orders from this office to leave the auditorium; you ignored the orders and stayed . . . what's to explain? You screwed up, Jones! Now tell me why you screwed up? Why did you screw up?"

Ferguson's face was barely an inch from Dexter's, their noses almost touching.

"Sir, if you'll let me explain."

"Explain? Explain! What's there to explain? Just tell me this; what in Turkish camels were you thinking of by ignoring my orders?"

Dexter took a breath before trying to explain.

Ferguson didn't wait. "Do any of you realize what kind of trouble you're in? Huh? Any of you?" He looked around the room, first at Dexter then to Chris. When he looked over to Tim, who was still lying on the bed, he noticed Doctor Omri glaring at him, visibly upset by the intrusion.

"Oh, sorry, Doc. Didn't mean to break in like this. Some pretty serious business here though, and these three might be up to their chins in trouble. Could you excuse us, please? Just for a few minutes?"

"I will not! This patient is suffering physical trauma induced from a terrible fall that caused his right collarbone to fracture just below the extended lower deltoid region. If he's not admitted into surgery soon, the healing process may suffer irreparable damage!"

Tim jumped when he heard the word "surgery." Attempting to lean on his right side to get off the table, he quickly changed his mind as a jolt of pain shot through him.

Ferguson laid his arm around the doctor's much smaller shoulders as he slowly, but deliberately, guided him towards the door.

"Right, Doc. Gotcha. I understood everything you said, and believe me, this will only take a few minutes, then you'll have as much time to cut into Dopler as you want."

Standing at the opened door, he gently nudged the Doctor out as he finished his last sentence. "But for right now, I need to talk to the three of them in private. Okay? We'll be done in just a few. Promise." Then he closed the door.

Ferguson turned to face his three news people. They were sitting erect in their seats, ready to leap out the door at the first opportunity.

"Don't even think about it. None of you are going anywhere." He looked over to Dexter and resumed his interrogation.

"So tell me, Jones, just what happened out there? Why did you screw up? Why did you ignore my orders? Why?"

Dexter had had enough. After everything he and Tim had been through, the last thing he felt like doing was apologizing. On the contrary, he wanted to convince his boss to view the disk, and then play it on the evening news.

"Mr. Ferguson, you wouldn't believe it without seeing it with your own eyes. So I recorded it, and here it is." He held the disk out.

"You recorded it? Who told you to record anything? Not me! As a matter of fact, you were supposed to pack up your recorders and leave! Remember?"

"Sir, you have to stop and listen for a minute! I'm trying to tell you that we witnessed a massacre! A massacre at the hands of HEdge soldiers! Sir, they literally slaughtered thousands of innocent people! With no reason! I have it right here on disk! You have to see it to believe it, sir!"

Ferguson looked down at the disk and grabbed it from him.

"Everything you saw at the auditorium is right here on disk?"

Combing his fingers through his short, curly hair, Dexter considered how to answer his boss.

"No. I wish it was, but the outside of the auditorium was just as bad as the inside, if not worse. Death. Just . . just . . . more death than you can imagine. For no reason! None! HEdge soldiers just wiped the place clean. It was tragic, it was macabre, it was . . . ." Dexter searched for the right word. "It was evil. Pure evil."

"Jones, do you know where you work? Who employs you? Let me tell you just in case it's a little blurry. You work at HRS Studios, Jones. And do you know what HRS stands for? Huh? Do you know?"

Without giving Dexter a chance to respond, Ferguson volunteered, "HRS stands for HEdge Reported Stories. That's what it stands for!

"Now, since we work for HEdge Reported Stories, and HEdge ordered us not to report a story, do you suppose it was a smart thing to go ahead and try to report it anyway?"

Dex had finally heard enough. "HEdge! What is HEdge!" He yelled at his boss. "HEdge is just ten people, no different than you or me, sitting up in their paradise dictating to the world how to live, how to think, and how to act! Just ten people telling billions how to live! Down to the smallest detail!

"Gods, they think they are, every one of them. But they aren't! They're just tired old warped people living in a fantasy world. A world we're more than happy to prop up for them. We let them get away with murder, Boss. At least we did today.

"Mr. Ferguson, you couldn't believe it. The soldiers, HEdge soldiers, killing innocent defenseless people! Just killing them . . . for no reason! Thousands . . . dead.

"There's no way HEdge wants this disk published, and you know why? Because it shows just how out of control they are. It would reveal to the world what chaos, what utter madness controls our lives! The whole planet, we've all fallen prey to an uncontrollable monster! And that monster is HEdge! And now, we have to show this to the world. We have to warn them!"

Ferguson looked down at the disk in his hand. Was it believable?

Looking over to Tim, he asked, "What's your part in all of this?"

Struggling against his pain, Tim answered, "Boss, it's just like Dex said, totally unbelievable, but true. We saw mutilations that would frighten the staunchest horror movie buffs. We are lucky to be alive. If it weren't for Lombard, old Dex and I would be a couple road-kills right now. We were only seconds from kissing this wonderful life good-bye."

Ferguson finally looked over to Chris.

"Talk to me, Lombard. What happened?"

Brushing aside a cute wave of hair draping the side of her face, Chris answered, "Boss, all I know, is after returning to the studio, I only had two of the three recorders we took with us. I figured something was up, so I headed back to the auditorium. Once I got there, I saw these goof-balls running for their lives outside in the parking lot, dodging HEdge bullets! They were lucky they didn't get killed.

"I didn't see much of the stuff Dex was talking about inside the audi-torium, but I saw enough to believe he's telling the truth. The place was a mess. Soldiers everywhere, everyone packing rifles and not hesitating to use them."

Then the door burst open. Twelve soldiers stood outside while the lead HEdge officer strolled in.

"Mr. Ferguson," Lieutenant Baumgartner spoke, "Have you got the recorder and disk yet?"

Strangely, Ted felt tied in a knot. He told the soldiers he would be back with the disk in a minute; apparently they didn't feel like waiting. But now, he wasn't so sure he wanted to turn it over. Could his reporter's be telling the truth?

But it was too late. The soldiers were here. If he didn't hand the disk over, they would take it anyway. And besides, he promised to keep his reporters quiet about what they saw, or the soldiers would take them too.

Ferguson handed the disk over.

"And the recorder," the Lieutenant demanded.

Dexter was watching all this happen right before his eyes. He could-n't believe it. His proof! The only proof of the massacre he and Tim had witnessed was now in the hands of the enemy! Without that disk, no one would believe him. He wouldn't be able to warn the world of HEdge! All was lost!

Dexter bent over and reached down to lift the recorder. As he picked it up, he said, "You want the recorder too, huh? Well here it is!" as he threw it with all his might into the wall right beside the Lieutenant, shattering into pieces.

No sooner had the recorder hit the wall, than the soldiers out in the hallway bolted in and pointed their weapons directly into Dexter's face; each of them itching to pull the trigger.

"There! There's your recorder!" Dexter yelled. "You slaughtering, malicious animals!"

Baumgartner chuckled. "You really need to get a grip of yourself, paperboy. Just be happy your boss pledged your silence concerning this little matter. Otherwise, we'd be taking you with us."

He grinned. "And make sure you do remain silent, otherwise we'll be back. And I promise you, next time we won't be so nice."

At that, he started for the door while motioning his soldiers to follow. Keeping wary eyes on Dexter, they lowered their rifles and began filing out.

As they left, Chris jumped from her seat and went to Dexter. She wrapped her arms around him. "It's all right, Dex. We're still alive. Be thankful of that."

Dexter was lost. After all he had seen, after everything he and Tim had been through, he couldn't believe it was all for nothing. But it was. The evidence was gone. All he had left was the memories; the sick, sick, memories.

Returning her embrace, he sighed, "Thanks, Chris. You've saved me twice today." He looked down into her soft brown eyes. She returned his gaze. A silent moment passed as they held each other, neither capable nor desiring to break the visual bond. Finally, Dexter bent over and kissed her. She responded as her arms held him even closer.

Ferguson left to get the doctor.

Tim breathed a deep sigh as he continued lying on the table. He closed his eyes.

Dexter and Chris held each other. They both needed this. In fact, they've wanted this for a long time, longer than either realized. They secretly felt a desire for each other, but the time never seemed right, the situation never rendered itself to comfortably discuss their feelings for one another. Until now, that is. Now they were communicating perfectly, expressing their mutual feelings in the ultimate language—the language of love. They were communicating so well, they could do it without uttering a word. Their eyes said it all. They came together like a perfectly molded sculpture waiting for the final dab of clay. Now it was complete.

They hugged again, and kissed. Holding their kiss for as long as the world would let them.

Chapter

13

Her dark slender arms reached up to fold the wash towel over the porcelain bar above the kitchen sink. The evening meal was finished, the dishes loaded into the washer, leftovers wrapped and stored in the refrigerator and the trash disposed in the recyclable trashmaster. All was done, now it was time to relax.

She lifted the cooking apron over her wavy brunette hair, carried it to the hook beside the small pantry door and hung it up. Then, turning gracefully on her white sneakers, she headed into the living room.

Her son was way ahead of her. He had already finished his chores and was plopped in the center of the beige carpet waving a cumbersome game in her direction, pleading for her to sit and play.

"Oh, all right, just one. But then you have to finish your homework."

"Great, but if I win, we get to play another game, okay?"

"No. Just one game, then homework."

His shoulders drooped for a second, but realizing the pity display wasn't going to help, he perked back up and began setting the game-pieces together.

Melody smiled inwardly. She enjoyed playing with her son and didn't mind his persistence. He was a good kid, and she loved him with all her heart. But even so, right now all she really wanted was to get comfortable by the videophone and wait for her husband's call. She hadn't heard from John in a few days, and was sure he would be in New York by now.

Half way through their game, the videophone rang. She hurried over to it. Matthew was right on her tail. He was hoping it was his dad too. He was bursting to tell him about a high score he got in a new game he and his best friend, Joshua, had played.

Just as Melody reached the videophone, she heard knocking at the front door.

The choice was easy. She answered the videophone first.

Pressing the pickup button, John's face instantly appeared on the screen, crisp and clear, but distressed.

"Honey, what's wrong?" she asked.

The knocking on the front door was getting louder. Who ever it was, they weren't going away.

"Hi, Dad!" Matthew excitedly yelled into the videophone.

"John, sweetheart, wait one minute, please, someone's at the front door. I'll be right back."

"Don't! Don't answer the door. Melody!"

She stopped. The strain in her husband's voice was apparent; he was serious.

"John, what's the matter, dear?"

"Melody, you've got to get out of the house right away. HEdge knows our address, or at least we think they do."

The pounding on the door was getting louder and quicker.

"Melody, fast, get Matthew and leave the house. Go out the back door. Go to Karen Riggins house. I'll call you there."

Melody hesitated for a second. Then, looking into John's stern blue eyes, she understood completely.

"I love you, John. Bye, sweetheart."

"I love you too, Baby. God be with you."

The screen went blank.

She turned and grabbed Matthew's hand, "Hurry, we have to leave!"

"Why, Mom? Is Dad okay?"

She reached the back door of their two-story townhouse with

Matthew in tow. "Yes, he's fine." Turning the knob, she swung the door open. Just as she was about to step onto the small porch, she was confronted with a host of armed soldiers in blue HEdge uniforms, rifles aimed at her and her son.

She screamed. Letting the door slam shut behind her, she frantically ran back into the living room. Matthew was right behind, "Mom! Who are they?"

The knocking at the front door stopped.

She rushed to it, stood up on the tips of her toes and peeked out the small rectangular window at the top. She was shocked to see even more soldiers lined up in front of her house. The street was covered with HEdge cruisers.

Matthew ran to the front window and peered through the curtain. "Mom! They're everywhere!"

Melody began to panic. Crouching down, she held her son close.

"Mom, what's going on?"

Trying to control her fear, she answered urgently. "Matthew, remember when your father and I told you how some people don't like your father because he teaches about Jesus?"

Matthew nodded.

"Son, some of those people are outside right now, and they want to take us from our home."

"But, Mom! Where will we go?" he asked with all the innocence of a spry, naive eleven-year-old boy.

"Son, I don't know. They might put us in jail."

"In jail?"

Holding Matthew by his young, boyish shoulders, she said, "I don't know what's going to happen, son, but you're a strong young man, and no matter how tough things may get, you can handle it, okay? And remember, you can always pray to Jesus. He'll always listen, son . . . always."

She hugged him while saying a quiet prayer.

Suddenly the front door crashed open. Wood splinters shot through the air as the door broke from its hinges.

HEdge soldiers exploded into the house, wielding their rifles recklessly as they scrambled through the front room and up the stairs to the bedrooms. Others stood firm inside the door, with guns aimed at Melody and Matthew.

Melody remained kneeling on the floor, holding her son tight while watching the soldiers ransack her home. "Dear God! Please stop this madness. Please help us, Lord?"

"That won't be necessary!" a robust, flaming-red-haired female HEdge officer snarled as she marched in through the broken doorway.

The haughty middle-aged woman was Major Harker, Commander of the Western Sector HEdge platoon ordered to apprehend John Rex's family. A witty and devious woman, she held the nervous respect of most of her peers and many of her seniors. The Major's clout was carried largely on her ability for nonstop, self-serving reprimands and snide remarks. An ability she flaunted whenever appropriate. Which, in her way of thinking, was most of the time.

She held a cool stare as she faced Melody and Matthew. Her pencil thin eyebrows rose to an arch as she faked a croon. "Oh, you poor little girl. My, my, calling to your God for help. Isn't that special."

Melody looked over to this female officer mocking her. *What kind of idiot is this*, she wondered.

Stiffening her expression, the officer callously announced, "You can save the prayers for your cell, honey. Because that's where you'll be spending the rest of your days." She snickered. "And there's no telling how long that may be. Some have been known to live long healthy lives in our comfy little cells. While others," she poked the barrel of her gun into Melody's stomach, "don't seem to last long at all."

Melody knocked the gun down and glared. "Who gave you the right to come in here and tear my home apart?"

The corner of Harker's mouth twisted as she yanked the gun back up and struck Melody solidly across her face with it.

Melody stumbled back then fell, her face burning with pain. On the floor, she instinctively reached for her son.

"One more word out of you and John Rex's son will witness his mother's execution," Harker scowled. "That is, if he is Rex's son. I've heard you Christian women get around."

"How dare you insult my family! You have no right! Why don't you leave us alone?"

A soldier shouted from upstairs. "Major Harker, we've found something interesting. I think you might want to see this."

She ordered her soldiers to keep guard over Melody and Matthew, and then went up the stairs. As she reached the top, two soldiers rushed from the master bedroom and presented some books to her. She took one and read its cover.

"Holy Bible! Ha! Are they all Bibles?"

"Yes, ma'am."

She took a few and read the inscriptions stenciled on their front covers; 'Happy Fathers Day', 'With all my Love', 'Happy Anniversary'.

"Charming," the Major scoffed. "Just charming." She slapped the Bibles back into the soldiers' hands. "Box them up, along with any other evidence you find. We'll take it all into Headquarters."

Returning to the living room, she saw Melody and Matthew standing side by side, embracing one another, and looking over to her.

"My, don't I have your attention now?"

Turning to the soldiers guarding the two criminals, she ordered, "Take the boy into juvenile detention. He's a delinquent. If he can be rehabilitated we might find him a good, law abiding home.

"Take the wench downtown and lock her up. She's seen the last of her family. And I'm sure the Eastern Sector would like to have a few words with her."

"No, please! Don't take my son! Please, let us stay together!"

Two soldiers grabbed Melody and tried to yank her out the door as she fought to hold onto her son. Another was trying to pry Matthew's fingers from his mother's waist, cursing as Matthew's tears sprinkled onto the back of his hands.

Trying to push them away, Matthew kicked one in the shins.

Matthew's eleven-year-old frame was a solid stocky one, with strong legs capable of inflicting considerable pain in such an instance.

The soldier was furious as he hopped on one good leg. "Any more of that you little brat, and I'll give you the beating of your life!"

Matthew looked up to his mother. "Mom, don't let them take me. Mom!"

Pleading with the soldiers, Melody cried, "Don't take my son! Please don't."

"Shut up, trash!" the soldier with the sore shins roared.

At that, Matthew kicked him again. "Don't talk to my mom like that!"

"You little rodent!" he swore as he struck Matthew fully across his face. Matthew spun around from the impact, wincing in pain, blood spurting from his lips, yet somehow continuing to grip his mother's waist.

As the soldier cocked his arm, preparing to land a second, even heavier blow, Melody cried out, "Stop it! Stop it!"

With tears streaming down her face, she began prying Matthew's hands from her side. "Matty, you have to let go, son, you have to let go. Or they'll hurt you even more."

"No, mom, please, no . . ."

"Son, I have to . . ."

Finally the soldiers succeeded in ripping the two apart.

Matthew reached out desperately for his mother, bawling as the soldiers briskly carried him out the front door.

"Matty, I love you. I love you, son."

Major Harker was amused by the whole affair. Sort of like open heart surgery, except not as bloody.

"Don't worry," she laughed, "think positive . . . today is the first day of the rest of your life." Melody was dragged out the front door, pulled in the opposite direction from where her son was carried.

Suddenly, the videophone on the living room table rang. A soldier went to press the pickup button.

"Don't touch it." she ordered. "I'll answer it."

Obeying, the soldier stepped aside.

She pressed the pickup button and was amazed to see John Rex appear on the screen. *So this is the mysterious Mr. Rex*, she delighted. *It's been years since anyone in HEdge has gotten a good look at him.*

John was visibly shaken when he saw the Major's face.

"What are you doing in my home? Where's my family?"

"Mr. Rex, I presume?"

"Yes, Major Harker. Where is my family?"

"My, my . . . so you're up on who's who inside HEdge, I see. Quite impressive. Gives me a little appreciation for the power you seem to wield over your simple-minded friends."

"Major, you're quite an over-achiever yourself. But the blood you've drawn to get in your position is a pathetic statement on HEdge's hierarchy. Now I don't care to discuss backgrounds, Major, I want to know where my family is!"

Chuckling, she answered, "No need to worry. They're both alive and well. Though I must say, they were a bit too spunky for their own good. I'm afraid they needed a short lesson in respect . . . you understand," she quipped.

John's heart dropped. What has she done to them.

"Major, where are they?"

"Just like a man," she taunted. "Always calling at the last minute and expecting his woman to jump. Well you're too late, bucko."

Harker broke into a wicked smile, "Now if you had called only a minute sooner you could have watched your dear wife and son part ways. But trust me, you didn't miss much; just a lot of tears and crying. You know, mushy stuff."

John was devastated. Anger was beginning to override his senses. Hatred began to envelope his every thought, and the Major could sense it. She could see it in his eyes. And she enjoyed every bit of it.

"I'm sure if you contact the Eastern Sector, they'd be happy to let you speak with your wife. That's where we'll be sending her. That is, after she gets a few more lessons in respect from me."

John felt a desperate loss for words. How could he protect his family from this heinous woman?

"Don't harm them! Please! I'll do anything! Just don't harm my family!" John was nearly screaming into the videophone.

"Don't worry, Mr. Rex. Or is it Mr. Brown?" she snickered. "Whatever, you can make your deals with the Eastern Sector. You're their business now, not mine. Have a good day."

Without letting John respond further, she leaned over and disconnected the call. The screen went blank.

Without pause, she pressed the operator button.

A young lady appeared on the screen.

"Operator, this is Major Harker of the Western Sector HEdge Forces. I want the number and address of the other end of the communication just finished on this line."

"Yes, Ma'am. Just a moment please."

After punching several buttons on her keypad, the following information appeared on-screen.

```
Phone number: 212-668-788-8214
Location: Public Phone booth No. 578
302 Park Ave
New York City, NY
```

"What?" the Major griped. "A public phone. That doesn't help any." After a moment of contemplation, she relaxed, "Well, we've got his family. Can't hurt much more than that I suppose."

The operator's voice returned, "Can I help you with anything else?"

"Yes. I want a playback of all conversations made on this line within the past twenty-four hours."

A polite frown formed on the operator's face. "I'm sorry, but we only store private communications for an hour before the system automatically sweeps them clean. Our data storage capabilities are somewhat limited. However, I can replay any communications made within the last hour if you'd like. Also, I'll need your HEdge Communication Authorization number, please."

Flustered at the inconvenience, Harker jabbed into her pocket and pulled out her HEdge Forces Identification Card, then read aloud the authorization number on its reverse.

"Thank you very much," the operator acknowledged. "I apologize for any trouble," then began tapping more buttons on her keypad. In a matter of seconds she was finished.

"Thank you for using Western HEdge Communications. If we can be of further assistance, please don't hesitate to call."

The operator's face left the screen and was instantly replaced by John Rex, as the entire conversation between he and Melody - made only minutes earlier - played out on the screen.

At its conclusion, the Major rubbed her chin. "Hmm. Karen Riggins. She must live nearby."

Turning to the nearest officer, she ordered him to contact headquarters right away. She wanted a complete listing of names and addresses of every person in the neighborhood. "I want this Karen Riggins captured. Sweep the neighborhood if you have to, but I want her found."

"Yes, Ma'am." The soldier went right to business.

A minute later, Harker was sneering wickedly as she turned to leave, "Two catches in one afternoon. Not a bad day's work."

Chapter

14

Distraught, Rex slammed his fist into the wall inside the phone booth on Park Avenue. He pounded it a second time as his jaws grinded, every muscle in his body tightening.

"How dare you take my family!" he shouted into the videophone. "I want them back!"

Refusing to walk away from the still-illuminating screen, he stood staring, seething at the vision of the female HEdge officer imprinted on his mind, a spiteful woman whose entire countenance seemed to lust after his anguish. She seemed to enjoy the whole affair, from the taunting and teasing, to forcing the last word, and finally breaking the connection.

But her nasty character aside, what concerned John the most was her apparent eagerness to feed that lustful appetite on the scourges of his family.

"God," John prayed as he closed his eyes, "why is this happening?"

His mind raced over everything, trying to sort it out, to make sense of it all. Surely there was some reason for this, some purpose.

He jabbed his index finger onto the videophone's 'Off' button. The screen went dead. Slumping over, he rested his elbows on the high stainless steel shelf that supported the videophone, and planted his forehead into the palm of his hands.

There he stood, succumbing to his emotions, stewing over his family's predicament, feeling tormented. As he did, every deceitful, antagonistic urge available in Satan's demonic arsenal played itself out on his psyche. He felt hatred tugging at him, thirsting for immediate and thorough revenge; he felt despair begin to settle in, making everything appear hopeless and meaningless. He was distraught. He felt a sense of betrayal from his friends' carelessness, and worse, he felt a wedge cutting deep into the very bowels of his faith.

Clamming his eyes tighter, he whispered in a barely audible voice, "How could this be happening, Jesus? Why is it happening? Why? Please show me, Lord. Please reveal your mysterious plan to me. Have I failed you somewhere, somehow? Is this a punishment, Lord? What have I done? What have I done?"

John continued questioning God's purpose, questioning His reasoning, even beginning to question the very basis of his own faith. He begged for a revelation of some kind to explain the tragedy that had befallen his family; first asking, then telling the Lord to account for it, to rationalize it, to justify it.

Finally, at the end of his patience, completely exasperated, John pushed his arrogance to the limit, as he demanded an explanation from the Lord, God.

But an answer never came. Only silence, and pain. He wept.

Andrew, Keeyon, and Jose waited anxiously on the corner of 39th and Park Avenue, eagerly waiting the results of John's phone call.

As soon as they saw him step out of the phone booth they knew the worst had happened. John's family was in the hands of HEdge.

"My God . . ." Andrew cried out as he looked to the heavens. "My God!" Then dropped his vision to the sidewalk, drooping his shoulders. He couldn't help but feel responsible for the pain his friend was suffering. There were no words to express how sorry he was for his negligence. How could he have been so careless!

He turned as he sensed John coming near. He couldn't look him in the eyes. Lowering his vision, he swiped a tear off his cheek.

Keeyon was in no better shape. He glanced over to John and met eyes with him, but likewise, couldn't hold it. What could he say? What could he possibly say?

One of them, either Keeyon or Andrew, had dropped the photograph of Melody and Matthew back at the restaurant before rushing out, but neither was sure who did. Both were willing to take the blame; not that it mattered at this point, the damage was already done; Melody and Matthew were gone, taken by HEdge. How much more devastation could a person heap onto a friend's life?

Both Andrew and Keeyon desperately wanted to express their remorse, their sorrow, but didn't know where to begin.

Jose remained silent, sensing the awkwardness and severity of the moment; understanding this was a matter that John, Andrew, and Keeyon needed to resolve amongst themselves.

John approached Keeyon and Andrew.

"Hey, come on you guys," he said as he reached out to both men. "You two look about as bad as I feel."

Looking up, Andrew said, "John, I'm so sorry. I don't . . ."

Keeyon also began apologizing.

"Listen, both of you," John interrupted, "you can't tell me anything I don't already see on your faces. And I love you both for it. Yes, Melody and Matthew are in HEdge's custody, and yes, it hurts. I can't begin to tell you what despair I just went through inside that phone booth.

"But this isn't the end; it's not over. We must believe they'll be back. The Lord will see them through this. Only He can wipe away these tears. He knows my love for them, and we know His love for us. He will uphold us. Praise God. He will uphold us."

Andrew and Keeyon listened as John recited his words of compassion, wisdom, and hope. As he spoke, the guilt that weighed them down so heavily gradually lifted and transformed into a spirit of camaraderie and love. The sorrow was still painfully there, but an undercurrent of peace rested between them. A peace only the Holy Spirit could provide.

As John finished, all three men joined together in a tight and healthy hug, with tears being shared among them. And they prayed.

Chapter

15

Samuel Treppin's lumbering body lay sprawled out on the lengthy davenport sofa in the center of his large office. He was dizzily recuperating from the drunken stupor he had indulged in the day before that prevented him from giving his speech at the New York State Auditorium.

Lying on his back, he held a cold compress to his forehead as a belly full of anti-toxin medicine fought off the aching effects of his hangover. His free arm dangled lifelessly over the side of the couch.

He was in no condition to do anything beyond simply existing today. He had exerted every ounce of energy just to get bathed, dressed and groomed in a presentable fashion.

In a strained voice, he called out to his secretary. "Jennifer, could I have another glass of orange juice, please?"

His pounding head barely survived the desperate plea for juice. He continued to lie as a fallen timber, without motion or sound. The only sign of life, aside from the constant thumping of blood beneath his scalp, was his roving eyes, watching with keen interest, searching the doorway for his secretary.

"Ugh," he moaned. "I'll never touch another bottle as long as I live."

There was no one else in his office. He wasn't speaking these words of commitment to anyone in particular, least of all, himself. And as he would reflect on this moment later in the day, he would come to the same conclusion he had come to for the past several years: his drinking really wasn't so bad, nothing he couldn't handle; in fact, he didn't really have a drinking problem. He just needed to put things in perspective, to drink in moderation. That's all. Nothing more than that.

So the cycle would continue; that evening or maybe the next, he would find another bottle of liquor titled over an empty glass, readying itself for proper disposal into the craving jaws of his thirsty dry mouth, absorbing the cursed fluids as a man possessed, without a care in the world, and, at least for the moment, without a care for the world.

And therein lies the problem. As Samuel Treppin immersed himself deeper into the life-draining anesthetics of alcohol, the concern for his constituents in the Eastern U.S. Sector tapered and ebbed. If gone unchecked, the days were not too far off when he would resemble the other thirty-nine Sector Chiefs in more than just a title, when his primary concern would become none other than himself. While the populace he was sworn to represent at the world financial tables of HEdge, would be fortunate to receive back-seat honors. It was something he had sworn would never happen, yet something that inevitably must. For it was the way of the world. And, as Samuel Treppin was most definitely of the world, it was to be his way as well.

"Jennifer, where's my juice?"

Ms. Bajon came around the corner as he cried out the second time. She was carrying a large glass of his favorite morning beverage, orange juice, with two ice cubes clanking against the glass.

Her dark blue skirt tugged at her shapely legs as she hurried over to him. Her cute, clear-complexioned face was pinched into a frown as her eyes locked onto his; purposely presenting an expression that was anything but conciliatory.

She leaned over to hand Samuel the tall glass.

"Mr. Treppin, you're going to become an old man before your time if you keep up with this nonsense."

Samuel ignored her. He has heard it all before, with the same disciplinary and motherly tone. He knew Jennifer meant well, it's just that he really didn't care to hear any of it right now.

Slowly lifting himself to a sitting position, he waited for his equilibrium to catch up, and then carefully reached for the glass of juice. He wrapped his fingers around it, making sure of a tight grip, and then guzzled.

Releasing a contented sigh, he closed his eyes as he finished the vitamin-enriched beverage. This was true medicine, life savoring orange juice.

After a moment of sheer pleasure, he opened his eyes. As he did, the room began losing definition again; the alcohol's lingering effects persisted as a floating sensation took over, the walls seemed to shift angles. He steadily handed the empty glass back to Ms. Bajon, and then slowly dropped himself onto the sofa.

Jennifer watched in dismay as her once health-conscious boss slumped back into the leather sofa and closed his eyes.

What a shame, she thought to herself. She wondered how a world-renowned figure like Samuel Treppin, a man who had gorged himself early in life with more academic achievements than most people could hope for in a lifetime, could fall for the predictable addictive qualities of alcohol. With his intellect, he should have seen it coming. He should have turned it around, before it turned him around, but not so.

His eyes crawled open as he turned toward her.

"Jennifer, I know what you're thinking. So don't, please. I'm fine. Really. I just need a little time to recuperate, that's all. I'll be ready for business in a couple hours. Promise. Okay?"

Jennifer looked down at him in sadness.

"Mr. Treppin, I don't mean to sound motherly, or preachy, or anything like that. But I'm really not so sure you will."

She hesitated a second. "And please forgive me for saying so, but I really think you should see someone about your drinking, a professional. Someone you can confide in. For your own good."

"Jennifer," he sighed, "I really appreciate your honesty and concern. I don't know what I would do without you. There aren't too many people who could come close to filling your shoes."

"None that I know of," she added with a touch of attitude.

He forced a smile.

"I really appreciate the great job you do around here, Jennifer. But even more than that, I appreciate your honesty. I need that perhaps more than anything."

He paused briefly.

"Jennifer, I'm going to take your advice. As soon as I return from the World Finance Conference at the end of the week, I'll see about talking to someone, a counselor. Okay?"

She looked somewhat pleased, though not entirely convinced.

He continued, "Maybe you're right. Maybe I do have a problem of sorts. We'll see. But in the mean time, could you have the staff make up a list of the best clinics in the city, with references? We can go over them together when I return."

For the first time in months, Jennifer felt a sense of hope for her boss. He actually sounded sincere this time … or was it just the booze talking?

"I hope you mean it, Mr. Treppin. I really do. For your own good."

Samuel forced a smile as he winked at her. He could see the sparkle of hope gleaming from her eyes. *Good*, he thought to himself, *maybe she'll leave me alone now.* He was drained.

"Jennifer, please cancel any appointments scheduled for this morning. I don't want to see anyone until after lunch."

"Yes, sir." Then added, "Oh, and just a reminder, sir, your jet will be ready at 7 p.m. for the flight to Geneva for the finance conference."

Samuel was feeling queasy. The thought of going to the World Finance Conference in Geneva didn't help any. He took a deep breath and then exhaled impatiently as he began complaining. "Too many bean counters these days, Jennifer," he muttered. "Always trying to think up new ways to confuse things."

Jennifer knew right away where Samuel was headed. If she didn't stop him, he was sure to once again delve into his accountant-bashing lecture.

"Sir, maybe you should try forgetting about the conference for right now. I'll bring in another glass of orange juice, and then you can get some rest."

"Yes, you're right, Jennifer. It's just that, I don't know how the other Sector Chiefs put up with it. Do they even look at their financial reports?"

He gingerly began sitting up while holding the cold-compress to his head. His body ached, but he just couldn't lie down when discussing his least favorite subject: Hedge accountants.

"People talk about lawyers, Jennifer, like they're some kind of pariah; a plague on society; parasites feeding off other peoples' misfortunes. But they're nothing, Jennifer. Absolutely nothing."

Squinting, he waved his right index finger toward her, emphasizing his next point.

"The lawyers, Jennifer, they're mice; just little mice chasing each other around fighting for whatever morsels they can get; but Hedge accountants, ah yes, now you have the big shots, the sharks. They don't settle for crumbs, Jennifer. Oh no, not on your life. They don't even settle for chunks. They aren't happy until they get the whole three course meal!"

Samuel was getting louder as he feebly stood, swinging his free arm through the air. "With a moved decimal here, a deleted zero there, before you know it, some well-to-do accountant held up in some lofty office has magically wiped out complete portions of Hedge finances for an entire sector!

"The parks, the schools, hospitals, everything suffers, and everyone suffers, just because one accountant had to adjust a ledger to get the preposterous thing to balance in column twenty on page ten.

"They're the heartless ones, Jennifer; the Hedge accountants. They love their numbers but don't give a hoot about the people!"

Jennifer took a step back as Samuel rambled on about the heartless doings of Hedge accountants. She wasn't listening so much as observing. She noticed the color in his face begin to drain as he stood, and could hear the strength in his voice gradually slipping away as he pushed even harder to get every frustrated word out.

He had been drinking at a reckless pace over the past several months and was starting to really show it. There was no telling how much longer he could continue without suffering heavy consequences.

"Sir, you'd better lay down. You're looking awful pale."

Samuel felt an instant jarring in his head. The sudden flurry of emotion left an immediate mark on his pounding headache. He felt faint. Carefully, he laid himself back down on the couch.

"Ugh," he moaned again. "Jennifer, you're right, I feel terrible."

"Sir, not to change the subject, but I need to know when you want to close for the day so I don't schedule any appointments too late."

While answering, he tried to ignore his thumping headache. "Not later than five. Now I'm going to follow your second piece of advice and take a nap. Wake me at eleven if I'm not already up."

With that, Samuel closed his eyes as he tried forgetting the World Finance Conference in Geneva and the HEdge accountants. "Retched bean counters," he mumbled before dozing off.

Jennifer walked calmly out of his office. She wasn't sure what to make of their conversation. Was he serious about seeing a professional for his drinking problem? She hoped so. Samuel was a good man and she hated watching him deteriorate like this.

Considering his present state, she was glad he didn't bring up the one subject that would have made his headache even worse. She figured he would be better able to cope with the news of the auditorium fire once he had a chance to recover.

The news flash that had come across the HEdge network first thing this morning had left her completely shocked, and she could only imagine what effect it would have had on him.

According to the HRS report, the fire was most likely an assassination attempt on the Sector Chief's life, and the coincidental appearance of the infamous John Rex, the Christian renegade from the Western U.S. Sector, had stirred up more than a little suspicion among HEdge authorities. The general consensus was that the auditorium fire was Rex's handiwork.

Jennifer was shaken when she considered how close Samuel had come to actually dying in that blaze. Now her primary concern was getting him to see a counselor about his drinking.

Leaving the office, she considered the chances of that happening. She closed the door behind her. "We'll see."

Chapter

16

As the traffic light turned green Jim Talbot put his unmarked HEdge vehicle into motion, driving slowly around the corner of Eighth Street, making a right on Sixth Avenue. Completing his turn, he pulled the cruiser to the curb, inched up to a parking meter and cut the engine.

He reached over to the passenger's seat, lifted the small videocomm and tucked it into his midnight-blue dress coat. Pressing the driver's side door release, it opened on one steady swing. The bright afternoon sunlight gleamed off his smooth leather boots as he stepped out of the cruiser. His tightly cuffed wool pants wavered as the afternoon breeze latched onto them.

Lingering beside the cruiser, he examined the busy intersection, searching the area for anything out of the ordinary.

He threw his sunglasses over his wide-brimmed nose as he continued scanning. Finally, with nothing interesting to report, Talbot decided it was time for some self-indulgence, which was the real reason he made this stop in the first place. His stomach had been grumbling for the past forty-five minutes and he knew exactly what it needed.

Across the sidewalk was a popular bagel restaurant, serving hot, "fresh from the oven" bagels to New York's most dedicated bagel connoisseurs. Jim Talbot was one of its frequent customers. Part of his daily ritual was to pick up a baker's dozen on his way to work.

Returning to his cruiser a few minutes later, Jim swung the drivers-side door open, tossed the bagels inside and climbed in. Almost before he could close the door, the bag was open with his fingers fumbling through for just the right one.

The videocomm inside his coat pocket suddenly sounded off. Nonchalantly moving the bag off his lap, he pulled the videocomm out. The small color screen sparked to life as the blond-haired, blue-eyed face of Bob Netherland appeared.

"Bob, have you see anything yet?" Jim asked.

"Naw, just a few knuckleheads. How bout you?"

"Same. Pretty boring. I had to stop and get something to munch on to stay awake."

"Bagels, right?" Netherland chided. "What is it with you and bagels anyways?"

"What's it to you? You don't have to eat em."

"Who say's I want to. Give me a pretzel smothered in mustard any day. Now there's a treat!"

"Yeah, if your taste buds are comatose."

"Give me a break," Bob smirked into the screen. "The only thing comatose around here is your brain."

Jim nodded slightly at the remark.

"Bob, is there something you called me for?"

"Actually, I was just bored. I needed someone to kill time with."

"Do me a favor will you?"

"Sure, what's that?"

"Next time you need someone to pass time with, call Joe Barnes. He's more your gum-chewing, simple-minded type. I'm sure the two of you could strike up some deep intellectual conversation over gum-wrappers or something."

Bob chuckled. "Real funny, Jim. Got any more stale jokes?"

Tired of the discussion, Jim concluded, "Naw, I'll talk to ya later."

The dialogue ended. Bob Netherland and Jim Talbot both snapped their videocomms to 'Off.'

Bored, there was nothing much to do except continue surveying the old Greenwich Village neighborhood, as hundreds of other undercover agents were doing.

After a few minutes, Jim snapped his videocomm back on and called Bob Netherland back.

"What?" Bob pompously asked as his face shot on the screen.

Jim thought to himself, *why did I call this jerk back?*

Oh well, "Is everyone in place? I saw agents over on Christopher Street a few minutes ago, but that's it. Have you seen anyone? They better not be boozing it up in the pubs."

"Yeah," Bob agreed, "some of them have real reputations, you know, real lushes. If they get caught, they're mincemeat. Banchard will kill em."

Neither man doubted this last statement. They knew Banchard, they knew his level of patience, and they knew his limits.

"You bet," Jim agreed. "Banchard's nervous enough with Rex in town. Wouldn't take much to set him off."

"Why's he so nervous?" Bob asked arrogantly. "Rex isn't stupid. He's not going to start any trouble. I'm tellin ya, we're all wasting our time."

"Fine, you tell Banchard that, okay?" Jim charged. "Then maybe we can all go home. Go ahead, man. Call Banchard and tell him we don't need to be out here looking for Rex and his gang. Then maybe we can go home."

Bob rubbed his nose nervously. "I'm tellin ya, Rex is probably just meeting up with some old buddies, and then he'll be gone before we know it. Headed back west. Trust me."

"Don't bet on it," Jim countered. "The intelligence network says Rex is trying to expand his network out here. That's why Banchard is so up in arms. The last thing he wants is John Rex spreading his business into our sector. The HEdge Council would have plenty of tough questions if the Christians infiltrated this sector the way they did out west. You know the trouble they caused out there. It'll be years before the Christians are completely filtered out of their ranks. If ever."

"Oh come on, Jim," Bob guffawed. "Rex isn't going to make a scene today, not after all that trouble over at the auditorium yesterday. He knows we're on the lookout. Besides, he's probably on the run right now. Like I said, Rex will be out of town before we know it, and without a peep."

Jim thought for a moment. He wasn't so sure.

"Bob, I'm going to drive over to Christopher and McDougal. There's nothing happening here. If you see anything, call me right away."

"Sure, but relax, nothing's going to happen. Trust me."

"Right."

T he radio blared from the cab of the eighteen-wheeler tractor-trailer as it barreled down Interstate 80 heading east toward the George Washington Bridge. Enrico Sanchez and Steven Labbs were listening to the latest HEdge broadcast concerning the New York State Auditorium blaze.

According to the special report, HEdge investigators had already concluded that John Rex and his Christian cohorts were responsible. The report went on to say the assassination attempt on Mr. Treppin's life was thwarted only by the Sector Chief's sudden illness that forced him to cancel his speech—doctor's orders, which ultimately saved his life.

Although the assassination attempt had failed, the Christian rebels were still responsible for the lives of thousands who had perished in the flames. The reporter quoted a high-ranking official within HEdge as promising that, "John Rex and his friends from the western sector would be found and prosecuted to the fullest extent of the law."

The reporter also announced that the wife and son of John Rex had been captured and taken before the authorities in the western sector. Rex's wife, Mrs. Melody Brown, was to be transported to New York City under heavy security by the end of the week. The western sector needed time to question her on other serious matters such as obstructing justice, assaulting an officer, and possession of illegal contraband.

The report concluded with a stern warning from a certain Colonel Dirk Reynolds, who was on-scene at the auditorium. "If you can hear my voice, Mr. Rex, if you are anywhere within the sound of this broadcast, you should be trembling with fear; because the full power of HEdge has been unleashed to find you, and you will not escape. You will be found, and you will be punished for this heinous crime against society!"

"Off!" Enrico snapped, causing the radio to instantly shut off.

"The only one who's going to be trembling will be the HEdge Council and their lackeys when they meet their Maker!"

Steven Labbs concurred, "They're blind, Enrico. Blind and deceived."

Enrico and Steven realized there were awesome powers at work here; powers beyond the tangible realm of natural human understanding. And within those powers, they knew that without a single public announcement or official decree, a full-scale war was underway. A war that had been raging for thousands of years, steadily increasing in momentum and intensity with each dawning day.

Enrico prayed aloud as he sat behind the steering wheel watching the road ahead. "Father Almighty, let them see past the lies and deceptions of the media. Let them see the truth, let them search out the truth that only You can provide."

"Amen!" Steven added.

Enrico pressed the accelerator a notch, speeding the truck ever closer to the George Washington Bridge. He was more determined than ever to complete this mission.

Glancing into his rear-view mirror, Enrico saw the other fourteen semi-tractor trailers tearing up the road behind him, each carrying the same special cargo, and each sharing the same purpose: to spread the Word of God to the residents of New York City; the heart and soul of the Eastern U.S. Sector.

The semi-tractor trailers had come together the night before, all traveling from different directions, but each originating from the Western U.S. Sector. Each trucker had driven separate routes on the old interstate system to avoid any unwanted attention a convoy might draw. They converged at a scheduled highway rest area right outside the city.

John Rex intentionally wrote into the plans for everyone to come together for this one last night. The purpose was to provide fellowship and encouragement before continuing on the last leg of their journey. The night's rest would be an evening of camaraderie, humor, and prayerful discussions.

The stop had served its purpose. The drivers were energized and invigorated; their spirits aroused from the group-readings of the Bible; their goals edified and illuminated. Any final trepidation over the perils that lay ahead was smothered with spiritual confidence. They were now ardent soldiers of God, valiant and stouthearted, eager to do the Lord's bidding.

The drivers were ready to take the final lunge into the core of one of Satan's many workshops. HEdge would have to step aside because these holy soldiers were coming through, full throttle.

Finally at the George Washington Bridge, Steven got on the truck's intercom and bid farewell to the other drivers as they all parted ways. Each truck had to follow their own separate routes through Manhattan to their individual destinations.

Enrico and Steven were scheduled to make their stop in Sheridan Square, the heart of Old Greenwich Village. After pulling away from the convoy, they followed the Henry Hudson Parkway south.

The traffic was horrendous, which was not a surprise. Enrico juggled his attention from the accelerator to brake pedal, making constant adjustments to the steering wheel as small cars darted in and out of their path.

The last few miles were more wearing on Steven and Enrico than the entire trip east. The gloom and despair of the city weighed heavily on them. They could sense a deep spiritual hunger everywhere; the life of the city had been drained, while a facade of humanism existed in its place.

"There's 34th Street." Steven exclaimed. Only a dozen more blocks and they would be at their stop.

A few minutes later they were finally pulling over to the curb on South Broadway in the center of Sheridan Square. Steven cut the engine. They both took deep breaths as they stepped out of the truck's cab.

Circling to the back, Enrico removed a thick metal key from his hip pocket and slipped it into a metal box right above the rear bumper. He turned the key a full 360 degrees then removed it. Nothing happened. Then he and Steven both walked along opposite sides of the long truck, pulling switches underneath as they did. There were twenty switches on each side, approximately three feet apart. Each needed to be flipped. Once completed, they met at the front of the truck, took a quick glance around the square, and then together, conspicuously hurried to the sidewalk.

J im Talbot was in the middle of a cinnamon raisin bagel when he spotted the Sloan Business truck pull up to the curb. Then he watched as two men stepped out, went to the back of the truck and fiddled with a box. A minute later they were each walking along opposite sides of the truck, reaching for something underneath every few feet of the way.

That's odd, Jim thought to himself.

Just then, the two men finished whatever they were doing, met at the front of the truck and speeded their pace to the sidewalk.

This is not good, Jim decided. *Something's wrong.*

He tossed the remainder of his bagel out the window. His fingers danced over the numeric keypad on his videocomm as he sent an urgent signal to every HEdge agent in the area.

"Everyone, this is Jim Talbot. I'm in Sheridan Square. Come out quick. We've got a red semi-tractor trailer out front with Sloan Business painted in green; two male drivers acting strange, one's got dark hair, looks Hispanic, wearing blue jeans and a white shirt; the other's brown haired, Caucasian, black pants, blue shirt, headed for the sidewalk. This is it boys and girls! Come out to play!"

Jim pressed the door release. The door opened too slowly. He pushed it as he flew out. From all around he could see HEdge agents spilling into the streets, each brandishing their weapons while running towards the Sloan Business truck.

Jim saw the two drivers start running down Bleeker Street. He knew he had them now. He took off after them. Knocking people over, he leaped up and down, shouting to the other agents as he pointed to the two running men.

As soon as the agents saw him, they understood, and immediately took up the chase; which was exactly what Enrico and Steven wanted.

"This side of the street's got even-numbered addresses. Must be on that side," Steven said as he ran down the sidewalk, pushing to keep pace with Enrico.

"Should be two blocks up, in the middle . . . 2315 Bleeker," Enrico shouted as they swung across the street, dodging between cars and pedestrians until finally on the opposite sidewalk, sprinting as fast as their legs would take them.

"We're at 1713 now," Enrico said.

They flew up Bleeker as fast as they could, trying their very best not to run into the dozens of pedestrians along the way. They trained hard for this part of the mission, day and night, through the worst of terrains, running until they could run no more. So physical endurance should not be a problem as long as no surprises pop up.

A couple blocks later the HEdge agents were starting to slow, losing their wind. But Enrico and Steven continued their fast pace through the clutter of people. The agents couldn't shoot with the lunchtime crowds everywhere, which was another factor included in the plans. They continued running as best they could. They were almost there.

Suddenly up ahead scores of agents spun around the congested corner, knocking people over as they raced through, trying to cut off the two men's escape route.

Enrico and Steven weren't sure if they could make it to the building in time. Their lungs were heaving. The agents behind were tiring fast, but the ones ahead were fresh, with fire in their eyes. They wanted Enrico and Steven; they wanted them bad.

Scanning the addresses as they ran, Enrico and Steven were desperate for 2315 Bleeker. Without it, they wouldn't have a chance.

Enrico saw it first. He pointed to an old brownstone building. Steven followed as they ran across a lawn onto its front steps.

The agents were almost on them. Enrico and Steven rushed through the front door of the old brownstone. As they passed the entrance, the door automatically closed behind them. An electronic device mounted above the door clicked at the sudden vibrations, causing two solid metal bars to drop into place on top of four iron hooks. The front door was now secured, and would remain so until a force stronger than those metal bars could break them free.

The agents swarmed at the front door just as it closed. They struggled to open it, but it wouldn't budge. They ran around back. There was another door, also bolted shut. There were no windows on the lower three levels of the building either. They were furious. Soon, all of the two hundred and fifty HEdge agents including Jim Talbot and Bob Netherland, along with every cop in the area, were at the building, all trying to force the doors open. An agent finally ran to a car and pulled out a box of plastic explosives. That would do it. But by now it was too late.

Enrico, you almost ready for the code?" Steven asked as they rushed into the basement, heading towards a hidden cellar that led into a maze of subway tunnels beneath the building.

Just as they got into the tunnel, Enrico stopped and said, "Let's do it!"

Pulling up his right shirtsleeve, Steven uncovered an elaborate electronic cuff wrapped around his arm right below the elbow. He pressed a few digits on it and was done.

"Okay, buddy. Your turn."

Enrico rolled up his sleeve, uncovering a miniature videocomm. He pulled it off and pressed a few digits causing the tiny screen to come to life. Then, he and Steven watched as the sides of their semi-tractor trailer began folding up into the roof in an accordion fashion. In a minute, every side was open, exposing rows and stacks of over five hundred thousand Bibles. Steven and Enrico listened as the speaker on the back of the videocomm recorded the announcement booming from the top of their tractor-trailer.

"Repent, New York, repent. Salvation is at hand. Please take one of these Bibles for your personal reading. Let Jesus into your life, New York! Only through Him can there be eternal salvation. Accept Jesus into your hearts! He is the Alpha and Omega, the Beginning and the End. Don't be deceived by HEdge lies. Jesus is Lord. He is the only way to eternal life and true happiness. Read these Bibles. Learn the truth! It's all here, the truth is ready for you; are you ready for the truth?"

Enrico and Steven watched as thousands of people scrambled for the Bibles, whisking them off the truck, running away before the authorities could return to stop them. A near riot was breaking out as the masses engulfed the trailer, grabbing Bibles for themselves and family members.

After years of being choked away from God's Word, forced to swallow the false teachings of HEdge, the crowds were rabid for the Truth, drawn to it like wayfaring children returning from a long senseless journey. Their spirits hungered for the Lord's Word and the salvation it offered, while their flesh only knew that something remarkable was finally within reach. And reach they did, by the thousands! The starvation was being fed, God Almighty, the starvation was being fed!

"It worked! It worked!" Steven shouted at the top of his lungs. Enrico joined in with exuberant cheers as they both leaped into the air, hooting and hollering.

Chapter

17

Several joyous minutes later, sitting quietly on the cool stony floor of the dark subway tunnel, Steven and Enrico were enjoying the security of their surroundings. Tickled smiles covered their faces as they reflected on the day's events. Having completed their mission, they were now waiting for their tunnel-guides. Neither of them could navigate the tunnels on their own. They needed someone to lead them through the endless maze back to sunlight and to their fellow drivers. Their instructions got them to this point, but from here on they were at the mercy of their Christian brothers and sisters in the eastern sector.

Enrico thought he heard a noise escape from deep inside the tunnel. He whispered to Steven, "Did you hear that?"

Steven looked over to where Enrico was pointing. He couldn't see a thing. The lighting was too poor. The black steel-casings that enclosed the tunnel wall-lamps were badly rusted over, allowing precious little light to escape.

Steven listened intently, straining to hear anything besides their heavy breathing. Only silence echoed back. The dark chamber of tunnels seemed to intentionally hold back any sounds.

For a minute, Enrico questioned himself; did he really hear something, or was it his imagination? An active imagination could have a field day with all the shadowy images dancing across this blackness.

Then he heard it again. This time Steven heard it too. They both sat still, straining their ears toward the sound, gazing into the darkness for any hint of motion.

An image finally began taking shape within the recesses of the tunnel. Still a distance away, but close enough for them to make out a blurry silhouette of someone moving towards them. They felt excited as the image got nearer, hoping it would be their guide, but keeping a cautious vigilant just in case. Stories of underground terrorists violently staking out their claims in the New York subway system were common.

Whoever it was, they weren't being secretive about their approach. The closer the image got, the faster it seemed to move. Finally, Enrico and Steven heard an excited man's voice call out to them.

"Enrico Sanchez? Steven Labbs? Is that you guys?"

Steven happily responded, "You got it, buddy! Are we ever glad to see you!" They hurried towards the man's voice, eager to meet the person who would lead them through this underground trap.

As he got closer, they saw he was a young man, perhaps in his mid-twenties. He looked as if he had been running a good distance. His clean-shaven face was sweaty and his T-shirt was soaked against his chest. "Thank the Lord, you guys made it okay!" the young man blurted between gasps. "I was on the street when your trailer opened up. The crowds went berserk. I doubt if there's a single Bible left."

The young man took another deep breath. "You guys are fast. I can see why they couldn't catch you. I thought my lungs were going to burst before I got here." He leaned forward to catch his breath.

Enrico put his hand on the man's shoulder. "Seven months ago we would've been no match for those guys, but we've been training for this and knew we had to be quick on the stick once we got here. Every hour of training paid off."

"Have you heard from the other drivers?" Steven asked. "Have they made it yet?"

"I don't know. Once I managed to get through the riot up there I ran straight down here. Haven't heard a thing about the others. We'll know soon enough though."

Having caught his breath, he stood up straight and reached his hand out to greet Enrico and Steven. "I'm honored to meet you. My name's Nick Sartucci. I can't thank you enough for risking your lives to bring God's Word to our people. God bless you both."

Ignoring Nick's outstretched hand, Enrico gave him a big hug. "Thanks, brother. God bless you too."

Steven hugged him next. "It's a pleasure, buddy."

"Pleasure is all mine, friend," Nick intoned. "Mr. Rex gave us a run-down on what to expect when you guys showed up. And I'm really impressed. You did a great job."

"Glory to God," Enrico said. "It got pretty close a couple times."

"Amen to that," Steven added.

Just then, a loud explosion went off above them. Pieces of ceiling-plaster rained down over them. Nick immediately started running back into the tunnel. He called Enrico and Steven to follow behind. "Quick, we've got to get out of here before they find the cellar."

"We're right behind you." Enrico shouted as he and Steven dodged the falling plaster.

In a few minutes the three men were out of that tunnel and into another, safely away from any danger of being caught by the authorities. The explosion was still ringing in their ears when they finally stopped to rest.

"Whew!" Steven exclaimed. "That was some blast!"

Nick was once again bending over to catch his breath.

Enrico held his palms over both his ears as he said, "I feel like some-one just blew my eardrums out. You guys okay?"

Nick straightened back up and nodded towards Enrico. Breathing heavily, he said, "You guys ever think about joining the Olympics? You should!"

Enrico and Steven laughed.

After taking another deep breath Nick started walking again, leading the way down the new tunnel. Enrico and Steven fell in behind.

Nick turned to face them as he marched. "This is a live tunnel so we have to keep an eye and ear out for any incoming trains."

"My eyes are fine," Enrico teased, "but I can't promise I'll hear anything after that explosion."

Steven gave him a friendly slap on the shoulder.

And so the three men started down the dark and forbidding tunnel, Nick in the lead with Enrico and Steven close behind. The tunnel seemed to be without end, but Enrico and Steven had confidence in their new-found friend, and trusted he would guide them to safety.

Chapter

18

The huge concrete playground encompassed an area large enough to hold two square city blocks. Although it got more than its share of use, it hadn't been blessed with the labors of a good groundskeeper in years. The playground reeked of neglect. Tall spindly weeds stretched forever from the hundreds of twisted streaming cracks in its ruptured concrete base.

Swing sets and seesaws were scattered about, their appearances only a shadow of their former selves. The bright and inviting colors that once caught the playful eyes of children in years past were all but gone, replaced instead with the less alluring attributes of rust and corrosion.

But even with all the decay and negligence, the playground remained a busy hive of activity with children of all ages making the most of what it had to offer. Regardless of how worn or dilapidated the equipment might get, the young imaginative minds could always find ways to make them seem new and exciting again. That was a gift children of all ages seemed to share; a gift of simple, unstructured and freewheeling imaginations. A gift well suited for this playground.

After all, it wasn't as if there was anywhere else these kids could go to burn off their energy. This playground was the only show in town, which of course was no secret to the thousands of children that played in it every day. A simple glance up toward the electrically charged barbed wire fence circling its perimeters drove that point home all too well. But then, no one ever claimed that living in one of HEdge's older juvenile detention centers didn't have its drawbacks, not the least of which was a serious lack of modern playground equipment. But such was the life in this western sector Juvenile Behavior Modification Center (JBMC), located on the outskirts of Oakland California.

The JBMC was an obscure, outdated juvenile penal institution that had seen its better days. It was christened nearly twenty-five years ago on a fateful rainy afternoon with an inmate population of just under six hundred; not even half what it was designed to handle. But now, almost a quarter century later, it was bursting at the seams with well over fifteen hundred inmates, crammed to the hilt, every bunk taken, every space accounted for. The JBMC was overcrowded and its staff over-worked. It needed a reprieve, and it needed it badly.

But that was not to happen, at least not today. Because today like most days, the JBMC would open its doors to another deluge of neglected, abused, or unlawful children. Police hauled some in after being picked up for loitering; others were apprehended just as they were committing one of a myriad of crimes. Good portions of the incar-cerated children were placed there at the direction of social workers that had literally ripped them out of dysfunctional families.

With over fifteen hundred kids crammed inside the stone walls of the JBMC, and more being admitted every day, a large expansive play-ground was a necessity. The kids needed somewhere to stretch their legs and exercise their young muscles. Without it, they'd release their hormonal wiles and anxieties in other, less desirable and certainly more rebellious ways.

Of course recreational exercise was the farthest thing from the minds of some of the newer inmates to the JBMC. These kids were barely beyond the stage of drying their young eyes, still suffering through the traumatic emotional upheavals of insecurity, disorientation, and ostracism.

They hadn't overcome the shock and fright of finding themselves stowed away in a barricaded juvenile fortress, locked away from their families, abusive or not.

These kids were still wondering when they would be able to go back home. They had not yet realized that for most, home was no longer an option. From here on, home was only a state of mind, changing from one month to another, depending on where HEdge's juvenile penal system decided to place them.

Quiet and reserved, these children normally kept to themselves, withdrawn, hopelessly trying to understand why and how they got into such a predicament.

One such boy was sitting by himself, sulking on the rusted edge of a badly dented metal slide located in the farthest corner of the playground.

Seven children: three girls and four boys, were circling the large slide, chasing each other while noisily calling derogatory names to the quiet boy, laughing at him as they ran by. He ignored their callous remarks. He sat with his head lowered and shoulders slumped, acting as if he didn't hear a word. But he did. He heard everything they said, and it hurt. Their remarks sliced through his frail ego, leaving only the few tears he had left to roll down his puffy rounded cheeks. But nobody noticed and nobody cared.

Matthew was still an emotional wreck from the day before when he watched his mother being roughed up by the bullying soldiers, and when one of the soldiers smacked him across the face before ripping him away from his mom. The whole experience left him feeling numb. He didn't sleep last night, and doubted if he would tonight. He couldn't. How could he sleep with his life suddenly turned upside down?

He realized his father was a man of God, and he knew some people didn't like his father because of that, but how could they dislike him enough to put his family in jail? What was the big deal? So what if his dad believed in God; why should that be enough reason to lock someone up?

He wondered if his mom was safe; it hurt so much to see her crying. If only there was something he could do. Maybe dad could come and rescue them; but how? How could he do that? Guards were everywhere!

The question kept riding through his young mind, what should he do? What would his parents want him to do? Then he remembered: "Pray."

That's what his mother was telling him before the soldiers took him. But what good could prayer do now? If prayers were the answer, why was he even in this place? *After all*, he thought to himself, *didn't dad pray before he left for New York? Didn't he ask God to keep his family safe while he was away?*

But here he was, in this dungeon. Is this safe? Is mom safe? Is dad safe? None of it makes any sense. How can prayer help now?

But what else could he do?

Pray … to Jesus? "Mmmm."

"That's what dad would do," he finally resolved to himself. "Must be right. Yes, that's the only thing to do … pray."

Matthew put his hands together over his lap, interlocking his fingers, holding them together in a tight clasp as he closed his eyes.

"Jesus … Jesus," he said in slow determined syllables.

His mom and dad taught him to start every prayer with praise and thanksgiving, but right now he couldn't think of anything to thank Jesus for.

After a moment, he continued, "Thank You, Jesus, for giving me a mom and dad who love me. And thank you for helping my friend Joshua find his turtle last week. It really made his day."

Pausing briefly, he started, "Jesus, why is this happening? Why am I here? And why is my mom and dad in such trouble? Why do all these people hate us for loving you? You are God. They should thank my dad for teaching about you, not hate him. Why do they hate us, Jesus? Why?"

Just as Matthew prayed those words, a verse from one of the Gospels he had recently studied with his dad stormed into his mind. It was verse thirteen, from the thirteenth chapter of the gospel of Mark. The verse rang in his ears, getting his complete attention.

> *"And you will be hated by all men for My name's sake.*
> *But he who endures to the end shall be saved."*

It was a verse his father had recited to explain why some things were the way they were. The verse drifted through his mind, taking its time to register.

Suddenly a spark lit in Matthew's mind. For the first time in his life Matthew felt a deep yet simple understanding sweep through him, a revelation of sorts. Suddenly he grasped the basis of his dad's teachings, and realized the Bible was not just a lot of empty verses for meaningless times, these words were real and alive. More alive than young Matthew had ever dreamed possible.

Then another familiar verse came to him, from verses twenty-seven and twenty-eight, the sixth chapter in the gospel of Luke.

> *"But I say to you who hear: Love your enemies,*
> *do good to those who hate you, bless those who*
> *curse you, and pray for those who spitefully use you."*

Matthew felt overwhelmed. The verses came to him like clamoring bells, ringing with God's truth and love.

He finished, "Please let mom and dad be okay. And please get me out of here soon. Thank You, Jesus."

He opened his eyes while unfolding his hands. Strangely, the children who had been circling and ridiculing him minutes earlier, were now standing in front of him, staring.

The verse came to him, "*Love your enemies* . . . *Bless those who curse you.*"

Matthew looked over to the seven children, and said, "Hi. God bless you."

Matthew's greeting surprised the kids, yet they accepted it gratefully.

A thin stalky girl with stringy, unkempt, shoulder length blonde hair and a pretty dose of freckles, asked, "What's your name?"

"Matthew," he answered.

A young boy standing beside the freckled girl, asked, "What were you doing?"

Matthew suddenly realized what had caught their attention; his praying surprised them. *How strange*, he thought to himself.

He finally answered, "Praying to God for help."

The blonde haired girl looked at him in astonishment, her eye's opened wide.

"I've never known anyone that could do that. Is it hard?"

Matthew chuckled. "Na, not once you get the hang of it. Wanna try?"

The girl looked even more stunned. "No, no, that's against the law."

Matthew considered her comment for a moment. He knew praying to God was against the law, that was no secret, his dad had told him that years ago. But his dad also said no man could top God's law. And God said to pray.

Matthew asked, "Do you know why it's against the law?"

The girl looked confused. She shrugged her shoulders. "Not really. Just that it is."

Matthew tugged at a small thin strip of rusted metal hanging from the edge of the slide. He yanked it off then tossed it over the heads of the seven kids. They watched as the rusted piece flew over their heads and dropped silently into a hill of grass.

"What's your name?" Matthew asked.

Returning her attention to Matthew, she replied, "Sandra."

Then the other six kids automatically began listing off their names, one after the other. As each stated their name, Matthew had a good chance to really see them for the first time. And instead of seeing the bullies and brats he expected, he was surprised to see seven children about his age that looked as fragile and insecure as he felt.

Peering at them, he couldn't escape the feeling that he was looking at himself, seeing his sadness in their eyes. He realized they had already experienced what he was now going through. And they survived it.

Matthew felt an instant bonding to these kids, tattered clothes and all.

He asked Sandra, "Why are you here?"

Looking sheepishly to the ground, Sandra rubbed a tiny circle in the sand with the tip of her worn shoe. She seemed to be debating internally whether to answer. After a minute she replied while continuing her downward gaze, "My mom didn't want me anymore, so they brought me here."

Her answer startled Matthew.

"Your mom said that?" he excitedly asked. "She doesn't want you anymore?"

Sandra looked back up to him.

"She didn't tell me that, exactly. But Ms. Hawthorn, our family counselor, told me my mom said that to her. Ms. Hawthorn has been helping our family ever since I got hurt and had to go to the hospital."

"Hospital?" Matthew blurted. "Why did you go to the hospital?"

"I fell off a ladder when I was helping my mom paint my bedroom. I hurt my arm real bad and had to go to the hospital. Ms. Hawthorn came every day to see how I was doing. She's a nice lady. I like her."

"Didn't your mother come to see you?"

"Ms. Hawthorn said it would be better if my mom didn't visit. She thinks my mom pushed me off the ladder so I could come here to live. She said the only reason my mom wanted to visit me was to stay out of trouble."

Matthew needed to know more. "Stay out of trouble? Why would she be in trouble?"

Sandra was getting frustrated. Her body language clearly indicated she did not want to discuss the matter any further.

Prodding her to finish, the young boy beside her nudged her with his elbow. "Go ahead, Sandra. You never told us the whole story."

After a minute of fidgeting in the sand, she gave in. "Okay . . . about a year and a half ago I did something really stupid." And at that, she assumed an arrogant pose while raising her left hand toward Matthew, exposing her open palm.

Matthew was surprised to see a small scar on her hand.

"I grabbed my mother's curling iron when I was seven. I burned my hand real bad and had to go to the hospital. They gave my mom a warning to not let that happen again. They thought she burned my hand. Anyways, after I went back to the hospital, this time for falling off the ladder, they told Ms. Hawthorn to make sure I wouldn't get hurt anymore. Ms. Hawthorn kept telling me how much she cared about me, and how important it was that I leave home. She said my mom was dangerous, and it would be better if I didn't live there anymore. So she brought me here."

"What about your dad?"

"My mom and dad got divorced right after I was born. I never met him. I don't even know what he looks like."

Matthew was at a loss for words. Her story seemed so incredible. "Do you miss your mom?"

Sandra started to answer, but stopped short. She took a deep breath before going on.

"Yeah . . . I do, I guess. I haven't seen her since I came here." Her voice cracked. "I don't see Ms. Hawthorn much anymore either. I guess she has other kids to look out for." Her voice cracked again.

Matthew sensed this conversation had turned down a road Sandra had not traveled in quite some time. As he caught himself, he wondered if it wasn't too late to change course. But looking at her face, he realized it was indeed much too late.

Sandra attempted to say something else, but stopped as her composure began melting away. Her lips quivered as tears welled up in her eyes. Turning her back to Matthew, she brought her hands to her face. With her shoulders trembling, she wept.

The other six kids shifted their position, suddenly feeling uncomfortable around her.

Watching her cry reminded Matthew of his mom the day before. He felt sad for this girl. Getting off the edge of the metal slide, he walked over to her. He couldn't help his mom, but maybe he could somehow help this poor girl. He took a step closer, touched her on her narrow freckled shoulders, and then whispered, "Can I say a prayer for you?"

Attempting to stop the flow of tears, Sandra tried to answer Matthew, but there was no way. She hadn't cried in months, and now that the floodgates were open, they weren't going to close easily.

She nodded, "yes."

It took everything he had to concentrate on prayer instead of joining in her tears. Pulling on his inner reserves, he began whispering a prayer for her. The other six kids moved closer, straining to hear.

"Dear Lord, please help Sandra stop crying. Please let her mom visit so they can talk to each other again, and maybe even live together again. Sandra really needs her, Lord. Please let her come and visit.

Thank You, Jesus. Amen."

He softly squeezed her shoulders before stepping away and returning to his seat on the edge of the slide. The other kids stepped back as he walked past them.

Sandra continued softly crying while the others stood, fidgeting in their pockets or kicking dirt, trying to avoid her, yet peeking every so often to see if she was all right.

After a few moments, Sandra finally stopped. She lifted the bottom of her shirt to wipe her eyes, getting the last few sniffles out as she did.

Matthew was relieved. Watching her cry put a lump in his throat. He couldn't believe Sandra's mother really didn't want her any more. How could any mom say such a thing to her own child? Well, at least Ms. Hawthorn still cared about her. That's better than nothing.

Sandra finally returned to her friends, apologizing for her tears. They brushed aside her apologies and went on to other more urgent matters; like playing.

Henry, a small agile dark-skinned boy with a bright smile and playful eyes, tapped Matthew on his shoulder, and shouted aloud for everyone to hear. "You're It!"

Just then, all seven kids took off in every direction, leaving Matthew on the edge of the slide, looking like an outcast. But it didn't take long to realize his role in this game. If he didn't catch someone quick and pass 'It' on, he would be stuck with being 'It' forever, or at least until the game was over; an intolerable proposition that he was not about to let happen.

Matthew leaped up and chased after Henry. Might as well give 'It' back to the person who gave 'It' to him. Seemed fair enough.

Henry was a fast young lad. Matthew tried beating him in a straight out run but Henry handily out-distanced him. Matthew's only hope was to catch him as he ran around the swing set. Matthew took up the chase, having fun for the first time in what seemed like years. He needed this.

Henry's feet slipped as he turned too sharply around the bottom edge of the ladder. He grabbed onto its base trying to keep from falling. The delay was just long enough for Matthew to catch up.

Swinging around the corner, he tapped Henry squarely on his back, shouting, "Now you're It!" as he rolled to the ground in a cloud of dirt.

Henry shouted, "No, no, this is base! You can't get me! I'm on base!"

Sandra hollered over, "We never called a base. That's not base. You're 'It', Henry!"

Henry realized the futility of his claim and burst into a mad dash after Sandra. She was the closest to him. And besides, she was a girl. He could catch her easily.

Sandra was in full stride, smiling with excitement as she struggled to out-pace Henry, her stringy blond hair flying in the breeze. But Henry was gaining, and he was gaining fast.

Suddenly, the playground bell rang out, loud and clear, bringing their fun to a screeching halt. Playtime was over.

Matthew's smile left his face. He threw a handful of dirt into the ground as he stood and walked over towards Henry and Sandra and the other kids. As he approached, Henry said teasingly, "You're lucky I slipped. You never would'a got me."

"Yeah right." Matthew snickered as he joined the small band of kids heading toward the main JBMC building.

These new found friends, acquired under the worst of conditions, were no replacement for his family back home, but for the time-being, they were a blessing and an integral part of his life. And he thanked God for each and every one of them.

As the eight children walked together, they noticed a woman standing outside waving in their direction. Matthew had no idea who she was or what she wanted, but when he looked over toward the other kids, he saw Sandra's face light up with joy. Jumping up and down, Sandra waved back to the woman.

She had to be either Sandra's mom or Ms. Hawthorn. Matthew hoped it was her mom.

"That's Ms. Hawthorn." Sandra excitedly announced. "She's come to visit me!"

Sandra immediately chased over, her arms waving. Henry and the other kids took off behind her.

Ms. Hawthorn was a pudgy woman with tightly cropped black hair sprinkled with gray.

Sandra attempted to leap into her arms but was stopped as Ms. Hawthorn grabbed her by the shoulders and held her at arms length. Forcing a wide smile down to Sandra, she exposed a mouthful of large white teeth.

"Hi, Ms. Hawthorn! I'm so glad to see you. Did you come to visit me? Will you be here long? I miss you, Ms. Hawthorn. Have you seen my mom? How's she doing?"

Ms. Hawthorn waved her index finger in front of Sandra's lips. "Not so fast, sweetie. I can't answer all your questions at once. Now take a deep breath, then ask away."

But before Sandra could finish her deep breath, Ms. Hawthorn started speaking.

"Sandra dear, you're looking quite healthy. They must be feeding you well. Do you like their food, Sandra?" she asked while patting Sandra's tiny belly.

Sandra blushed. "It's okay, I guess," then started back with her questions.

"Ms. Hawthorn, where have you been? I haven't seen you in such a long time. Have you seen my mom?"

Ms. Hawthorn smiled as she took Sandra's smaller hand into hers.

"Little darling, I am so happy to see you. I was in the neighborhood and wouldn't dream of passing by without stopping in to see my special little Sandra."

"Ms. Hawthorn, I've been thinking about you so much lately. I thought you'd never come to see me. Are you going to stay awhile, like before when we spent so much time together, and we'd go places and eat ice cream cones."

Ms. Hawthorn looked out over the hundreds of kids lining up outside the JBMC building. Patting Sandra on her back, she said, "Sandra dear, you and your friends need to get in line before the second bell rings, or else you'll all get in trouble. I wouldn't want my little Sandra to get in any trouble just because of me. So off you go, sweetheart, back in line."

"But Ms. Hawthorn, I just . . ."

"Not now, sweetie, back in line." Ms. Hawthorn cut her off while gently nudging her away.

Sandra grudgingly turned with the other kids and headed towards the lines.

As an afterthought, Ms. Hawthorn added, "Oh, and Sandra?"

Sandra swung back to her. "Yes, Ms. Hawthorn?"

"Can we have lunch together today, sweetie?"

"Sure, Ms. Hawthorn. Sure, I'd love that. I'll see you in the dining hall, okay? That'll be fun!"

Ms. Hawthorn gave a cutesy wiggle as she smiled back to Sandra before returning to her business of shooing the other kids away. "Hurry up now children. I don't want to see any of you get in trouble."

Sandra skipped merrily to the end of the long line, delighted in her prospects for lunch. Once there, she turned to wave to Ms. Hawthorn, but was too late. She had already gone inside.

Sandra frowned for a moment, then got excited again as she considered her upcoming lunch-date. This was something to look forward to. *Lunch with Ms. Hawthorn*, she thought happily. *Wow! Maybe she'll stay for a long time. Maybe she can tell me all about mom and how she's doing. Wow!*

Chapter

19

The second bell rang just as the last child jumped into line. All thirty lines were now formed. Staffers took charge of each, ordering the children to follow, which they did in procession formation, single file, back into the heartless, stony corridors of the JBMC.

Once inside, the lines were broken into two groups, half were taken back to their respective squad bays, while the rest continued to the dining hall for lunch.

Much to Sandra's joy, the line she was in, along with Matthew, Henry, and the other five kids, was headed right to the dining hall. Sandra could think of little else besides having lunch with Ms. Hawthorn. She could hardly wait to hear about her mom.

When the fifteen lines reached the huge entrance to the dining hall, the staffers ordered them to stop, then directed the children to shimmy up close so people could get by.

Matthew was right behind Henry, smudged between him and the kid behind him. Up front he could see Sandra looking around, searching for someone. Probably looking for Ms. Hawthorn, he figured.

A staff worker finally motioned for their line to enter the dining hall.

Good! Matthew relished. He hadn't eaten since he was taken from his home. He had to admit he was famished.

Matthew followed his line into the dining hall, mimicking the kids ahead. This was only his second time in here. Yesterday he was too grief-stricken to have an appetite.

Ushering past a large stainless-steel cabinet stacked with metal trays and plastic eating utensils, Matthew pulled the top tray from the stack, along with a plastic fork, knife, and spoon. He then shuffled down the busy serving line, sliding his tray across the counter.

Galley workers were standing behind large pots with metal shovels ready to scoop whatever foods the kids wanted onto their trays.

Matthew progressed, ordering mashed potatoes, corn, a piece of fried chicken, and some cornbread stuffing. At the end of the long counter he picked up a bowl of jello, then, balancing his tray in both hands, jockeyed for a position near the juice fountain.

Grabbing his drink, he scanned the dining hall searching for his new friends. As he looked across the bustling floor he saw rows of white rectangular tables quickly filling with young, energized and hungry children. He noticed a solitary red table at the far corner of the dining hall, positioned apart from the other tables. There were eight kids sitting at the red table, slouched over their trays, quietly devouring their meals. Not so much as a whisper passed between them. A huge burly guard stood nearby, keeping an eye on the unhappy bunch.

Matthew couldn't help but wonder what those kids did to have to sit at that table.

Henry's voice called out, "Hey, Matt, over here."

Matthew's attention was diverted away from the brooding red table, toward the center of the dining hall. Henry was waving to him. "Come on, Matt, I saved you a seat."

Matthew rushed over to where Henry, Sandra and the other five kids were sitting. As he walked, he noticed Ms. Hawthorn sitting next to Sandra. He thought it odd that they weren't talking to one another. Ms. Hawthorn's attention seemed preoccupied with her food.

After he was seated, he asked, "Anyone know why those kids have to sit at the red table?"

"They were in trouble," Cynthia, a dark-skinned girl sitting opposite him volunteered. "One of them was caught fighting in the squad bay.

And I know that kid over there too; the one with the brown hair, see him?" She held her arm out straight, pointing to the young boy at the end of the red table.

"He was cussing at one of the playground guards last week; real loud too. Saying all sorts of nasty things. But the guard wasn't havin it, so he took him inside for a talk. This is the first time I've seen him since then. I guess they taught him to shut his mouth up.

"And he probably wonders why he's here. Hmmff." Cynthia finished her discourse with a nod of disdain, as she spooned a large helping of wobbly green Jell-O into her mouth.

"I know one of them too," Henry said. "The one in the middle with the thick glasses." He pointed. "That's Alex. We used to play tag a lot. At least until he got weird."

"Weird?" Matthew repeated.

Henry took a big bite of his drumstick, and then elaborated between chews. "Yeah, weird. All of a sudden he didn't want to be alone anymore, he wouldn't go anywhere by himself."

Henry leaned closer to make sure no one else could hear. Cynthia was engrossed in her meal. Other kids were carrying on their own discussions as well. No one was eavesdropping.

Henry confided, "Alex told me not to tell anyone this, so you have to keep it a secret, okay?"

"Sure," Matthew promised.

"Alex told me that one day after gym class he was in the squad bay all by himself changing clothes when one of the adults came in. At first Alex thought the adult was calling him for lunch, but instead he took him into a small room somewhere in the basement. Alex wouldn't tell me what happened there, but he's been acting strange ever since. He's not the same kid he used to be. He doesn't want to play or do anything."

Goose bumps ran up Matthew's spine as he listened to Henry's strange tale about poor Alex.

"So why is he at the red table now?"

Henry shoveled a large scoop of mashed potatoes into his mouth as he looked seriously over to Matthew, answering, "I heard he got caught trying to escape. Once you try that, you can forget it. They keep a real close eye on you then."

Matthew took another bite of his chicken breast then chased it with a big gulp of juice.

"That's terrible."

"Yeah, it sure is," Henry agreed as he finished his chicken and potatoes, then started on a bowl of chocolate pudding.

Before putting the spoonful of pudding into his mouth, he turned to Matthew and asked, "So tell me, Matt. Why do you pray anyway?"

"Oops," Matthew suddenly remembered, "I forgot to say grace before eating. Thanks for reminding me."

"Sure . . . no problem," Henry responded curiously.

Matthew bowed his head, clasped his hands together and began a quiet prayer of thanksgiving.

Through the corner of her eyes, Ms. Hawthorn saw Matthew fold his hands and bow his head. With a sudden jerk, she dropped her fork onto her plate, thrust herself up from the table and screamed over to Matthew, pointing at him. "You stop that right now! That's against the law and you know it. You must be that derelict kid, Rex's son. Aren't you?"

The volume of her scream caught everyone's attention. Kids all through the dining hall stopped and turned to see what was happening. The guard standing by the red table rushed over to her.

Ms. Hawthorn continued her pointing and staring as she boisterously informed the guard of the terrible deed Matthew had just committed. "He started praying, right there, right at the table in front of everyone, as though he owned the place. He's going to be trouble, I tell you, a lot of trouble. Just like his old man."

Matthew didn't know what to do. He was stunned by Ms. Hawthorn's outburst. He sat looking over to her as if asking, "What did I do?"

The tough looking guard stomped over to Matthew. Looking scornfully down at him, he asked with a growling voice, "What's this all about, kid? What were you doing?"

Matthew was at a loss for words. He was shocked. What had he done? What? Then it dawned on him . . . he prayed. He looked up to the sweating angry face of the guard towering above him. The hulking guard looked bigger and meaner than anyone he had ever seen in his life.

"I was just giving thanks to God for . . ."

At that, the guard grimaced angrily as he lifted Matthew by both his armpits, ruggedly yanking him free of the table.

Ms. Hawthorn stood scowling.

The guard pulled Matthew up to within an inch of his nose. Matthew's legs were dangling above the chair. He could feel the guard's thick breath exhaling over his face.

"You listen to me you little runt. I catch you doing that again, and you'll be sorry! You hear me, boy?"

He sniffled out a response. "YYYes sssir . . , but you're supposed to thththank God . . ."

The guard was furious; this kid was testing him. "Well, we'll see who passes this test." The guard flexed his bulky muscles as he heaved Matthew into the air. Matthew's arms and legs were flailing as he shot through the air like a bird that's lost flight, until tumbling to the floor with a heavy bounce a dozen feet away. He rolled to a stop at the legs of some children sitting at a table across the aisle. None of them offered any help. They were too frightened.

The guard laughed heartily as he thumped his way over to Matthew. Leaning his top-heavy frame over, he lifted him up again, this time by only one arm. Matthew was once again dangling in the air, crying while his free arm was swinging out, reaching, stretching for something to hold on to.

The entire dining hall was the guard's audience, and he loved every second of it. He's been waiting for an opportunity to remind these young hooligans who was in charge anyway. And a reminder they got, as everyone sat in awe of the cruel exhibition playing out in front of them.

"Stop it," Matthew pleaded, his voice echoing through the nervously silent dining hall, tears gushing from his eyes. The guard cursed as he tossed Matthew again to the floor. He landed on his shoulder as he gave out a pained cry, tumbling another five feet before coming to a stop at a table-leg, more bruised and battered than before.

The guard hollered, "Get to the red table, punk! You don't belong at this table, and won't until you straighten your act up!"

Trying to lift himself off the hard-tile floor, Matthew could barely hear. He shook his head to get the ringing out.

Wearily hobbling over, Matthew wiped his face on his shirtsleeve, sniffling, trying to suppress his tears. Everyone in the dining hall watched as he finally reached the red table and painfully sat down.

Once there, Matthew realized he didn't have his tray with him. No matter, he'd lost his appetite anyway. Slumping over, he hid his face between his arms, and cried.

The guard proudly stomped away between rows of scared, intimidated children. Once at the exit, he glanced over his shoulder at all the stunned faces, children sitting frozen in the silent dining hall. He gave a satisfied grunt as he walked out the door for a breath of fresh air.

Henry felt terrible for his new friend. He lifted Matthew's tray to carry it over to the red table. Ms. Hawthorn saw what he was up to and scowled over at him. "Don't you dare. That boy deserved what he got. He'll learn his lesson."

Sandra was completely upset. She had become increasingly aware that Ms. Hawthorn had no intention of answering any of her questions about her mom. She was only there for a free lunch. She had no right to scream at Matthew like that, and the guard had no right to pick on him.

Sandra had seen enough.

She stood at her seat, marched straight over to Henry, took Matthew's tray from him, and then, in clear view of everyone in the dining hall, defiantly carried the tray over to the red table.

Ms. Hawthorn's mouth dropped as she watched Sandra parade across the hall.

Once at the table, Sandra rested Matthew's tray beside his crossed arms.

Henry came running after, carrying Matthew's grape juice with him, and laying it on the table next to the tray.

Lifting his head from his arms, Matthew looked up to his two friends. A swelling bump was visible on his forehead along with a puffy bleeding lip.

"God bless you, Matthew," Henry said.

Sandra added with heartfelt emphasis, "I'll say a prayer for you, okay?"

Matthew smiled weakly up to both of them, his face bruised and bleeding. Sandra took a napkin and wiped his lips.

With Henry and Sandra rising to Matthew's defense, albeit after the guard had left the dining hall, the other children received a sense of hope for themselves. An unknowing, unintelligible sense that perhaps there was some good in this place after all. The caring example set by Henry and Sandra left them all feeling a little bit better about themselves, and maybe even gave them something to think about. After all, they heard what Matthew had said about thanking God. Yes, they heard.

Suddenly, from somewhere deep within, an eruption of gratitude forced itself out as the children in the dining hall began clapping their hands. They felt good for a change. Didn't really know why, but they felt good.

In a few seconds their voices joined in, loud and vibrant, "Hurray! Hurray! Hurray!"

But then, slamming the door open, the red-table guard rushed back inside. He roared over the kids' cheers, "One more sound and everyone will get the same treatment! Just one more sound!"

The guard's voice was heavy and powerful. It left a noticeable dent in the high spirits of the children. The cheering stopped. Sandra and Henry rushed back to their table, but only after giving Matthew a friendly tap on his back.

No sooner had Sandra sat back down, than Ms. Hawthorn grumpily lifted her tray and unceremoniously departed the table. Sandra didn't even say good-bye.

Matthew was sore everywhere; his head ached; his arms ached. Every muscle in his body was throbbing and crying out for attention. But even with all his pain, Matthew retained an inner peace. A spiritual peace; something the guard could not take away, no matter how many times he tossed him across the room.

Because Matthew knew he was not alone. Somehow, he just knew that his Lord, Jesus Christ, was sitting right there at the red table alongside him. He could almost feel Jesus' powerful arms wrapped over his bruised shoulders. And he could almost hear Jesus' peaceful, life-giving voice, whispering in his ear, "Rejoice and be exceedingly glad, for great is your reward in heaven, for so they persecuted the prophets who were before you."

Matthew cried again, except this time, with joy.

Chapter

20

The dimly lit subway tunnel dragged on for as far as the eye could see. Shadows leaped through the darkness taunting at Steven and Enrico's imaginations, creating stealth images where none existed. Nick Sartucci hardly noticed his friends' apprehension as he easily led them through the darkened labyrinths, guiding them past the many turns and divisions along the way.

Nick was a veteran traveler of the New York City subway system. When he was a young boy he attended Sunday services in underground chapels with his parents and grandparents. The chapels were hidden deep within the lost corridors of unused, outdated tunnels, dug out and cleaned up just for the purpose of worship and fellowship.

As Nick matured, he followed in his parent's footsteps of accepting Jesus Christ into his life. Eventually he became an active member in one of the many underground Christian networks in the Eastern U.S. Sector. This affiliation had forced him to expand his knowledge and expertise of the New York tunnels to an even greater proficiency. Few peers could equal his knack for finding the shortest and most direct routes to most any location.

Now if only Enrico and Steven could hold as much confidence in Nick's abilities as everyone else did. A couple hours ago they were enjoying their new tunnel-sleuthing experience, but now, after treading mile upon mile of train tracks, dodging incoming and outgoing subway cars, and jumping around nests of lively subway rodents, the two were beginning to lose patience with their one and only tunnel guide.

"Hey, Nick?" Steven had to ask. "Where's the sunlight, buddy? Do we have much farther to go?" He tried to ask without appearing too anxious, but wasn't very successful.

Slowing his pace, Nick glanced back. He heard the underlying concern in Steven's voice. It was common for people to feel out of place, worried, even panicky on their first venture deep inside the tunnels. It's to be expected. The eerie darkness and constant drip from leaking pipes, not to mention the infamous rats, leaves many first time travelers fidgety and spooked.

"Won't be long now, guys. We're getting close."

Enrico had to express his concerns. "Nick, I'm usually pretty good at knowing my north and south from my east and west, but to be honest with you, right now I couldn't tell you if we're going up or down, much less what bearing we're headed."

Nick chuckled. "Well guys, to ease your minds I'll tell you, we're going north in the city, but heading down in the tunnels."

Steven had to ask for clarification on the 'down' part. "Huh, Nick, what do you mean we're going down in the tunnel? Aren't we supposed to be going up . . . like to the sunlight n' all?"

"Oh yeah, we'll be going up in time. But first we have to meet with everyone. You'll see."

Enrico and Steven remained silent. This was not exactly what either wanted to hear. They suddenly felt very vulnerable to this guide with his mole-like tendencies. This may simply be another day out for Nick Sartucci, but for them, it was like plummeting through a bad dream with no chance of waking up.

Suddenly, Enrico thought he saw movement behind one of the large pillars that made up the tunnel's infrastructure. Excitedly tapping Steven on the shoulder, he pointed to the suspect pillar.

Steven jumped at Enriqo's unexpected tap.

"Chill out, brother," Enrico whispered. "Take a look over there. See anything?"

Steven's tenseness surprised even himself. He released a nervous laugh as he looked over to where Enrico was pointing. He couldn't see a thing.

Neither could Enrico now.

Steven whispered back, "Don't feel bad. I've been seeing things ever since we got down here. The place gives me the creeps."

"Amen to that!" Enrico agreed while continuing to study the shadows near the pillar. He finally gave them up to an overworked imagination, and directed his focus ahead.

Just as Steven and Enrico were beginning to feel somewhat relaxed in their extraordinary surroundings, a low-pitched rumbling reverberated through the darkness, setting their nerves off again.

The noise wasn't loud. In fact, if not for the dead quiet of the tunnel, they never would have heard it.

Nick immediately stopped and held both arms up, motioning for them to halt.

"What was that?" they asked in unison.

"Shhhh," Nick whispered.

When they all came to a stop, they could hear even more sounds. This time Steven and Enrico also heard voices, just slightly.

At first they thought another train was coming their way, even though Nick had said this was an abandoned tunnel. But even a train wouldn't explain the barely recognizable sounds of voices.

But if it wasn't a train, what else could it be?

Both Steven and Enrico were getting a serious case of the willies. They were doing all they could to keep their feet planted while every nerve in their bodies was primed to run. Of course without Nick to lead their way, running would only make matters worse. Getting completely lost was hardly an option either of them wanted to explore.

Turning to face them, Nick said in a hushed voice, "It's okay, we're almost there."

Enrico and Steven exchanged doubtful glances as they fell silently in line, following him down the track. The mysterious rumbling and voices continued getting more audible with each forward step.

After a few minutes, Steven thought he saw someone in the distance moving toward them. Visibility inside the hazy tunnel was poor, but still, Steven was sure he saw someone. He tapped the others on their shoulders to make sure they saw it too. They did.

In a second he realized it wasn't just one figure coming towards them, but several; and the figures weren't simply walking, they were running!

Steven froze, as did Enrico. Not noticing the sudden grip of fear that had over-taken his friends, Nick continued on his way, even speeding his pace as he headed right toward the group of people rushing at them.

Enrico and Steven didn't know what to make of this. They stood frozen, locked in place, their minds racing, desperate for understanding of this latest calamity.

Nick turned back and saw them standing stiff in the center of the track, gaping out with panic-stricken faces.

He couldn't help but smile. "C'mon guys. I know them. They're good people."

Enrico jabbed Steven in his side, "Yeah, c'mon, they're good people."

Steven found his feet again as he followed behind.

As the figures got nearer, Steven and Enrico heard them calling out greetings, with Nick responding in kind. Then much to their surprise some of the people started calling out to them as well.

"Enrico Sanchez? Steven Labbs? Is that you two over there?"

Nick volunteered their answer with a loud holler, "Yep, it's them, and take it easy, it's been a busy day and they're worn out."

Before Steven and Enrico could say a word, several excited men and women surrounded them. Each taking turns offering their hands in congratulatory shakes.

Nick could do little more than glow as he watched his friends express their appreciation and gratitude to the two men. He understood their enthusiasm. He felt the same when he first met them.

The exuberant group overwhelmed Steven and Enrico. The apprehensions and doubts they had harbored for their young tunnel-guide evaporated in the flurry of joyous outpourings.

Soon, Enrico and Steven, accompanied by their newest friends, resumed their trek through the tunnel, with Nick shepherding the way.

The rumbling sound the original three travelers had faintly heard earlier was now much clearer. They could hear well enough to know it wasn't so much a low pitched rumbling, as it was a rhythmic repetitious beating, more in the way of heavy musical notes dancing away. They heard voices that seemed to be flowing in sync with the music's melody.

But so loud? Enrico questioned. The source of it must still be a good distance away.

The group moved forward in the tunnel, everyone seeming to know exactly where they were headed, except of course, Enrico and Steven.

After another half kilometer, the tunnel widened and the ceiling began sloping up, rising higher with each turning bend. Most noticeable of all was the sudden introduction of lights. At first they were dim, but as the small group journeyed beyond a couple more bends, bright lights appeared everywhere, lining the tunnel ceilings from one end to the other.

Rounding the last turn in the track-laden tunnel, the small group finally arrived at their destination. Steven and Enrico unintentionally slowed their pace as they witnessed the tunnel's wondrous transformation from a narrow, constrictive tube, into a vast, outdated, underground subway station.

The two men's eyes darted freely about as they stepped slowly down the middle of the train tracks, straight through the center of this ancient subterranean depot.

Bright, gigantic spotlights illuminated hundreds of kilometers of spacious red-bricked walkways on both sides of the tracks. The walkways extended all the way back to towering walls where several archaic store fronts stood as remnants of decades past. Antiquated yet gracious, these stores appeared ready to open for business, just waiting for the first customer to step through their sealed doors.

The depot was a well-preserved ghost of a time long past. A time when anxious shoppers roamed freely through, eager to spend the loose change jingling in their pockets. It was a time when thousands of New York commuters carried their energies and excitements through this once-hectic station on their way to jobs, families, or entertainment.

The two men marveled as they swallowed the sights. After a few electrifying moments, Enrico and Steven came out of their trance and moved along with the group.

The noises they heard further back in the tunnel were now blaring. The musical notes were slurring away with an aggressive yet peaceful melody, joined in with a powerful choir of angelic voices.

Enrico and Steven craved to find the source of this beautiful music. Coincidentally, that was exactly where Nick was leading them.

He walked fifty meters across the expansive redbrick platform, directly up to a tall, eighteen-foot plain white door. Aside from its enormous size, the door was simple and unadorned. It's only distinguishing feature was a shiny golden knob positioned at its left most edge.

Steven and Enrico had little doubt the source of music was coming from the other side. They could almost see the door vibrating with the pulsating waves of gospel music surging through it.

Nick was finally at the golden knob. He rested his right palm on it, then looked back to his friends and offered a warm, compassionate smile. He turned the knob, and slowly, joyously, opened the door. "We're holding a celebration service for you guys," he said.

As the door opened, an immediate avalanche of thundering gospel choruses drenched over the small group of men and women. An explosion of unbridled, free spirited, praise music, flooded over their beings!

As powerful as the music seemed with the door closed, it was now double the might.

Smiling broadly, Nick motioned for Enrico and Steven to accompany him up the long carpeted aisle between the hundreds of rows of singing parishioners.

As Enrico and Steven feebly let one foot lead the other up the aisle, the incredible dimensions thrust upon their senses once again took them in.

They were awestruck as they looked out over the enormous hall with its overhanging balconies and several-tiered seating levels. Thousands of men, women, and children were standing in their cushioned pews, cheering and singing praises.

Steven and Enrico now realized how the powerful music had resonated so far into the tunnels. Mere walls could not withhold such a fierce onslaught of heavenly music.

Overwhelmed by the energies and songs pouring through their spirits, Steven and Enrico were brought to tears. Enrico reached over and shouted, "Where sin abounds, grace abounds much more!"

Steven wrapped his left arm around Enrico and hugged him. "This is great, brother! Praise God!"

Nick lifted his arms toward the front of the hall, then hollered, "There are some friends up there you may want to see."

They both looked to where Nick was directing their attention.

At the very front of the large hall sat an elevated, light-blue carpeted stage. An older, gray haired, ebony-skinned pastor was standing beside a polished wooden lectern, clapping hands and singing boisterously along with the rest of the congregation.

Behind the pastor were two long rows of chairs lined evenly up against the wall. Standing and singing in front of the chairs were the other twenty-eight truck drivers from the western sector.

Enrico jumped when he saw them. He shouted, "They made it! Alleluia! They all made it!"

As Steven saw what had caused his friend's exhilaration, he swung his arms out, giving out a loud hoot. "Thank God, they made it! They made it!"

Glistening tears flowed as the two men rushed up the long aisle to greet their western sector brethren.

Nick watched with a heavy heart as his two friends rushed past. His job was now complete. Rejoicing, he sang along with the congregation as he headed for a seat in the back.

The twenty-eight drivers on stage spotted their two brothers rushing up the aisle toward them. Just as thrilled, they left their chairs and streamed down the stage one after the other, hurrying to greet their friends.

Half way up the aisle, the two parties met. The drivers surrounded their two brothers and embraced them.

The congregation reacted enthusiastically to the reunion, bellowing their songs and praises with all the might they could.

The pastor shouted into his microphone, "Praise be to God!"

The crowd shouted with glee in response. The entire hall was a wild, thundering, pandemonium of praise and cheers, everyone standing and singing in celebration.

And so the uproar continued for a good while as Enrico and Steven were taken with the other twenty-eight drivers to their appointed seats on stage.

After all thirty drivers were in place; the pastor raised his hands to quiet the congregation. The musicians responded by gradually slowing their tempo and lowering their volume until the music had rescinded. The congregation reacted similarly as they quietly waited for the pastor's direction.

"Please, everyone take your seats."

The entire congregation, along with the thirty truck drivers standing behind the pastor, took their seats.

The stately pastor strolled patiently in front of the podium as he waited for everyone to get comfortable. He was a medium sized man, about five foot eleven with rich dark brows riding above his blissfully energetic eyes.

Shortly, he turned to the rows of drivers behind him and said, "Welcome to our little chapel under the city." A wave of chuckles passed through the group of drivers at the deliberately poor choice of words to describe this mammoth hall.

His face aglow, the pastor stated, "I thank the Lord for each and every one of you. We're overjoyed to have you with us, and we thank you for accepting this challenge God has laid before you."

Then he directed his attention out over the congregation.

"And I would like to give a very special thanks to all of our tunnel-guides who diligently led our western sector friends out of harm's way.

"Would all of the tunnel guides please stand to be recognized?"

At the rear of the hall, fifteen men hesitantly stood in their pews.

"On behalf of the entire church, I extend our heartfelt thanks. You did a great job. May God bless you dearly for it."

At that, all thirty drivers on stage stood at their seats and cheered for their tunnel guides. Enrico and Steven were first to stand and cheer. Nick saw them and waved.

The congregation accompanied the drivers in their show of appreciation, standing while clapping for each of the guides.

After a few moments everyone was back in their seats.

Ready to continue, the preacher looked out over the church, and then began speaking.

"We began this celebration prayer service over three hours ago. We joined together, asking our Father in Heaven to oversee the successful completion of His mission. And as we now know, the Lord has answered those prayers and blessed our city with the delivery of thousands of volumes of His Word. Souls will be saved, salvations will be had, and lives will be turned around. Isn't God great?"

The congregation broke into applause.

After a few minutes, the pastor's eyes narrowed, his voice became somber and determined. "And now, as you know, Mr. Rex's family is in HEdge's custody. At this moment we aren't sure where his wife or son are being held. We've received scattered reports that Matthew might be at the western sector's JBMC facility in Oakland, California, though we haven't been able to confirm it."

The thirty drivers were especially attuned to the Pastor's words. They haven't heard any reports on Mr. Rex's family other than what the secular press had to say. They were hoping and praying the situation had improved, or at least wasn't as dire as the press had made it out to be. Unfortunately, that was not to be the case. The press was correct on this one.

The entire congregation listened intently to the pastor. Not a sound passed, not a cough nor whisper.

"We know Melody is being transferred from the western sector to somewhere within this city, but we have no word exactly where."

"Mr. Rex is in our mid-Manhattan office right now working with our staff searching through archives, checking names and locations of every prison in this sector, along with the types of prisoners detained in them.

"Mr. Rex asks for our prayers on behalf of his family. And so I ask all of you, anyone that can, to stay a while longer as we lift his family in prayer.

"But anyone who needs to leave, you are dismissed, and thank you for sharing your time. May God bless each of you."

No one could be seen leaving their seats. Not a one. The pastor smiled broadly as he asked everyone to open their Bibles to the book of Nahum. And there he began preaching about strongholds and God's power and strength to those who believe.

The church listened, they prayed, and they worshipped; and strongholds were being affected as they did. God almighty was listening!

Chapter

21

Fragments of light seeped into the boys' north-wing squad bay of the Juvenile Behavior Modification Center in Oakland, California.

The steel doors of the crowded hundred-rack berthing area were opened just enough to allow a teasing morsel of hallway light to sneak in, providing a thin layer of visibility in the otherwise impenetrably dark room.

Young boys of varying ages were cuddled under their respective linens, sleeping soundly, enjoying their nightly reprieve from the harsh, cynical world that the JBMC flaunted on them throughout the day.

Some of the boys slept with their legs tucked up to their stomachs, their still-moist thumbs resting innocently on the lower lip of their open mouths. Others laid sprawled out nonchalantly across their mattress, arms and legs spread in every possible direction, above and beneath the sheets.

Little snores could be heard ruffling from under some of the thin-layered coverings, sometimes manifesting into loud obnoxious snorts, ending ultimately with someone in a neighboring rack nudging them to stop.

Every so often a scrambled one-way conversation could be heard bursting through the still night as someone became overly involved in a dream-state discussion.

The second hand on the bulky government issued wall-clock shifted from 2:33 a.m. to 2:34 a.m. The faint clicking sound penetrated the quiet squad bay, echoing all the way to a bottom bunk twenty feet away where young Matthew was lying, his eyes propped open and ears on full alert.

Matthew was the only boy that heard the clock's announcement of the changing minutes. Everyone else was fast asleep, and had been for hours; but not Matthew. As hard as he tried, and as badly as he needed, his mind just couldn't shut down for the night. He was too busy worrying about everything.

Was his mom okay? Was his dad safe? Where was that horrible red-table guard? Would the guard leave him alone tomorrow? When would he see his mom and dad again?

Matthew's young mind was a pinwheel of rotating worries, repeatedly going over the same problems and troubles. As he did, his tired mind became even more confused and distraught. The two days lack of sleep was taking its toll, wearing him down.

The lunch-hall episode with the red-table guard kept playing itself over in his mind too. A couple times Matthew actually dozed off to sleep, only to be startled awake again in the middle of a bad dream where he saw himself being flung through the air, hitting the hard floor, then crying out in pain, awakening just as the red-table guard leaned over to pick him up again.

Terrified, he would jump up in bed and quickly scan the room to make sure the guard wasn't anywhere in sight.

Still sore all over, it hurt even to lie in bed.

Then he remembered Sandra bringing his tray to him at the red table, and Henry bringing his glass of juice. The pleasant memory laid a touch of comfort onto his fatigued mind.

His heavy eyelids began closing slightly. He pictured the sincere faces of Sandra and Henry looking over to him, extending their friendship at such a desperate moment.

He began drifting off to sleep, beautiful, restful sleep.

Just as he was about to go out for the night, the haggard face of the red-table guard crashed through the fond memories, snarling back into his dreams. Shuddering under his blanket, Matthew's eyelids popped open. He wasn't going to sleep. No way! That guard could be anywhere, behind anything, hiding, waiting for another chance to beat him up. And so the night continued, unending and unmerciful, with Matthew always watchful and always on the alert.

Suddenly the doors to the squad bay opened. A flood of hallway light slipped into the room briefly, and left just as quickly as the door swung closed again.

Matthew heard footsteps walking in the squad bay, slow, crisp, footsteps. They were moving in his direction. Pulling the covers up just under his eyes, he turned on his side, facing the oncoming steps. His breathing was shallow and quiet, but it still seemed too loud.

The footsteps continued, heavy and direct, without ceasing, one step, then another.

He listened as the steps came closer and closer, until finally, they were at the very end of his rack. Then they stopped.

Sucking in his breath, Matthew looked to the foot of his bed through the shadows and saw what looked like tall pant legs. They turned towards him.

Scared senseless, he pulled the blanket up another inch until it was over his eyes. Praying desperately, he clenched the bedspread tightly over his face.

He heard the steps moving between his rack and the next one over. His knees began trembling. He heard the stranger bending over; he thought he heard the pants crinkle as the stranger kneeled down.

Too frightened to lower the blanket, he laid there in total panic.

Suddenly, he felt a warm palm lay atop his forehead. The instant the palm touched, somehow he knew this was a friend, and that everything would be okay.

"Be calm, young Matthew," the voice seemed to say. "I am an angel of the Lord, sent from the great I Am. Be at peace. Rest, and be assured that your God loves you and will not forsake you."

The fear that had encompassed Matthew suddenly vanished. The burdens of the last couple days lifted from his mind, his breathing relaxed, a deep peace of divine origin comforted him. His heavy eyelids became as light as feathers, his fears and anxieties withered away, replaced instead with a sense of love, a love he had never before known, or felt. The words of the stranger soothed him. Before he could open his eyes to explore their source, sleep overtook him.

The stranger removed his palm.

Matthew's tired, beaten body pulled him into a much-needed slumber as he collapsed into a deep, restful sleep, respite of any negative thoughts or feelings. Only good, happy dreams would follow him through to morning.

The angel smiled as he looked lovingly down on the little boy. The message was delivered, and the Lord's blessings were with Matthew.

He turned, and as legions of angels joined him, he walked from the room.

Chapter

22

In the formative years of HEdge's gradual rise onto the world scene, conditions were set in place by the HEdge Council to lay a solid foundation for future growth. Some of these conditions received less than enthusiastic support from the communities directly affected by them. As such, isolated political skirmishes broke out from time to time, causing short periods of bad press for HEdge, though seldom forcing HEdge to back down from its original stand. On the contrary, HEdge attacked these insignificant bands of insurgency with the force of a high-powered steamroller, ultimately driving them into submission, and then devouring them in complete and undisputed victory.

One such case involved a ten square kilometer landmass on the southern tip of Staten Island, New York, known as the 'Great Kills'. This relatively small plot of land became the hotbed of conversation on the New York rumor mill as word got out that it was mysteriously being put up for grabs by some powerful land broker. As rumor had it, this broker wanted to purchase the land to support a private venture into some clandestine government project.

However, there was no wealthy land baron involved in this hostile real estate maneuver. Instead, the party interested in procuring this rich plot of U. S. soil known as the Great Kills of New York was none other than the HEdge Council itself. The ten member Council recognized early on the strategic advantage this suburb could hold for their soon to be activated New York based HEdge Forces. In fact, the location so impressed them that they ordered an immediate excavation of every household in the area, and the hasty construction of state of the art office buildings and warehouses, which would eventually make up one of the largest HEdge military installations on the eastern coast of the United States.

The Governor of New York became the heavy in this highly contested HEdge land takeover. Governor Koumral pleaded passionately with the rich tenants of Great Kills, trying to appeal to their heightened sense of world awareness, bolstering what an honor it was to have the HEdge Council personally interested in their property. But all the logic invoked and all the petitious speeches given, not a single homeowner wished to voluntarily part with their small portion of land.

Ultimately, Governor Koumral had to call in the Norfolk based HEdge Forces to physically remove the thousands of Great Kills tenants from their homes and businesses, then relocate them into what many resident's later claimed to be squalor-like conditions on the northeastern tip of the island.

However, a spokesperson for the HEdge Council was quick to point out that if they had surrendered their property without the government's intervention, and abided by the HEdge Council's wishes, they would have enjoyed a much greater outcome with profits to be had by all.

With the old neighborhood now gone, progress towards renovation quickly began. Once the area was fully redeveloped and buildings hoisted up to meet the high standards of HEdge building specifications, the newly activated New York based HEdge Forces quickly moved in and assumed ownership.

For the Governor's sake, in failing to successfully convince the Great Kills township of the need to voluntarily sell their property and relocate, all for the benefit of the HEdge Council, she was promptly removed from office, replaced by the incumbent Lieutenant Governor and forced into early retirement. Adding insult to injury, the HEdge Council saw to it that once her household goods were removed from the Governor's mansion in Albany, the moving company was instructed to transfer her entire belongings to the northeastern tip of Staten Island, where she would be forced to dwell alongside her recently displaced Great Kills population.

The citizens hardly noticed the sudden change of Governorship, and needless to say, the once peaceful and tranquil residents of the old Great Kills neighborhood were thrilled at the prospect of welcoming their old nemesis into their fold.

History has an eerie way of reminding political leaders of the dire consequences adjudged upon them when turning on their own people, no matter the reason. Ex-governor Koumral never had a chance. She had barely finished moving into her comfy little condominium high-rise when an explosive blast took out the southwest corner of the building, killing eighty-seven.

At the time of the blast, the ex-governor was enjoying a pleasant afternoon lunch, lounging on her eighth floor terrace overlooking the beautiful city harbor.

Unfortunately for her, the bomb that created all the havoc was planted above a ceiling tile just outside her entrance. When it went off, she was one of the first to feel its deadening affects as her body was instantly vaporized from the powerful explosion. It didn't take long for the police to come up with a motive for the crime. The case was closed almost before it was opened.

Thus, an era of questioning HEdge's authority quickly came to a close. The Great Kills feud was small in nature, but profound in its political fallout. This battle, along with hundreds of other similar skirmishes across the globe, clearly set the world on course for a complete and unadulterated HEdge domination.

Accordingly, the newly established Great Kills Eastern U.S. Sector HEdge Forces Base became the premier military installation of the eastern United States, and one that would play a large part in eradicating other unpopular movements within their borders.

Chapter

23

Lieutenant Thomas Benson stood motionless outside the Great Kills HEdge Forces office building, his eyes propped upward toward the large pane-glass window of Colonel Dirk Reynolds third-floor office. The Lieutenant was hoping and waiting for his division chief to walk past it.

The late-afternoon sun hovered calmly behind him with its radiant beams reflecting sharply off the building's windows.

Benson looked haggard and dazed as he stood fixed in that position, his arms hanging listlessly to his sides, his normally spruce uniform wrinkled and baggy, crumpled especially at the elbows and knees. Even his patent leather dress shoes begged for a polish.

This was not the Lieutenant Benson of old. This was not even the Lieutenant Benson of a week ago. This man was different, different in every way imaginable. The bouncy personality that once made up his lively character was now sluggish and reticent. Only the sparkle of his wire-rimmed glasses hinted of the bright disposition that once was his trademark.

Life held no meaning for Benson anymore, or death. His existence was merely a fact he had to reckon with daily. He had become an oasis of existence onto himself, not bound by any peripheral obligations or expectations. He was a lone man driven by a lone cause . . . a worthy cause, but one that would surely bring an end to his now decrepit and solitary life.

But he knew that, and he accepted it willingly, he even looked forward to it. What other way could he rejoin his wife and son?

Ah yes . . . , he thought as he stared blankly into the third floor window. *The flames . . . she's still waiting.* He knew she was waiting with his son, both of them, waiting in the flames.

"Won't be long now, baby. I swear it won't be long now!" In his mind's eye, he visualized both his wife and son watching, waving to him through the flames, and smiling.

He smiled back; his top lip quivering.

Thomas Benson was getting close to the edge. His mind was delicately teetering on the crevice of another world, a nether world, where he was ready to plunge at any moment, to join his family once and for all.

Suddenly, the Lieutenant's face lit up, his breath speeded. Someone just traipsed in front of the Colonel's window. He could see a figure; looked like a man, a tall man, yes that's him. That's him!

The wait was over. His limp, spiritless body sprang to life. His right hand lunged into his baggy uniform pants pocket, gripping the small rounded barrel of his miniature HEdge pistol. The pistol was similar in design to the nineteenth century derringer, but the bore was smaller, and the aim more accurate. Not to mention it packed ten times the punch. He had a full round of high caliber, shaved, metal-piercing bullets loaded into its small cylinder. A little overkill perhaps, but better too much than not enough.

He ran his fingers over the barrel one last time before starting towards the building. He was ready.

"Here I come," he murmured, patting his right trouser pocket over the hidden pistol. "First I'm going to make things right, baby, just like I promised. Then I'll be joining you and my boy."

With much effort, he walked rather than ran, steadily towards the building, admiring the professional landscaping that surrounded it, appearing as normal as possible, while actually pondering his assassination plans for Colonel Reynolds.

The plan was not complicated. He would step into the Colonel's office, start a conversation over some mundane topic, then, as a passing consideration, he would ask him one last, very important question: Who was responsible for the auditorium riot?

Of course the Colonel would have no idea how important his answer to this question would be, but that was no concern of Lieutenant Benson's. He just wanted to hear the answer. He wanted to hear him pride-fully boast how everything went just as planned, and that all the proper seeds were planted in the right places, and how the peaceful crowd was successfully converted into an uncontrollable, raging mob.

Benson knew how these things worked; he's been involved in seeding crowds before. And he understood the reason behind it; the State had a compelling interest to have the crowd eradicated. Didn't matter what the interest was; it wasn't his job to ask questions. He just followed orders.

But when he did, he made sure no HEdge families were involved. That was the problem here. A HEdge family was involved, and that family was his.

The Colonel's inevitable answer to that question would surely be the last answer of his life. At which, Benson would calmly remove the pistol from his trouser pocket, point it to the Colonel's head, and kindly advise him that his wife and son were slaughtered in that riot; only before pulling the trigger.

From there, all time would stand still, he was sure of it. Once the Colonel's head and torso were fairly saturated with bullets, and his body was lying sprawled out on the floor bleeding over the carpet, then the Lieutenant would turn the pistol to himself.

He only had to finish what was started a week ago. For all practical purposes, when his family was massacred, his life ended with them. He was already a dead man; a walking corpse; one of the living dead. There was only one problem . . . the job wasn't finished. So he had to finish it himself. Then, and only then, would his mission be complete. And only then could he rejoin his family . . . in the flames.

The large glass doors opened as he stepped inside the Headquarters building, a second set opened as he continued through the entrance-way. Entering, he presented his HEdge Forces Identification Card to the security officer at the front desk.

Attempting to be funny, the guard bellowed, "Looks like you spent the night on the curb. Wife throw you out of the house or something?" The guard laughed as he waved him through.

Benson froze at the mention of his wife. How dare the guard use her in the butt of a joke! His first impulse was to take his pistol out and shoot him right then and there. Only his need to follow through with his plans prevented him from doing so.

The security guard caught the Lieutenant's flash of anger and quickly retracted his remarks. "Hey, sorry, buddy. I was just kidding, okay?"

The Lieutenant managed to reel his anger in before creating a scene. Brushing the security guard's weak apology aside, he stalked over to the elevators, the guard's leery eyes following behind.

Stepping into the first elevator, he mumbled, "Third floor."

"Third floor. Thank you," the computer's digital voice confirmed as the doors closed.

Benson saw the number '1' light up on the screen above the elevator door; then '2' as they ascended up towards the third floor.

Small beads of perspiration began forming across his forehead. For a brief moment he felt jittery and nervous, actually considering changing his mind and going home. But the moment was fleeting as visions of his wife and son entered his mind, excitedly dancing through flaming embers, happily laughing and waving; intoxicated with the joy of know-ing they would soon be together. Even the flames seemed to come alive as they arched wildly through the air, madly licking his family with long weaving strokes as they danced around them.

Benson took a deep breath as he timidly smiled back to his halluci-natory family, becoming more unstable with each passing minute.

Once at the third floor, the elevator stopped. He got out and walked to the right. The Colonel's office was half way up the brightly carpeted hallway.

Getting past the Colonel's secretary would be the first challenge, but he could do it. He has known Margaret since he arrived on base three years ago, and they've been flirting-friends ever since. But that was history now. Anymore, Margaret was simply a wall to be hurdled in order to get to Colonel Reynolds. If he had to, he'd shoot her to do it.

As he made his way down the long hallway, a steady stream of nicely clad men and woman were rushing from one office to another. Some were dressed in blue HEdge uniforms, others in formal civilian attire. Many took a dim view as they noticed his shabby appearance and despairing gaze. A balding, gray-haired old man accidentally spilled some of his coffee when he noticed the ragged looking Lieutenant heading towards him. He stepped aside to let him pass.

Benson ignored them all. His mission had nothing to do with any of them. He wanted only one person in this building, and he was determined to get him. Nothing else mattered.

Only a few more steps and he would be there.

Margaret surprised him. Just as he was entering the Colonel's outer office, she came rushing out the door. Her smaller five-foot-three slender frame hit him full bodied, almost knocking him over. Thrown completely off balance, he reached for the doorframe to anchor himself. Margaret latched on to his waist to keep herself from going down.

After a moment of clumsiness, the two recovered from their untimely collision. Frantically straightening her clothes, Margaret apologized, "Oh, I'm sorry, Thomas. I didn't see you coming. I'm so embarrassed."

Benson regained his balance in no time. The incident happened so quick his narrowly focused mind wasn't sure how to react. Angry? Playful? Nothing . . . he couldn't feel a thing. All he knew was that she was in the way.

After her clothes were straightened, Margaret looked up from her cotton blouse and finally got a good look at him. Her feminine instincts instantly recognized something was wrong.

"Thomas, what happened? Are you okay? You look dreadful!"

Avoiding her stare, he looked past her into the Colonel's office. Reynolds was lounging in his richly upholstered leather chair, feet propped up on his larger-than-life oak desk, reading a magazine.

"Thomas, are you all right? Can I get you anything?" Margaret was beginning to worry. This isn't the same Thomas Benson she's played and laughed with over the years. His expression was off, he didn't have the same zeal or energy. He looked lost.

"No. I'm fine, Margaret," he answered blandly, void of any emotion whatsoever.

His hollow response was all the additional evidence she needed. This man was a stranger. Something terrible had happened to her friend, something unthinkable. And she wanted to know what it was.

Taking him by the arm, she led him to a comfortable chair next to her desk, and gently sat him down.

"Listen, Thomas, I really have to go to the lady's room, but I won't be long. You just sit here until I get back, okay? Don't move. I know something's wrong, Tom, I can read it all over your face. But relax. I'll be back in just a minute, then we can talk."

She gave him a final glance before rushing out of the office, closing the door behind her.

Benson was pleased at the sight of the closed door. It would only make things easier.

He stood up at his chair.

His mission was almost complete. He was in the Colonel's outer office, only yards from the man he had vowed to kill. A promise he had made to his wife and son the day they were taken out; a pledge to end the life of the person responsible for their deaths. And that is exactly what he intended to do.

He stepped slowly toward the opened door of Colonel Dirk Reynolds' private office. Gazing in, he saw the Colonel was still engrossed in his magazine, oblivious to his presence.

What an imbecile, Benson thought to himself. The Colonel can lead hundreds of thousands to a massacre, yet he can't even sense when his own life is about to end. *Amazing.*

Rapping his knuckles a couple times against the opened door, he tried to get the Colonel's attention.

Arrogantly ignoring Benson's knocks, the Colonel continued reading his flimsy magazine. Thomas just stood, waiting for the appropriate sign to enter. Just as he was about to knock again, the Colonel closed the magazine, and with an agitated expression, turned to face him.

A moment of uncomfortable silence followed while Benson stood as a mannequin, waiting for the Colonel's invite. Finally, Reynolds laid the magazine on his desk and dropped his feet to the floor.

His eyes closed into narrow curious slits.

"Lieutenant, come in, please. Have a seat."

"Thank you, sir."

Entering the expansive, highbrow office, he walked across the burgundy carpeting over to a nicely finished armed chair in front of the Colonel's desk. The chair's leather cushion squeaked as Benson's weight pressed onto it.

A heavy aura of power permeated from the mahogany-walled office. Everything in it seemed beyond touch, beyond feel, as if it were off limits to all but the most affluent.

"Well, Lieutenant, you're looking rather shallow today, aren't you?"

To an untrained ear, the Colonel may have appeared to be trying his luck at a bit of humor. But Benson knew better. This was a clear reprimand from one of the top military officers in the Eastern U.S. Sector Forces. A reprimand from this level would normally bring a shudder to the person being addressed. But in Lieutenant Benson's current state, it was like water straining through a porous colander, leaving no trace of its existence.

"Yes, sir, I apologize for that. I'm afraid I've run into a few snags in my personal life. Can't seem to get anything right these days. I expect things will be improving very soon though." He couldn't help breaking a smile at that.

Reynolds didn't see the humor. "I certainly hope so. Now tell me, what brings you into my office?"

"Well, sir, it just occurred to me that I haven't been able to discuss my platoon's performance during the New York State Auditorium riot last week. You had wanted a report from all the platoon chiefs. Remember?"

Reynolds looked at him curiously.

"Lieutenant, that report is due in my office tomorrow. I hardly feel a need to discuss the matter individually with each platoon chief."

"Yes, sir, I realize that, however, I, uhh . . . feel a need to discuss certain ramifications of that riot to you directly, sir. I, uhh . . . feel there were certain factors that may have been, uhh . . . overlooked, that perhaps could be avoided in the future."

Reynolds leaned forward over his desk while looking directly into Benson's dark, detached eyes. After a brief study, he pulled open his top desk drawer, reached in and took out a fountain pen with a small pad of paper. After a few seconds of scribbling, he laid his pen down and handed the paper over.

"Lieutenant, take this referral slip to medical. I don't know what's happened to you, but it doesn't take a Ph.D. to realize you need some medical attention. You look and sound terrible. A good rest with a few days off might do some good."

The Lieutenant took the slip from Reynolds' hand and slipped it into his shirt pocket.

"Any recommendations you might have concerning the auditorium riot can be included in your report. Have a good day, Lieutenant."

Reynolds was through with this unscheduled visit, and was anxious to get back to more urgent matters, such as his magazine.

"Sir, thank you for your concern. May I ask one last question before I leave?" He reached into his right trouser pocket, wrapping his fingers firmly around the grip of his pistol. He slid to the edge of his seat ready to leap.

Openly agitated by the request, the Colonel impatiently obliged, "Yes, one last question. Then I really must get back to work."

The HEdge pistol was at the edge of the Lieutenant's pocket, his index finger pressed lightly over the trigger.

"Thank you, sir. Yes, I would like to know one thing if I may. Referring back to the auditorium riot, how did it start anyway? Who was responsible for the riot? I mean, uhh . . . were there seeds planted in the crowds?"

Sweat began streaming down Benson's face; his left foot began tapping uncontrollably on the carpet. Every nerve in his body was burning as he waited for the response.

Leaning forward a trifle more, Reynolds took an even harder look at the Lieutenant. "Why are you asking me this? Is there a reason you need to know?"

Benson's patience was being pushed to the limit. He wanted an answer. Nothing more.

"Actually, sir, I was just wondering, I uhh . . . was sort of surprised at how quickly the crowds became unglued. I mean, when our troops first arrived at the auditorium, everything seemed pretty calm . . . but then, all of a sudden . . . everybody went nuts, then I heard shots go off.

"I was just wondering if seeds were planted. I uhh . . . know I didn't plant any. I was just wondering."

Reynolds burst into laughter as he fell smoothly back into his chair, dropping his arms on the leather arm rests.

"No, Lieutenant, you have it all wrong. First you heard the shots, and then the crowd went berserk. Remember?"

The Lieutenant thought for a second, replaying the horrible incident in his mind. Yes, the Colonel was right, the shots did come first!

"You're right, sir, now I remember. There were shots fired first, and then the crowd lost it! Yes, I remember now."

Hesitating for a second, Reynolds continued in a mocking tone, "Well I'm so glad you're up on current events. Now would you please leave?"

On the contrary, Benson had no intentions of leaving. There was too much at stake; his family's revenge and the Colonel's death, not to mention his own.

He asked his question one more time, pronouncing his words clearly while rising from his chair, keeping the gun concealed in his pocket.

"Sir, you haven't answered my question. Who was responsible for the riot?"

Also rising behind his desk, Reynolds leaned toward him, and raised his voice as he roared an answer to the burning question.

"Lieutenant, if you really must know, I did not plant any seeds in that crowd. Got that? Not one! And I don't know why I should be telling you this, but for the sake of getting you out of my office, I will!

"Seeds were planted, Lieutenant, but not by me; they were planted by Mr. Banchard's people! Banchard wanted the place destroyed, burned to the ground. He said the Christians were using it for secret meetings. Besides, the local population needed a little downsizing anyway. So it had to happen. The riot was just the most convenient way to do it. Banchard sent snipers to take out a few civilians and get the crowds and soldiers panicky.

"And I'd say they did a pretty good job." The Colonel chuckled.

Benson's eyes went wide, his pulse quickened, his stomach tightened. He was shocked. It never occurred to him that Roderick Banchard was the cause of his family's tragedy.

All of his plans, all of his dreams to avenge his family's death! Everything wasted . . . wasted . . . for nothing!

He felt lightheaded. The walls began spinning. The realization that life had once again played a dirty trick on him was too much. Suddenly, his weight became too much for him, his knees began giving out, he couldn't hold himself up any longer. Dropping to the floor, he passed out. Margaret ran into the office just in time to catch his head from hitting the coffee table. Her smaller frame could do little more than guide him to the left of the table and soften the impact.

Startled by Benson's collapse, Reynolds hurried from behind his desk to help his secretary.

"What happened, sir?" Margaret appealed.

"I don't know. He kept pushing me for information about the auditorium riot. That's all he would talk about. I think he saw more than he could handle, Margaret. I really do. Anyway, I gave him a referral slip for medical. If anyone can help him, they can. Better give them a call so they can take him right down for an evaluation."

"Yes, sir. I hope he's going to be all right," she said while heading out to her office phone, leaving Benson on the floor.

Reynolds looked grudgingly down at Benson, studying his worn out appearance while wondering what it was that had pushed him over the edge. Just as he was about to turn away, the Lieutenant's eyelids snapped open, sending a chill through the Colonel.

While fixing his gaze on the Colonel, Benson sat up on the floor. His movements were surprisingly smooth and agile. Looking sympathetically to the Colonel, he asked one last, endearing question.

"Colonel Reynolds, may I have a transfer? I'm afraid I need a change in my life. I have to confess, the riot threw me off a little. Battle fatigue I guess. The truth is, I haven't been the same since. If I could get a transfer to another division, somewhere else, I'm sure I would be better off."

Standing over him, Reynolds considered the request. *If anything, this man needs hospitalization, not a transfer.*

"And where do you suppose you might want to be transferred to?"

Benson was waiting for this question. The moment the idea sprang into his mind, he knew exactly where he wanted transferred . . . the only place he could complete his mission.

"The Manhattan division, sir."

"You mean you want to work in Mr. Banchard's building? That's not exactly known for easy living, you know. More people are trying to get out of that building, than into it."

Walking around his desk, Reynolds chuckled at the request. "I think you really have lost your mind, Lieutenant."

Pleading for consideration, "Yes, sir. But I know Manhattan like the back of my hand. I could do exceptionally well there, sir, exceptionally well."

The Colonel had to admit the request was tempting. Getting rid of Benson was not a bad idea. But he wasn't sure if unloading his deadwood into Banchard's building would be a good move. If something went wrong, it could prove to be a serious mistake. But on the other hand, who's going to notice one quack in a building of over four thousand? Besides, with a little medical attention and a few days rest the Lieutenant would be back to normal.

The idea was intriguing. He could dump a retread and get a fresh lieutenant in its place, someone more capable, and more stable.

Tempting . . . very tempting.

Benson waited patiently in front of the Colonel's desk, desperate for an answer, but only one answer would do; none others.

Finally, Reynolds stopped pacing behind his desk and looked directly over to him. "Okay, you got it. But only after a medical checkup and a few days rest."

"Thank you, sir. Thank you," he groveled happily.

Margaret returned to the office with some medical personnel.

"Thomas," she stated with glee. "You're all right. Thank goodness, you had me worried."

Benson wasn't even aware she had entered the room. His mind was somewhere else. A dumb smile lingered across his face.

Addressing his secretary in a business manner, the Colonel ordered, "Margaret, get me a transfer slip. I have some work for you concerning Lieutenant Benson. In the mean time, they can take him down for an evaluation."

"Yes, sir," she answered, while leading Benson to the door.

The three medical-staff members introduced themselves to the Lieutenant as they calmly took him from Margaret and helped him out of the office.

Benson just kept smiling. He could see that his wife and son were disappointed with this delay in their family's reunion, but he knew they understood. They paused their dancing and waving, but their chins were still high. And they smiled to him.

Yes, they understood.

Chapter

24

Samuel Treppin scuttled across the rooftop of the eighty-story, Eastern U.S. Sector HEdge building in mid-town Manhattan, hurrying towards his private, vertical lift-off jet scheduled to fly him to the World Finance Conference in Geneva.

Jennifer Bajon, his prized secretary, was rushing alongside trying to keep pace with his longer strides, while urging him to heed the advice of his eleven Advisors.

Ignoring her, Samuel continued hastily toward his jet.

She finally stopped and lowered her arms in surrender as she shouted, "Samuel, didn't you hear a word they told you? You could be in danger! You need more security!"

The Sector Chief was exasperated. He had listened to enough warnings from his Advisors; the last thing he needed was his secretary picking up where they had left off. The incident at the New York State Auditorium was a catastrophe. And quite possibly foul play was the cause. So investigate it and see where it leads you. Don't sit around creating imaginary monsters to hide from.

Stopping abruptly, he turned to her. "Jennifer, please. I'm fine. See?" He swung open his dress coat and spread his arms out wide. "Not a bullet-hole in sight. And no one's jumped from behind any walls yet."

Ms. Bajon wasn't amused. She folded her arms and glared. Samuel held the pose for a second, and then started towards the jet again, but at a slower pace. She followed.

"Thanks for your concern, Jennifer. I'm flattered and grateful, but please don't over do it. Yes, I heard everything the Advisors told me. I sat for over an hour listening to their babble, didn't I? But they're wrong. Whatever caused that fire at the auditorium had nothing to do with me. I just know it. I can sense it in my bones."

The Sector Chief's face took on an angry, yet saddened expression as he finished his remarks. "Besides, you heard what Greg White said: The auditorium's management called for HEdge support because their crowds were getting restless waiting for me! Can't you see, Jennifer? If anyone's to blame for that riot, it's me!"

"Samuel, you also heard the first reports from the auditorium when the troops arrived. The crowds were calm and under control. It wasn't until those Christians started shooting and set the fires that everyone went nuts. That's not your fault!"

She paused a second, allowing the Sector Chief time to absorb her logic.

"Samuel, if those Christians would kill that many people to get to you, I'm afraid what they might try next."

Totally frustrated, Samuel countered, "How do you know it was Christians that started the fires? Who saw them? Who? The fact is, we don't know who started them, or why. And besides, I didn't help the situation by not showing up."

"And I'm grateful you didn't. Or you'd be lying somewhere in a pile of ashes like everyone else that died in that inferno."

The Sector Chief waved her comments aside. He's heard enough. The argument was over. No winners, no losers.

Finally at the short stairway leading up to the jet's opened door, they stopped.

Two of the aircraft's crew members stood attentively beside the stairs, holding their salutes proudly as they waited for Samuel to board.

Turning towards his secretary, he looked over her shoulder and saw his Advisors congregated just outside the rooftop entrance, with

Gregory White and Lester Ellis crowding at the front.

Each of the Advisors were yearning out to him, forlorn expressions draped over their loyal faces, hiding the indifference or contempt in some cases, they actually felt for him. The sight was almost comical.

Samuel waved to them as he held back a chuckle.

Each of the eleven ambitious technocrats threw their arms up, waving excitedly back, bright smiles returning to their faces.

Samuel couldn't watch them any longer. He turned to his secretary.

Ms. Bajon looked devoutly up to him, her moistened brown eyes gleaming with reverence.

He wondered if it was a put-on, or if she really was concerned.

"Jennifer, if I thought I was in some kind of danger, I'd stay right here instead of going to that boring conference. Believe me.

"But I'm not in danger. Any more than if I didn't go at all. So please, take it easy."

Samuel paused briefly. "Besides, someone has to keep an eye on those crackpot Accountants. That's my job."

Reaching out, he pressed the padded shoulder on Jennifer's red blouse, trapping several strands of her auburn hair under his palm.

"I promise. I'll take good care of myself. You just take care of this zoo while I'm away. All right?"

She cracked a smile. "Samuel, do you promise? Really? You'll be careful?"

Samuel raised his right hand as if taking an oath. "So help me, HEdge, I promise." Then smiled warmly to her.

Jennifer looked down for a second, and then raised her attention back to her Sector Chief.

"All right, Samuel. Have a good trip. But if you need anything, give me a call. Okay?"

"Great. Thanks, Jennifer. See you in a week."

Turning towards the stairs, Samuel walked up. Jennifer didn't budge. She stood at the base of the steps watching.

The two crewmembers scurried up the stairs behind him, then lifted the retractable steps back inside and closed the hatch.

Jennifer grudgingly turned from the jet and walked towards the rooftop entrance where most of the eleven Advisors had already disappeared into. Following behind, she didn't exchange words with any of them, or them with her.

Silence accompanied the group as they filed down the hall and loaded into the elevators. Within minutes they were all back inside their respective offices, pursuing their individual tasks, with most of them sharing the happy consensus that their drunken, starry-eyed Sector Chief was finally out of their hair for a week.

Just as Jennifer Bajon reached the doorway outside her office, the booster engines of the Sector Chief's personal jet fired off their massive 400 horsepower thrusters. In no time the 2.5-ton luxury, three passenger, three crew member, ultra speed aircraft, was lifting gracefully off the tarmac rooftop.

The jet's smooth, vertical ascent continued for several seconds until two hydraulic clips engaged on both sides of the fixed wing aircraft, causing the angle of the booster propulsion engines to dip six notches, taking the jet from a steady vertical motion, into a forty-five degree forward momentum above the city.

In a second, the Sector Chief's state of the art aircraft was hurling across the New York City skyline, beginning its long global journey to a HEdge installation in the southern tip of Geneva, Switzerland.

In less than half a minute, a dozen HEdge Force jets, carrying the Sector Chief's personal security force, swooped down to escort the solo aircraft, with everyone on board sworn to protect the life of the eminent passenger inside.

The trip from New York to Geneva would be relatively short in duration, cruising at an average speed of .87 Mach, or 661 miles per hour. He would arrive in Geneva before early morning, where he could rest awhile before meeting up with his own accountants who had arrived three days earlier.

Sitting alone in his confined, yet luxurious cabin, Samuel tried to unwind. He needed a good night's sleep but wasn't ready to call it a day just yet.

Forcing his mind off work, he sat comfortably back in his reclining chair, gazing out the window to the fluffy clouds drifting freely through the sky.

After a short while of daydreaming, he leisurely reached across the small counter beside his chair and lifted a tall glass of gin and tonic from it. Carefully balancing the full glass to his lips, he casually tilted it, and then heartily swallowed the contents down.

It had been a hectic day to put it mildly. A little nightcap was exactly what he needed to clear his mind of the day's troubles. And that it did, as he closed his weary eyes and listened to the mellow classical tunes flowing from the ultra-digital sound system inside his cabin.

He didn't forget the promise he made to Jennifer about laying off the booze. He fully intended to cut back; it was just a matter of time. But the time just wasn't there yet.

He promised himself that after the week was over, he would find a counselor to help wean him off the bottle like Jennifer wanted. That's when he would get serious about quitting. But for right now, there were other concerns on Samuel's mind. Kicking his drinking habit would have to take a back seat to the conference.

Though, even the conference wasn't the heaviest concern on Samuel's mind at the present. What troubled him the most were all the crazy warnings his Advisors dumped on him before leaving.

Was it conceivable that John Rex really wanted him dead?

"How could that be? John Rex, trying to kill me?" He laughed.

He considered it for several minutes before dismissing the idea entirely.

Chuckling to himself, he realized how unlikely it was that Rex would ever want him dead. But he understood why his Advisors might believe otherwise. They didn't know what he knew about Rex. And that made all the difference in the world.

Samuel continued pondering the mystery of John Rex well into the night, until tipping a few glasses more than intended, and finally dozing off. Oblivious to the lights in his cabin and the soft-playing music, he was out for the evening, or at least until his flying convoy arrived in Geneva.

Chapter

25

A storm was brewing in the skies above the eastern seaboard. Shadowy gray nimbus clouds were clustering overhead, permitting only scant rays of sunlight to break through to the city below.

Short bursts of thunder roared through the heavens, warning the millions of city dwellers of the raging tempest that was moving in from the west. Light-sensitive street lamps were switching on all over town as the gray overcast filled the skies.

The storm was a surprise to the international weather services. None of the meteorologists saw it coming. It materialized in less than three hours, with the majority of the populace completely unaware until it was right on top of them.

It began when a northerly cold front shifted south colliding into a northbound heat wave. The two weather fronts met above the central-eastern United States where an unusually high humidity had already settled in over the last couple days.

With the three atmospheric extremities merging, each battling for a niche in the skies, something had to give; a storm was inevitable. It was just a question of how powerful that storm would ultimately be.

By the time the weather services collected the data and made their educated guesses as to the size, force and direction, it had already reached a full-fledged gale and was rapidly beating a path eastward over the Atlantic coastline.

The storm demonstrated an endurance and destructive nature unseen on the east coast for decades as it thrashed violently over entire communities, washing out cities unfortunate enough to be caught in its path.

In the storm's wake, billions of dollars worth of property was left destroyed, and multitudes of lives perished.

But even as the casualties mounted, not everyone agreed the storm was such a bad thing. One such person found it especially exhilarating, even entertaining.

Standing on the covered terrace outside his office on the sixty-sixth floor of the HEdge Forces building, this tall lanky man stared down on the darkening city. He leaned dangerously over the black cast-iron rail of his terrace as he snickered, watching citizens scatter in every direction, rushing for shelter.

Even from his high vantage point, he could see mothers pushing their strollers at breakneck speeds, while swerving-taxicabs worked overtime offering expensive rides to anyone that could pay the price.

The hate-driven man leaned even more daringly over the rail, straining to see the people scurrying as heavy rain pellets shot down on them.

The tail of his long dark cloak whipped back and forth as the erratic breeze played wild cat-and-mouse games with it. Angry gusts blew his stringy black hair in every direction, sometimes slapping down over his face.

"Hurry you insignificant peons!" he screamed above the roaring winds, waving his right fist over the terrace's rail. "Run! Run! Before you get caught in the storm!"

Speaking in a low sinister tone, "Are you people ever prepared for anything?"

"Of course not," he answered, stifling a laugh. He snickered again as he took in a lung full of fresh blustering air, then walked back into his extravagant private office.

Just as Roderick Banchard closed his doors, a chiming sounded from the videophone atop his desk. It chimed a second time before he could get to it. Pressing the connect button, his male secretary's handsome face appeared on the screen.

"Mr. Banchard, you have two visitors waiting outside the lobby for you. Mr. Gregory White and Mr. Lester Ellis. May I show them in, sir?"

Roderick paused a second. He didn't want to see either one of them.

"Do they have appointments?"

"Sir, I believe they do, let me check please."

Roderick watched the screen as his young secretary leaned forward, searching through the appointment ledger.

"Oh yes, here they are, for three o'clock, sir."

"I don't remember putting them in my schedule. Don't they know it's storming outside? Why aren't they back in their offices where they belong?"

Roderick realized there was no proper response to his question; he was simply raging to rage. Besides, he enjoyed putting his new secretary on the hot seat. The worthless lad wasn't good for much else.

"All right, let them in. But don't bother me with anything else. I plan to nap through to evening. I might need you later though." His lips parted as he released a sickly grin.

"Yes, sir. I'll show them right in, sir."

The videophone shut off.

Standing behind his enormous desk, Banchard rubbed his pronounced chin. "It's been one day since Treppin left for the World Finance Conference. So far he hasn't stirred any contention between our accountants." He smirked, "Thank the stars for small favors."

Roderick's solid oak door opened as Gregory White and Lester Ellis entered. Roderick ignored them until they walked directly up to him and extended their hands to shake.

Staring coldly down at both of them, he finally took their hands.

The enmity between the two parties had obviously not withered since their last meeting, and was in fact, quite alive and well.

After shaking hands Roderick sat uncaringly in his leather-upholstered chair behind his desk, resting his long thin arms on its cushioned armrests. Mr. White and Mr. Ellis sat in the two chairs across from him.

With a callousness in his voice, Roderick asked, "Gentlemen, what do you want?"

Gregory and Lester glanced at each other through the corners of their eyes. Neither man enjoyed sharing the company of this monster, but some things had to be done, like it or not.

Gregory was first to speak. "Roderick, let me start by saying, on behalf of Lester and myself, we deeply regret that the New York police were unable to apprehend John Rex the other day. I assure you, we both would have preferred a different outcome.

"However, circumstances being what they were, we had no choice but to deny your request. We hope you understand."

Gregory waited to give Roderick an opportunity to respond. It would be best to bury the hatchet now so they could get on with business.

But Roderick showed no sign of answering. Sitting motionless and silent, he stared bitterly at Gregory; his festering hatred all too evident on his face.

Gregory realized he was getting nowhere. He had hoped Roderick would have gotten over the matter by now but apparently that was not to be the case.

Lester sat quietly in his seat, wondering what could be going through Roderick's demented mind; what possible thoughts of retribution were lying dormant just under that sickened exterior. He felt a chill run up his spine. Banchard was truly a grotesque human being.

Gregory started back up. "Roderick, we are extending a peace offering to you. We hope you accept it, if for no other reason than maintaining a congenial working relationship between your office and ours. But if you do not, that's all right too. We will survive. I trust you will also. Albeit much less secure in your position, I'm sure."

That was a threat, pure and simple! Roderick caught it before it left Gregory's mouth, and was livid.

"You measly reptile. How dare you come into my office laying petty threats around!" Roderick stood behind his desk. His jaw muscles jittered under his pale skin. "You're the reason John Rex is not my prisoner today. You and that lap dog of yours. Believe me, someday you will both regret that mistake. Someday soon, I promise you."

Gregory bolted out of his chair. "You don't think I could have your head rolling out that door if I wanted? You don't think I know your connections with the Council? Well I do! And believe me, I can checkmate any move you think you can lay on me! I'm no fool, Banchard! You would do well to remember that."

Gregory stomped away from the chair, heading toward the door. Lester understood; it was time to leave. Good!

Once again Gregory spoke the right words to get Roderick's attention. All of a sudden Roderick felt apprehensive. How much did White know about his connections to the HEdge Council? Did White really know, or was he bluffing? Dare he ask? No. That could open him up to further questions. He's probably lying. He doesn't know a thing. But if he does, that could mean he's got closer ties to the Council than he does, and that could spell disaster.

Roderick almost leaped from behind his desk to prevent Gregory from leaving. Just as Gregory was reaching for the door handle, Roderick slipped in front of him.

"Gregory, Gregory," Roderick slithered out. "Why must we always play these silly games? We're both grown men, we both have the interests of the organization at heart. All this arguing is solving nothing. It really is silly."

Extending his hand, Roderick forced a humble expression. "Please accept my apology. I do get a little rattled at times, I admit." Pushing his humility to the limit, Roderick lowered his eyes just slightly, and then said, "Please forgive me. Please?"

Gregory realized he had won yet another argument with Roderick Banchard. And like the last one, it felt good. He shook Banchard's hand.

"All right," Gregory gave in, "that's water over the dam. Now let's get on with business."

Following Gregory's lead, Lester returned to his chair.

"Looking out that window I'd say we don't have much time," Gregory began, "so I'll get on with it. We came to discuss a couple issues dealing with your favorite subject: John Rex. We've run into some problems that perhaps your Forces could help us with."

"Sure, whatever you need."

Gregory turned to his fellow Advisor. "Lester, tell him what we know about Rex."

Lester suddenly came to life. "Roderick, to put it bluntly, we don't know anything about John Rex . . . nada . . . nothing."

He got up from his chair and started pacing as he began his story.

"When the western sector's intelligence people combed Rex's house in Alameda, they couldn't find anything to help identify John Rex. Not a thing."

Roderick was slightly amused. "What do you mean, nothing? Did you really think his name was going to be John Rex? C'mon guys, get with the program. Of course it's not John Rex. I'm sure he works under an alias name."

Gregory looked impatiently over to his fellow Advisor. Their eyes met. "Go ahead, Lester, tell him the rest."

Lester continued, "Roderick, you don't understand. They took every kind of evidence that they could find from that house. They took prints, they took DNA scans, scent studies, voice scans from the phone, every-thing, you name it they took it. But after all was said and done, they still came up with zilch."

Roderick looked confused.

"Let me explain another way. After taking every intelligible piece of evidence they could find in Rex's house, they tried matching them up with the ID's in the World Data Bank on the Belgium Mainframe, and you know what they found?" He paused to make sure Banchard was with him.

Roderick sat gawking, waiting for the obvious answer.

"Nothing." Lester finally said. "Nothing. They didn't find a thing. John Rex is not on record, anywhere, by any name or face, anything! None of the prints or scans matched any identification in the network. None of them.

"In short, we have nothing to prove the man was ever even born!"

Roderick rose slightly in his seat. This was getting interesting . . . and weird.

"Are you sure? How could that be? Obviously someone made a mistake, they had to. Rex is alive, we have witnesses that saw him; he's got a family for HEdge's sake! Don't tell me we don't know who he is!"

Lester realized the point had finally hit home with Banchard. Things were rolling now.

"Roderick, that's exactly what I'm telling you. We don't know who he is. We can't even confidently tell you such a man exists."

Gregory intercepted, "Roderick, every piece of information they had on Rex was scanned, then scanned again, each time by experts, searching for any kind of identification link possible, and they found nothing. The Intelligence people are stumped. They don't know what to make of it. He's just not there."

Roderick was getting excited. This didn't make any sense. No sense at all.

"But how could that be? Every person born on this planet is numbered and recorded. Records made and stored in several data banks worldwide, with the Belgium mainframe storing them all. It is inconceivable that John Rex, or someone using that alias, is not on record. It's impossible!"

Lester continued, "We agree with you, Roderick. We don't see how this could be happening either, and yet, it most definitely is."

With his part over, Lester returned to his seat.

An extended silence filled the room as Roderick tried to come to terms with this impossible revelation. Gregory and Lester had already spent hours trying to figure it out, as did the people over at the ID lab. They've all given up on it.

Roderick finally broke the silence. "I find this very hard to comprehend, gentlemen, and disturbing. But with that being said, what exactly do you want from me?"

Gregory sat up straight and took in a deep breath. "To be honest with you, we don't know. This whole thing has got us so baffled we don't know what to make of it. Your people were the closest to him in the old Greenwich Village neighborhood. They almost got him. Did any of them actually see him? Or catch anyone that was with him? Did they come up with any evidence that perhaps we don't know of? Anything that might help?"

Roderick sat still in his chair. This was getting too bizarre. These guys are serious. They really have no idea who John Rex is. This is unbelievable!

"Gregory, trust me, if we had something on him, if we found anything interesting, I'd let you know. But we have nothing, nothing at all."

Something just occurred to him.

"Have you talked to his wife or son? Surely they can tell you something. I mean, they are on record, aren't they?"

Gregory slumped back in his chair. This was not going well. He looked over to Lester and sighed.

"Well . . . yes, they're both in our data banks. But they haven't helped at all. We've talked to his wife," Gregory said. "But she hasn't talked to us. All she'll do is pray and ask her God for help. Really pitiful sight let me tell you."

Lester joined in with a chuckle. "They had to tape her mouth shut, she was driving everyone crazy with her prayers. They've got her chained to a wall, arms spread apart to keep her from folding her hands together. It's sort of comical; like an old renaissance dudgeon. You'd be impressed."

Gregory added, "A certain Major Harker from the Western Sector apparently worked her over pretty good. She wasn't looking too healthy when we got to her. I guess she figures her time is almost up. Probably right too."

Roderick snickered while holding his hands over his mouth. "I know Major Harker. If she had anything to do with ordering a beating, you can rest assured a beating took place. She's not one for squandering a good opportunity. Our Mrs. Rex is lucky to be alive, believe me."

Roderick continued, "Have you talked to the kid?"

Lester's face became even more perplexed. Turning towards Gregory, he offered him a chance at it.

Gregory accepted.

"This one's even stranger, Roderick." He hesitated as he searched for the right words to explain what had happened to Matthew.

Roderick sat forward in his chair not wanting to miss a single word. Anxious to hear what on Earth could possibly be stranger than what he had just heard about Rex.

Speaking at a deliberately slow, clear pace, Gregory began, "The JBMC in Oakland wants to get rid of the kid. Fast."

"Why?" Roderick snapped.

"Well, apparently something's happened out there, something odd. I guess, well, they claim that Matthew is different from the other kids, really different."

Roderick was getting upset with this staggered, incomplete story. "Speak up, will you? I want to know what you know!"

"Okay. The day after Matthew got arrested and put in the JBMC, he caused quite a stir from praying in the cafeteria. I guess a guard had to come in and straighten him out. Anyway, the guard supposedly roughed him up pretty well. The kid had a few bumps and scrapes, and from what I understand, the ordeal of being torn from his mother and manhandled by the guard, left him about as down and out as any kid could be.

"Well, the very next morning when he went back to the cafeteria for breakfast, it was as if he was a new kid. Bursting with energy, smiling and as full of himself as if he had just won a race. And he was moving like he'd been in training for a marathon. The guard really freaked out when he saw him. Scared him to death. They say Matthew even tapped the poor slob on the shoulder and greeted him with a big smile. Told him that Jesus loved him.

Roderick listened intently to the incredible report, partially waiting for the punch line as if the whole thing were just a joke. But none was to come.

"Whatever's happening out there is causing other problems too. Some of the children sharing the same wing as him haven't been the same since he showed up. Everyone's walking around . . . happy."

"Happy? So what?" Roderick fumed.

"Listen to me, Roderick." Gregory pressed. "I mean happy like you've never seen.

"You have to remember where these kids come from. Most of them are nothing but young scoundrels, criminals in their own right, and of the worst kind. Many have come from the worst dysfunctional families imaginable, beatings, incest, you name it and they've been through it.

Now they're locked up in that JBMC hellhole. They've got nothing to be happy about. Nothing!

"But now, all of a sudden, they say some of these kids are like a bunch of little saints. They say Matthew's been sharing something with them but no one has the guts to find out what it is or to try and stop him.

"Anyway, the staff out there doesn't know what to make of it. They're scared to death of the kid. They think he's got some secret power or something. And to make matters worse, he's praying in the cafeteria again, before every meal. And most of the kids in his wing are praying with him. The staff's afraid to stop them, afraid for their lives. It's really quite strange. Quite distressing."

Roderick had heard enough. Roaring with laughter, he bellowed, "You don't mean to tell me you believe all that hocus pocus stuff? Secret powers, oh please," he laughed. "That staff has always had more than its share of quacks. They're loaded with them." Roderick laughed himself dizzy before continuing. Composing himself, he leaned across his desk and looked directly at Gregory

"You don't believe these cock-and-bull stories, do you, Greg? You're a logical man with common sense. Please tell me you don't believe a bit of it."

Gregory sat straight up in his chair, unsure exactly what to say. After all he had discovered, or rather, did not discover about John Rex, and then this, he was beginning to feel a little spooked. Roderick saw the apprehension on his face.

"You mean to tell me you believe this nonsense? You really do!"

Smirking with disbelief, Roderick said, "Gregory, the fact that you believe their story is almost as incredible as the story itself. How could you buy into such a fairy tale? How?"

"I'm not saying I agree with them or believe everything they told me, Roderick. I am simply telling you that *they* believe what they told me. And I must say, I've known several members of that staff for years, and they've never struck me as the type to go off the deep end easily.

"To tell you the truth, Roderick, I don't know what to make of it. Between Rex's mysterious identity, and the strange happenings with his son, I'm at a complete loss."

Roderick couldn't believe what he was hearing.

"What did Treppin have to say about all this?"

Lester spoke up. "We didn't tell him. He slept through most of the day, another hangover of course. But when he did wake up, we barely had enough time just to brief him on the auditorium fire."

Mildly surprised, Roderick asked, "So Treppin doesn't know we have Rex's wife and son?"

"That's right. But he'll be back in a week. We'll tell him then if he doesn't hear about it in Geneva first. If he stays sober long enough, that is."

A strong wind slammed against the windows, distracting the three men from their discussion. The full gust of the storm was about to hit.

"We'd better go, and fast," Gregory exclaimed as he got up from the chair. Lester followed. He had no desire to spend any more time with Banchard than was absolutely necessary.

Before opening the door, Gregory stopped and turned back to Roderick.

"What should we do with Rex's son? Bring him out here, or let him stay put?"

Roderick tilted his head towards Gregory, locking eyes with him, as if trying to read the other's mind. Finally, he answered in a firm sober voice, "No. They can keep him . . . for now."

Gregory nodded in agreement.

"We'll stay in touch," Gregory offered as he opened the door. "If you hear or find anything helpful, let us know. We'll do the same."

"Right," Roderick answered. "You'd better hurry, this storm is nasty."

In no time the two Advisors were in their limousine and on their way back to their office, with little to show for their trip other than a sincere apology from Roderick Banchard. Just how sincere was anyone's guess.

Chapter

26

Private First Class Frank Arpell stepped out of the elevator on the ground floor of the Great Kills Base Headquarters on Staten Island. Tucked snugly under his right arm was a sealed brown envelope given to him by Colonel Dirk Reynolds with explicit instructions to deliver posthaste to HEdge Forces Headquarters in lower Manhattan.

Standing outside the elevator, Arpell struggled trying to put his uniform-issued rain parka over his military shirt while being careful not to drop the envelope with its precious contents. His left arm fumbled clumsily through the maze of flapping synthetic nylon as he searched for the correct hole to slip his arms into. His first attempt at donning the parka ended in failure with his arms in the wrong sleeves and the zipper opening on his backside.

A passing soldier noticed the trouble he was having and offered to hold the envelope so he could use both arms. The Private hesitated at first, not wanting to compromise the envelope's security, but after another failed attempt at aligning his sleeves correctly, had no choice. He gladly handed it over to the obliging soldier who stood watching as he continued fumbling with his parka.

In a matter of seconds he managed to slip his arms into the correct sleeves with the zipper lined up front. With some glee he tugged down on the bottom of the parka while pulling the zipper clear up to his throat.

Relieved, he thanked the soldier for his assistance, then retrieved the envelope and started towards the front doors. The helpful soldier grunted an acknowledgment as he continued on his way, shaking his head as he left.

Aside from the difficulty he had with his parka, Private Arpell was normally a fast dresser, and a sharp one. His shoes were always polished to a luster and his uniform always nicely pressed, even when the next personnel inspection was weeks away.

Arpell was the first person that came to mind when his supervisor was ordered to have someone deliver a package from Colonel Reynolds to the Manhattan office. Not only was he one of the few soldiers presently available for the job, but also his immaculate uniform made him the obvious choice.

Admittedly, Frank Arpell would not have been the first choice if the mission were any more complicated than delivering an item from point A to point B. For that matter, he wouldn't have been the second or third choice either. Frank wasn't exactly a genius among his peers, even with his impeccable uniform.

Walking hastily towards the exit, he kept the brown envelope snuggled under his arm. The duty HEdge vehicle was parked at the curb right outside, waiting.

Stopping at the front glass doors, he gazed up to the darkened rain clouds outside. A bawling thunder roared down sending a chill through his back. Even with his less than brilliant I.Q., he realized going anywhere in this weather was not a good idea. Not that he had any choice in the matter.

Stepping outside, a strong wind gushed into him, lifting the bottom of his parka into the air, flapping it around wildly. Undeterred, he fought against the wind to get to his cruiser. He pressed a button on his wristband activating the driver-side door release. The door rose above his head as he quickly stepped in and sat down. With his body weight pressing fully on the seat, the door automatically closed and locked shut.

Within seconds he was revved and rolling out the front gates of the Great Kill's base on his way to the Manhattan HEdge Command Headquarters.

Watching the road ahead, Arpell reached over the passenger seat and pulled the brown envelope closer, balancing it partly on his lap and the seat beside him. He remembered Colonel Reynolds counseling him on the importance of the package. "It was vital that it be delivered as soon as possible." (Or ASAP as the Private liked to say.)

Arpell loved acronyms and abbreviations. Made him feel smarter, and he knew people were impressed when he used them; he could tell by their expressions. He learned early in his six-month career that knowing them was a critical part of being a good soldier; almost as important as a sharp uniform.

The Verazanno Narrows Bridge was coming up. He stayed in the right lane following close behind hundreds of other vehicles trudging forward. Another thunderous roar screamed from the heavens followed by a thick curtain of rain. The automatic windshield wipers jumped into action managing to swipe some of the moisture aside, but missing the bulk of it.

He considered returning to base. Colonel Reynolds might understand; but then, he might not. Holding the steering column in a death grip, he decided to keep going. No need taking chances with the boss.

Arpell took the cruiser slowly over the bridge. Heavy wind gales rammed him trying to push the cruiser across lanes, forcing him to make constant adjustments to the steering column.

After another forty-five minutes, he was finally in Manhattan; but the weather and road conditions were no better there, in fact they were worse. By now the storm had increased in intensity, and the traffic had responded by slowing to a snail's pace.

With only a few blocks left to go, the rain finally succeeded in shutting the roads down. Deep puddles had turned into flowing streams, stalling vehicles everywhere.

Arpell was desperate. He had to make his delivery and return to base; but had no idea how he was going to do it.

Feeling disgusted, he decided his only hope was to get out and walk. The idea lacked zeal, but what else could he do? His cruiser wasn't going anywhere; of that he was certain.

After a few minutes trying to stir up enough nerve, he finally opened his door and jumped out, the envelope grasped tightly under his arm.

Dashing across the sidewalk he pressed his wristband to activate the cruiser's door-locks. He didn't bother turning around to make sure they worked. If the doors didn't close, that was just too bad. He wasn't running back in this raging tempest for anything.

Do you think Banchard is hiding evidence about Rex?" Lester Ellis asked his fellow Advisor as he glanced out his limousine window to the dozens of pedestrians scrambling on the sidewalks.

Gregory considered the question. "Lester, I don't believe he is. Did you catch his expression once he understood the enigma Rex had turned into? He looked startled, didn't he?"

"Yes, he did seem a bit perplexed. I enjoyed that. Any time we can stump the old-beast is a moment worth treasuring." He chuckled.

Gregory hesitated. "I'll bet if we play our cards right, we may be able to rid ourselves of that hideous individual. I suspect Samuel doesn't like him any more than we do."

"I know, Gregory, but Samuel doesn't have what it takes to kick that freak out!" Lester snorted. "If I were the Sector Chief, that devil would be out peddling newspapers on a corner. I wouldn't give him enough authority to blow his nose without asking."

Gregory understood his partner's resentment, but he also understood the reality of the situation.

"Lester, remember, Banchard's position is under the Council's complete purview. Samuel can advise and suggest, but he cannot hire and fire. His opinion might weigh heavily in the Council's final decisions, but that in no way assures his feelings will be the determining factor. As you well know, many times the Council contradicts Samuel's opinion entirely."

Gregory paused before finishing his line of reasoning. "Which of course brings us to the awkward situation we currently find ourselves. An incompetent Sector Chief near the end of his seven year reign; a maniacal HEdge Force's Chief who has demonstrated time and again a lusting slant for maliciously evil acts; and, our fellow Advisors who absolutely could not care less so long as their hallowed positions are not threatened."

He raised his eyebrows. "Interesting times we find ourselves in, Lester. Most interesting indeed."

Lester took a deep breath as Gregory finished. He agreed whole-heartedly. Yes, these were certainly interesting times.

Lester finally asked, "So what do you think happened at the auditorium? Do you really think the Christians burned the place down to get to Samuel?"

Gregory grinned as he reached up to scratch the tip of his nose. "Lester, I don't know."

After a moment of introspection, he added, "Probably not. That's something Banchard thought up, I'm sure. I mean, as ill-versed in Christianity's primitive doctrine as I am, it would seem to me something as diabolical as that, would not fit well into their methodology.

He continued, "I'm sure if the Christians really wanted Samuel Treppin killed, they wouldn't have to slaughter thousands to do it. Call me naive if you wish, but I don't buy it."

"Well, if they weren't responsible," Lester intoned, "who was?"

Gregory laughed. "My, my, aren't we living a sheltered life? And I was afraid you might think I was naïve.

Gregory paused a moment as he whimsically studied his partner's face. "Lester, that auditorium fire and all the deaths that resulted from it, looks more the handiwork of our friend, Roderick, than it does those simple-minded Christians. Don't you think?"

Lester agreed of course, he just wanted to hear Gregory say it first. He didn't want to be the one to invoke such an accusation . . . just in case.

Lester leaned comfortably back into his cushioned seat and stared out the window.

The storm was getting worse; the wind was wrestling with the limousine.

"You know, Gregory, you are absolutely right. It is pretty obvious, isn't it?"

"Very."

"Well, I suppose some good came of it," Lester said. "Last time I checked, this sector's population was just a notch above acceptable levels. If not the fire, something else would have had to happen. So all's well after all."

"Exactly," Gregory agreed.

After a few seconds, Gregory added solemnly, almost as if talking to himself, "You know, Lester, it's scary sometimes how alike we are to Banchard. For instance, we wouldn't dream of wiping out masses of people even though we understand it has to be done from time to time. But when Roderick steps in to do the dirty work, we easily accept it as a necessary part of doing business . . . of governing the masses."

"Yes," Lester accepted. "I know what you mean. It is a little frightening isn't it? We recognize the need for such brutality, yet wouldn't kill even a single person on our own, at least not without ample justification."

"Precisely. So Banchard does serve a useful purpose, doesn't he?"

"Yes, he's an excellent goon. Whom I don't trust."

"Nor I," Gregory finished.

Suddenly the limousine slowed to a steady, yet definite halt. Gregory flipped a small switch, opening the privacy window that separated the driver's seat from the passenger's section. Both men gazed ahead through their driver's front windshield to see why their limousine had stopped.

Seeing the red traffic light ahead, Gregory shouted, "What's the matter, Ed? If we sit here we'll get flooded in like everyone else."

"Sir, there's a man crossing the street," the driver answered. "Looks like a soldier. I would have hit him if I didn't stop."

Gregory peered out his window to see the soldier. He wondered why anyone would be out in weather like this, let alone a soldier?

Lester took a second look; he could barely see the soaking blue colors of the HEdge uniform. Struggling against the winds, the soldier stomped through the puddles until finally making it across the street.

"Why would he be out in this mess? In uniform?" Lester asked.

"No idea," Gregory said. "He's having a rough time of it though, isn't he?"

"I'll say. Looks like he's got something pretty important under his coat. You see that, the way he's keeping his right arm pressed against his side. He's holding onto something for dear life."

"Yes, I see. Wonder what it could be?"

The driver started up the limousine. "Hold it, Ed," Gregory ordered. "Swing around and offer our little soldier a ride."

"Yes, sir."

The limousine spun around, blocking off cars in both directions. A few inconvenienced drivers blew their horns.

The limousine pulled up to the curb only a few feet from where the soldier was fighting against the torrential downpour.

Lowering his window, Ed covered his face as he shouted to the soldier, motioning him into the limousine. Not having to be told twice, the soldier gladly accepted the offer.

The back door flew open as Gregory shouted above the storm, "Hurry, get in before we all get soaked!" Before he finished giving his order, the soldier was inside and sitting comfortably across from him.

Gregory flipped the door-release back causing it to snap down and lock shut. He tapped the switch closing the privacy window between the driver and them.

The torrid rain and noisy winds were suddenly gone, replaced instead with the subdued peace and dryness of the opulent limousine. The soldier shook from the wet chill that had saturated his uniform. His right hand pressed against the envelope tucked beneath his parka.

Gregory hit the intercom. "Thanks, Ed. Start back to the HEdge Command building."

The soldier perked up, "What luck! A limousine ride to HEdge Forces Headquarters! Thank you!"

Gregory and Lester sat quietly observing their soldier.

Feeling awkward, the soldier decided it was time to be introduced to these kind people.

"Hi, I'm Private Frank Arpell. Nice to meet you."

He swished his arm out to shake their hands, throwing a fine spray of water in every direction.

Gregory and Lester sprang back to avoid the soldier's splash.

"Oh, sorry bout that. Have to dry off I guess. Thanks for the ride though, I really needed it. Especially with you guys going to the HEdge Forces building. That's where I was headed to."

Gregory spoke up. "I'm afraid you're a bit confused. We're not going to the HEdge Forces Headquarters, we're going to the Eastern Sector Command in mid-town."

"Oh, I can't go there. I have to deliver a package to Mr. Banchard in the HEdge Forces Headquarters right away. It's very important."

Gregory and Lester sat up at the mention of Roderick Banchard.

Lester asked, "What could be so important to deliver in such terrible weather, may I ask?"

"Just an envelope, sir. I don't know what's in it, but Colonel Reynolds told me it was very important that Mr. Banchard get it ASAP. That's my Colonel back at the Great Kill's base."

Gregory turned to Lester. "Colonel Reynolds? Isn't that the colonel who presided over the recent auditorium catastrophe?"

"Yes, I believe it is," Lester answered with more than a little curiosity.

They both took new interest in this young Private . . . and his important package.

"How did you get all the way over here from Great Kills?" Gregory asked. "Where's your vehicle?"

"On the West Side Highway. Traffic's all clogged up over there. Roads are flooded and cars stranded everywhere . . . including mine. I had to get out and walk."

Gregory hit his intercom again. "Ed, avoid West Side Highway, take the FDR Drive."

Suddenly the limousine shifted to the right lane and turned up the next street.

Arpell felt a little conspicuous as the two men continued staring at him.

"Excuse me, please. If you don't mind, I really need to get out so I can deliver this package."

Gregory spoke up first. "Private, do you know who we are?"

Arpell hesitated. He thought for a second. No, he had no idea. They looked oddly familiar but he didn't know why, and to be honest, didn't care. He just wanted out so he could make his delivery.

"No, sir. I don't."

Lester volunteered, "We are the two senior Advisors for your Sector Chief, Mr. Treppin. I'm Mr. Lester Ellis, and that's Mr. Gregory White."

That's it! He knew these guys looked familiar. He's seen their pictures at Headquarters. Wow! He's actually sitting in a limousine with HEdge Advisers! He suddenly felt a need to impress the two men.

"Nice to meet you, gentlemen. I'm actually on a TEMDU assignment from my C.O.; gotta deliver this P.K.G to H.Q. ASAP."

Gregory and Lester remained silent as the Private rambled on.

When he finished, Lester simply said, "I see."

Arpell thought to himself, *Yeah, there's that expression again. They think I'm really smart. Good. Maybe they'll stop the limousine so I can get out.*

He asked again, "Excuse me, I really need to go. This package has to be delivered ASAP. Can you stop the limousine, please?"

Ignoring the request, Gregory stared at the obvious bulge protruding from beneath the Private's cloak.

"Let me see that, please."

Arpell was at a loss for words. "Sir, I ... I don't know if I can. This stuff is supposed to be secret . . . I think."

"Private, I understand. But you needn't worry. I am far superior to your Colonel Reynolds. If there are any problems, you can relay the complainant to me. I will see to it that no harm comes to you. Now, let me see the package, please. Now." Gregory held his hand out expectantly.

Arpell knew something wasn't right here. He hesitated for a moment, unsure what to do. He realized that a HEdge Advisor was senior to a Colonel, but did that make this right? Arpell would give anything to be back outside in the storm. Even that didn't look so bad now.

With deep reservations, he handed the envelope over.

Gregory politely received it. Lester looked on with intense interest.

Rubbing his hands smoothly over the medium sized brown envelope,

Gregory felt something hard and flat inside.

"Mmm." He considered what to do with it.

"Open it," Lester coaxed.

Arpell tensed up even more. "Sir, I know you're an Advisor n'all, but I really don't think that's supposed to be opened by anyone other than Mr. Banchard. That's what my Colonel told me before I left."

Gregory ignored the Private's remarks. He forced his index finger beneath the edge of the top flap, and, much to the dread of Private Arpell, who by now realized he was in deep trouble, proceeded to rip the envelope open.

Lester watched with genuine curiosity as Gregory slipped his fingers inside and gently pulled out a small plastic box. After fondling it for a couple seconds, he lifted the mysterious box's lid. Inside he found a disk surrounded with soft rubber foam.

"A video disk?" Gregory asked curiously. "What could be so important about a video disk?"

Lester saw a small note fall out of the envelope. Leaning over, he retrieved it, and then read it aloud.

Mr. Banchard, you'll love this. It's from the NYS Auditorium fire. Have fun with it.

Sincerely,

Colonel D. Reynolds

"What do you suppose he means by that?" Lester asked.

"I don't know. Here, put it in the player."

Taking the disk, Lester fed it into a small slot on a monitor against the limousine's back wall, and then turned it on.

Shortly, a picture appeared on the screen.

Then, with no forewarning or narrative build-up, Gregory, Lester, and Private Arpell found themselves watching, in vivid colors and screaming audio, the gruesome beginnings of the New York State Auditorium massacre.

All three men sat spellbound as they viewed the macabre scene. First they saw whole sections of the audience getting up from their seats, moving orderly to the rear exits. Then, for no apparent reason, all the back and side doors of the auditorium crashed open as wild, frantic mobs charged inside, stampeding over the hundreds of people still bolted at the doors trying to get out.

Unbridled chaos erupted as the crowds inside became terrified, running to and from the blocked exits, converging in mad packs trying to find a way out.

Then, to the amazement of the three spellbound men, firepower suddenly blasted into the auditorium, followed by hundreds of unrestrained HEdge soldiers, gunning down innocent civilians in a wild frenzy of brutal insanity.

The three men listened in horror as the lone voice of Benjamin Gordon bellowed out over the sound system, trying to retain control over the melee, but without success. They saw him crumple to the stage as a bullet struck one of his legs. Then crawling to reach his microphone, they saw him knock over as a second, more lethal shot, blew off part of his scalp.

Sitting in awe, they watched thousands of men and woman scrambling to escape the gunfire while the soldiers continued their insane attack, shooting mercilessly, killing without cause or reason.

The scenes of real life horror playing out on the monitor was as graphic as any movie ever made, but worse; this was not fiction. These HEdge soldiers, in their ready blue uniforms, were really slaughtering countless people, ruthlessly gunning them down without remorse, without compassion.

The deafening chorus of desperate screams echoed through the auditorium, coming over the monitor all too clearly, sending chills up the spines of all three men.

The stark reality of Private Arpell's chosen profession was suddenly all too much for him. He hated the uniform he was wearing and despised the day he ever joined the Forces. Without warning, he leaned over and began vomiting.

Gregory and Lester quickly scurried aside, neither of them wanting their clothes soiled.

As the horrific scenes continued across the monitor, Gregory looked over to his fellow Advisor and wryly asked, "Would you suppose Mr. Treppin and the HEdge Council might take offense to such a sloppy method of handling this sensitive a material?"

Lester felt a spark of ingenuity from Gregory's question. He knew exactly where he was headed.

"Yes, I would think having a recording of this nature being delivered in such a compromising manner would stir quite an alarm with our Sector Chief, not to mention the HEdge Council."

The meaning of their conversation was hidden deep within their words. Someone listening in might not catch it, but there was no misunderstanding between the two Advisors. They knew precisely what the other was thinking, and to that point, realized this recording presented an ideal opportunity to rid themselves of the likes of Roderick Banchard, once and for all.

They knew Treppin would be appalled once he saw the recording. And even more shocked when he discovered Banchard engineered the entire massacre, then had the audacity to tape the grotesque killing and have it lugged around town like a sack of groceries. If a recording of this nature ever reached the public domain, HEdge would suffer incalculable damage to its public relations. The propaganda wars would take years to discredit the recording and claim the public's confidence back. Yes, this could easily ruin Banchard's career, if not his life.

The two Advisors glanced over to the still-regurgitating Private.

"Now what?" Lester calmly asked.

Gregory's face was without emotion. He knew what had to be done. There was no question of it.

Lester fully understood. Grinning, he asked, "Are we on the same page?"

"Yes, my friend, we most certainly are."

With that, Lester reached down and opened a small drawer beneath his seat.

Arpell heard the Advisors' brief dialogue, but missed its meaning entirely. He glanced over just as Lester was opening the drawer.

An alarm suddenly went off in his head. He needed to get out right away.

Lester pulled a small item from the drawer. The Private couldn't see what it was, but had a bad feeling about it.

"I really have to leave now. Could you please stop the limo?"

"Private," Lester began. "I want to thank you for the important services you have rendered this sector, and the world for that matter. If this recording had gotten into the wrong hands, I shudder to think what the consequences could have been."

Arpell forced an appreciative smile, the alarm still ringing in his head.

" . . . and you have definitely prevented a terrible mistake from occurring. Again, I want to thank you on behalf of your Sector Chief and the HEdge Council."

Lester paused.

"No problem," Arpell nervously answered. "Now, can I leave?"

Gregory turned to him and answered regrettably, "I'm sorry, private, but unfortunately, that will not be possible. I'm afraid you know much more than your short career has prepared you for."

Arpell was getting panicky. What did all this mean?

Lester ended the conversation, "Private, do you know what D.O.A. means?"

Arpell's eyes went wide. Of course he knew what D.O.A. meant. Dead On Arrival! He jumped for the door release and jabbed the switch to the up position. The door flew open.

Just as he leaped from the limousine, Lester pulled up a HEdge revolver and unloaded three rounds into his back. He never had a chance. Private Frank Arpell was dead before his body hit the pavement.

The limousine didn't even slow down.

Lester pushed the door release. The door swung closed and locked shut.

The two Advisors looked at each other.

After a brief silence, Gregory uttered, "You know, I could almost see how Banchard could get to like this sort of thing."

Lester nodded in quiet agreement.

Chapter

27

The nervous security guard punched the classified six-digit code into the electronic keypad beside the door. In a second, the massive solid-steel door began slowly grinding open over its worn hinges, creating a slow grating noise that echoed through the hallway.

Impatient, the jittery guard pounded his thick forearm against the heavy door causing it to swing open, banging noisily into the gritty wall behind it. The metal clanging sound reverberated through the cellblock, attracting the curiosity of inmates confined nearest the entrance.

A medium sized, ebony-colored woman, dressed in captain's regalia, marched through the large doorway and into the brightly lit maximum-security wing of the Redhook District Prison in Brooklyn, New York. Her steel-tipped boots clamored noisily across the concrete as she made her way past dozens of private cells, none of which held her interest in the least.

Two male soldiers, one dark as night, the other blazing blonde, followed in stride, stomping belligerently down the hallway; their taller, broader features hovering behind hers.

Several grungy faces of weary prisoners, male and female, peered out from the small holes cut into each cell door to see who had invaded their quiet misery. Their sorry eyes followed the three HEdge military

members, straining to watch as they marched past their limited peripheral vision.

The Captain began reading the cell numbers posted above each door
as she hollered back to the bulky security guard, "Where is she? I was
told she was in cell 95. Now where is that?"

The guard nearly tripped over his tongue as he blurted out an answer.
"Ma'am, are you sure you're looking for the right person? We have
several by that name; maybe you're looking for someone in a different
wing?" His right hand began twitching nervously.

Furious, she argued, "First you said she was in the east wing, then the
south wing! Now you're saying we may be looking for the wrong person
altogether! Do you know what in the world you're talking about,
Sergeant?"

Scanning the numbers above each cell, she didn't wait for an answer.
"Of course you don't."

The guard forced a second response as his left hand began jerking
along with the right. "Ma'am, I didn't say she was in the east wing, that's
what the main office was telling everyone; beats me why. But now that I
think about it, I'm pretty sure she's right here in this wing. You can trust
me, ma'am."

"Do you take me for a fool?" the Captain snarled. "I'll trust you when I
find her, until then you're on my hit list!"

Suddenly, the guard volunteered directions as he picked up a slight
twitch in his neck. "Actually, the more I think about it, I'm almost positive she's in the last cell all the way down this isle around the corner to
your left. You can't miss her."

"She'd better be," the Captain grunted while leading her small
company down the isle.

Just then, the guard stepped discreetly out the doorway back into the
main corridor leaving the Captain and her two partners on their own.
Dodging across the open floor, he grabbed the videophone mounted on
the wall. He rapped a sequence of digits across its keypad, and then
waited anxiously for someone to pick up on the other end.

A deep gruff voice cursed through the phone line. "We don't want to
be disturbed, you idiot!"

"Shut up!" the security guard snapped. "We've got visitors and they're coming your way. Hurry and clear out!"

The man's face turned red as his muscular jaw grinded, "Who are they?"

"I don't know; some captain from the Western Sector Forces. Mean one too. Said she's here to check on her prisoner."

"A captain?" Without another word, the man at the other end broke the connection.

The intemperate Captain with her two hulking soldiers marched indignantly down the hall, giving the appearance of three hapless individuals performing the same rotten task. Finally at the end of the hall, they made a left. As they turned, the Captain looked behind and noticed the guard was gone. Slowing her pace, she relaxed her uptight posture and exclaimed, "Praise God." Her two brawny soldiers also released a quiet but celebrated "Alleluia," as they noticed his absence.

The last isle extended a good seventy meters back and was strangely dimmer than its adjoining rows. As they marched down they heard a rustling noise echo from the opposite end. The sounds were getting clearer as they speeded their pace. Suddenly, a woman's desperate scream rang out, followed by a heavy slap and a curse.

Without hesitation the two soldiers charged past their Captain, running full stride. Almost at the end of the hall they saw the cell door fly open. Three men scurried out, tucking in their shirts. Slow to see the Captain's two soldiers barreling down on them, they reached for their guns, but were too late. The two larger soldiers were on top of them before they had a chance. They all went down in a wild scuffling pile.

As fast as it started, the fight was over with the three men lying unconscious on the floor, the two victors hurriedly wrapping them in nylon cuffs.

The Captain surveyed the roughhouse scene in front of her.

"You guys really need to play with someone your own size."

They continued binding the three sergeants.

Turning her attention toward the cell door, she peered in. But it was too dark; she couldn't see a thing. From somewhere inside she heard a faint cry, a woman's cry.

The Captain pulled a small quarter-inch disk from her belt and slapped it on the door as she stepped inside. As soon as the disk made contact, a bright light sparked from it, illuminating the room.

In the rear of the cell the Captain saw a woman laying on the dirty floor, her bruised body curled in the corner. She was weeping pathetically as she covered her face with both her scratched hands. Her ragged clothes were partially ripped off, exposing much of her backside with shreds of cloth hanging sporadically around her waist.

Hurrying over, the Captain removed her HEdge uniform coat and covered the pitiful woman with it. She knelt down and laid her hands gently over the woman's trembling back.

Jerking slightly at the touch, the woman cried out feebly, "Leave me alone, please . . . don't hurt me."

"It's okay, sweetheart, it's okay."

Combing her fingers through the woman's crumpled hair, the Captain said, "Let me see your pretty face, dear. I won't hurt you. I promise."

After a moment of tender coaxing, the grieving woman slowly and painfully turned around. As she did, the Captain got a good look into her battered and swollen face, and immediately recognized her.

"Melody. Melody." the Captain cried softly. "My Lord, Jesus. Melody, what have they done to you?"

Melody just lay there, unable to do much else. The repeated beatings she had endured over the course of the week left her numb and defenseless. She was beaten to within an inch of her life, and she looked it.

Finished tying up the three soldiers in the hall, the two sergeants entered the cell. Their hearts sank at the sight before them.

Through tear-drenched eyes, the Captain spoke. "Melody, we're here to help you." She waited to see if Melody could hear.

A soft straining voice broke through Melody's lips, little more than a whisper. "Thank you for coming." Her voice was weak and frail. "God bless you."

Gazing through teary eyes, the Captain said, "How do you feel, sweetheart," while slowly caressing her forehead.

Melody tried hard to get the words out. Her face was in agony, her lips puffy and bleeding, her cheeks were camouflaged in various shades of purple, and her left eye was swollen shut. What had once been an adorably beautiful lady, was now a beaten, trampled-down woman, barely capable of sustaining consciousness.

Finally, after a tortuous inner-struggle, Melody quipped, "I've been better."

The Captain smiled.

"Melody. It's so good to see you. These young men with me are Sergeants Kenny Drake and Jerome Franklin."

The two gentlemen nodded respectfully to her.

"I'm Captain Riggins. We came from the Western Sector to help get you out of here."

She paused for a moment to see if Melody was following her.

Looking up through her one good eye, Melody asked, "Captain Riggins? Karen Riggins?"

"Yes. Your husband said you would be expecting me."

Melody remembered back to what seemed a lifetime ago, before the soldiers broke into her home. She remembered John telling her to go to Karen Riggins' house. So this was Karen.

"Thank you for coming," Melody managed, then struggled to add, "You are in grave danger by being here."

Riggins smiled, "We'll be fine, dear."

Melody closed her eye and painfully licked her broken, swollen lips. "How is my son? How is Matthew?"

Riggins had no idea how Matthew was doing. No one had been able to get inside the Oakland JBMC yet to see or talk with him. But against everything she had been taught from childhood on, Riggins looked compassionately down to her limp patient, and lied.

"He's doing fine, just fine. They're taking real good care of your son." She didn't regret a word of it either. Under the circumstances, she only hoped someone would have done the same for her.

Melody's head rested into the Captain's arms. A strained smile brightened her beaten face. "Thank You, Lord, thank You."

Then, looking back up, she asked, "Karen, is John all right?"

Struggling, "Is he free?"

The labor in her voice hurt to listen to. They wanted only to carry her out of this ungodly place. But they couldn't. Not yet.

"He's doing fine, Melody. They haven't caught him. He's in the city right now working on plans to rescue you."

At that, her face beamed. Even under all the bumps and bruises, they could see the confidence and love Melody had for her husband.

Melody forced a smile. "Praise the Lord. With God's help, he'll find a way. I know he will."

Melody rested her head back into Riggins' arms.

As Karen looked upon her, she wondered if she should follow through with the original plan. They had brought a miniature video-comm for John to speak with his wife. But after seeing her condition, Riggins wasn't sure Melody could handle it.

After a silent prayer asking for God's direction, she decided to go ahead. Melody's well being was her primary concern, and she knew nothing would brighten her spirit like speaking to her husband.

Looking over to Sergeant Drake, she nodded. He understood. He unwrapped the instrument from under his sleeve.

"Melody, we've got a videocomm with us. Would you like to see your husband?"

Her face lit up. "John?" The excitement in her voice was evident, and the pain.

Riggins knew she would have to keep the communication short.

"Yes, dear. As soon as I key in your husband's code we'll have him on the screen. He's waiting to see you."

Melody's entire countenance sparked to life. The three of them could feel her excitement as she struggled to sit up. They leaned forward to help.

Once she was up, Riggins asked both men to check on their three comatose victims outside.

"All right, Melody. Here we go."

Focusing her one eye on the videocomm, her shallow breathing quickened. Riggins pressed a few incremental numbers across the small keypad then handed the videocomm over. Melody received it happily, holding it in front, waiting for it to come to life.

A flash of static shot across the screen, replaced with the exuberant face of her husband, John Rex. Melody gasped. A tear started down her cheek.

The two stared at one another for a long, hushed silence, waiting for the other to speak. Neither could find the words to express their feelings. Melody closed her one eye as tears filled it.

John finally said, "I love you." The only words that came close to expressing his deep feelings for this wonderful woman he's devoted his life to.

"I love you," Melody struggled to whisper back. "I miss you so much, John." She trembled. The excruciating pain combined with the joy of seeing her husband was almost too much for her.

"Honey, I'll get you out of there. I promise. Please be patient, Darling. I haven't stopped praying for you since the day they took you." John's voice broke as he began to openly sob. Melody's appearance had gotten to him. He hurt for the pain she must have endured to look as she did.

Riggins turned away. Her heart broke as she listened. Her eyes also began watering.

"Melody, the Lord will see us through. Believe that, Darling. We'll be together soon."

Melody tried to speak, but the growing pain in her jaws and lips made it unbearable. To even open her mouth had become sheer drudgery. Instead, she carefully handed the videocomm over to Karen. Holding back tears, Karen held it up while Melody began painstakingly using every fiber of energy left to communicate to John with sign language. Using sluggish hand gestures, she told John she loved him with all her heart, and to continue praying.

They both knew sign language fluently. It was a special ministry they used to teach the Gospel to the deaf. As she finished the last painful gesture, her weak body finally reached its limit. Her quivering arms dropped to her sides, her eyes rolled up; then she collapsed. Karen caught her just as she was about to hit the floor.

The videocomm fell upside down on Melody's lap. "Melody! Melody!"

came John's muffled voice. "Melody! Are you all right? Baby, talk to me!" Weeping, he cried out to his unconscious wife. "Melody . . . Melody!"

Karen picked up the videocomm as she cradled Melody in her arms.

"Mr. Rex, she's okay. The day's been too much for her . . ."

John cut her off mid-sentence, "Get a doctor to her right away, Karen, and some food. Call me as soon as you can. Thanks for being there, sister. May God keep you safe."

"Thank you, Mr. Rex."

She broke the connection.

"Jerome, Kenny, come here! Quick!"

The two men rushed in and helped Karen maneuver Melody to the thin mattress along the wall, then covered her.

"All right you guys, it's time to finish the job."

"Let's do it!" Sergeant Drake agreed.

Sergeant Franklin offered, "You two go ahead, I'll keep an eye on the three goons outside."

"Okay, Kenny, lets go," the Captain concurred.

Before leaving the cell, Riggins wiped the tears from her cheeks and prayed no one would notice the redness in her eyes. Then her and Sergeant Drake charged out of the cell and headed back down the long hallway. Once they got to the heavy door, Riggins kicked her steel tipped boots into it with all her might, creating a loud bang that vibrated through to the other side.

The door popped open, with the same nervous security guard standing outside. His whole body seemed to be caught in one convulsive twitch.

Hustling through the door, Riggins swung her right fist into the Sergeant's face, punching him square in his left eye. The shocked Sergeant fell back a couple steps, reaching up to his burning eye, uttering curses. Recovering quickly, he lurched forward to attack her. "Why you short . . ."

Just as he let loose his swing, Sergeant Drake reached out and caught his fist, pulled it down and responded with a left upper cut, jabbing him fully into his ribs knocking the wind out of him. The blurry-eyed Sergeant rocked back another step then fell to the floor, holding one jittery hand over his chest, the other over his eye.

Riggins pounced over to him, her steel tipped boots planted firmly between his thighs.

"Listen, you filthy punk! You try pulling that stuff on me again, I'll have you thrown away for life!"

Jabbing her index finger into his face, "Now I know why you didn't want me to find her, and why you wanted us to go looking in another wing. You trash! It's not enough she's locked back there, but you sickos gotta take advantage of her too!"

Still covering his sore eye, the Sergeant responded brashly, "I wasn't taking advantage of no one."

"Yeah right. And I suppose those clowns back there were just delivering pizza!"

"I don't know what you're talking about."

"I had a hunch you might not."

"I don't!" He sounded sincere. *It must've taken years of practice to lie that good*, Karen thought inwardly. "What a shame," she said as she stepped over the Sergeant's legs and walked to the videocomm on the wall.

"What's the name of your supervisor? I'll take it up with him."

The Sergeant didn't like the sound of that. Quickly managing to get back on his feet, he pleaded, "Ma'am, why do you want to talk with him. I can take care of business. Honest."

"You can?" she laughed. "Like you did back there?"

"Ma'am, that was a mistake. I didn't know it would turn out like that!"

"You mean you didn't know you were going to get caught! Now who is your supervisor?"

Looking flustered, he answered, "Master Sergeant Timmons."

"What's his number?"

Gazing dejectedly down to the floor, he mumbled, "71203."

Riggins pounded the numbers into the keypad. In a second the Master Sergeant's face was on the screen.

"Can I help you?" he asked.

Not restraining her temper in the least, the Captain angrily introduced herself, and then stated quite vehemently how difficult it was to keep certain prisoners alive under the crass management of this cellblock, explaining how the three sergeants were found assaulting her prisoner.

The Master Sergeant's eyes narrowed as he asked his Sergeant for an explanation.

The Sergeant's twitching was picking up tempo again as he repeated the Captain's story almost word for word, with the exception of remitting his name wherever possible and twisting the story just enough to clear him of any responsibility.

Unconvinced, the Master Sergeant asked, "How on earth did they get inside without you seeing them?" Not waiting for an answer, he added curiously, "Sergeant is something wrong with your eye?"

"Huh . . . no, nothing, sir, just a little run-in with the door. That's all."

"As you can see," Riggins interrupted, "your sergeant has run into more than a few problems, not the least of which is taking adequate care of my prisoner. Now, before her condition gets any worse, I demand that she receive immediate medical attention."

Picking up a threatening tone, she warned, "This prisoner is our best link to capturing John Rex, and I'm sure you are aware of Mr. Banchard's desires on that matter. If this prisoner dies, I think it's safe to say Mr. Banchard will be looking for someone to blame. And I guarantee, that someone will be you!"

He answered cautiously, "Captain, as you know, we are not in any position to set guards around every lowly creep that lands in our cells, and we certainly do not want to set a precedent with Rex's wife.

"However, if you would like to assign your people to watch over her, by all means, you have free reign to do so."

Trying hard not to show it, the Captain was ecstatic. This was perfect.

Remaining disgruntled, she snapped, "Fine. If your people can't handle the job, then we will. Now, I want a doctor and a decent meal brought in. Remember, if she dies, you'll have to answer to Roderick Banchard."

"Not a problem, Captain. We'll have a doctor there in a minute."

Speaking sternly, he ordered, "Sergeant, you and I will discuss this matter later, but for right now, I want you to get a meal to that woman; I'll send a doctor right up."

As the Sergeant attempted to acknowledge the orders, Timmons cut him off. "Captain. I apologize for our shoddy security. I assure you, it won't happen again. You have my word."

"Master Sergeant, I assure you, if it does happen again, I'll see to it that your name is the first one on Banchard's report. Do you understand me?"

Timmons didn't respond.

The Captain concluded, "It's been nice talking with you." She snapped off the videocomm.

Keeping her angry composure, she turned to the Sergeant and ordered, "You get those monsters out of that cell block before I remember how much I don't like you."

He was in no position to argue. "Yes ma'am." Reaching for the videocomm, he ordered a meal for the prisoner. Then just as quickly, he called for additional security to take the three captive soldiers away.

As he made the arrangements Riggins smiled discreetly over to Sergeant Drake. He nodded and smiled in return. Things were looking up, praise God.

Chapter

28

Rex was slumped at the heel of the deadened videophone. Grief stricken, he searched for the strength to keep his mind focused, to keep his howling emotions from running amuck. The capture of his family had already brought havoc to his heart, but now, to see the brutality and hatred of the enemy borne out on his wife was more than he was prepared for.

A hand pressed softly on his shoulder. He looked up and saw Andrew standing over him, puddles under his eyes. Lowering his face, John asked under his breath, "Did you see her?"

Andrew took a few seconds before answering. "Yes, John, I did." His words broke. "John, have faith my brother, have faith."

John straightened a little at the words; they caught his attention. "*Faith?*" he thought, "Lord, did you see her? Why Lord? Why?"

John felt a hand on his other shoulder. He looked up to see Keeyon standing beside him, eyes closed, tears streaming down his face, praying.

He lowered his head again.

The two men remained standing at his side, praying; powerful men of God, standing strong for their brother, praying for God's mercy and strength on their friend.

John was desperate to help his wife, yet realized the impossibility of doing so. The sight of Melody, beaten and exhausted, carried him to a new depth of human understanding, to the unsought knowledge of what lurks deep within the bowels of humanity, the part reserved for things not good, but evil, the ugly side, where hatred dwells freely and revenge grows bountifully.

He felt an overwhelming need to inflict pain to another human being, for no reason other than to spread the suffering, spread the hate, to make everyone hurt along with him. He wanted to catch the people that had brought this agony upon his wife, and punish them, punish them himself! He wanted to be the one to inflict their pain! To hurt them; hurt them the way they hurt Melody.

As John became immersed in this wicked strain of thought, absorbing every lashing wave of justified retribution, the prayers of his friends began to be answered. He suddenly sensed himself being lifted out of the dark, spiritually heaved from the murkiness and brought back to the light.

Without further thought, a message of divine authority burst into his mind, revealing a well-studied verse from the Book of Romans, chapter twelve, verse nineteen:

> *"Do not take revenge, my friends, but leave room for God's wrath,*
> *for it is written: "It is mine to avenge; I will repay," says the Lord."*

At that, tears filled John's eyes. He realized the trap he had so easily fallen into; as if he had dozed off to sleep, then startled awake in the middle of a terrible nightmare. He was ashamed for what he felt, humiliated and disgraced for the thoughts that had infiltrated his mind.

Keeyon dropped to his knees and wrapped his arms around John, holding him firm, offering support in this impossible time. John cried unabashedly into his friend's welcome shoulder, grieving for Melody, mourning her pain and suffering, and weeping for his captured son, releasing every bit of emotion Melody's tortured appearance had stirred in him.

With Keeyon and Andrew offering their prayers and support, John continued his lamenting, unrestrained and uninhibited, crying freely for as long as he needed.

After a period of draining his heart, he wiped his eyes dry and stood from the desk.

John realized another grief had to be dealt with. No less deserving than the first, but much more dire in its consequences. This grief wasn't for Melody or Matthew. Instead, it was for the people who had inflicted their scorn and hatred upon his family. He felt a deep sympathy for those reckless individuals. Because he knew if they didn't repent for their sins, the punishment brought by God would be far worse than anything he could ever inflict, far worse, indeed. He felt a charge to pray for them, for each of them, however many there were, and to ask God to have mercy on their souls.

After finishing, John turned to his two friends and, pulling on every bit of godly confidence he could, said, 'Melody's going to be all right."

"Amen, brother," Keeyon helped.

"She's a tough cookie, John," Andrew assured him. "The Lord has blessed her with the will of a lion and the perseverance of a shepherd. She'll be okay, my friend."

Encouraged, John and his two friends headed out of the small conference room of the downtown Brooklyn office building, into the lengthy bare-walled hallway.

Advertised as a warehouse for retail supplies, the building was much more than that. This warehouse was a waiting station for the delivery of millions of Bibles making their way across the continent from the Western U.S. Sector. Soon, with the Lord's grace, all three floors will be stacked to the ceiling with cases of Bibles.

Walking down the hallway of the undercover Christian warehouse, Andrew said, "Captain Riggins has done an outstanding job getting inside the Redhook District Prison. She's quite a woman, John."

John smiled. "Yeah, she's a real soul winner. The Lord has opened many avenues for her, and she's used them all wisely. She's been more than a blessing to us, Andrew; she's been a miracle. I can't say enough for her, other than to thank God she's on our side. She'd be a terror otherwise."

They all chuckled.

"Do you have any idea how long it'll be before she calls back?" Keeyon asked.

"Well, I suspect she's got a guard posted outside Melody's cell by now, and probably has half the staff frightened out of their wits. She'll be calling within the hour, I would guess."

Keeyon and Andrew both nodded in respect for their Christian sister.

With uplifted spirits, the three men continued down the hall until they reached one of several gargantuan storage rooms where hundreds of Christian workers were busily operating heavy machinery, lifting crates and moving supplies, all for the purpose of making way for the future deliveries of God's Word.

Chapter

29

Roderick balanced his favorite ballpoint pen on the tip of his right index finger, playfully killing time as he sat listening to the bimonthly political dispatch droning out across his monitor. The taped program was being aired from the Eastern U.S. Sector's Security Administration office in downtown Manhattan. It provided the bimonthly analysis of contemporary trends and attitudes as observed by leading HEdge Analysts.

It was mandatory viewing for high-ranking HEdge officials, with the purpose of keeping them in touch with the everyday lives and opinions of their constituents. The program was a conglomeration of social commentaries based on worldly reactions to current global events.

Beyond their own personal observations, the primary tool these analysts used to form their monthly thesis was the HEdge Quarterly Survey.

The process for the quarterly survey was fairly simple: At three-month intervals, multiple-page questionnaires were downloaded electronically into millions of entertainment monitors in households all across the globe. The members of these households would simply key in their responses to the questions asked, and then close the document out. The completed survey would then be electronically uploaded through central data collection terminals located in various spots around the world, then further disseminated into HEdge's Central Security Establishment where the data would be compiled and analyzed.

This data gathering system was conceived in the early years of HEdge's development and quickly put into place once HEdge achieved its world dominance. The Survey was touted as proof of HEdge's insistence to open the political process to everyone, regardless of social status, race, wealth, or gender. After all, what better tangible evidence could HEdge offer to support its humanistic worldly causes than a quarterly survey which incorporates the opinion of every world-citizen?

As such, the Quarterly HEdge Survey became an instant success. People across the globe anxiously looked forward to the beginning of each new quarter so they could freely input their ideas and opinions into this world think tank. Then anxiously wait to see if large enough numbers to influence HEdge policy on the world scene shared their opinions.

The Survey and its process had been a raving success. No one had a bad thing to say about it . . . well, almost no one.

The black shiny pen dropped from Roderick's finger to his desk then bounced to the floor. He cursed as he swiveled his leather-upholstered chair back allowing himself to bend over stiffly and retrieve it.

Roderick cursed at the monitor as he sat back up. The HEdge Analyst blandly continued his commentary, oblivious to the reaction it was evoking from the Chief of Eastern U.S. Sector HEdge Forces.

Staring across his office to a digital clock on the wall, he was stunned to see he had already wasted an hour of his precious day listening to this drivel.

It wasn't that Roderick opposed the original concept of the Survey. On the contrary, he was amazed at its brilliance. The political maneuvering made possible by the diversion it provided, made it one of the greatest propaganda ploys of all time. But he realized the true purpose of the survey had long since past, the facade was no longer necessary, HEdge was now in charge and giving the orders . . . not the people . . . not even their national governments. And the window of opportunity for an effective dialogue on whether to permit HEdge's power-grab to continue was missed entirely, thanks in large part to the HEdge Quarterly Survey.

Roderick threw his pen into the middle of the monitor's screen where it ricocheted off and hit the wall.

"Shut up, you babbling idiot! Tell me something I don't know! Tell me something worth the hour I've wasted listening to your pitiful voice!" The Analyst continued his recorded presentation, unaware of the mockery Roderick was making of it.

After another minute of heckling, Roderick slammed his index finger on the connect button of his videophone. His secretary appeared on the screen. "Yes, sir, can I help . . ."

Cutting him off, "Of course you can help me, you fool, why else would I be calling you?"

The secretary sat blank faced.

"Make a note to recommend terminating that stupid quarterly survey. I've wasted enough time on that project. I want it done away with."

"Yes, sir, I'll remind you in the morning, sir."

"No you don't!" Roderick scowled. "You forward my recommendation to Security Administration NOW, with a note to solicit opinions from other HEdge Forces Chiefs. Then contact me with the results."

"Yes, sir."

"Right away!"

"Yes, sir, Mr. Banchard."

"Oh, and Michael, what was your excuse for being late today?"

The secretary looked timidly back into his screen.

"Sir, yesterday's storm flooded most of the subway lines. I had to switch trains three times, and then take a bus from Sheridan Square. Most of the city is still closed, sir. I wasn't sure if this building was even going to be open."

"Why didn't you call?"

"Sir, I was rushing from train to train, I didn't have time to stop and call."

Roderick was having fun with this one. He knew the mass transit system in the city was worthless today, and quite frankly, he didn't expect the young lad to show up at all. But since he did, might as well have a time of it.

Glaring sternly into his videophone, Roderick stiffened his jawbone and squinted, assuming the scroogiest affect possible.

"Don't let it happen again, Michael. Thousands of people are waiting in line to take your job. Thousands! Do you understand me?"

The cowering young man answered with his eyes lowered, his self-esteem reduced another notch. "Yes, sir. I won't be late again, sir."

Grunting in disgust, Roderick slammed the disconnect button, breaking the communication. Then he howled with laughter, enjoying the spiteful moment all he could.

Shortly, he was once again listening to the bimonthly analysis, his happy grin slowly mutating into a frown. Leaning back into his chair, he glared at the running monologue playing out across his monitor. He detested every word oozing from the Analyst's mouth, every syllable of every word. He hated them all.

Suddenly, Roderick was shaken out of his contemptible state as he heard the HEdge Analyst mention an interesting name, a name he had grown to abhor over the last few years, a name synonymous with enemy: the name of John Rex. He sat forward, suddenly interested in what this sloven bureaucrat had to say.

" . . . and the world has suddenly become aware of the misadventures of a certain renegade by the name of John Rex. A man no one can seem to identify or understand. Mr. Rex has been accused of organizing an underground network of fugitive Christians that has reportedly been growing in popularity and spreading into various sectors of the globe.

"Regardless of the illegal nature of his actions, Mr. Rex, and many of his followers, the numbers we cannot yet confirm, are secretly conspiring to usurp HEdge's authority, and attempt to infuse their intolerant ideological dogma into mainstream politics, with the ultimate goal of removing control from of the hands of all people, into theirs."

The Analyst's tone became more emotional as he spoke. "An alarming number of Surveys have shown an increasing glut of support for this underground zealot. Though not directly advocating his primitive orthodoxy, there does seem to be a certain appeal, if you will, to the success he has had in spreading his faith in the mythological figure known as Jesus Christ, all the while evading capture from the increasingly embarrassed HEdge Forces.

"When asked if they believe John Rex and his Christian cohorts were responsible for the recent New York State Auditorium catastrophe, many responded in the negative, perhaps rejecting the notion that John Rex had anything to do with it at all. We find this response particularly disturbing. If people disavow John Rex's responsibility for the fire, then who do they believe is responsible?

"The enigma of John Rex has proven to be a puzzling matter to say the least. Be assured, we will continue to monitor and report on this subject in future surveys.

"The next matter we wish to discuss is the . . ."

Roderick slammed his fist onto the desk. "What do you mean they don't believe Rex is responsible? You imbecile, who cares what they think?"

The Analyst continued unfazed.

Jumping out of his seat, Roderick began stalking back and forth, angrily staring at the monitor as if somehow it could feel his wrath. "Blasted survey! It needs to end!"

He continued introspectively, "Rex, I'll get you. I swear I'll get you. I'll find you. I know you're out there somewhere. I can almost smell you." He inhaled a lung full of air, then quickly exhaled.

"Yes, and I'll make you change all those people's minds, all those gullible fools, before they actually start believing your myths. And I have everything I need to do it." He grinned, "I have your family."

His wicked imagination began contriving the perfect plan for John Rex. "Yes," he grimaced, "when I'm finished with you, no one will believe a thing you say about your Lord, your God, or anyone else.

"Then they'll be ready for HEdge's god, the true lord, the master of darkness, the angel that should be king!"

The videophone on his desk chimed. His secretary reappeared on the screen.

"Sir, we just received a classified report, labeled, 'The Rex Investigation' in the electronic mail. Would you like it forwarded to your terminal, sir?"

Roderick felt an exhilaration shoot through him. This is what he had been waiting for: the investigation! There had to be something in it that everyone had overlooked, something to help capture John Rex, he was sure of it.

"Yes, send it through right away. I want to see it now."

"Yes, sir. It's on its way."

Roderick glanced over to his monitor, and in a flash, the HEdge Analyst, who was just concluding his remarks about the latest HEdge Quarterly Survey, disappeared, replaced instead with a bold-faced document, covered with large block letters spelling out John Rex's name and address, with a digitally enhanced photograph of John Rex's house in the background.

Roderick pulled the monitor's control board out of his top drawer, laid it on his desk, then began to operate it as he paged through the electronic documents on the screen. One by one, he scanned over every page, every word, every letter, searching desperately for something that was missed. He knew something was there, something obvious, he was sure of it. As he continued impatiently scanning the report sweat formed across his brow, he was close, he knew it, and he could sense it.

Then it happened! Flipping to the next page of the investigation, something finally tumbled out, something no one else had noticed, or at least pieced together. He read the page twice over. His eyes lit up, an idea came to him. Yes, this was obvious. Very obvious.

He considered it for a minute, wondering what the possibilities were, guessing, and then wondering some more.

Finally, at the height of anticipation, Roderick excitedly pressed the videophones connect button. His secretary appeared on the screen.

"Get me the Western U.S. Sector HEdge Force Headquarters. Now!"

The secretary heard the expediency in Roderick's voice. He quickly pressed a few numbers, and then responded. "Yes, sir, they're on the line, sir."

"Good!" Roderick was convinced he was on to something, something good, a breakthrough. At last!

The secretary's face left the screen as a representative from the

Western Sector HEdge Forces appeared.

Roderick didn't pause to catch a breath.

"I want to talk to Colonel Doschier."

"Yes, sir. May I ask who's calling, please?"

"Mr. Banchard, Chief, Eastern U.S. Sector HEdge Forces."

The person at the other end knew that name; she recognized his face too, and immediately wanted to end the conversation. Roderick Banchard's ill-famed reputation preceded him.

"Yes, sir, Mr. Banchard. I'll forward you right through."

In a matter of seconds Colonel Doschier appeared on the screen.

"Yes, Mr. Banchard, what can I do for you?"

"We need to talk, Colonel. I need to know something right away. But this is top secret. We need to talk on your secure line."

"Not a problem. Let me switch you over."

In another second the line was switched. Then the high level classified conversation began, with Roderick asking the questions, and Colonel Doschier answering.

In a few minutes, they were finished. And much to Roderick's pleasure, his hunch had played out, he was right, perfectly, exquisitely right! And now he knew exactly what he would have to do to capture John Rex.

Lounging back into his over-stuffed chair, he gloated. His lips stretched into a full-faced grin, a satisfying, hate-filled expression. His hands rested comfortably behind his head as he relaxed back into a reclining position, his legs propped on the edge of his pompous desk.

"Life is good," he exclaimed. "So good!"

Chapter

30

The cell door opened. The fair-skinned, decidedly feminine sergeant entered the small softly lit room carrying a dinner tray and a container of cool water. Extending a gracious smile, she gently lowered the tray onto a round table beside Melody's bed, politely offering her the afternoon meal.

"Here you are, Mrs. Brown. I hope you like it. I made sure the vegetables and toast were still warm. You might want to be careful around the sides; the plate's pretty hot to the touch."

Melody smiled gratefully as she sat upright on her thin mattress, still nursing wounds from two weeks earlier but feeling much better. The swelling in her lips had gone down completely, the bruises around her jaw had lightened in color to the point of resembling a shaded tan rather than a darkened bruise, and the swelling around her left eye had almost completely healed.

Making the process almost complete, she could once again eat solid foods without much pain. Still hurt a little but at least she could chew, thank God.

"Thank you, so much. I'm sure it'll taste just fine," her voice still a little tender. "In fact, every meal has been so good, I'm actually starting to enjoy myself here."

The sergeant chuckled at Melody's exaggeration. "You can tell that to someone who doesn't know better." Then laughed as she turned to exit the cell. With a parting thought, added, "And with God's grace, we'll get you out of here soon."

"You've all been so kind." Melody intoned.

"Ma'am, the pleasure's been all ours."

Melody felt a confident enthusiasm exuding from this sister-in-the-Lord. Exactly the kind of inspiration she needed.

"Thanks again."

"You're welcome," the sergeant responded as she stepped out the door.

Sergeant First Class Johanne Terrill was one of the many Western U.S. Sector HEdge Force soldiers that came over with Captain Riggins. And like so many of the others, she was brought to the Lord by John Rex, evangelized and baptized into the Kingdom by Melody's husband.

Closing the cell door behind her, Terrill strolled purposely into the lobby outside the long row of cells, keeping an alert eye out for anything suspicious.

Melody said a quiet prayer over her meal. After a sincere "Amen," began to eat, enjoying every scrumptious bite.

After finishing, she rested back into her bed and began reading from a week-old HRS newspaper Sergeant Terrill had brought for her. The paper was a daily rag steeped in gossip and loaded with HEdge propaganda. Flipping quickly over the gossip and horoscope pages, she went straight to the political editorial section.

She was surprised to see a picture of herself on the first page. The photograph was taken as she was rushed past a barrage of reporters at Kennedy Airport. The large bold-print caption above the picture, read:

"REX'S WIFE, CAPTURED! BROUGHT TO NEW YORK!"

Critiquing the photograph, she decided the reporter couldn't have picked a worse time to snap the picture; her hair looked a wreck and her clothes weren't much better. She chuckled, amused at herself for taking notice of such a trivial matter at a time like this.

Reading the article, she saw that Major Harker was quoted excessively throughout, running down a laundry list of charges against her, everything from assaulting a HEdge officer, to storing illegal contraband and instigating treasonous acts against society. Frustrated, she laid the paper down.

Turning her thoughts to her husband, she delicately stood. She wondered how John was doing. She's spoken to him twice since her timely rescue by Captain Riggins. She missed John and Matthew so much.

As she was getting ready to sit back down, Sergeant Terrill rushed in, her breath short and her eyes wide with excitement. Speaking in ecstatic whispers, she quickly informed Melody of a phone conversation she had just finished with Captain Riggins. The Captain told her that Melody was being transferred to a maximum-security prison on Roosevelt Island in two days. She said Mr. Banchard wasn't satisfied with the level of security at Brooklyn's Red Hook District Prison, and felt the isolation and heightened security of the Roosevelt Island prison would better serve their needs.

Terrill could hardly control her excitement as she explained that Captain Riggins was put in charge of the transfer, adding that it would be a perfect opportunity to escape. John Rex was already working with the Captain on an escape plan.

Elated by the good news, Melody wrapped her arms around Johanne, giving her a hug. Johanne responded with equal fervor.

"And Matthew is being transferred too," Johanne continued her report. "They're going to bring him to New York. We're working on a plan to take him before he gets on the plane at San Francisco. Everything could happen like clockwork, on the same day and almost at the same time!" Johanne was beaming with enthusiasm. "Melody, you could be back with your family in just two days!"

Melody could hardly believe the good news. "Two days? Praise God!"

Johanne continued, "Captain Riggins said she and your husband are mapping a route to Roosevelt Island. They plan on overtaking Banchard's people somewhere along the route, then taking you underground with them. Captain said the Christians in the western sector already have soldiers ready to escape with your son. The whole plan should take only a few minutes."

Melody was astounded. Everything was happening so fast.

"Let me know as soon as you find anything else out, okay, Johanne? I can hardly wait."

"You bet." Joanne was ecstatic herself. She was as anxious as anyone to get this show on the road.

Chapter

31

John pressed the disconnect button on the videophone ending his conversation with Captain Riggins. It would be the last time they would speak to one another until meeting at the designated point where John and his men would intercept the HEdge security vehicles carrying Melody. And to anyone who didn't know better, the two would appear to be bitter enemies; which, of course was necessary if Captain Riggins was to continue as a covert presence in the Western U.S. Sector HEdge Forces.

The plan called for John and his men to block each corner of the intersection on Fifth Avenue and Tenth Street in Brooklyn, then over-power the HEdge soldiers and grab Melody along with a half dozen undercover Christian HEdge soldiers, and head into the tunnels. The entire operation should take no more than a few minutes.

Captain Riggins had given explicit instructions to each driver of the three vehicles as to which routes to travel to get to the prison. The drivers weren't Christians and weren't privy to Captain Riggins' plot, but that didn't matter; they were simply following orders. Right now Captain Riggins was the person giving the orders.

Andrew would accompany John, while Keeyon and his men would be setting up the first line of defense inside the tunnels to ward off any

HEdge pursuers who might get too close once the chase begins.

With the last stages of the plan finally in place, and all the players at their designated posts, the mission was ready to be set in motion.

Keeyon and Andrew sat patiently on opposite sides of the conference table, facing John. Both men were silent and still, eager expressions across their faces, ready to spring from their seats and get on with rescuing Melody.

Sitting there, John thought about his family, praying they would be spared any harm in the escape.

"It's that time, my friends. Melody will be on location in less than an hour; and Matthew should be on his way to the airport in thirty minutes. The time of reckoning is almost at hand."

Rising from his seat, Andrew asked, "What was the name of our man that's going to pull Matthew out?"

"Lieutenant Brad Lewis," John answered as he headed towards the door.

"How many soldiers are escorting Matthew to the airport?" Keeyon asked.

"Three."

"In that case, Matthew's escape should be pretty simple," Keeyon followed. "We've got twenty soldiers working with Brad to get him out. With only three escorts, it should be a cakewalk. I'd say the odds are in our favor."

John paused for a brief introspection, "Yeah, this is really working out perfect. With Matt and Melody both being transferred at nearly the same time, we should have them free before the east coast knows what the west coast is doing. We couldn't have asked for a better arrangement."

Keeyon asked one final and telling question as he started down the second floor stairwell behind John. "How did we know the number of soldiers escorting Matthew, anyhow?"

Giving out a hearty guffaw, John answered, "Karen got it right from Banchard's mouth. Couldn't ask for a better source than that. Right?"

Andrew remained silent as he followed the other two down the stairs. Something struck him as uneasy, an uncertain feeling, indefinable. Was it John's seeming overconfidence? Or was it something else? He could-n't put his finger on it. But one thing he was sure of was that all of a sudden something didn't seem right. In fact, something seemed terribly wrong. But he had no idea what, or why.

He followed John and Keeyon down the stairwell and out to their cruisers in the front of the building. Climbing inside along with John, he waved a thumbs-up to Keeyon who got into another cruiser that would take him to where his men were waiting underground.

John and Andrew were scheduled to meet with fifty men and eleven cruisers, and then drive in a convoy down Sixth Avenue to Broadway, where they would carry out their mission—and confront their destiny.

Captain Riggins, Melody and Banchard's people, were all heading to the same location, but with radically different objectives; different in the truest sense of the word.

Chapter

32

Matthew was running as fast as his young eleven-year-old legs would carry him, dodging around clusters of children, keeping a steady pursuit of his friend Henry who was sprinting through the ragged playground of the Oakland, California JBMC, in yet another splendid game of tag. The fun-filled chase took the two boys around a corroded metal swing set, over the rusted end of a dented slide, and through an old rubber-tire obstacle course, before finally showing signs of fatigue. After nearly falling over a rubber tire, Henry had to give in; his lungs were about to burst. He slowed then stopped altogether as he bent over to catch his breath, laughing in broken spurts as he did.

"Gotcha!" Matthew shouted as he flew past, tapping him on his shoulder before rolling down into a cloud of loose earth.

"You didn't catch me! I stopped!" Henry protested, his breath still short.

Matthew sat up while spitting dirt. "You didn't stand a chance. I was right on top of you! You would have been 'It' in another second anyways!"

"You weren't even close," Henry managed between breaths.

"Was so! I was right behind you!"

"Was not!"

As the two boys continued their light-hearted exchange, the other dozen kids started yelling in, whimsically venting their displeasure with the sudden delay in game.

After a few idle minutes Sandra finally offered a solution. "Listen guys, one of you either volunteer to be 'It,' or I'm going to volunteer. I'm tired of waiting, and I want to play." She finished her threat with an emphatic exhale as she tossed her stringy blond hair over her left shoulder and poised herself directly in front of them.

The two boys looked at each other in surprise as they considered Sandra's offer. The idea had merits. After a quick read of each other's calculated expressions, they burst into laughter, their young bodies heaving forward in a short period of glee. There was only one possible answer to Sandra's offer, only one, and the fact that they both came to it at the same time was hilarious.

Henry winked to Matthew, then turned to Sandra and shrugged his little rounded shoulders as he merrily said, "Okay, you're 'It'.

Sandra remained calm and motionless, acting as if she hadn't heard the response and was still waiting for an answer. But in truth, she was shocked. She didn't think the two boys would actually take her up on the offer.

"Hey, wait a minute. I didn't want to be 'It'! You know what I meant. I want one of you to be 'It'."

They ignored her.

Losing control of the argument, she blurted out, "C'mon you guys, which one's it going to be? Who's going to be 'It'?" But she was too late; they were already happily walking away, laughing and waving. "You said you'd be 'It'," Matthew playfully chided. "Now, you're 'It'." He slapped Henry on his shoulder as the two broke out in laughter again.

Sandra realized she had been had. In a moment, she found herself in the center of an increasingly large vacant circle as the other kids darted away in every direction. The consensus had decided; she was 'It'.

"Of all the nerve." She grunted under her breath, throwing her hand on her hip as she stood in disgust.

Matthew and Henry were still cheerfully walking away, chuckling and talking.

"Well," she defiantly exclaimed. "They won't be laughing for long." She took off after them, running with the conviction of a wild cheetah bearing down on its prey, determined to nab one, either one, it didn't matter which; and then give 'It' back to its rightful owner.

She was just about on them when the two happened to turn around at the same time and catch an ominous glimpse of her no-nonsense expression. They were shocked into action. Dodging apart in opposite directions, they hoped the diversion would slow her down. But Sandra was not to be deterred. Without a second's hesitation she dashed after Matthew.

He wasn't sure if he could out-run her with his late takeoff. It would be close. Hustling, Sandra caught up and slapped him on his back. Matthew whooped with joy as he felt her hand briskly hit him. He knew he had it coming; Henry would be next to get 'It'.

After her successful pickup, Sandra continued her fleet-footed jog across the field as she let out a victorious hoot, exaltedly waving her slender freckled arms through the air. Henry shouted happily behind her; better Matthew than him.

Sandra heard Henry's mirthful outburst and looked back toward him as she continued her celebrated trek forward. In the process, she became careless. As her eyes met Henry's, she saw his face contort into an alarmed grimace as he tried to shout something to her. But before she could understand, her young lanky frame ran full-force into a solid metal slide.

She let out a "woomf" as her body collided, knocking the wind out of her. Her head and chest received the majority of the blow.

She dropped hard to the ground in one painful, silent thump. Her head snapped back onto a barren splotch of dirt as her arms and legs flopped out across the ground. She was out cold.

Henry and Matthew were aghast, calling for help as they ran to her aid. The rest of the kids rushed to the scene.

"Sandra! Are you all right?" Matthew pleaded. "Can you hear me?"

After no response, he looked around to see if any guards were coming. None. He ran in the direction of the main JBMC building in search of a doctor or guard, anyone who could help.

As he raced through the mass of children converging on the scene, he spotted a woman running in his direction. Hollering over to her, he pointed back to where Sandra was laying on the ground. Meeting halfway, the woman slowed enough to ask Matthew for the name of the child. "Sandra," he blurted. "She ran into a slide, real hard. She's unconscious!"

The woman gasped. She told Matthew to run to the building and find a doctor; then she took off in Sandra's direction. Matthew continued his rapid pace towards the building. As he finally reached it, something occurred to him. That woman's face, it looked a lot like Sandra's, an awful lot as a matter of fact. Could it be? *Nah.* He dropped the thought, realizing it was too good to be true. He headed straight into the main JBMC building to hunt down a doctor.

The pretty, blond-haired woman leaned over Sandra's unconscious body, tears flowing from her rich-blue eyes. Touching Sandra's petite shoulders, she bent over and whispered something into her ear. Next, she placed a hand delicately under Sandra's limp head, and held it there as she observed the blue and purple bump swelling on her forehead. She gently caressed the bump with her soft fingers, then leaned over and kissed it.

More children were gathering around, crowding in, trying to get a closer look. The woman ordered them back so Sandra could have some breathing space. The children obeyed.

The woman's plea for the children to move seemed to have an affect on Sandra, as her eyes slowly began opening. At first only a tiny bit, then, gradually, feebly, her bright blue eyes opened wide as she looked straight up to the woman who had come to her aid.

At first Sandra had a dazed, confused look to her, but as her vision cleared, and she realized this wasn't a dream, she shouted with joy. "Mom! It's you!" Ignoring any pain she might still feel from the accident, she threw her arms around her mother.

"Sandra . . . I've missed you so much."

Tears flowed freely as mother and daughter became family once again. Sandra could hardly believe it. Her Mom! She was really with her Mom!

Sandra cried into her mother's ear, "I was afraid you'd never come."

"Honey, I've tried," she wept. "But they wouldn't let me. Mrs. Hawthorn dropped our case. She didn't want it anymore so another counselor got it. After a fresh review, the new one disagreed with Mrs. Hawthorne's analysis and saw no reason for you to be here."

She looked directly into Sandra's moist eyes. "They're letting you come home with me, sweetheart . . . for good." Tears ran down her cheeks onto Sandra's waiting forehead

"Please, Mom, don't let them take me again. Please don't ever let them take me."

Sandra's mother pressed her daughter gently into her bosom as she answered, "Don't worry, sweetheart, I won't." Then the two held each other for the first time in what seemed like ages.

As mother and daughter sat embraced on the hard patch of dirt inside the JBMC compound, the attention of most of the kids became temporarily distracted as a sudden commotion was heard coming from behind. Shortly, Matthew could be seen charging through the crowd, tugging three adults behind. Doctor Alred from the children's dispensary came first, followed by two playground guards.

As Matthew broke through, his distressed eyes were treated to the wonderful sight of Sandra and her mother in each other's arms. The angelic look on Sandra's tear-drenched face said it all. This woman had to be her mother.

The doctor shoved his way past the children as he briskly knelt down next to Sandra's mother. Reaching over, he gently rubbed his hand over Sandra's forehead, delicately sensing the size and pressure of her lump. He glanced over to Sandra's mother and asked if everything was all right.

"Couldn't be better," she answered with a glowing smile.

"May I examine her?" he asked.

"Oh, yes, of course." Loosening her hug, she asked Sandra if she could sit up.

"Sure. I feel fine." She reached up to rub the bump on her forehead.

The doctor asked, "Do you hurt anywhere else?"

"No. Other than this bump right here."

"Can you stand?"

Wincing slightly, Sandra stood. Her mother got up with her.

As she stood fully erect, the doctor stepped behind and ran his fingers methodically up her spinal column. "Does this hurt?"

"No." Sandra answered while wiggling her slender girlish waist. "Tickles a little though."

Children standing close by also giggled.

The doctor asked if she could walk. She obliged as she smiled shyly, embarrassed for the attention being lauded over her.

After a moment of contemplation, the doctor pronounced that she appeared to have survived the accident with no damage, aside from the swelling lump on her forehead.

With the diagnosis complete, Sandra's mother introduced herself to the doctor, and told him she was getting ready to take Sandra home with her.

"Just keep an icepack on her for about twenty minutes." He reassured her, "She should be fine. If there's any complications give us a call."

Thanking him, she led Sandra through the crowd, holding hands as they walked. Matthew and Henry followed close behind. They were saddened when they heard Sandra's mother say she was taking her home. On one hand, they couldn't ask for better news for their friend, but on the other, they would miss her a lot. Sandra was a real joy and had become a main part of their little clique. She was the closest thing most of them would ever have to a real sister.

Even though Matthew was a newcomer to this small group, he had developed a fond relationship with her; he would miss her dearly.

As they were almost at the main JBMC building, Matthew saw a large contingent of HEdge soldiers marching into the playground, heading in his direction. *Must be over a hundred soldiers.*

Strangely, as the soldiers got nearer, he began to suspect they were coming for him. Pushing in to Henry, the two boys hugged up closer to

Sandra's mother. He wanted to hide, and felt an instinctive draw to his friend's mother.

As the soldiers marched to within a couple dozen yards from the two boys, the one in charge spotted Matthew.

Sandra's mother was alarmed when she noticed the soldiers marching toward her, afraid they were coming for her daughter. Sandra saw a couple of them pointing behind her. Turning around, she was startled to see her two good friends; Matthew and Henry. Matthew looked frightened. Right then she knew whom the soldiers were coming for; they wanted Matthew. But why?

As she stopped to face her two friends, Matthew almost walked into her, his mind preoccupied. He and Henry exchanged glances, and then looked over to Sandra. She looked at them. They all realized their little clique was about to break up. Somehow, they sensed they would never see each other again. Sandra would be going home, Matthew would be following the soldiers somewhere - no idea where, and Henry . . . well, Henry would remain here as a regular client of the Oakland California Juvenile Behavior Modification Center.

Silently gazing back and forth to one another, they quietly poured their love and sadness into each other's eyes, passing on feelings their young, immature minds were not fully capable of expressing through verbal means.

The three children instinctively reached their hands out to one another, forming a small circle. Matthew quietly led them in a short prayer. Sandra and Henry followed with a sincere, "Amen."

"That's him. Get him!" the lead soldier ordered. Two soldiers grabbed Matthew while the others pushed the other two children aside. Then, the soldiers all formed up as young Matthew was once again taken into custody.

Being tugged away from his two friends, a tear dropped from his right eye, but he retained his composure. This time he was determined not to let his sorrow show.

Matthew was developing toughness at his young tender age. An emotional barrier was growing inside that would cheat him of much of his youth, but at the same time, provide him the means to cope with the difficulties that were only starting to come his way.

And in his young uncomplicated mind, he was fairly certain things were not going to get better any time soon. He was growing up fast.

Glancing back he saw Henry and Sandra were doing their very best to control their emotions too.

He remembered the first time he saw them. They were running circles around the metal slide he was sitting on, ridiculing and calling him names. He thought they were such bad kids back then. But he's learned; he's grown to appreciate the hard knocks and bruises they've had to experience.

And he realized now more than ever, the only saving grace these kids had was the knowledge they now shared in Jesus Christ. Without which, they would be the same now, as the day he first met them; lost, confused, and rebellious, in need of a loving shepherd to lead them home. Now they have that shepherd.

Henry and Sandra watched as Matthew was pulled into the middle of the platoon of soldiers, hidden from view of everyone else.

Before he was completely out of sight, Matthew looked back and saw Sandra break down in tears as she hid her face in her mother's arms.

A second tear fell, but that was it, he wouldn't let any more escape. He would miss Sandra and Henry. He would miss them dearly. But he couldn't let it show. That would allow the soldiers to see his weakness, and who knows what that could bring. He wasn't going to take the chance.

And so, young Matthew marched through the JBMC with his head up high, his boyish shoulders pressed back, as his stocky little frame struggled to keep pace with the longer strides of the soldiers. But he could do it. If nothing else, the experience in the JBMC made him realize he could handle a lot more than he ever thought possible. He was tougher and stronger than he was before. He would keep pace with these soldiers if he had to run to do it. But he would do it.

A third tear managed to slip out as he gave his thoughts over once again to Henry and Sandra. He would miss his two good friends very much.

Once outside the main JBMC building, Matthew saw hundreds of soldiers covering the grounds. He saw HEdge military cruisers lining the streets, all of them waiting for him. He wondered why there were so many.

Off to the side, a startled HEdge officer stepped back into a doorway-cubbyhole and viewed the enormous gathering of HEdge Forces outside the JBMC, all for the purpose of escorting this lone, eleven year old prisoner to the Eastern U.S. Sector.

Confounded by the surprising turn of events, a horrible thought entered the officer's mind. A thought he prayed would be wrong, but from what he was now witnessing, feared it probably wasn't.

Pulling his miniature videophone off his belt, he slammed a few incremental digits across its keypad. Another soldier's face appeared on the screen. Without offering the soldier any time for niceties, he hurried with his message; he had to get it out quickly, time was of the essence.

"This is Lieutenant Brad Lewis. Abort the mission to rescue Matthew Brown. I repeat, abort the mission. There are over two hundred HEdge troops formed outside the JBMC, with cruisers armed to the hilt. Our intelligence has been corrupted somehow. Whoever the source was that said three soldiers were escorting Matthew, was only baiting us.

"I believe we've been set up. You need to warn John Rex right away. I suspect he's walking into a trap. Relay this message immediately!"

The voice on the other end acknowledged the Lieutenant's report, and immediately punched his relay switch to transfer the message to the east coast and try to get it to John Rex before it was too late.

Chapter

33

John and Andrew sat in the front seat of the four-passenger metallic-blue cruiser alongside their driver, Rob Hendricks, who was navigating them through the congested mid-afternoon traffic. Their concentration was keen as they led the eleven-vehicle motorcade down Sixth Avenue heading into old Greenwich Village.

To avoid calling attention to themselves, the vehicles kept a non-conspicuous distance apart from one another; enough room for a car or two to slip in between.

The four-lane road narrowed as the convoy edged its way through the shadows of the downtown streets, herding obediently along with the rest of the southbound traffic. After sifting through dozens of busy roads and intersections they were finally beyond of the Village and heading south on Broadway.

Each person traveling in the eleven-vehicle motorcade had their prayers raised to a higher, more intense level, as they steamed ever closer to their destination. There was no mistaking the dangers inherent in their mission, but they had no qualms with it. None. Any chance to rescue Melody from the clutches of the enemy was not to be denied.

John sat quietly by the passenger-side door, barely uttering a word. His eyes monitored the traffic and congestion around them, alerting him to anything suspicious, while his prayers continued, asking God's blessings over his family and every person involved in their rescue.

Andrew offered some small talk to help loosen John up. But that wasn't the only reason; it was also to help ease his mind. Ever since leaving their office in mid-town, a strange ominous feeling seemed to cling to him. A feeling he couldn't shake.

Afraid it was some kind of grim premonition over Melody's rescue attempt, he toyed with the idea of warning John to cancel the mission, but decided against it. He wasn't confident enough about the odd feeling to bring everything to a stop. If there was a chance to rescue Melody and Matthew, he certainly was not going to step in the way.

But he kept returning to the same question: What was this odd feeling? What was wrong?

He felt perplexed. Everything about the mission seemed so perfect. To most anyone else the whole affair may actually seem a preordained gift from God; with Melody and Matthew being rescued at almost the same time, on the same day. It was almost too good to be true. And for some strange reason, Andrew knew that it was. *But why?*

After much soul-searching he decided to keep the strange intuition to himself, and, to stay close by his friend's side. That much Andrew did know for certain, he was to stay close by John's side. Somehow, he knew that's where the Lord wanted him, and so, that's exactly where he intended to stay.

The eleven-vehicle motorcade passed sluggishly through the bulk of the finance district in the Wall Street area. Its destination was the Manhattan side of the Brooklyn Battery Tunnel, about one kilometer up.

The tunnel was one of the many transportation links between Manhattan and its sister borough of Brooklyn. But more to the point, it was to be the route for transporting Melody through the New York harbor. A route the Christian motorcade intended to intercept before the afternoon was over.

Nearing their destination, Rob Hendricks pulled the cruiser over to the curb, and then waited in neutral while the others caught up. In no time everyone was lined up behind him.

Rob pressed the videocomm button, "Okay, folks, we're nearly ready to roll."

Andrew glanced at his watch. "I've got 1800."

John checked his watch. "They'll be here in about ten minutes."

"Yep, it's almost time," Andrew said.

John folded his hands together, clenching them tighter as Rob revved the engine.

Pulling the miniature videocomm from inside his shirt pocket, Andrew pressed a few digits, and then spoke to the convoy.

"Okay, guys, we've got less than ten minutes to form up. Remember; keep your prayers and eyes on alert. If we stay with the plan, we should be able to pull this off without a snag. So let's do it. God be with us all."

He pressed another button on the videocomm. "Keeyon, we're moving into position, buddy. Everything okay down there?"

"We're doing fine, big guy. We've got your tunnel ready and waiting. No one's getting through this tube except God's people. What's it like up there?"

"Couldn't be better," Andrew acknowledged, unintentionally voicing the comment with a tone of uncertainty. "Keep us in your prayers, brother."

"Always."

"Okay, Rob, let's do it," Andrew ordered.

"You got it, Andy. Hold on to your Bibles, it's deliverance time!" He snapped the cruiser into drive and pulled sharply away from the curb. The other ten vehicles followed suit. Turning past the corner, the convoy picked up speed and headed straight to the Brooklyn Battery Tunnel. As they arrived at the lip of the tunnel's exit an intermittent string of traffic was rolling out.

Finding a gap in the outbound traffic, Rob led the way as each cruiser in the motorcade positioned themselves on opposite sides of the tunnel's exit. Shortly, they were all parked and idling, eager for Melody's cruiser to come through.

The tension inside each vehicle was high; the excitement was fever pitch. Each man in the motorcade gripped their steering columns or clasped their door handles, ready to jump into action at any moment. Now it was just a waiting game. Andrew would give the signal when it was time to move. The sooner he did, the better.

Barely tapping the accelerator, Roul Johnson painstakingly prodded his HEdge cruiser slowly through the glutted Brooklyn Battery Tunnel, inching it steadily forward, taking advantage of every open space.

Oddly, the two HEdge cruisers ahead and the one beside began picking up speed, increasing the distance between his cruiser and theirs.

Not to be out-done, Roul pressed his accelerator to keep pace. He couldn't be left behind. After all, he had the prisoner in his back seat. As he approached the halfway mark in the tunnel, Roul glanced passively into his rear-view mirror; more out of habit than necessity. What he saw caught his immediate attention. He asked Sergeant Townsend, "Hey, what's happening to the traffic behind us?"

Townsend glanced through the back window, past Sergeant Terrill who was sitting stiff in the back seat beside her sole prisoner, Melody.

Both lanes of traffic behind them was slowing down and falling back.

"Beats me," the Sergeant grunted. "Guess they're tired of reading our plates."

Roul spoke excitedly as he scanned his rear-view mirror. "Those two cars back there, see them? They're slowing on purpose, blocking the rest of the cars from passing. See that?"

The Sergeant took another look. "Yeah, go figure. Probably Jersey drivers."

The distance between them grew until their cruisers rounded the final bend, losing sight of the traffic behind them.

"This is weird," Roul voiced suspiciously. "Why in the world would they be slowing down? Doesn't make sense, does it?"

Sergeant Townsend grunted, "No."

"Then why are they?"

"Relax Buddy. Who cares what they're doing? We got a job to do, that's all that matters."

"Yeah, I guess you're right. It just seems kind of strange, that's all."

"Don't sweat it. They can pitch a tent for all I care, just so they're not slowing us any. Know what I mean?"

Roul grinned, "Yeah."

Finished with their discussion, the two men rode in silence.

Sitting quietly in the back seat, Sergeant Terrill discreetly tapped Melody on her left knee. Her time was getting close. Melody's freedom was only seconds away. Terrill was feeling edgy, even nervous. She knew very well why the traffic behind had slowed down. It meant they were nearing the end of the tunnel. Christians drove both of the vehicles behind them. No one wanted to risk innocent civilians getting hurt, just in case things got out of control, so the two drivers purposely held the traffic back.

The tunnel's opening was just ahead.

Melody couldn't help herself. She reached over and held Sergeant Terrill's hand. The Sergeant returned her grip happily, yet discreetly, as the two women looked at each, then ahead to the tunnel's opening, both anxious for what the next few minutes would hold.

Both feeling the cry, "Here we go!"

Chapter

34

Andrew and Rob recognized the lead cruiser in Captain Riggins' motorcade as it began nosing out of the tunnel. With the videocom to his lips, Andrew shouted to his men, "Now!"

With that, Rob squealed his cruiser backward into the middle of the ramp, offering itself as a sacrificial cushion for the first target.

A loud crunching sound penetrated the air as the lead HEdge cruiser rammed uncompromisingly into Rob's rear bumper, shoving it clear to the trunk. The three men inside felt their bodies jerk back, but they were well protected as thick nylon straps held them firmly in place and exploded air bags offered any cushion they needed. The passengers in the HEdge cruiser were also spared any harm as large air bags ignited inside of each.

The rest of the Christian convoy sprang into action as vans hurled into the intersection, bouncing over curbs and blocking any avenues of escape.

Realizing they were being ambushed, the driver of the lead cruiser reached for his gun. But before he could get it, the soldier sitting beside him got it first and aimed it directly at him. Their eyes met. Right away the driver knew his struggle was futile. The battle was over before it began.

The other cruisers shared the same experience. Undercover Christian soldiers disarmed them before they realized what had happened.

In Melody's cruiser, Sergeant Townsend snatched Roul Johnson's pistol just as Roul was about to unsheathe it from his shoulder harness. The struggle for the weapon was short. In seconds not only did Sergeant Townsend have the gun, but he also had Roul handcuffed to the steering column, his eyes wide and mouth hanging open in shock.

"Catch flies like that," Townsend jested as he ripped the ignition keys from the dashboard. "Nothing personal, Roul, really. We just serve two different masters."

Every vehicle traveling in the Christian convoy emptied as men leaped out and sprinted to the four HEdge cruisers to help their Christian brethren.

Everything was happening fast, confusion and gridlock crippled the intersection, horns were blaring, and angry motorists shouted curses to the men scrambling through the street. Johanne and Melody jumped out and ran. Sergeant Townsend turned to his still-surprised driver and said, "Jesus Christ is the way, buddy. Think about it." He winked, then leaped out the cruiser and followed behind Melody.

Rob, John, and Andrew had finally unstrapped themselves and squeezed out from their demolished cruiser. Once freed, they ran towards the tunnel where the last two HEdge cruisers were sitting under the overhang.

Melody saw her husband right away. She took off after him, limping desperately across the chaotic intersection, her wavy hair tossing behind her.

"John!" she called, working every muscle in her still-tender body as she tried to run. Her erratic gait was a visual reminder of the beatings she had endured over the last few weeks.

Bittersweet tears welled up as John saw his wife struggling through the road, hobbling toward him. He couldn't hear above all the racket, but that didn't matter. He returned her call, shouting her name while dodging around trapped cruisers.

At last, hardly a minute after the whole episode began; the two long-separated lovers were once again united. John gently lifted his beautiful wife off her feet, cheering, "I love you!"

Tears rolled down Melody's cheeks. "Johnny," was all she could say before kissing him and squeezing her arms around him.

Suddenly a loud, rambunctious voice could be heard above the racket, "Stop this, what are you doing!"

It was a raging woman's voice. "You'll regret this! Every one of you!"

John turned to see Captain Riggins putting on her performance, standing beside her cruiser, handcuffed to the doors.

John wanted so much to walk over and thank her for everything she's done. But he couldn't. For her safety, he could only ignore her and run in the opposite direction, with Melody in his arms.

Behind John, Andrew took off also. Intending to stay close by his friend's side. A lump formed in Andrew's throat as he watched John holding his wife in his arms. The reunion put a joy in his heart.

Yanked from his thoughts, his videocomm suddenly rang. He unlatched his pocket, pulled out the miniature videocomm, and pressed the 'On' button.

An alarmed man's face flashed across the tiny screen. Andrew knew right away they were in trouble. The man hurried with his message. "Mr. Hoyte! We just received a call from Lieutenant Brad Lewis from the western sector. He thinks we've been set-up! They couldn't rescue Matthew; there were over two hundred troops at the JBMC guarding him. The Lieutenant thinks it was a trap to get you, Keeyon, and John out in the open!"

The man finished with an urgent plea. "Hurry and get out of there! You're in much danger!"

Of course! Now Andrew knew! He understood! Everything was clear to him! This is why he's been feeling so apprehensive!

He shouted above the screams and noise, "Everyone! To the tunnels! Now!"

At that, all but a handful of HEdge soldiers started running across the road to a nearby subway station to escape to the tunnels below.

Only Captain Riggins and four HEdge soldiers, along with four of Banchard's people remained by the pile of wrecked cruisers and vans, handcuffed and spitting angry. Most of them cursing the day they ever volunteered for this duty.

Trapped motorists were screaming at the Christian marauders, waving fists at them. Andrew took it in stride as he looked around to make sure all his people were accounted for. John was beside him, carrying Melody in his arms, struggling to keep pace. Once Andrew had everyone in his sights, he turned to John and Melody to see if they needed help. John just kept running, fighting for every spare bit of oxygen he could. He had waited a long time for this and was not about to slow down until Melody was safely out of harm's way.

Oh Melody, Andrew thought fleetingly while dodging across the road. After all these years, he was finally going to meet her. He flushed with compassion as he saw her contented face settle over John's chest, her arms holding him, as if she would never let go. Andrew's heart went out to her. He longed for the opportunity to finally sit and spend hours talking with her, rehashing childhood experiences of him and John. He already loved this woman as the sister he never had.

Andrew smiled as he ran through the street. Yes, soon he would experience for the first time, the family he's always felt such a part of.

Then, without warning, sirens began screaming from everywhere as rows upon rows of HEdge cruisers charged out from several obscure side-streets, tearing over the bumpy roads and cutting off the escape paths of the Christians. Up above, helicopters appeared from nowhere, hovering over the buildings, their propellers pounding waves of air pockets over them.

Caught in the fear and confusion, the Christians scattered in every direction, running for their lives, shocked and panicked. They scrambled to out dodge the roadblocks thrust in front of them. Many tried their luck at running straight through the center of the now-waiting HEdge cruisers, hoping beyond hopes to run past them and into the tunnels without getting captured.

Andrew was aghast. He saw John running with Melody, her head now up and crying for him to put her down so he could run for his life. John refused. He continued vainly sprinting as best he could, holding onto his love, determined to do everything in his power to protect her.

Andrew realized against all fears that John was running straight into the blockade, along with others trying to make a break for it. There was no way he could make it. Some of the younger men might have a chance, but he was carrying his wife and was already winded.

"John, back this way!" Andrew shouted. "To the West Side Highway!"

But John couldn't hear above the sirens and helicopters. Andrew didn't know what to do. Truthfully, neither option held much promise.

Realizing John was not going to turn around, Andrew bolted after him.

The HEdge cruisers were now firmly in place. Husky, grim soldiers jumped out, ready to stop anyone trying to pass. A loudspeaker roared above the clamor of the street noise, booming out from the roof of a bright blue HEdge van.

"Stop! You've been caught! Give yourselves up, or we'll shoot!"

None of the Christians heeded the advice, realizing their chances for survival were just as slim if they surrendered as if they continued in their efforts to escape.

The thundering voice sounded again. This time the edict was shorter and more to the point.

"Stop, or we'll shoot!"

Some managed to race through the HEdge blockade, dodging faster than the HEdge soldiers expected, but many were still on the other side, running against time and hope, with only a prayer to make it to safety.

Melody cried to her husband, to put her down. There was no way she could make it, but John had a chance.

Try as she might, her tears were in vain. She watched his strained face as he held her tightly in his arms, running as fast as he could. He agonized for air as his chest heaved under her weight, his mouth straining open, fighting for every breath of oxygen.

Giving up, she laid her face against his sweaty neck and held on. Whatever was to come was to come. She cried for her love.

Andrew saw that John wasn't even considering slowing down. Then, without further warning, the travesty exploded as rapid gunfire roared out from the standing line of HEdge cruisers. The barrage of gunfire tore into the closest of the Christians, throwing them into the air as the impact of the lethal bullets lambasted them, then dropping to the ground.

Andrew looked on in horror as his fellow Christians were sprayed with HEdge ammunition. All around, his friends were falling, dying in heartless fractions of seconds. He looked ahead to John and Melody, yelling to them to get down. But John was beyond panic, he was beyond reason, all he knew was that he finally had his wife, and he had to run, he had to run to keep her safe, he had to run, run, run!

Looking behind, Andrew noticed a HEdge soldier in the middle of the pack. The soldier had his aims cocked and ready, intent on only one target, and that target, Andrew knew, was John.

Out of instinct and love, Andrew leaped forward with all the strength remaining in his tired legs as he tried to get to his friend. But before he knew it, Andrew felt the pressure of several lead cased bullets puncturing into his backside, ripping through his lungs and lodging deep inside his rib cage. At the same instant, he saw John's left arm being riddled with gunfire. The added momentum from the bullets carried Andrew's body forward, slapping into his old friend's back, slicing him down into a rolling heap on the ground.

John was thrown forward. He held onto Melody as best as he could, trying to protect her from the fall, but ultimately losing his grip. As John tumbled to the ground, Melody fell out of his arms and rolled several feet ahead. Her head pounded onto the concrete as she tumbled forward, knocking her unconscious. John stopped a short ways behind, only partially conscious himself.

Lying in the middle of the road, he could hardly move. He was out of strength, his legs exhausted; his breath had been depleted to the point of barely maintaining consciousness. He sobbed aloud as he saw his wife spread out on the pavement beyond his reach, not moving.

A few feet over, laying flat on the ground, bleeding heavy, with barely a breath left in him, Andrew called out to John. He had to know that his old friend had survived. "John!" Andrew called again.

John heard him. Turning, he saw his friend lying in a puddle of blood. He struggled to get to his knees and crawl over.

Andrew coughed as blood streamed out of the corner of his mouth, his eyes closed in pain, then opened again, alert and determined.

John was finally at his side. He knelt next to him, taking Andrew's hand weakly into his own. Tears fell as he looked into his friend's dying face. "It's okay, Andy. We'll make it, buddy. We'll make it."

Gazing through moist eyes, Andrew strained to say what needed to be said. "John . . . do you remember when we were kids?" He struggled, "When you . . . asked Jesus into your life?"

John fought to hold back tears as he nodded, unable to speak.

Andrew released a labored gasp as a drop of blood fell from his mouth. "The Holy Spirit has used you mightily since then." A gurgling sound emitted from his throat. "There are many more . . . John, who need to hear the Gospel." Andrew's eyes closed in pain. "Stay with Him, John. Don't lose . . . faith. Stay in the race . . . John . . . stay in the race."

John could only bite his lips as tears gathered. He searched for the right words, but none came.

"Tell Melody and Matthew . . . I'm sorry I didn't get to meet them. But tell them, I loved them . . . as if they were . . . my . . . own."

As the last painful word escaped his lips, Andrew laid his head back into John's arms, and finally, comfortably, died.

And with his death, John felt his life siphoned out, his existence coming to a meaningless, empty, end. He was devastated.

"Andrew! No!" he bawled, "You can't! You can't go!"

Andrew didn't respond. His lifeless body hung limp in John's trembling arms.

Realizing his old friend was really gone; John gently laid his body down. At the end of his rope, he looked up to the heavens and hollered, crying at the top of his strained lungs. "Lord! Why Lord? Why? How much more do you want? How much more?"

Then he fell next to his good friend, and cried. He cried hard for his wife and his son, he cried for Andrew, he cried for all the men and women who had died in vain trying to rescue his family, and as he did, he pounded his fist violently against the pavement.

Blood from both he and Andrew splattered as he continued slamming his fist, harder and harder, taking his anger and frustration out on the uncaring cement, pounding until his hand lost all feeling. By continuing, John was increasing the blood-flow out of his body through the wounds inflicted by the HEdge bullets. First his hand was numb, then his arm, until finally, driven beyond his physical and emotional endurance, John's body shut down as he collapsed in the road, laying unconscious beside his best friend, and a dozen feet from his unconscious loving wife.

The last thing John heard before losing complete consciousness was a pair of heavy footsteps moving toward him across the hard pavement. Accompanying the footsteps was a bizarre giggle. He didn't have the energy to look up to see who it was. It didn't matter at this point. He had lost all hope. His best friend was gone, and now, he would probably lose his wife and son too.

Nothing mattered anymore. Nothing.

John closed his eyes and fell desperately to sleep. Whether he would ever again awaken, he didn't know, or much less, care.

Chapter

35

The alarmed voice burst from the hand held videocomm gripped in Keeyon's dark fisted palm. There was no mistaking the urgency in the man's words as he spoke, pausing only to catch his breath. A dozen men huddled anxiously around, listening intently to every word pouring from the pocket-sized device, becoming more distressed as the message wore on.

"Mr. Webster, I just spoke with Mr. Hoyte; the rescue mission for Matthew has been aborted, HEdge Forces are swarming the JBMC in Oakland, our people can't get close to him."

As the man delivered his rapid-fire message, disappointed sighs could be heard rumbling through the small cadre of men, dissipating into a hushed silence as the message's ominous underpinnings began taking hold.

"Lieutenant Brad Lewis from the Western Sector thinks we've all be set-up. He thinks this is a trap! Mr. Hoyte is taking his people off-scene right now.

"We believe you may all be in grave danger!"

As the message played out, Keeyon quickly glimpsed across the faces of every person standing inside the tight circle, reading their expressions, swiftly deciphering what he could from their visible thoughts.

Finally, after a few closing words, the tiny screen went blank. Keeyon stood holding the videocomm in the middle of the dim tunnel, exchanging concerned glances with his men, all of them sharing his anxiety.

Just then, before a single word could be uttered, Keeyon felt a hammering jolt against his spirit, a harsh vision sweeping through him like a burning singe against his flesh. And at that very moment, a single thought crashed into his mind, "Andrew!" he cried out, "Lord, God Almighty! What's happened?"

Without thought, he began running to the tunnel's exit, shouting for his men to hurry. They took off after him, each feeling the same dreadful premonition sinking over their spirits.

Finally at the tunnel's opening, Keeyon jumped up off the tracks onto a narrow ladder, and raced up the stairwell to the world outside.

Standing on the sidewalk by the subway's entrance, he was shocked as he saw the chaos in the street; fellow Christians scrambling for their lives, struggling to make it to the safety of the subway's shelter. Further up he could see soldiers raising their guns, leveling them at the dashing crowds.

Some fleeing Christians recognized Keeyon and shouted for him to return to the tunnel. A female sergeant screamed, her face contorted in fear. "Keeyon! Go back! Go back!"

Keeyon's heart jumped as he saw his friend, Andrew, running through the street, chasing behind John and Melody. Andrew seemed to be shouting something to John, trying to get his attention.

Keeyon impulsively stepped out of the subway's sheltered entrance into the street, intending to rush against the stampede to help his friends.

Drastically, just as Keeyon took those few steps, the unmitigated horror of the moment struck. Without warning, an incredulous stream of all-out gunfire stormed through the scattering Christians, tearing them down several at a time, brutally killing them in rapid-fire succession. Keeyon jumped back in shock as the earsplitting firepower exploded into the air.

Several Christians managed to hurdle themselves to safety as they flew past, exhausted and terrified. Many tried to pull him into the shelter with them, but Keeyon resisted, still in shock, dazed from the raging cyclone whirling around him. His eyes remained fixed on his good friend, Andrew, still wanting to go to his aid but paralyzed where he stood.

He watched Andrew leaping forward with every ounce of energy, desperately stretching out to protect John and Melody from a shower of ammunition. Then, in a dazed horror, he saw Andrew's body jerk forward with the deadly projectiles plundering into his back, riveting through him with life-ending madness.

Keeyon's despair sunk even lower as he saw John and Melody plunging forward into the filthy road, violently crashing into an excruciating heap of torn and bloody flesh; both of them ending the assault in a prone position, flat on the ground, separated once again.

Outraged, Keeyon exploded from his daze, whipping himself into a wild cacophony of mad, heated screams. He ran uncontrollably into the street, shouting bloody murder, intent on avenging his friends at all costs, even if it meant dying in the process.

"Keeyon! Don't!" one of the men shouted from behind. But Keeyon couldn't hear. His mind was absent of reason, all deductive logic had been swept away in the bloody furor, and only a crazed need to vindicate his friends' lives remained.

Capturing the instant attention of several HEdge soldiers, Keeyon became an easy, upright target. The soldiers gladly fixed their sights on his rabid, maniacal march through the street, and, accordingly, opened fire.

Just as he was about to receive a shower of ammo, two huge men ran up from behind, seemingly from nowhere, and tackled him. The siege caught him by surprise. He tumbled with a heavy thud, slamming his head against the pavement, knocking him unconscious. The two powerful men effortlessly grabbed his arms and legs and ran him back across the street into the protective confines of the sheltered subway entrance.

Gently handing his body over, the two men motioned the group of Christians to escape into the tunnels. Heeding their advice, everyone scrambled down the stairwell with Keeyon's men carrying him at the front.

The two silent men remained behind, keeping a dire watch over the HEdge soldiers, who by now had become strangely confused and unsure of where all the surviving Christians had disappeared.

After a few moments, with the job finished, the two men departed the scene. They didn't bother with the stairwell though; there was no need of that. They had their own means of escape, if escape were the proper word; which it wasn't. Nonetheless, the two men were suddenly, no longer there.

Chapter

36

A nervous giggle escaped Banchard's lips as his jet-black boots carried him another step closer to the defeated, unconscious body of John Rex. Splattered bloodstains surrounded the motionless figure lying in the grease-slicked road, with more of the precious fluids soaking the pavement another foot over where a second victim lay.

Roderick knew the unconscious figure was John Rex. The second he spotted him running through the street clenching onto his wife, he knew it had to be him.

He giggled. The thought of John and Melody reunited after so long a separation, only to be torn apart again, but this time for good, punched a tender nerve in his demented funny bone. The thought was hilarious. With the ecstasy of the moment over-taking him, his giggle exploded into a scornful wail as his head tilted back and his chest heaved with glee.

Roderick couldn't be happier. Things had gone just as planned . . . well, almost. Rex wasn't supposed to be injured, but at least he wasn't killed. A little bleeding but he'll survive, which is more than he could say for the trigger-happy soldier that fired on him. That hapless individual would pay a heavy price for his little error; a heavy price indeed.

But *Melody*, he dreaded inwardly. *Where is she?* Jerking completely around, he probed the area where she had fallen, eager to see if she had survived the melee. His dark eyes gleaned out from beneath their shadowy sockets, a hungry scavenger searching out its prey.

He found her a dozen feet over, lying prostrate in the road, her back rising slightly as she breathed.

"Good!" he mumbled triumphantly. "I can still use her."

Satisfied that his two primary subjects were still alive, he relaxed. Gloating freely, he surveyed the gruesome scene around him, bloodied corpses strewn about, downed Christians, his mortal enemies, reduced to a pathetic string of lifeless cadavers.

He took yet another step closer to the unconscious body of John Rex. "What kind of godly man is this," he sneered. "Filthy pig!"

Standing tall and lordly, he kicked John once in the side, not vehemently, just enough to make a point, to satisfy his own imperial ego, to prove to himself this lying figure was nothing more than a lowly servant of a lesser god; and accordingly, that evil had once again, in fact, triumphed mightily over good.

John's unconscious body reacted nimbly to the kick, recoiling involuntarily with a strained gasp emanating from his lips.

Feeling more empowered than ever, Roderick turned to a small group of soldiers standing nearby. Pointing to John and Melody, he hollered, "Get these two out of here. I want them treated immediately. They must live! Do you hear me? They must live!"

Looking down to John's unconscious figure, he jeered, "I've got plans for these two. Big plans."

Jumping at his orders, the soldiers had John and Melody carted away on stretchers, separately tucked into two vans then hurried off to base where a medical staff waited to treat them.

With that taken care of, Roderick had one last piece of business that needed tending to. He turned to the remaining soldiers and barked, "Get me Captain Riggins! Now! And I want her cuffed!"

As they dashed off to get her, Roderick had some time to spare. He decided to entertain himself by strolling through the minefield of fallen bodies up and down the street.

Stopping at the first bloody corpse, he recognized the lifeless face of

Andrew Hoyte. A surge of hatred coated with joy rushed through him, blasting him with self-gratification. The identity of the fallen evangelist only complemented Roderick's already secure sense of victory. Giggling, he began a perverse discussion with the still corpse.

"Andrew Hoyte, so you're having a bad day, I see." He giggled. "Taught you not to play with fire, didn't I? Yes, indeed, Andrew knows not to play with fire now."

He waived mockingly, "Now if you could only show me where your friend Keeyon disappeared to. But don't get up on my account, oh no, I'll find him myself, thank you very much."

Then he started towards the next body, finding more choice words for that one, and still the next, continuing his sarcastic euphemisms on down the line.

Almost a block and a half from where he started, Roderick was interrupted.

"Here she is, sir," an aggressive yet spiritless female soldier announced as she presented Captain Riggins in cuffs. Two male soldiers stood by.

Karen Riggins was visibly struggling within herself. Moist, red circles surrounded her eyes as drying tears left their marks across her smooth brown cheeks. She tried to conceal her devastated emotions, to hold back her tears, to appear upbeat and victorious; but she couldn't. The defeat was too much. The open brutality thrust upon her friends was more than she could take. Her chin trembled.

Trying to look up to this beastly monster gloating before her, she lifted her face, then looked back down in sorrow. Her emotions were sagging along with her posture.

Roderick's expression took on a sly, cunning aura as his eyes pierced into her flushed face. A rippled sneer formed across his lips. This was going to be fun.

"Good afternoon, Captain." he slithered out, fomenting each syllable as they left his tongue.

Karen remained silent, eyes focused on the ground.

Pacing slowly yet purposely in front of her, Roderick started his oration.

"You know, Captain, you had me puzzled at first. But I wasn't the only one. It seems most everyone that reviewed Rex's phone messages the day of his wife's capture missed it too. Sloppy work. Sloppy, sloppy, work."

Roderick brushed his hands aside, disgusted with the incompetent efforts involved in conducting Rex's investigation.

"It was the strangest thing though, Captain. After Major Harker combed the neighborhood in search of this mysterious Karen Riggins, they came up empty handed. They never found her."

He jostled with her a bit. "Can you imagine that? I mean, why would John Rex tell his wife to go to Karen Riggins' house if there was no Karen Riggins living nearby? Doesn't make sense, does it?"

After a short pause, he continued. "Our Major Harker, still in her ecstasy over capturing Rex's wife and son, eventually disregarded the issue, ignoring it completely. Just blew it off to some meaningless mispronunciation or something. It didn't matter, she was happy just to have Melody . . . and of course, to play her games with the poor girl."

Looking directly at Karen, he pried, "I understand you've seen the results of some of Major Harker's games with Melody, haven't you?"

Karen looked up. The burning memories of the tortured and desperate condition she found Melody at the Red Hook District prison brought a revived sense of meaning. Her eyes were off the ground and firmly on his.

Realizing he had struck the desired nerve, Roderick moved on.

"Yes, you remember." He giggled. "As if it were only yesterday. Poor child, wasn't looking too well when you found her, was she?"

Not saying a word, her fiery brown eyes pierced through his over confident facade, her contempt for him visibly evident.

He glimpsed into her eyes, then just as quickly moved on. The connection made him uncomfortable.

"It wasn't until I had a chance to review the investigation myself, that the name Karen Riggins once again became an issue. And of course, you know why, don't you, Captain?"

Karen's teeth were clenched tight, her jaw twitched.

"Yes, of course you do. Because you are that Karen Riggins."

Karen only stared at him. There was no point in arguing; she had been discovered, the guise was over.

"I suspected as much when I first saw your name on the investigation. I remembered the name from years back when you were assigned to this sector, working in this very building. Was it five, six years ago when you transferred west?"

She didn't answer.

"To tell you the truth, I'd forgotten all about you, that is, until I saw your name appear on Rex's investigation. That's when the bells went off. I was more than a little surprised." He clasped his hands in exuberance.

"But even then, I wasn't sure. I had a hunch, but nothing more. I had to confirm my suspicions. So I spoke with your division chief, Colonel Doschier.

"Kindly gentleman, he was very helpful.

"Oh, and by the way, the Colonel sends his regards. He said you were always one of his favorite officers, though, unfortunately, he said you did seem a bit passive toward the Christian movement. Not enough to cause alarm mind you, just subtle statements here and there that caught his attention. But after I explained my suspicions, it became very clear to him.

"Anyway, after our conversation, the Colonel said if my hunches turned out to be true, he didn't want you back. I could keep you for myself."

He paused for a brief smile.

"So naturally, I had to discover the truth myself. I had to know for certain just whose side you were on. That's why I put you in charge of this little prison relocation escapade. I figured if you were the same Karen Riggins mentioned in the report, you'd make the most of the opportunity and find a way to get Melody to freedom. And in the process, I was hoping you might even get her dreary husband, the infamous John Rex, out in the open also."

At that, Roderick broke into congratulatory laughter while espousing, "And you did a splendid job, my dear, just splendid."

Roderick's expression then melted into a gentle, warm texture of congeniality. He took on a kinder mood and attitude. His countenance softened.

He slowed his pacing and began speaking in a friendlier tone.

"First and foremost, Captain, I want you to understand, I am a firm believer in sharing the fruits of my people's labors. I strongly believe in giving credit where credit is due. If my officers perform well, I insist on rewarding them in kind.

"After all, don't you think good work deserves comparable recognition?"

Karen wondered where this was going. Banchard wasn't the type to ramble on for nothing.

"And now, Captain Riggins, or, Karen? May I call you Karen?"

She ignored him.

"All right, Karen. Now, before I share all the credit for this outstanding victory, I need to make certain that we are on the same side. Is that all right?" He gestured politely, offering his friendship openly.

He stood in front of her, his tall, lanky presence towering over her smaller, feminine frame. Staring compassionately, almost lovingly down to her, he spoke, "Look up to me, Karen. Please?"

Feeling strangely drawn up, Karen slowly raised her focus to Roderick. His sickly, pale complexion trying its best to convey a caring, even fatherly image; as though he were genuinely concerned with her little fall from grace, his grace.

"That's it, my dear. Now, to share in all the glory of this day, I ask one thing of you, only one."

Karen's moist eyes stared up to this diabolical rogue hawking over her, wondering what this was all about.

With a simple, yet direct order, he oozed out, "All you have to do is denounce this Jesus Christ. Admit he's a fraud; that no such person ever existed. He isn't God; it's all just a hoax. That's all you have to do."

Surprised, Karen smirked; the demand caught her off guard. She was not going to answer. There was no way.

Roderick's expression changed slightly as he struggled to maintain a friendly composure, a necessary level of compatibility to help coax this renegade captain back in line.

"Go ahead, Captain, just a sweet little denouncement. Then you can go your merry way. I'll even give you the lion's share of credit for orchestrating this superb victory. So let's have it. Okay?" He finished the request with a leering emphasis, his patience beginning to wane.

Karen stood firm. The idea was absurd.

"C'mon Captain. I offer you freedom. I offer you credit for this victory; credit that will place you in an ideal position for the upcoming promotion cycle. All I ask in return is a simple little statement; a spoken gesture of allegiance on your part. That's all."

She didn't budge. Her composure became more serious, sterner. She knew this game was nearly over.

At Karen's abstinence, Roderick became frustrated, angry; his persona became more expressive, more outwardly hostile. His voice rose with the growing tide of hatred cutting through his flowery facade.

"Captain, I don't think you understand. The fact of the matter is, you are my prisoner. I am offering you clemency for your outrageous behavior. All you have to do is denounce this Jesus Christ. That is all."

He resumed his pacing, his anger rising.

Standing perfectly still, she dropped her focus back to the ground.

Roderick was exasperated. "Captain, look up at me. Speak." he ordered. "Why don't you speak?"

Her eyes burning with determination, Karen slowly raised her focus; her tough, solid character rising up with the spirit of truth and eternal victory washing through her. Finally, looking Roderick squarely in the face, she blasted, "I don't cast my pearls to swine."

Roderick fell back a step, startled. Rebounding, he pulled himself together. He was furious! Enough games! He ordered the nearest soldier to come over. The soldier rushed to his side.

"Get your gun out!" he fumed. "Point it to her head!"

The soldier was surprised. He didn't expect this. He hesitated.

"I said pull out your gun!" Roderick cursed. "Hold it to her head!"

Slowly, the soldier obeyed the awkward order, steadily reaching into his shoulder harness, smoothly pulling out his shiny revolver.

Karen began praying. She closed her eyes.

The soldier nervously fumbled with the revolver until it was firmly gripped in his right hand. Gradually, he raised the gun, leveling it at shoulder height, his arm weakly extended towards her.

Several soldiers standing nearby became suddenly still as they watched the bizarre scene unfold in the middle of the street. This was a senior HEdge officer being held at gunpoint. A Captain no less! Highly unusual, highly unusual!

Roderick scolded the soldier. "Raise it. Higher! Closer to her head! Can't you understand me?"

Soldiers further up the street suddenly stopped as they became aware of Roderick's anger, hearing his hateful curses echo down the dead calm street. Looking over, they were surprised to see Captain Riggins handcuffed, with a gun aimed at her head.

But they knew Banchard was in charge, and that's all anyone needed to know. They watched, but did nothing else.

Gradually following the order, the soldier raised his gun higher, until it was perpendicular to Captain Riggins left temple, just above her ear. His knees weakened as he stood holding the position.

Roderick's thin veneer of compassion was completely gone. The mirage of seeming to care in the least for the Captain's well being had dissipated. Gone. He cursed with all the loathing and revulsion he'd been holding inside.

"Captain Riggins, you will denounce this Jesus Christ. Or you will die!"

Karen stood firm, her eyes closed in prayer. Not a muscle was flexed, not a nerve aroused.

Roderick stomped his feet in anger as he stooped down to face her, his nose touching hers.

"Captain, is this the way you want it to end?" His hate-filled breathe blowing across her face.

She remained quiet and steadfast.

Roderick was furious. Suddenly an idea came to him. He reached behind the soldier and yanked a small instrument out of his back pocket.

"Give me that!" he shouted as he pulled the tool out.

Reaching behind the Captain, he shoved the instrument between her hands, slashing the nylon cuffs from around her wrists, freeing her hands completely.

"Now, are you happy? You're free. Now denounce this Jesus Christ once and for all! Get this thing over with!"

The soldier continued aiming the revolver at her head.

But to Roderick's utter shock and dismay, Captain Riggins did no such thing. Instead, she raised her free hands to the sky, lifting them above her head. With both hands raised, she began praising the Lord, thanking Him for allowing her to lead so many lost souls to salvation.

Roderick was beyond hatred, he was beyond revulsion, this was truly more than he could handle. In fact, it was having the effect of ruining his entire day. His supreme confidence was being swept away on a passing cloud of righteousness. He suddenly felt defeated, conquered, as if this wonderful day had turned into a horrid nightmare. He felt a creeping mediocrity slip into his soul, exposing a wasted, empty void, without solace or purpose. A powerful spirit of depression began consuming him, leaving his exaggerated ego crushed beneath a stockpile of doubt. Roderick was suddenly frightened beyond measure. He had to do something, and he had to do it fast, before all was lost!

"Shoot her!" he screamed at the soldier. "Shoot her!!!"

The soldier held his arm out straight, locking his elbow in place. He applied pressure to the revolver's trigger, but not enough. He couldn't do it. For no apparent reason tears began rolling down his cheeks. Much to Roderick's dread, the soldier lowered the gun to his side, in surrender.

Without hesitation, Roderick savagely ripped the gun from the soldier's hand, pointed it at him, then cursed as he fired. The soldier's body dropped to the ground with a quiet thump.

The many soldiers standing nearby, jumped, shocked at what they had just witnessed.

Roderick then pointed the gun directly into Karen' face. He screamed, the blood vessels in his neck pressing out against the flesh, twitching with rage. "Denounce Him! DENOUNCE HIM NOW!!!"

As a tear fell, Karen spoke her final words, arms extended to the Heavens, "Lord Jesus, receive my spirit."

"ARGHH!" Roderick screamed as he pulled the trigger, once, then twice, then a third time as Karen's body flew to the ground.

Soldiers all around stood silent and still, unbelieving, lost.

Roderick pummeled the entire round of ammunition into the lying corpse at his feet. The empty, spiritless shell of Karen Riggins jerked back and forth as the powerful bullets tore through her flesh.

Finally, Roderick was finished. The revolver was spent and so was he. What started out to be a wonderful day had now been completely laid to ruin. Something went wrong, terribly wrong, something he had no control over. And whatever it was, it left him devastated.

Dropping the gun clumsily to the ground, he drooped his shoulders in despair, and then slowly, lethargically trudged toward his cruiser.

Moping past several nervous soldiers, he mumbled his last order of the day. "Clean up the mess."

No one moved. They waited for him to enter his cruiser, and leave.

Karen Riggins was elated, she was tingly all over, as was Andrew.

Both of them, truly aware for the very first time, fully cognizant of the awesome, unfathomable joy and happiness only the presence of God could bring. The two saints, along with the rest of the martyrs from this day's events, were blissfully rejoicing in the splendor and unimaginable ecstasy of being in the divine presence of the Almighty One. A more enthralling experience than they could have possibly conceived or dreamed. And now, they were thoroughly absorbed in it!

As they gazed starry eyed into the stunningly beautiful face of their Creator, brilliant lucent beams of glory flooded over them, bathing them in pure unfiltered treasures of God's all encompassing, everlasting love, serene gold of the ultimate kind. They were happier than they ever could have imagined.

And as they were being embellished with the awesome, miraculous presence of their Lord God, one word continued flowing repeatedly from their joyous spirits; only one word.

"Holy, Holy, Holy . . ."

And the glory of God continued to shower over them.

Chapter

37

Only fifteen minutes since his morning shower and Samuel Treppin was already tipping his glass to a second helping of the chilled, pre-mixed blend of gin and tonic. The hotel's top maitre 'd stood poised in complete etiquette as he tilted the fancy carafe over Samuel's tall narrow glass, watching as the tart alcoholic beverage gushed over the rounded molds of ice.

With the tall receptacle now bursting with zeal, Samuel was ready to hunker down and quench his thirst. But first, social amenities had to be observed. He lifted his glass in thanks. The maitre 'd politely smiled, bowed, then turned and walked to the door, and left.

No sooner had the large sculptured door closed than Samuel had the mildly shaking glass raised to his dry lips. And finally, within the seclusion of his extravagant quarters in Geneva, thousands of miles from New York City, Samuel attacked the sullen, addictive fluids.

Fully satisfied, he placed the used container on a counter top, and then strode casually toward his cavernous bedroom where his shirt and silk tie waited.

In no time, he was fully dressed and standing before his full sized bedroom mirror adjusting his tie. Gazing passively into his reflection, Samuel couldn't help but notice the shadows under his eyes, dark, wrinkled bags of fatigue. They caught his attention; he looked tired and worn.

Was it possible that the pressures of being Sector Chief were getting to him? He chuckled at the thought. He liked his job and wouldn't trade it for anything. The pressures could be intense at times, but nothing he couldn't handle.

So why the shadows? he wondered.

He pondered the subject as he straightened his tie.

Sleep? Did he need more sleep? If so, that could be remedied easily. After the conference was finished he'd start going to bed early, say, around 9 p.m. That should take care of it.

Finished with his tie, he took a final sweeping glance into the mirror, getting an overall appraisal of himself. But this time, he inadvertently locked onto the eyes of his reflection, holding the view, stealing a longer, more intimate and absorbing look than intended. And much to his chagrin was not at all comforted with what he saw.

Staring despondently back from the mirror's sad reflection was an unhappy, insecure, middle-aged man; melancholy in spirit, empty of life, shallow. Not the man he knew seven years ago. Not even close.

Samuel felt a flush of disappointment, as he turned ashamedly away from himself, timid and disgraced, unable to face his mirrored image any longer.

Deep down he knew what the real problem was, but to face that, to really claim his alcoholism for what it had become was just too painful. He wasn't ready yet. And maybe never would be.

Haunted by his gloomy reflection, Samuel haggardly went about slipping into his black patent leather shoes and throwing his dark blazer on.

Heading to the door, he stopped at a short walnut cabinet and yanked the top-drawer open. He reached in and pulled out two small bottles of alcohol, small but powerful doses. Fondling each with care, he placed them into his coat pocket, and left his hotel room.

A few listless steps through the hall and he was at the elevator. He stabbed the Call-Button while contemplating the day's upcoming events. He wished he had taken Jennifer's advice and stayed in New York. An entire week of dealing with accountants could be the one thing to push him over the edge. "Accountants! Bean counters! Hate 'em all!" he grumbled.

The elevator arrived with a chime. The bright gold doors opened on a whistle. He plodded in, his head lowered, debating internally whether he should even bother with the conference or just stay in his suite, alone, relaxing with his two bottles.

Startled out of his depression, Samuel was surprised to see a tall well- dressed, bronze-skinned man looking amiably over to him. The quiet man stood with a relaxed smile, his light brown eyes exuding a genuine friendliness, an aura of tenderness.

"Good day," the tall man offered.

Samuel agreed cautiously, "Yes, it is."

The elevator doors closed.

Samuel muttered, "Ground floor."

A soft animated voice responded, "Ground floor." The elevator began its smooth descent down the long, seventy-story shaft, carrying the special passengers inside.

Casually surveying the tall man through the corner of his eyes, Samuel noticed a small package under his right arm. He wondered what it could be.

Suddenly the warnings given by his Advisers before he left New York popped into his mind, and immediately, he knew the package had to be a bomb. Fear washed over him. He was convinced the stranger was a terrorist involved in a plot to kill him! Jennifer was right; his life was in danger!

Samuel froze. He regretted ever getting on the elevator. He should have waited for the next one. Trying to remain calm, he instinctively caressed his coat pocket, gracing the two small bottles hidden inside, wanting to pull them out and guzzle.

"You don't need those," the stranger admonished gently.

Samuel was shocked. How did the stranger know what was in his pockets? "Huh?"

"I said you don't need those."

Samuel's mind was a swirl of confusion; his knees felt strangely weak. "Who are you?"

"A friend," the man answered, offering a welcome smile.

Now Samuel was even more confused. How is that possible? He's never met this guy before.

This was getting too weird. Samuel discreetly glanced up to the numbers flashing above the door. They were just passing the 60th floor, which meant they had a ways to go yet.

He considered getting off on an earlier floor; anything to get away from this killer. Maybe he should call building security. All it would take was pressing the red button on the wall next to him. The elevator shaft and every floor along its route would instantly be swarming with security personnel.

He sneaked another glimpse of the small package tucked under the stranger's arm. *Was it a bomb?* Beads of sweat formed across Samuel's brow as he became plagued with anxiety, his emotions battling between reason and paranoia. His right hand began inching over to the red security button. He decided it was the safest thing to do, the ONLY thing to do!

"You needn't worry," the stranger said. "It's just a gift."

Samuel caught his breath. "Huh? How'd you . . ."

"It's okay, Samuel." the stranger gleamed. "You don't have to worry. You worry enough already."

Samuel's eyes went wide. "Who are you?"

The stranger smiled. "Samuel, your time is nearly at hand."

Samuel gasped, "What?"

The stranger continued speaking as he removed the small package from under his arm. "Everything must work in the fullness of time, Samuel. God's time. And now, that means you are almost ready. But you need not worry."

Handing the package over, he said, "This is for you."

Slowly, hesitantly, Samuel received it.

"W-why?" Stammering, he looked up to the stranger. "W-what is it?"

The stranger raised his voice slightly as he advised, "Don't worry, Samuel. It is something you have desired for a long time."

With hardly a second gone by, the stranger abruptly said, "Third floor." The elevator's digital voice confirmed with a soft tone. "Third floor."

Samuel was falling into an emotional dither. They were on the tenth floor descending fast.

He didn't want the stranger to go. He needed to know more.

They were passing the fourth floor.

The stranger stepped from the back wall, past Samuel to get to the door.

The elevator came to a gentle, controlled stop on the third floor; the doors opened.

Samuel was desperate; he couldn't let the stranger leave, not now, he had too many questions.

"Wait! Don't go!" Samuel ordered. "What's this all about? What does it mean?"

The tall stranger looked back before stepping out. With a calm, friendly voice, he answered, "I am a messenger, Samuel. You have received the message, and the gift. Remember, you must follow through when the time comes. It is important."

The stranger finished his words of instruction, "May you ask the Lord for strength. He is the Way, Samuel. And with Him, all things are possible."

Then with a parting smile he stepped out, the doors closing behind.

Samuel was trembling. He didn't understand any of it. What did it all mean? He scrambled to open the door, slipping his hand in just before they shut. At that, the doors flew back open.

In a frenzy, he leaped out of the elevator; he had to stop the stranger, he had to!

Once out, he gazed down the hallway in the direction the stranger had turned, but to his amazement, the hallway was empty. Completely, utterly, empty!

"What?" he shrieked.

Staring disbelievingly down the long red-carpeted hall, no one, not a single person was in sight. The nearest door to the elevator was at least twenty yards away. The stranger couldn't have reached it so fast! No way. And yet, if not, then where did he go!

Samuel was dumbfounded. His mind was a whirl of emotion. A nervous quiver started up his spine. He shouted in vain, hoping against hopes the stranger would appear from somewhere, anywhere. "What does this mean? Where did you go?" But there was no answer. None.

He gazed down at the mysterious package in his hands, almost afraid of it; afraid to open it. But he knew he must. He fondled the strange gift, tilting it slowly in every direction, caressing it, trying to guess at what it might be.

Finally, he began unwrapping it. The paper came off easily, no rips or tears. He continued until the paper was completely off, exposing a small, two-inch thick box. He carefully, gently lifted the cardboard lid while trying to get a peak inside.

Then he saw it. A cold sweat ran down his back. His knees felt wobbly, shaking slightly. His hands trembled as he gazed inside the box.

Almost losing his composure, Samuel needed to sit. He carefully laid the strange gift on the floor as he positioned himself next to it, leaning weakly against the wall.

Reaching into his coat pocket, desperate and confused, he felt the two perfectly shaped bottles mold into his palm, and yanked one out. He snapped off the cap and jammed the bottle to his lips. In seconds, the contents were gone. Guzzled down. He repeated the process with the second bottle.

With both containers tossed carelessly across the floor, Samuel's attention returned to the strange gift, his mind bewildered.

In a daze, he muttered, "Was John right all along?"

Then he reached over and touched it. And for the first time in decades, the first time since his mother left with his younger brother to move to California so many years ago, leaving him to live with his rich father in New York City, he held the strange, yet powerful gift.

In awe, Samuel read the inscription on its cover:

"*Holy* BIBLE.

To Samuel, with love. Mom."

A tear dropped, then another.

"No," he cried softly. "No. It can't be . . . It can't."

Chapter

38

The two muscular soldiers marched noisily behind their drug induced, partially-conscious prisoner, barking orders and making lewd comments as demented thoughts entered their minds. The bigger of the two slammed his fist against the prisoner's sweaty back, almost knocking the wind out of him.

"Hey Rex!" the soldier jeered. "Are we having fun yet?" Not waiting for an answer, "You bet we are!" Then burst into laughter.

The second soldier couldn't resist. Following behind, he pressed his boot into John's left foot in an effort to trip him. John got caught up and stumbled forward. He tried to catch himself, but in his drugged condition there was no way. He crashed to the floor, face-first, bloodying his nose. The two soldiers broke into hysterical laughter as they saw him sprawled out, groping to get back up.

With a surprised face, the guilty soldier bolstered sarcastically, "Oh my! Can you forgive me?" Then bellowed out with more laughter.

Just as John was almost standing again, the first soldier grabbed him under his arm and heaved. "C'mon chump, your cell's down the hall. Even an oaf like you should be able to make it that far without too much trouble. Let's go!" Proceeding with another round of shoves, they manhandled their woozy prisoner down the corridor, keeping themselves in stitches all the while.

For his part, John lumbered sluggishly forward, his mind a blur. Drugged and feeble, he had no control over his body and very little over his mind. He had no choice but to follow the directional prodding of his captors.

While his body was being pummeled down the hallway, his mind was dizzily trying to piece together the events of the last few hours. He vaguely remembered the chaos in the street, but couldn't grasp the details.

As John stumbled forward, the dismal lackluster eyes of prisoners locked away eons ago inside their concrete hell peered out from behind thick bars. Apparently recognizing their newest cellmate, some of them spewed out contemptible hisses, mocking John for his faith, while others, at the risk of increasing their own personal torment, offered their sympathy, asking John to pray for their sorry lives. But John could hardly decipher their requests, much less respond.

Nearing the end of the row, one of the soldiers grabbed him by his ripped shirt, jerking him to a stop. "Hold it, Rex."

The other sergeant removed a small disk from his pocket and pressed it flat against an adjoining circular plate on the door. The door started swinging open.

"Ready," the soldier announced as he slipped the disk back into his pocket.

"Good," the other acknowledged.

Suddenly a sound emanated from inside the dark cell: a grunting noise, followed by an angry man's voice. "Hey! What are you guys doing?"

A grubby, middle-aged man stepped out from behind the cell's shadows. Sloppy and unkempt, a belly the size of a world globe wobbled over his belt as he rushed to the door. One of the soldiers laughed as he saw the hefty man charging towards him.

"Don't even think about it, Duncan!" he threatened. "You're not going anywhere."

The obese man grunted with disgust as he carried his disheveled body closer to the door. "Hey! I didn't do anything. Why am I here anyway? What'd I do? Tell me, what'd I do?"

The other soldier pulled the withered frame of John Rex from behind, and propped him up to the cell door, right in front of Herb Duncan.

"Remember him?"

Herb instantly recognized the face of the ragged prisoner.

"Yeah, I know the bum. So what?"

Ignoring him, they heaved John into the cell. He stumbled forward, then fell right at Herb's feet.

"Hey! What's going on here?" Herb hollered in objection. "What d'ya mean puttin' him in here with me? What's this all about?"

"There, he's all yours, Duncan." They laughed as the cell door banged shut.

Herb stood in shock. He looked down at John's collapsed body, then back to the soldiers. They smirked, the amusement obvious on their faces.

"Have fun, Duncan," the one chided. "Maybe he can teach you something."

Totally frustrated, Herb jumped to the cell bars and held on. "You can't do this! Let me outta here!"

They gave Herb one last jeer, accompanied by a sarcastic chuckle, and without another word, headed away down the hall.

"Wait a minute!" Herb pounded his fists on the bars. "You can't do this to me! You can't leave me with this kook!" His desperate voice echoed through the cellblock. The place became encumbered with his cries of anger, screaming with an intensity that surprised even himself.

The soldiers continued on their merry way, ignoring him. There was nothing they could do for the slob. Banchard was the one that ordered him locked up, so Banchard would have to be the one to order him free. Scream all he likes, he wasn't going anywhere.

Meanwhile, John Rex sank quietly into an unconsciousness slumber, oblivious to Herb's rantings. He was buried in a drugged bliss that would carry him mindlessly through the next several hours, with the stark reality of the day's events nestled safely away.

Chapter

39

Gregory White and Lester Ellis made their way giddily down the plush seventeenth-floor hallway of the Eastern U.S. Sector HEdge Headquarters in mid-town Manhattan. Sneaky, prankish grins glazed their faces as they strolled side by side, both caught up in an uncharacteristic case of the giggles.

The two felt like young schoolboys preparing for the biggest class prank of the year. Excited and energized, their hearts seemed to pound in unison, beating faster with each passing step. They were anxious to set their plan into motion.

Finally at the end of the hall, the two Advisors reached Gregory White's office. The lights clicked on automatically as the room's sensors recognized the two humans entering it's high-security domain.

A stifled giggle escaped Gregory's lips as he stepped into his sumptuously furnished office, his mind racing with thoughts of seeing their plan carried out. Trailing behind was Lester Ellis, who was struggling with his own excitement as he also let loose a round of excited giggles.

Gregory took a beeline to the opposite side of the room where his sleek-sculptured desk with its three dimensional computer screen waited for his ready use. He rolled the chair out from behind his curvy desk, stepped around and plopped himself into it. Without pause, he leaned forward and hit the computer's mode switch.

The monitor's screen pitched to life. In a fraction of a second an infrared optical scanner locked onto Gregory's retina, confirming his identity; a simple procedure causing no discomfort, but necessary for security reasons.

The retina check was complete. A perky, digitized female voice sounded from the computer, wishing him a good day and offering any help needed. Before the last digitized word was spoken, Gregory was spewing out his instructions.

"I want access to our HEdge mainframe. I want parameters formed around every module tagged with HEdge Forces information."

The computer replied instantly. "Thank you. It is finished."

"Take the module leading to the Eastern U.S. Sector HEdge Forces Command, and open it."

"Thank you. It is finished."

"Inside, find the module to the Chief, Eastern U.S. Sector HEdge Force's electronic mail system, and open it."

"I'm sorry, I cannot help you. That module is accessible only by Mr. Roderick Banchard. It is protected."

"Yes, yes." Gregory interrupted irritably. "Of course it is. Listen, here's the code; 6-2-5-7-8-6-9-J-B-X-6."

"Thank you. It is finished."

"Whew!" Gregory breathed aloud.

"Okay, now, prepare to load a video file from Drive A, into this module. And I want it sent directly to the Sector Chief's personal mail system in Geneva."

"Ready to receive," the computer prompted.

Gregory gave a sigh of relief; he was actually inside Roderick Banchard's electronic-mail system! With no glitches!

Banchard's password cost him a fortune in credit. But it was worth every bit. A professional hacker of the quality needed to crack his security system was literally worth his weight in gold. Every sensible HEdge Advisor had a hacker on their payroll. It was just a matter of who had the best and brightest. He, no doubt, had a charm.

Gregory held his opened palm out to Lester Ellis, waiting for the one remaining item needed to complete the job. Lester obliged as he removed the small diskette from his pocket, complements of their late departed friend, Private Frank Arpell, and laid it into Gregory's hand.

Gregory took the small diskette and slipped it into the appropriate slot in the monitor's side.

He ordered, "Load it."

The animated voice acknowledged, "Thank you. The file has been received and is ready to send."

He looked up to Lester and offered him a mischievous, wicked, smile. Lester returned the same.

Gregory sat gloating, soaking in the splendor of knowing that the conspiracy to topple Roderick Banchard from his coveted perch was almost complete. When Treppin receives the recorded file of the New York State Auditorium massacre, and sees that the incident was orchestrated entirely by Banchard's HEdge Forces instead of a group of Christians, and then filmed no less, he'll bring the curtain down on Roderick Banchard! And not a moment too soon!

Gregory paused cautiously before giving the final order to transmit the file. He looked over to Lester, as if to make sure his comrade was still with him. Wouldn't be as much fun otherwise, or as safe.

"Go ahead," Lester coached. "We've gone this far. Send it."

Before giving the order, Gregory commented, "You know, Lester? This is probably the most fun I've had in years." Adding in a terse voice, "This should put an end to that miserable wretch!"

Growling inwardly, he ended, "I hope he burns in hell."

Lester rebutted curiously, "What do you mean? I'm gambling there is no such place. Let's just say we hope he doesn't discover we have his password. Okay?"

Gregory squinted. The thought passed without comment.

He gave the order, "Send it."

The computer responded instantly. "Thank you. It is finished."

The file was gone.

Lester looked down to Gregory - Gregory looked up to Lester. They shared a moment of reserved joy at their success. Then slowly, guardedly, began to laugh. At first sedate; a gentle chuckle rolling off their tongues, but gradually growing and compounding, until soon, they were bawling out in explosive celebration.

Their main antagonist would soon be out of business, for good! The person they hated the most and trusted the least would become an irrelevant fixture in HEdge's history! Both men were elated with the idea. They laughed for a good fifteen minutes. It was truly a moment worth relishing.

Chapter

40

J ohn groggily raised his head just slightly as he lay sprawled on the floor. His legs shifted an inch, bending a little at the knees. His eyes opened slowly, allowing a hazy flood of images to drift in, at first fuzzy and translucent, gradually sharpening into recognizable shapes and hues.

With his visual clarity returning, John began taking notice of the objects nearest him. He spotted the tall narrow bars a few feet away stretching to the ceiling. Gaping through the dim lighting, he saw a room across the hall where similar bars lined its darkened entrance.

At first, he couldn't make sense of it all, but as the blurry images continued filling his mind, he began to understand the reality of his situation, and with a sudden revulsion, grasped the inescapable meaning of the bars: he had been captured, and was in the hands of the enemy!

As John's vision cleared, so did his memory. Puddles began gathering under his eyes as he recounted the horrible scenes of his friends being ruthlessly shot down.

With glaring detail, he replayed the traumatic incident through his mind. Everything, all the pain, all the sorrow, everything, revisited again, playing mercilessly through his senses. Tears ran freely, mourning anew for his lost friends and family, lamenting over their plights, and dreading the fact there was nothing he could do for any of them.

Shifting to a sitting position, he leaned the bulk of his weight on his left arm. As he did, a jolt of pain shot through his arm to the rest of his body. He dropped over on his right side, wincing in agony.

As the pain subsided, he gazed at his arm and was surprised to see it covered with gauze from his wrist to his elbow. As he studied the wrapped appendage, a revelation came to him. His memory shot back to the street, back to when Andrew rammed into him. Just then, John knew the bullets that ended the life of his very best friend, were actually intended for him. Looking down over his arm, he realized Andrew had saved his life.

John lowered his head, and wept.

A few feet behind laid a solitary figure, silent and still, lying in the shadows of the bottom rack, quietly observing John. The figure had a blanket pulled clear up over his nose, exposing only his eyes.

Herb Duncan was watching and enjoying every bit of it. He chuckled quietly when John leaned on his left arm and painfully fell over. Then watched cynically as he lay on the floor sobbing.

Serves him right, Herb thought to himself. *The scoundrel!*

In a semi-prone position, John cried out, "Lord, you suffered and died on the cross, the cross of our sins. You said that by your stripes we were healed. You said it, Lord. So why is my family suffering? I beg You, Lord, why? Why have so many died trying to rescue them?"

This was quite a show for Herb. But as John's weeping lessened and his words became clearer, Herb began feeling dismayed, even baffled. He couldn't understand why John would still be praying to this God of his. After everything he'd been through, Herb figured God would be the last one John would care to speak to, except maybe to finally admit that no such being existed in the first place. But instead, he was carrying on as if this God were sitting right there, listening to every word.

Herb was dumbfounded. John wasn't denying his God at all; on the contrary, he was asking his God for understanding and mercy!

This caught Herb totally by surprise. It didn't make sense! Why would a person still believe in someone who had only brought pain and suffering into their life, with nothing but a broken family and a few dead friends to show for it? It didn't make any sense. Something had to be missing, something; but what?

As Herb continued listening and questioning, something inside began to click. Like the gears of an old locomotive stirring to life, something was being set into motion, something which Herb had not allowed to fill his mind in years; in fact, not since he was seven years old, barely old enough to remember. But now he did remember, and the memories hurt.

The truth is, this wasn't the first time Herb had witnessed an intense devotion to God. The person who had the most influence in his childhood was his mother; a Bible believing, God loving woman if there ever was one. And Herb loved her so much.

A morning wouldn't go by that she didn't pull out her bible and read to him, and pray over him. Afterwards she would spend time with him, playing in the yard or just smiling like an angel, beaming over him.

But that was before a drunken motorist, plowing crazily down their street, decided she was a good target. Herb remembered seeing his mother's broken body, as if in slow motion, being pressed between metal and metal. Her death was quick, but the fallout had yet to be fully realized.

She died that instant, and with her, Herb's desires for anything to do with God. If this was how God treated people, Herb didn't want anything to do with Him.

From then on, Herb's life was a dismal existence of rebellion and bitterness. Academics, friends, everything fell apart. He drifted through life without any rules, other than watching your back.

But now, for reasons beyond his understanding, thoughts began filtering through again. Things he hadn't considered plausible since childhood. Things which prior to this very moment would have been laughable, and yet, right now for some uncanny reason, seemed about as real as the day.

Then finally it hit. For the first time in decades, Herb actually got a sense that maybe, just perhaps, there really was something to life after all, something profound; but what?

Herb wanted to hear more. Tilting his head, he strained to hear every word John uttered.

John raised his voice. "Lord, my wife was hurt! I saw her in the street, she wasn't moving, Jesus! Please . . . Jesus!" He let out a final, desperate cry, followed by a river of tears.

Wiping the moisture from his face, he adjusted to a kneeling position, clasped his hands over his chest and raised his face to the heavens.

"Jesus, Your Word said we would not be given more than we can handle."

Tears rolled freely. He took another deep breath.

"Lord, You know the limits of my strength. You know my weaknesses, you know Lord, You know." He wavered as he wiped a tear. "Right now, Lord, I have to be honest, I don't even want to live. Take this life, please, along with everything else that has been taken away."

He lamented, "You've always provided someone for me Lord: a helper, an interceder, Melody, Andrew, other believers, but now, I'm alone. Who is there, Lord? Who can help my family? Our world has collapsed."

In a spirit of defeat, John finished his discourse. "Who can help us, Lord? Who?"

He remained in a kneeling position, his mind weary and searching, lost in a quagmire of hopelessness.

Startled from his prayers, John heard a sound from behind; something had moved. Turning, he peered into the shadows. A double-bunk bed was hidden against the wall. Gazing down to the lower rack, he saw a dim outline of a person. Someone was in the room with him, and whoever it was, they were awake and listening.

Getting over the initial shock, John fell back into his state of turmoil, debating if he even cared who was sharing the cell with him. Finally, after a long silence, he felt convicted to offer whomever it was, a greeting.

"Hello," he said without much sincerity.

Herb didn't respond. To be honest, he was a little startled himself. His mind was lost in thought, absorbed in a torrential state of indecision. He had heard John's prayers, he saw his grieving, and strangely enough, he even considered the notion that perhaps there was a God after all. But at the same time, his intellect, conditioned by his secular world's view and buried by the bitterness from the loss of his mother, simply prevented him from grasping the concept.

Herb was in the midst of a spiritual battle. A battle he was ill equipped to recognize, much less fight. He wasn't prepared spiritually or emotionally to do battle with the forces raging through him.

A moment of silence passed.

John persisted, this time with a little more certitude. "Bless you, brother."

Herb's lips finally broke as the warfare raging inside revealed itself.

"Don't try anything!" Herb threatened. "I know who you are! I don't want you here! I don't want to talk to you!"

John sat quietly, considering the situation.

Another moment of silence slipped by.

Determined to break the impasse, John offered an introduction.

"I'm glad you know who I am. I'm afraid I can't share the pleasure. Can I ask your name?"

Several seconds passed before Herb grudgingly responded. "Herb Duncan."

That's a start, John considered, suddenly taking a strange interest in this person.

"Do you have any idea what time it is?" John asked.

Answering slowly, Herb grinded, "Two or three in the morning. The guards haven't made a round in awhile."

"Thanks."

Straightening his legs from under him, John got into a more comfortable position. After a couple minutes, he attempted conversation.

"I guess the top bunk is mine?"

Herb didn't respond.

With hardly a minute passing, John asked, "How long have I been asleep?"

Sounding tense and on edge, Herb answered. "Since yesterday. About noon."

Obviously, Herb wasn't thrilled with sharing his cell. John assumed he wasn't a Believer. With that in mind, John understood part of the source of Herb's anxiety. But oddly, he discerned something else as well; something more significant than just carnal paranoia. There was more.

Without further thought, John began praying, asking God for insight into the situation. What was it he sensed? A spiritual hunger? Was God prompting him towards something? Finally, he prayed for God to open Herb's eyes, to give him revelation. He prayed for spiritual discernment to come over Herb, that he could see through the muck and haze of a deceptive world and openly desire the Truth buried deep beneath the lies.

John prayed quietly, his eyes closed.

"What are you doing?" Herb interrupted.

John opened his eyes and gazed forward. "Praying."

"Why?"

"You need the Lord."

"Why?"

John stood, took a few steps to the bed, leaned over, and laid his hand on Herb. "Because you do!" Then proceeded to pray aloud.

"Lord, I ask for your mercy on this lost soul. Save him, Lord. Let him see from whence he came, and to where he needs to go. Lord, his spirit is eager, but his flesh is weak. Take him, Lord. Take him and cleanse him. In Jesus' almighty name, I pray."

Herb's first reaction was to draw back, to knock John's hand aside. But an inner desire prevented him. Something inside wanted this, wanted John's prayers; something at the innermost core of his being, a spiritual embodiment crying for freedom from the bondage that's wracked his life since childhood.

Herb didn't resist. He couldn't.

John's voice grew stronger; a stirring power arose in it, forceful, overwhelming authority consuming him.

"Jesus, You're the Alpha and the Omega. You've seen this man from his inception to his final days. If it is your will, if his name has been laid down in the great Book of Life, so let it be, let him become FREE!"

From nowhere, Herb felt a tear pushing to the surface, then another, then more, and before his pride could stop the flow, a cascade of water began gushing from his eyes. He became succumbed by love, he felt the peace, he felt the awesomeness, and along the way, he saw his life for what it had become, and was immediately shamed by it. He saw the ugliness, the selfishness, and yet, he saw hope. He saw the hope his mother had once prayed for, which he had long since abandoned.

He broke down. His entire body quaked as he sobbed; his arms, his legs, every part of his being were taken into the Spirit as he relented willingly.

And it all happened in the blink of an eye. At one moment Herb was resistant, steadfast and rebellious. The next, he was fully engorged in surrender as the Holy Spirit washed through him, driving unworthy sentiments aside. Before Herb could catch up, he was being transformed into a new creation, with a new beginning, in Christ Jesus.

Inwardly the battle had been won, his salvation was at hand, but a decision still had to be made. Herb had to accept Jesus Christ into his heart. It was a decision afforded to every person; a decision God provides as a way to eternal life, or, eternal death.

As Herb cried, John sat next to him, continuing in prayer.

As the exhilarating moment came to a close, John watched Herb begin to gather himself, wiping his tears in embarrassment, understandable but unnecessary.

Sitting beside him, John looked directly into Herb's eyes, and without pause, explained the way to salvation.

He spoke firmly. "I don't know you, I don't know anything about you, but Jesus does. You've been a sinner your whole life, and God knows that. I know that. But now, you have to know it."

John prayed.

"And now, I believe that you do."

With a discerning mind, John continued. "You needed your eyes opened Herb. But only the Holy Spirit could do that for you. And praise God; I believe He has done just that. But now you need to know about salvation."

Herb sat up in his bunk. His eyes still moist, his countenance open for knowledge.

"You must accept Jesus Christ into your life, Herb." He paused, waiting for the right moment.

Finally, he asked, "Are you ready to do that?"

Herb was at a crossroads in his life, and he knew it. He remembered his mother's scripture readings, all the stories about Jesus Christ. But since then, Herb had ridiculed people for considering such tripe as even remotely possible. Now he knew how wrong he was, and regretted every faithless word he had spoken.

But he didn't stop to reflect; instead, he kept his sights on the future. He saw the opportunity; he caught a glimpse of what life could be. And he wanted more of it.

He answered, "Yes."

John closed his eyes, sighing, "Thank you, Lord." He smiled, "All right, Herb, to receive salvation you have to make a pronouncement of faith. And remember, this is the beginning of a new life, so don't sweat your past. You're a sinner. So am I. But God is a forgiving God. He made a way for us long before you or I ever took our first breath."

He offered, "And now, are you ready to share in God's gift?"

Visibly eager, Herb snapped, "Yes."

"I see," John smiled.

Then with a clear, doctrinal voice, John continued, "If you confess with your mouth that Jesus Christ is your Lord, that he died for your sins, and believe in your heart that God has raised Him from the dead, then you will be saved."

Herb looked confused. "That's it? I don't have to do anything else? I mean I've heard all sorts of stories about ancient ceremonies, rituals 'n' stuff. You're sure that's it?"

"Book of Romans, Chapter 10, verse 9, you got it buddy. But remember, this is just the beginning. There's much to follow, and much to learn; water baptism, the great commission, and plenty more."

"Once you make your confession of faith, expect your life to change, because it will. You'll see things differently, new perspectives, new outlooks. It'll all come in time. But getting into the Bible and learning His plan for your life is the first part. All right?"

Herb swallowed. He looked up to John. It was time. He was ready. But first . . .

"John?"

"Yes?"

"Before I do, I have something to tell you. You'll probably hate me for this, but I can't go on without saying it."

John wondered what it was that could possibly make Herb think he would hate him.

"Sure, Herb. What do you have to say?"

With a crackly voice, Herb timidly broke the news.

"I'm the reason you're here, John. It's my fault."

John took a deep breath. He didn't like the sound of this.

"Why do you say that?"

Herb swallowed hard. A tear formed in the corners of his eyes. Then he began his sordid tale.

"I'm a bartender, John. I work in the Village. I'm the one that reported you to HEdge. I saw you and Andrew Hoyte and Keeyon Webster outside my pub. I called HEdge." He stammered. "I'm . . . the reason . . . you're in here. It's my . . . fault." Then he looked down in shame.

John just sat there, despaired. How could this be? The person that brought this terror into his life, the person ultimately responsible for his wife and son being locked up, beaten, humiliated, and scorned.

John lowered his face. This was too much. This was a definite curve ball. There was no way he could have prepared for this kind of challenge. Pictures of his wife flashed through his mind, her bruised face, her limp walk, and her tender smile. And his son, Matthew; was he even alive? He hasn't heard from him since he was taken away.

And the person responsible for all this is right here!!

The pictures were too much for him. He had to fight the images; he had to clear his mind. He had to, because if he didn't, something terrible was going to happen.

Suddenly, John was under attack on all fronts. Anger tried to rise up and consume him. Hatred reared its ugly head trying to get a piece of the action. A bitter wrath began to rage just beneath the surface. He wanted to kick this man, to spit on him. He wanted to hit him hard, over and over again. The venom was flowing, the hatred surging like a dam broken free.

And so, the struggle for John's soul was on. The forces of the nether world saw their moment of opportunity and ravaged it, while John, in his emotionally weakened state, was precariously girded to do much about it.

But he fought nonetheless. And in so doing, took the battle directly to the Lord, knowing full well he didn't have a chance on his own. And there, the battle was won as the forces of evil were stymied, then crushed altogether by the supreme authority of God's power. The match was over.

Ultimately, John refrained. He knew what had to be done, and violence had no part in it.

Slowly, steadily, he placed his hands on Herb's shoulders. Herb looked up to him, their eyes met, tears flowed.

"I . . . forgive . . . you."

Herb trembled, "I'm sorry. So . . . sorry."

John's eyes gushed with more tears than he thought possible. He reached over to Herb and hugged him, holding him tight, sprinkling his sorrows onto his shoulder.

Herb cried openly.

After several minutes of emotional healing, the two finally separated. They sat quietly in the cell for a while, both of them collecting their thoughts. Finally, with a renewed sense of purpose, John was once again ready to pursue Herb's salvation.

Staring Herb in the eyes, he whispered, "You need to receive the Lord, Herb. Ask the Lord for strength. He'll help you."

Herb nodded. Then, with the seriousness of a broken soldier, he spoke the words that needed to be spoken, and felt the sincerity of each in his heart as he did.

"Jesus Christ, is my Lord," Herb paused as he gathered his strength, "who died for my sins, raised from the dead, and now sits in glory forever." Adding emphatically, "And now, I am His. ALLELUIA!"

With tears, John reached over and gave Herb a congratulatory hug, welcoming him as a Brother in the Lord.

Ending the moment, John took Herb's hands and said a quiet prayer of thanks. Herb listened to John's wondrous words, foreign to his ears, but tender to his soul. He felt alive and renewed!

John was rejuvenated. His spirit was vibrant and strong once again. His situation hadn't improved, he was still in the belly of the beast, and his family was still beyond reach, but through it all, he took comfort in knowing the Lord was still in control, and with that, John knew there was still hope.

Looking over to Herb, he said with a broad smile, "I've got a lot of teaching for you, brother."

Herb returned the smile. His whole life had been changed. For the first time since his mother died, he knew the feeling of love. He felt God's love, and he knew he belonged.

Herb wanted to learn everything John could teach him about God. And more!

"Where do you want me to start?" John asked.

Taking a minute to consider, Herb finally answered, "It's been so long. Please, just start at the beginning."

Smiling, John said, "Oh, what I would give for a Bible right now!"

"That's okay," Herb offered, "just tell me what you know, from the beginning."

John looked reassuringly to his new friend. He beamed with encouragement as he cleared his throat. He began his lesson.

"In the beginning, God created the Heavens, and the Earth . . ."

And there the two sat for hours on end, teaching and learning.

All the while, God remained in control.

Chapter

41

Standing at the foot of his mammoth bed, Samuel gazed down at the leather bound Bible resting on the edge of his mattress, his hands tucked deep inside the pockets of his dress slacks.

A chilled carafe of liquor gleamed from the middle shelf of a nearby bookcase, the spirited contents vying for his attention. He had guzzled half of it after storming back into the suite from his strange encounter on the elevator; no doubt, the rest would soon follow.

Through the haze of the alcohol, Samuel stared at the enticing book sitting on his bed, his eyes fixed on the rich golden letters ingrained in the crevices of its shiny black cover.

It was the Bible his mother had given him when he was a youngster about ten years old. The "Good Book" she had called it. He remembered opening it for the first time; his youthful, eager fingers holding it steady as the thin pages ruffled under his curious eyes. As the pages settled in their place, young Samuel's mind was drawn to a verse at the top. A verse that even at his young, pre-adolescent age, struck him as unique.

And oddly enough, Samuel could still remember that verse, even after all these years:

"For God so loved the world that He gave His only begotten Son.
That whoever believes in Him shall have eternal life."

"Hmm . . ." He wondered how the verse could have stayed with him after so many years, and why? He gazed quizzically down to the holy book, contemplating it.

As he stood there, more childhood memories began stirring inside him, thoughts that haven't crossed his mind in years, even decades. He found himself reminiscing back to when he lived on Long Island Sound with his parents and younger brother, the now infamous, John Rex.

He could almost see John playing a game of Hide-&-Seek, playfully chasing their buddies around the huge weeping willow tree behind their house. And there was Andrew Hoyte, John's best friend, running behind the enormous tree, laughing while John scrambled in the opposite direction searching for someone else.

The monstrous willow was fondly named "Rex," after their favorite dinosaur, the Tyrannosaurus Rex. The tree was the biggest in the neighborhood, and its huge drooping branches made a perfect covering to sit beneath on a hot summer day, or to play tag around.

Continuing his reminiscent stroll though childhood, Samuel stopped on the day his mother left for California, taking John with her. His heart sank at the memory. It was one of the saddest days of his life. He felt cheated, betrayed by his parents for breaking up the family; bitter for stealing away the relationship he could have forged with his younger brother.

But those days were long past. He'd never know how things could have been, how they should have been. And that hurt.

Not to say that Samuel had had a bad life. On the contrary, with his father's wealth and political influence, Samuel had attended the best schools and was placed in the most politically astute government positions, grooming him for the ultimate position of Sector Chief. So life had been anything but bad. In fact it had been pretty good.

And yet, he still ached. He was still haunted by the lingering effects of his parent's divorce. It left an emptiness inside that he just couldn't fill. And with both parents now deceased, the likelihood of capping that void was impossible. His only living immediate relative was John, and Samuel knew how impossible that situation was: a renegade, a convicted felon wanted by every law enforcement agency in the world, not to mention HEdge Forces.

The only reason John had not yet been caught was because Samuel didn't want him captured. And with Samuel's access to the world data bank network, and his influence as Sector Chief, it was something he could prevent.

Samuel had destroyed every record of John's existence. No genetic, written, or pictorial record remained anywhere. He had even altered his family's records to show John dying in an auto accident as a child. His complete history had been wiped out. He was no longer a living person at all.

Samuel considered the many times he could have turned John in. Even with his alias name "John Rex" taken from the old weeping willow in their back yard, it would have been easy to track him down. Easy.

But he couldn't. John was still his brother. Maybe a little off balance, a little confused, but he was still his younger brother. And he still loved him. At least he thought he did. That's why he deleted all of his records, giving him a chance to remain free for as long as possible.

But for what? Maybe John really was a madman after all, a lunatic bent on killing him out of jealousy for his success. Maybe John really did hate him. Was it possible?

Samuel didn't want to consider the possibilities any longer. It didn't matter; the world has gotten so crazy, nothing made any sense.

He continued staring blank faced at the Bible, as if in a trance, while his emotions gradually slipped into a somber depression. He was despondent over the affairs of his personal life, and tired of the emotional emptiness he's had to endure for so many years.

He couldn't take the pain any longer. In desperation, he practically leaped for the carafe of gin and tonic waiting for him on the bookshelf. Grabbing the container, he tipped it forward, splashing the fluids carelessly into his glass, flinging drops to the carpet.

After chugging the contents down, he lapsed into a mild state of euphoria as the poisonous fluids took hold of him once again. A chill went through him. His breathing steadied. He felt better. Everything was going to be okay.

Samuel's bout with alcoholism had finally reached its pinnacle. The time for quaint social drinking was long past. The facade was now over. Even under the drug's spell Samuel recognized what he had become, and simultaneously realized he was powerless to do anything about it.

But that was all right. It was easier this way; so much easier. Why fight it? Why struggle? When you can wallow in its ecstasy? Just give in.

And that's what he did.

Somewhere deep inside, a final cry for help flickered out, smothered by the encroaching darkness that had been preying on him for so many years. The battle was now over.

With a sharp clang, Samuel plopped the empty glass back on the bookshelf. He trudged over to where the Bible rested on the mattress. In an intoxicated fit of rage, he swung his fist out and smacked it with all his might. The Bible flew into the wall and toppled to the floor landing upside down with several pages folded under.

"I hate this!" he cried in torment. "My life is a sham! I have no one!" His voice grew louder as he directed his venom toward the Bible. "Your words mean nothing to me! Nothing!"

After a moment, Samuel pulled himself together. He tucked his shirt back in, swung his coat over his shoulder, and swaggered a path to the door.

"I've got to get to the conference," he slurred pretentiously, "My people need me there."

Then proceeded haphazardly out of his room, eventually making it to the street below where his limousine waited.

The opening session of the World Finance Conference had already begun, and the HEdge Supreme Accountants were making their presentations. Samuel would be arriving late, but that was okay. He would still find the conference interesting, very interesting indeed.

Chapter

42

Herb Duncan sat on the edge of his bed, his eyes closed in prayer. John sat on a metal stool mounted in the floor across the room, also in quiet prayer. The two were preparing for another lesson in scripture.

Shortly, John whispered an ending to his prayer, but Herb continued in his own right, praying to God, asking Him for knowledge and understanding.

John felt a lump in his throat as he watched Herb, a young Christian and new Believer, praying so devoutly. He thought of Jesus' urging to never forget your first love. Sometimes you have to go back to your beginnings to fully appreciate the gift God has delivered to your door.

John heard a noise, a gate opening somewhere. He looked through the shadows of the cell bars. Nothing, he couldn't see a thing. It was late, the sun was down and the lights were dim. Most prisoners were asleep.

He ignored it.

Herb finished praying. He opened his eyes and looked over to John.

"So what's today's lesson?"

"Can't get enough, can you?" John chuckled. "That's what I like about you, Herb. You're the quintessential student - eager, energetic and demanding," he finished, "and a pain." They both chuckled. "But seriously," John added, "you're a blessing, and it's a pleasure to teach you."

"Pleasure's all mine. This is good stuff. So let's start."

Pointing both index fingers to the sky, John added, "Give me the words, Lord. And give him the patience. Amen."

"Amen." Herb chuckled.

Suddenly, they heard several footsteps coming down the hall. Herb stepped to the cell door, curious. John followed. They saw six HEdge soldiers in full military garb, about sixty yards away, marching toward their cell. Their pace was steady and swift.

John glanced over to Herb. He knew the soldiers were coming for him. So did Herb. John felt a sudden tension arousing in his spirit. The roller coaster ride was about to start up again. He took a deep breath.

Herb looked over to him, concern on his face.

"John, they're coming for you."

"I know."

"What do you think they want?"

"Doesn't matter. They won't get it."

John turned away from the cell bars as the soldiers came nearer. He walked to the rear of the small room, his mind in deep thought.

Herb began to feel desperate. He didn't want to lose John now. Not after everything they've been through. Besides, he needed John. He still had so much more to learn.

John spoke. "Herb, I don't know where they're going to take me, or if I'll be coming back, but whether I do or not, don't stop praying, and don't stop believing.

"You've seen God's miracle working in your life. You've felt His awesomeness and His love. Don't ever forget it, Herb. Don't ever let it slip away."

The soldiers were at their cell, unlocking the door.

Herb was almost in tears, as he looked John square in the eyes.

"Thank you, brother," he stammered. "Thank you so much."

John returned the expression. He felt a sorrow too. They both suspected they might never see each other again.

He placed his hands on Herb's shoulders. "Thank you. May God bless you and keep you growing in your faith."

A tear fell from Herb's eyes as he fondly wished his cellmate, "Good-bye."

John ended the conversation as the soldiers entered the cell.

"It's never good-bye, Herb. If nothing else, we'll see each other on the other side."

Tears streamed down Herb's cheeks. He smiled. The thought was comforting, and powerful. Yes, if nothing else, we'll see each other in Heaven. Thank You, Lord.

"Rex!" the first soldier barked. "You're coming with us," as he yanked John carelessly by his injured arm.

"Turn around!" he ordered as he slammed him against the wall. A second soldier latched a nylon cuff around John's wrists and pulled it tight. John cringed at the pain. His arm was pulled back too far. It hurt badly.

A third soldier hollered over to Herb.

"Duncan?"

Herb nodded.

"You're a free man. Get outta here!" the soldier ordered.

No explanation, no reason given, no nothing. Just go.

John strained, looking around to his friend as the cuffs were being tightened.

Their eyes met. John gave him a warm smile. This was the way it was meant to be, and they both knew it. Herb smiled back. A love passed between the two men, accompanied with a deep respect and admiration.

Herb's lips formed the word, "Thanks."

John closed his eyes softly as he mouthed the words, "God be with you."

Then he was off. The soldiers yanked him abruptly out of the cell and shoved him down the corridor, cursing him every step of the way.

Herb just stood there in the cell with the door open. His emotions were in a daze of melancholy and confusion. He was happy to have his freedom back, but that wasn't the point. In truth, he had received his freedom while he was still locked up; a freedom that only God could give. And now, he could walk out and share that freedom.

He felt pained for John. It hurt to watch the soldiers push him down the hall the way they did; and all this because John was teaching the Truth, sharing the gospel of Jesus Christ. Telling people what they needed and hungered to hear.

The revelation sank in . . . for the first time! He now knew that this was Satan's work against God's people!

Herb felt a jolt of anger rush through him; but not a worldly anger, a righteous anger. It was anger from watching a man of God abused at the hands of ungodly, lost men, blinded by the enemy.

This is wrong! And he knew it. It was so clear to him, so obvious. Why didn't he see it before? How could it have been so illusive?

With a stern countenance, he stepped from the cell into the hallway.

John was already gone with his captors. No one stayed around to see him to the door. *How ironic*, he thought. For days, he'd been locked up. Now all of a sudden, he's alone and free. Not a guard in sight.

Stepping down the corridor, he prayed, asking God to protect John and his family, to watch over them and keep them safe. He prayed that somehow God would get John's family together again, and free them.

Then he prayed for prisoners as he walked past their cells. He prayed that God would find a way to reach all of them as well. Then it dawned on Herb just how fortunate he was. Of all the cells in this prison, God brought John to him, to teach him, and to lead him to salvation. He was humbled; God even cared for someone like him.

With his newly found grace, he asked, "Please, Lord, reach the other prisoners too. Please, somehow, reach them too."

Walking through the exit on his way out, he whispered under his breath, "Amen."

Chapter

43

The elevator came to a steady halt as it reached the twentieth floor.

"This is our stop," a soldier announced as he nudged John out the door.

"Over this way," another ordered as he jerked him by the cuffs, almost knocking him over.

The soldiers formed a wall around him as they marched down the hallway, keeping the same swift pace as when they got him.

A soldier to his left sneered, "Listen punk, you're gonna meet someone real special today, and let me tell ya, patience is not his virtue, so don't push your luck. Keep your mouth shut unless he asks a question. Got that?"

"Why are you telling me this?" John asked.

The soldier shrugged. "Cuz it'll be a lot easier walking you out of there, than carrying you out!"

The other soldiers chuckled. How true.

Rounding a corner, the lead soldier pointed to a metal door at the end of the hall. A bronze plate at the top read, "HRS Video."

"That's where we're going, Rex."

John's curiosity peaked. He wondered what HEdge Reported Stories had to do with this?

The first soldier reached the door, opened it and walked in. John was not so cordially prompted to follow as the rest stepped in behind.

The office was large with a high-arched ceiling making it appear even bigger than it was. A scant inventory of two chairs and a sofa provided their seating—which the group ignored.

A malcontent sergeant, acting as receptionist, occupied a simple desk by the far wall. He cast a condescending glance over the small group before muttering, "Wait here." He got up and left through a back door.

The small entourage stood waiting, staring at the walls or each other. No one volunteered any small talk. In fact, the entire group seemed suddenly predisposed as a strained tension or edginess filled the air. John sensed their apprehension.

Shortly, the dispirited sergeant returned.

Sitting back at the desk, he mumbled, "He'll be here in a minute."

A soldier standing nearest, asked warily, "Is he in the building yet?"

"Yeah, just came in. They told me he's on his way up."

Another soldier prodded, "Did they say what kind of mood he was in?"

"Nah. Don't suppose it'll be any better than usual though."

"You've worked with him before?"

"Only once, and it wasn't much fun, if you know what I mean."

At that, the soldiers became quiet as their imaginations churned. Yes, they knew exactly what the sergeant meant. They've heard enough stories.

Sensing their uneasiness, the sergeant added, "Just stay quiet and keep out of his way, you won't have any problems."

They all nodded in agreement. The advice sounded good, stay out of his way, yeah, no problem there.

John watched their faces as they carried on the conversation. Their nervousness was evident, especially in the eyes. Even the sergeant at the desk seemed uneasy.

Just as they ended their conversation, a rumbling of foot soldiers sounded from the hall, storming towards them.

The sergeant jumped at his desk as he anxiously announced, "Must be him. He never travels alone." He sucked in his gut, threw his shoulders back and slapped his arms to his sides.

The six soldiers also came to attention, clicking their heals and standing erect as they listened to the oncoming rush outside the office, each gaping at the door.

The noise stopped. The handle turned and the door swung open. Everyone in the room, including John, held their breath as the intensity rose to a climax.

Just then, a stream of heavily armed soldiers swept into the room, visually interrogating everyone as they past. In seconds dozens of HEdge soldiers surrounded John and the six men that brought him.

Strangely, John felt pity for the six men. He could see the terror in their eyes, and was amazed by it. He wondered who would bring such fear into the hearts of their own men? But before he could guess at the answer, a soldier shouted, "ATTENTION!"

Then, in all his eloquence, the Chief of Eastern U.S. Sector HEdge Forces, strutted in.

John froze as he saw the pasty, gloom streaked face of Roderick Banchard. Without intention, John's hands folded into tight, white knuckled fists, his jaw muscles rippled beneath his cheeks.

Roderick made his way to the center of the room, his eyes skimming over every starched uniform in the office, until finally locking on the cold steel expression of the one person he had come to meet: John Rex.

Their eyes met. Roderick's face contorted into a wicked, devilish grin. John remained unmoved.

"So there you are," Roderick grinned passionately, his eyes not breaking for even a blink. "How positively exhilarating!"

He took a couple steps forward.

John's glare followed him.

"Mr. Rex," Roderick snarled, "after all the trouble you've put me through, it's hard to believe you're finally mine."

"Dream on, Banchard! What the Lord has claimed, you can hardly take away! And that won't change!"

"My, my, you don't miss a beat, do you? Are you always this direct?"

"Tell me, Banchard, what's your hatred grounded in? Is it fear of the Truth; the truth of Jesus Christ? Only He can set you free, Banchard! He is the way."

Furious, Roderick smashed the back of his hand against John's face, knocking him over a step. "Shut up! I'm not here to listen to your petty sermons! If I wanted preaching, I'd go to the archives!"

The six soldiers around John felt their knees begin to tremble.

Regaining his balance, a dab of blood found its way to the corner of his mouth. Realizing the futility, John calmed himself and spoke as plainly as he could. "Where is my family, Banchard? What have you done with them?"

The smirk returned to Roderick's face. His demeanor shifted. He giggled teasingly, "Your family? Yes, I have them, your wife and son as a matter of fact.

He chuckled, "Isn't it funny, Mr. Rex? Less than two weeks ago I couldn't even prove you existed! And now," he glimpsed boastingly to his soldiers, "I have you, and your loving family in my control!

"Isn't that fascinating?"

The soldiers chuckled nervously.

"It's hilarious!" he giggled. "And now, YOU are asking ME about your family!" Roderick howled with laughter. "This is too good! Just too, too, good!"

John remained mute as Roderick had his fun.

Finally, Roderick eased off the laughter.

"Mr. Rex, why do you suppose you have been captured? Has your Lord forgotten about you and your family? Is that the problem?"

"My God will never leave me nor forsake me. He's here Banchard! Right here with me!"

Roderick chuckled. "Ah yes, scripture. Quote it at will, can you? How nice. So tell me, Mr. Rex. Will you follow your god to the grave? Even to your death? Is it really worth all that?"

"Banchard, death lost its sting once I accepted Jesus Christ into my life. So tell me, where will you spend eternity? Have you given it much thought? Have you ever considered what eternal damnation will be like? Do you have any idea at all?"

Infuriated, Roderick bashed his arm fully across the other side of John's face, scowling as John toppled backwards into the arms of the two soldiers standing behind, blood gushing from his mouth.

Roderick fumed, "What must I do to shut you up! HEdge's sake!

He screamed, "Where is he, Rex! Where is your God now when you need him the most!"

John's eyes were on fire.

"Mr. Rex, I don't know. Your god doesn't seem very interested in your plight from what I can see. In fact, if this is the best he can do, I'd suggest you find yourself another god. There are certainly enough to go around."

John just stared. It was no use. He just wanted to see his family. He wanted to see Melody and Matthew.

As if reading his mind, Roderick interjected. "Yes, I see, you want that darling wife and son of yours?" he smirked. "Well, that just may be possible. Yes, I believe we could arrange for that."

Roderick began pacing.

"I've been waiting for this very moment, Mr. Rex."

He stared directly into John's eyes. "You see, I have a plan I've been wanting to put into action, but couldn't until you became available.

"It will give you exactly what you want, AND, give me exactly what I want. Best of all, it's so easy, it only requires a little effort on your part. And if all goes well, you and your family will be sent home, completely free."

He paused for John's reaction.

John was openly skeptical, and his expression showed it.

"You don't believe me, Mr. Rex?"

"What do you want, Banchard?"

Roderick raised his eyebrows. "You'll see." Then motioned for his soldiers to follow as he led the whole group down the hall into a much larger room. Once there, Roderick led them to a small stage at the front. A five-foot HEdge placard hung at the center of the platform, with a wooden lectern sitting a few feet in front of it.

"Come up here, Mr. Rex," Roderick ordered as he stepped behind the lectern.

John climbed the two steps to the platform, and walked over to Roderick.

"Right there," Roderick pointed impatiently.

John stepped behind the lectern.

With a self-indulgent grin stretching from ear to ear, Roderick cast a star-like gaze across the room.

"Mr. Rex, in just three days this room will be filled with excited reporters. And do you know why they will be here?"

"Tell me," John mimed irritably.

"They'll be here to listen to you! As you confess to the world that you no longer believe in your Jesus Christ. And that you're joining HEdge Forces to hunt down and capture all those Christian renegades still on the loose."

Roderick panted excitedly. "Isn't that fabulous? And your speech will be broadcast over the entire globe! As one of the most famous criminals on Earth, everyone wants to hear that you've turned your life around for the better, and finally denounced this ridiculous faith of yours!

"And best of all," he interjected, "the HEdge Council will know that I am the one who made it all possible!"

Gleaming proudly, "Could get me a Sector Chief's position when the next one opens up!"

"You're crazy!" John exclaimed while jerking away from the lectern. "There's no way I'll do it! This is preposterous!"

"Oh no, not preposterous at all, Mr. Rex. Like I said, I have a plan. And believe me, you WILL make your announcement. Let me show you why."

Pointing to the top of the wooden lectern, he explained, "Look at the screen to the right, the TelePrompTer. See it?"

John glanced over. He saw the transparent plate jutting out at an angle on top of the lectern.

"Yes," Roderick coached, then waved to the back of the room where someone was waiting for his signal.

Suddenly sentences began streaming across the TelePrompTer. Beneath the words was a picture of a small room with two odd looking chairs pressed against a wall.

Roderick's panting increased as he continued his explanation.

"You see, Mr. Rex. Your speech is already prepared and waiting. All you need do is read it."

"And if I don't?"

Roderick spun around in a tizzy as he clasped his hands together.

Grinning feverishly, he answered, "Look at the picture on the TelePrompTer, if you would please. You see those two chairs with leather straps? That's where your family will be seated, tucked nicely in place to hear your wonderful speech.

"They'll be able to see and hear everything you do, Mr. Rex. And of course, you'll also be able to see them as you read the text.

"But here's the important part!" Roderick exclaimed gravely. "You must read your speech very carefully, exactly word for word. Because if you don't, if you miss even one word, something quite interesting will happen to that loving family of yours." He pointed to a closed door in the back of the room.

John's eyes opened wide as Roderick got to the point.

"You see; the computer that runs our sound system also controls our security network. By linking the two, we've been able to rig up a nice little program we like to refer to as, the Cause and Affect Module.

"That is to say, if you should mistakenly misread your prepared text by even a word, thousands of volts of electric current will instantly rip through that darling wife and handsome son of yours. They'll both fry right before your eyes."

Giggling wickedly, "Isn't that exciting!" He clapped his hands together jubilantly.

"In the name of Jesus, you won't!!" With his hands cuffed behind his back John bolted for Roderick. Two nearby soldiers intercepted just before he reached him. Knocking him to the ground, they fought as John struggled to get back up.

Roderick continued giggling as he watched them wrestling on the floor.

As the soldiers managed to steady him, John promised, "I won't give your speech! Never!"

"Oh I think you will, Mr. Rex," Roderick chided. "When you see your pretty wife and darling son strapped to those cold metal seats, I do think you'll have a change of heart."

He giggled louder.

Roderick walked over to him and snickered. "Yes, when it comes right down to it, Mr. Rex, I believe you'll denounce your god to save your family."

"No!" John repeated, "I won't do it! I won't!"

"Oh yes you will." Roderick giggled as he stepped down the platform. "Just be prepared to read, Mr. Rex. Nothing more is required of you."

Heading for the doors, Roderick flippantly bid him good-bye with a flick of his wrist. "See you in three days, Mr. Rex. Get some rest will you. We wouldn't want you to miss any lines, would we?"

He giggled as he walked out the door. The soldiers that came with him trailed behind; leaving the original six to escort John back to his now-empty cell, to ponder and to pray.

Chapter

44

The towering HEdge Convention Center located in downtown Geneva, Switzerland, was a monstrous building that stood tall against the backdrop of the majestic peaks of Mount Blanc Massif.

The convention center consisted of dozens of conference halls, the largest of which was reserved for the semi-annual HEdge World Finance Conference.

Today, as usual, the lobbies and passageways were bustling as a marketing jamboree was once again in full swing. Thousands of civilians and HEdge officials were roaming the halls, eager to spend their monthly credit, while merchandisers were marketing their wears in every nook and cranny they could find.

Bright colorful HEdge logos were splattered everywhere. Anything and everything was up for grabs. Food vendors were the most prevalent, while clothing and trinket stands ran a close second.

Outside the building, a sleek, dark-blue limousine edged up to the curb. A spiffy red-coated chauffeur rushed to the limousine's rear door, along with two heavily armed security guards. The guards' eyes darted with mechanical precision as they scanned the streets, prowling for any potential threats to the honorable passenger sitting inside.

Just as the chauffeur cracked the door open, the passenger burst out, knocking him to the ground. The startled chauffeur watched from the curb as the stocky frame of Samuel Treppin stumbled out shouting to anyone within earshot. "Get out of my way! I need to be in there! My Sector needs me; they need me in there. Get out of my way!"

The startled security guards stepped back as Samuel teetered by on a crooked sway toward the building. Taking a whiff, they immediately understood, the rumors were true; he was an alcoholic after all.

With brows raised, they looked at each other as if to ask, "What now? Should we stop him? Take him back to his room?"

But as they considered the issue, Samuel had already reached the main entrance and was swaggering past the electronic doors.

Both men lurched forward, alarmed that the person they were assigned to protect was almost out of their sight. Drunken or not, he was still a Sector Chief, and if anything happened to him, they could kiss their futures good-bye.

Inside the entrance, an arrogant guard asking for identification confronted Treppin. Samuel plodded past, paying him no heed. But the guard wasn't about to be ignored. He reached over, grabbing Samuel by the arm and demanded an identification card.

Just then, Samuel's security guards caught up and slammed their High Security Badges in front of the guard's face.

Looking over to Treppin, he finally recognized the Sector Chief. Totally embarrassed, he released his arm and stepped aside, bowing his apologies.

Straightening proudly, Samuel slurred, "Fine! Don't let it happen again!" as he bobbed past, the incident already forgotten.

Without fail, a group of curiosity-seekers loitering in the area spotted the Sector Chief, and all at once shouted excitedly as they converged on him. Crowds immediately began gathering around.

The lobby was already amassing with confusion; Samuel's presence only compounded it. The senior guard clicked on his transceiver and called for more security. In seconds, scores of guards were teeming around Samuel, forcing a wedge between him and the crowds.

Treppin remained incoherent amidst all the ruckus and noise, ignoring the throngs of people following him. None of them mattered. The only thing important right now was getting inside the World Finance Conference to represent his constituents.

The guards managed to shove the crowds back beyond the security zone as Samuel rounded the final corner of the hall. He walked the last fifty steps with only his two security guards at his side.

Finally at the huge conference doors, four additional guards, armed to the teeth, posted to block any unauthorized entrance into the conference, met him.

Samuel was met with no resistance as the guards graciously stepped aside and unlatched the door to the auditorium. Samuel and his two guards were politely ushered in.

Trying to appear sober, Samuel pulled his shoulders back and strutted through the entrance as if the entire world were watching. The guards followed close behind, just in case he lost his balance.

The auditorium was a vast oblong shaped hall with hundreds of rows of tiered seating, enough for every primary HEdge accountant in the world. A rich marble stage stood at the front, with a large flamboyant lectern positioned at its center.

Samuel headed down the middle isle toward the privileged boxed off section reserved only for Sector Chiefs. The security guards followed half way, then turned and headed back to the doors, confident he could make it the rest of the way on his own.

Trying to deliver a speech from the lectern, a HEdge Supreme Accountant was doing all he could to ignore Samuel's erratic entrance and keep with the text of his speech, but was losing the battle as more and more people became aware of Samuel's entrance.

Heads turned and eyes rolled as Samuel floundered past rows of high minded accountants; his wobbly path leaving no doubt as to his intoxicated condition. As people recognized who was trailing past them, a chorus of shocked sighs followed.

Trying to contain the audience's attention, the HEdge Supreme Accountant over dramatized his speech, waiving his arms in concert with his dialogue, doing all he could to keep them involved; but was slowly losing the battle.

As Samuel finished his swaggering trek down to the Sector Chiefs reserved seating, all the audience's attention was on him.

Two other Sector Chiefs that had managed to attend the conference were carrying on a private conversation when they suddenly noticed Samuel at the end of their row. They stood up graciously and welcomed him while motioning for the Supreme Accountant to pause.

The accountant, visibly upset, finished his sentence then came to an abrupt silence.

"Welcome, Mr. Treppin," the first Sector Chief blared over the sound system, capturing everyone's attention.

The other Sector Chief motioned for all to rise as the presence of a fellow Sector Chief was to be cordially and respectfully recognized. The entire auditorium stood, and on queue, broke into a polite round of applause.

After shaking the hands of both Sector Chiefs, Samuel waved merrily to the audience in appreciation for their warm welcome.

In the process of waving his arms about, the alcohol got the better of him as he lost his balance and toppled over, falling right into the bosoms of the other two Sector Chiefs. Caught completely off guard, the two Sector Chiefs, with shocked faces and all, quite unsophisticatedly tumbled down with him. In a second, all three were rolling on the floor like three happy pigs splashing in the mud, the two struggling to get out from under the wider and heavier frame of Samuel Treppin, arms and legs swinging.

Pockets of embarrassed giggles spread through the auditorium, as eyes remained glued on the acrobatics in the Sector Chief's seating area.

Trying to save face, some leading HEdge officials ran over to help untangle the mess.

Finally, the two Sector Chiefs were back on their feet brushing themselves off. They glared over to Samuel, who by now had already seated himself and was comfortably waiting for the speaker to continue. Their eyes burned after him.

Grumbling under their breath, they found their seats and motioned for the speaker to continue, giving one last heated glance over to Samuel.

The HEdge Supreme Accountant rattled his notes against the lectern for effect, retrieving everyone's attention. Then he cleared his throat, and resumed the speech where he left off.

"As I stated earlier, besides the problem with counterfeit HEdge Citizen ID Cards, other matters are becoming increasingly alarming as well. Of particular concern is the recent flush of criminal activities by religious zealots that have been scourging our society. The latest of which was the failed assassination attempt at the New York State Auditorium against one of our finest and most illustrious Sector Chiefs, Mr. Treppin himself."

Again, on queue, the audience erupted into a chorus of cheers and applause as everyone stood in honor of Samuel Treppin.

He remained seated as he swung his arms through the air, thanking them for their kindness.

After another few seconds, the cheering died down and everyone returned to their seats. Samuel smiled warmly over to the other two Sector Chiefs, but was quickly rebuffed as they glared back.

Undisturbed, Samuel released a crude burp, and then turned to the front where the speaker was starting up again.

"These activities are an unnecessary drain on our financial resources, not to mention the dark clouds of stress and danger our world leaders are forced to live under.

"We feel this Christian movement must be stopped at all costs before any further casualties are inflicted on our great society."

The audience applauded spontaneously.

Suddenly above the stage, a red warning light began flashing.

Noticing it, the speaker announced, "Ladies and gentlemen, we are about to be blessed. It appears the HEdge Council will be honoring us with their presence."

He stepped over to the right of the lectern and turned to face the back of the stage. Finishing his dialogue with the audience, he politely asked, "I beg your pardon."

He then knelt and bowed his head in a gesture of submission.

A collective gasp emanated from the audience as everyone became suddenly nervous and excited at the same time. This was an unusual, yet thrilling surprise. The HEdge Council rarely does impromptu visits to the convention center, but when they do, it's always news breaking.

Everyone bowed their heads, including the Sector Chiefs, as a bright light consumed the stage.

Chapter

45

Radiant pulses of refracted light streamed through the auditorium with bright incandescent beams showering directly over the stage. The intense light forced the audience to squint, as they remained submitted in their seats. A steady rumbling accompanied the fierce lights, sending waves of vibrations through the floors and walls of the large chamber.

As quickly as it came, the lights and sounds vanished, leaving the auditorium as it was, quiet and still, but with one major difference: Planted center stage, immediately behind the lectern, were ten, massive, gold trimmed and jewel embedded thrones. Seated in them were the ten aged members of the HEdge Council, each clothed in royal apparel, staring proud and lordly over their restive and tense audience.

Lavish silk robes flowed from the ten elderly statesmen. Brilliant shades of red, violet, and gold, embellished their regal attire while outlandish jewelry adorned their fingers and wrists.

Anyone that didn't know better would be hard pressed to believe the holographic images on stage were not authentic; their texture and clarity were rife with detail, right down to the color of their eyes.

After a brief, heavy silence, the first of the kingly apparitions spoke.

"Welcome."

His single word roared through the auditorium, amplified several decibels above normal volume range. The other nine Council members sat quietly in their thrones, browsing discreetly over the nervous audience.

Waiting to be recognized, the still genuflecting accountant remained beside the lectern, bowed face to the floor.

"Rise, young man," a Council member ordered.

Without hesitation, the accountant stood, slapped his hands to his sides and gazed upon his rulers, the peremptory authority on Earth; or, as the HEdge Council came to consider themselves, gods of the world.

The Council member nearest the accountant became suddenly distracted. In disgust, he gasped while directing the attention of the other Council members to the accountant's uniform.

"Do you see that? Do you see it!" he screeched as his eyes laid into the increasingly distraught HEdge Supreme Accountant.

The other Council members looked on in dismay, baffled by their comrade's behavior.

"Do you see it?" the Council member repeated emphatically. "Look, right there! On his coat!" He pointed his diamond-garnished index finger toward the accountant, who by now was feeling faint.

The others strained unsuccessfully to see exactly what he was balking at. Finally, another Council member interrupted. "Come, come, Felix. Leave the poor heathen alone. He's only a human, after all."

At that, the upset Council member climbed down from his throne, and with some effort, carried his fragile, timeworn body feebly across the stage to where the accountant stood. Once there, he irately jabbed his finger into the panicky accountant's chest, and, since the Council member was only a holographic image, through his chest.

"There! Now, do you see it?"

The others squinted as they struggled to find the cause of their friend's concern. Then slowly, one by one, they spotted the aberration: a single strand of fallen hair that had clung haphazardly to the accountant's shirt.

"Yes . . . yes, I see," the first agreed.

"Mmmm. What do you make of it?" another pondered.

The flustered Council member admonished, "This is why we must keep ourselves apart. This is the reason I demanded we holograph into this place! Who knows what germs these barbarians may be carrying with them!"

That was it. The exasperated accountant's knees buckled under the weight of the high level criticism, as his collapsing body withered unconsciously to the floor into one clumsy heap.

The Council member simply chuckled as he watched the accountant drop.

"Positively captivating!" he exclaimed as he turned and started back to his throne. "Absolutely amazing."

The audience was mute. Not a cough or groan could be heard.

One of the Council members openly objected to his brethren's unnecessary flurry of emotion.

"Felix! Do you see what you've done? The poor lad has fainted!"

He added rebuking, "The next time you feel led to throw a tantrum, please have the courtesy to refrain for a more suitable moment; namely, when I'm not present! I could have been soaking in my hot oil bath!"

Climbing back onto his throne, the now amused Council member jested, "How was I to know the silly boy was going to pass out! My, what a soft minded imbecile." Chuckling, he finished, "Too easy! Where do they find these subjects anyway?"

A few of the Council members joined with tepid laughter, finding a strain of humor in the situation.

"Please have him removed," a Council member ordered.

Two guards bolted onto the stage to lug the comatose accountant off.

With that taken care of, one of the Council members finally got back to greeting the audience.

"Welcome. We are delighted to be here," he paused expectantly.

Without further prompting, the entire audience, along with the three Sector Chiefs, were on their feet applauding the ten members of the HEdge Council.

"Thank you . . . thank you," the Council members cordially acknowledged with half-hearted waves and royal nods.

After a few moments, a Council member raised his hands to quell the audience. Obeying, everyone in the auditorium immediately found their seats.

After a moment, another Council member spoke up. "We are here to make a very special announcement . . . and to honor a very special person."

The Council member then gazed straight down to the Sector Chiefs' seating area, offering an enthusiastic smile. With a slight wave of his hand, the Council member motioned for one of the Sector Chiefs to rise.

Ready to take the glory, the two Sector Chiefs sprang from their seats. But the Council member uttered, "Yes, Mr. Treppin. This is for you."

Embarrassed, the two quickly dropped back down, casting a frozen smile toward Samuel.

Slowly, Samuel rose, teetering slightly, a confused expression covering his face.

"May I have the lights dimmed, please?" the Council member requested.

The lights went down.

"Mr. Treppin, on behalf of the entire HEdge Council, I wish to congratulate you for your Sector's recent capture of one of the world's most troublesome, and, to be sure, most notorious state criminals."

A giant photograph of John Rex suddenly flashed above the stage in full dazzling color.

Samuel stumbled back a step in shock, his eyes riveted on the blown up picture of his brother.

In the photo, John's lips were swollen as a tired, yet determined stare shone from his eyes.

The Council member pointed upwards to the larger-than-life picture, and then boomed out, "This, ladies and gentlemen, is Mr. John Rex!"

A collective gasp escaped the assemblage as they gaped at the photograph of the captured evangelist. A stunned silence filled the room. Shortly, everyone burst into a wild, euphoric applause, once again directed towards Samuel Treppin.

Not to appear unmoved by the thrilling news, the two Sector Chiefs grudgingly clapped along.

The HEdge Council members joined in, all ten of them grinning proudly over to Samuel, then to each other.

Finally, one of the Council members stood at his throne and began speaking. The audience immediately silenced.

"The Chief of Eastern U.S. Sector HEdge Forces, Mr. Roderick Banchard, notified us yesterday of Mr. Rex's capture. And I'm pleased to say, we now have the entire Rex family in captivity; his wife, son, and now, him."

Another applause erupted from the audience, charged with even more emotion.

After a couple minutes, as the applause began dwindling, the Council member added gleefully, "Roderick Banchard also stated that Mr. Rex will be making a formal announcement tomorrow on HRS Global Network news, in which he will be denouncing his primitive faith!"

Samuel just stood, dazed, taking it all in, knowing what no one else knew, and tormenting inside because of it. He wondered how this could have ever happened. Anxiety was overtaking him. Oddly, the room felt as though it were starting to spin. He felt his pulse rising; his blood seemed to be exploding through his veins and arteries.

The Council member concluded with a bonus, "And I understand Mr. Rex has even offered to help HEdge Forces track down other renegade zealots and bring them to justice."

At that, the audience was swept into a frenzy.

In the midst of all the hoopla, Samuel's intoxicated mind was screaming out for understanding, fighting for a mental grasp of all that was happening. But time was racing by much too quickly. Events were climaxing at a break neck speed, and his confused, disordered mind, simply could not keep up.

At the edge of a mental breakdown, Samuel finally collapsed, fainting unconscious to the floor. Aside from a few paramedics who rushed over to resuscitate him, no one even noticed.

Chapter

46

No sooner had the HEdge Council finished sharing their news of John Rex, than they bid the audience farewell and flashed their holographic images back from whence they came.

The paramedics had Samuel revived in no time, after which, he immediately excused himself from the conference, much to the pleasure of the other two Sector Chiefs.

Resuming their escort duties, the two security guards met Samuel at the auditorium's door to lead him through to his limousine outside. Walking at a faster clip than earlier, Samuel made it a bit trickier for the guards to keep pace. Although casting off curiosity seekers was easier since people hardly had a chance to recognize him much less talk with him. Not that he would have stopped anyway; his concentration was on one thing and one thing only: his brother, John, and his family.

He strangely felt a maternal instinct rising up inside, as if John's family were actually part of his own. But then, he realized, they were! How odd.

Finally in the limousine, John ordered the driver to take him back to his hotel suite. Watching from the curb, his security detail was happy to be done with him.

Back in his hotel room, he was rummaging through the liquor closet, reaching for a fresh bottle of gin to mix with his tonic. Grabbing the now filled glass, he walked over to his computer and sat down. He needed information . . . he needed to know what's been happening since he left New York!

Finishing the first gulp, Samuel laid the glass down, and then prompted the computer to life.

"Yes, may I help you, Samuel?" the pleasant voice spoke.

"Do I have any messages?" he blurted.

"Yes, you have fifteen."

"Do I have any from Roderick Banchard?"

"Yes, you have two from Mr. Banchard."

"Subjects?"

"The first is a training fund request for his troops. He wishes to send five platoons to the HEdge Training camp in Babylon, Iraq. The second concerns the New York State Auditorium fire."

"You're sure that's it? There's nothing about John Rex?"

"There are only two messages from Mr. Banchard, sir. Neither discusses Mr. Rex."

Samuel took a second guzzle as he contemplated, *Why didn't Banchard send a report on John's capture?*

The computer spoke up. "There is a message from Mr. Gregory White concerning John Rex, sir. Would you like to see that?"

"Yes. I would."

"Thank you."

The computer displayed the message from Gregory White:

```
Mr. Treppin, We've captured John Rex.
Banchard caught him the day after you left.
He set a trap, using Rex's wife and son as
bait. A minimum number of troops were used
in the operation, with only two casualties.
A certain Captain Karen Riggins got caught
in some cross fire. The Captain's family
```

has already been notified. Aside from her, there was one other soldier killed, which appears to have been self inflicted.

Please call me as soon as possible. We have more information on Rex's son that might interest you. Thank you, sir.

Samuel thought to himself, *What's that about John's son? When did he get caught anyway? And John's wife! So much has happened in such a short time!*

He considered calling Gregory White, but decided against it for now.

"What were the two messages from Banchard, again?" he queried the computer.

"The first concerned training funds for HEdge Forces. The second concerned the New York State Auditorium fire."

Debating which to view first, he finally decided, "Let me see the message on the auditorium fire."

"Thank you," the computer obliged.

Then with no advance warning or preparation, the gruesome recording of the New York State Auditorium massacre, replete with graphic details and screaming sound effects, played out.

No filters or edits removed the unpalatable segments; there were no HEdge disclaimers, and worst of all, there were no credits to indicate this was a fictional motion picture with superb special effects.

No, this was real!

Instead, there were only gory, gut-wrenching scenes of HEdge Force soldiers painstakingly gunning down hundreds upon hundreds of innocent civilians, mutilating them with firepower, ruthless, wicked, and deadly firepower.

Shock and horror were the emotions ripping through Samuel's conscience. The cruel inhumanity thrust upon his citizens, senselessly, without cause or need, left him frozen in his seat. But the shock quickly deteriorated into depression as he realized these were his troops committing these barbaric acts. His troops!

The video left no doubt as to who was responsible for the auditorium's demise; and Christians certainly had nothing to do with it!

Banchard knew all along!

Half way through the gruesome recording, Samuel grabbed the opened flask of gin and shoved it to his lips. He didn't need tonic water or a glass, just the bottle, that's all.

He guzzled, and then guzzled some more.

At the video's conclusion, the computer asked, "Mr. Treppin, would you care to see the remaining messages, sir?"

But Samuel was well beyond coherence. He was passed out, again, in his chair, with the empty bottle resting peacefully in his lap. The computer repeated the question twice, and then automatically shut off. The remaining messages would wait till morning.

Chapter

47

The HRS news broadcast blared from the monitor in the Webster household's living room as Keeyon and his family sat cuddled together watching.

The anchorwoman seemed to enjoy herself as she blithely made her report. "Tomorrow at noon, eastern standard time, the world-renowned Christian renegade, dubiously known as Mr. John Rex, will make his first public statement since being captured at the hands of Eastern Sector HEdge Forces."

Staring directly into the camera, she continued, "Anonymous reports from HEdge Headquarters in Manhattan have indicated he may be giving a formal denunciation of his faith at that time. Other reports have even alluded to him offering assistance in tracking down Christian renegades still on the loose.

"More details will be provided as they come in."

Shifting subjects, the anchorwoman took on a more somber expression.

"As reported in yesterday's broadcast, there were only two HEdge casualties resulting from Mr. Rex's apprehension; one of which was Captain Karen Riggins. A funeral service was held for the heroic Captain at the Hine's Point Cemetery this morning. Her family was at the service, along with several high-ranking HEdge officials who offered their comfort during this sad time.

"Mr. Roderick Banchard, Chief of Eastern U.S. Sector HEdge Forces, offered a folded HEdge flag to the Captain's bereaved parents, extending his condolences for the ultimate sacrifice their daughter had given for freedom."

"Elsewhere in the news, a positive surge in the international commodities markets has been seen as a direct link to the crack down on the Christian underground in the Eastern U.S. Sector. The volatile trading is expected to carry well into the coming weeks . . ."

Keeyon ordered the monitor "off," then turned to his two impatient young boys sitting beside him. The five and six year olds smiled up to their dad, ready to play.

"Not yet," he motioned.

Then gazed into the gentle brown eyes of his pretty wife, Brandy, as she laid her sweet, bronze-skinned face on his shoulder.

Hugging her, he appreciated her warmth and love more than ever. He was hurting inside; suffering from the loss of his dear friend, Andrew. Adding to that, the capture of John and his family and the death of Karen Riggins and all his other Christian brothers and sisters. He couldn't believe things had gone so sour, and yet they had. For whatever reason, everything had just fallen apart.

Over the last couple days, he's struggled to understand how such a disaster could have occurred. But was only left with feeling the need to pray even more.

For once, he wished the war could pass him by. If only he could conveniently step aside and let it rage on without him. He wanted it to be so. To just languish away with his family, living a quiet, desolate life, praying in seclusion, letting others take up the fight while he enjoyed the solitude. He's done his part, after all. Can't someone else take up the scepter of battle for a while?

If only it were possible.

But it wasn't, and he knew it. Keeyon knew his calling in life. He's always known. His was to march the path that John, Andrew, and Karen had marched. The path of a righteous warrior, a soldier for Christ, standing up when the world wanted you to sit down, when the world demanded that you sit down! But, as Keeyon well knew, greater is He who is within you, than he who is in the world! It was wisdom to live by.

So, if that's where the Lord wants him, that's where he will stay.

But it wasn't going to be easy.

Looking into his wife's beautiful brown eyes, he felt a tear slip from the corner of his own. Brandy reached up and wiped it away, then kissed him.

His two boys giggled as mom and dad got mushy.

"I have to go, babe," he whispered.

Pressing closer, she sighed, "I know, sweetheart, I know."

Tears began to stream down her smooth cheeks. He pulled her closer, and gave her a tender kiss.

Seeing the tears on their mom's face, the two boys cuddled closer, trying in their own special way to comfort her.

Smiling lovingly, she gave each a peck on their cheeks.

They kissed her back with a giggle.

Looking over to her husband, she asked softly, "How will you stop them from making John tell that lie?"

A stern expression covered his face. "John will never turn from God. He'll never denounce Jesus as his Lord. Of that, I'm sure. What troubles me is how far they'll go to try and get him to do it. They have Melody and Matthew. I don't want to think of the threats they must be making if John doesn't say what they want."

Brandy shivered in her husband's arms as she imagined the scenario.

"We have to get John out of there, and his family. And we have to do it before noon tomorrow. That's the trick." He clenched his fists.

"But how, sweetheart?" Brandy looked into his eyes, concern on her face. "I don't want you to get caught too."

Keeyon chuckled. "I was sort of thinking the same thing, sugar."

The two boys giggled. "Dad won't get caught, Mom. He's too fast."

Then the boys leaped onto their dad's stomach, giggling and tickling him.

Laughing along, Keeyon wrapped his strong arms around them and happily announced, "That's my little men!"

He whooped as he squeezed the two bundles of joy. "I wouldn't do anything to miss out on you two growing up!" Then tickled under their arms as they both shook and delighted in their dad's love.

Watching them play together warmed Brandy's heart. She smiled contentedly, thanking God for blessing her with a loving family.

Keeyon caught her expression. Delighting in it, he bent over and kissed her again. The two boys giggled some more as they both pronounced, "Yuk!"

Keeyon gave his sons another hug, then instructed, "Come on, guys." Speaking firmly, yet playfully. "Dad has to talk with mom a little bit, okay? So go play in the other room for now."

They were off and running, chasing competitively to see who would be first to play with their favorite toy.

Keeyon and Brandy watched the two boys trot off. Once out of sight, Keeyon returned his attention to his woman, and, while caressing her shoulder, leaned over and laid a passionate kiss over her lips.

"I love you."

"I love you too."

They kissed again. This time, holding it for a couple minutes, enjoying each other's pleasure as long as they could, not knowing exactly when time would permit it again.

Ending the romantic interlude, a chiming sounded from their videophone.

"That time already?" Keeyon asked disappointedly as he reached to press the connect button.

Brandy caught her breath as her husband's attention was diverted, knowing what the call must mean.

A man's face suddenly appeared on the screen, timid at first, realizing he had interrupted a special moment between the two lovers.

"Oh, huh, hi, Keeyon. Hi, Brandy."

Both offered a mediocre greeting, "Hi, Tom."

"Sorry bout intruding."

Chuckling, Keeyon let him off the hook. "No problem. Are folks starting to show up?"

"Yep. And we posted the blueprints on the chapel's announcement boards so everyone could get familiar with the plan."

"Good." Keeyon glanced at his watch. "Make sure everyone's set to go at 6:00. I'll be there in about an hour."

"Sounds good, Keeyon."

Trying to be encouraging, Tom continued, "We'll have your husband back in no time, Brandy. Don't you worry."

Smiling appreciatively, she offered softly, "Thanks. I know you'll take care of each other."

"Oh yeah. You betcha, sister. See you later."

Keeyon ended the discussion, "See you, Tom. Thanks for the call."

"No problem."

The screen went dead.

Gazing over to her husband, dreading the moment that had finally arrived, Brandy asked, "Are you sure it'll work, honey?" Her countenance was struggling; yet trusting.

He looked soothingly into her eyes, realizing the stress she was under.

"Yes, dear, everything will be fine. We know John's brother will return to New York. With the conferences finished in Geneva he should be back anytime today. And when he does, we'll be there waiting for him. It rests on him."

"Samuel Treppin?" she asked, surprised.

"He's the one," Keeyon assured. "Samuel is the key. We need to get to him before he enters the building. Then we'll try . . ."

"Honey," she interrupted, her voice more distressed. "Samuel Treppin is a godless drunk. He hasn't talked to John in years. How can you put your trust in him! What if he doesn't show up?"

Hearing the hopelessness, Keeyon touched her lips with his index finger.

"Hold up, babe. I'm not trusting in Samuel Treppin. Not for a second."

With confidence in his eyes, "I'm trusting in the Lord, and only in the Lord. I believe this will all work out."

Hardly feeling comforted, Brandy laid her head on his shoulder, surrendering. Another tear fell from her eyes.

"I know, Keeyon, I know, but I just don't want to lose you."

He was silent, not sure what to say.

"Do you have to go?" she pleaded.

He gave a slight nod. There was no other way.

"What if you can't get them out? What then?"

Caressing her smooth shoulder, Keeyon finally said, "Just pray, sugar. Just pray."

At a loss, Brandy snuggled back into his arms, smothering in his warmth.

Then, quietly, she began to pray.

"Wait, honey," Keeyon asked lovingly. "Let's go to the Lord together, as one."

A tear escaped as she reached for his solid hands.

Then, holding each other, they approached the throne of God in prayer, two combined as one, coming into agreement, asking for God's power to manifest in the perilous hours ahead.

Chapter

48

Twenty minutes after closing his eyes, a cramp in Samuel's neck stirred him awake. Still reeling from the booze, his pink blood-shot eyes opened as the horrific scenes of the auditorium massacre snapped fresh to his mind. Staring ahead at the blank computer screen, he angrily choked, "Banchard's responsible; he knew all along!"

Gradually, sluggishly, he pushed his drunken body up off the chair and away from the desk, his head throbbing with every move. The empty gin bottle rolled off his lap and clanked to the floor. Paying it no mind, he trudged forward, his lethargic body looming closer to the bedroom.

Finally at the foot of his bed, he teetered. The glaring photograph of his brother stormed into his mind, hovering above the conference stage like a captured trophy. Cutting straight to his heart, Samuel's emotions exploded. Despaired and depressed, he was overwhelmed. The throbbing grew even harder against his skull; the room started spinning.

"That's my brother!" he cried aloud, "My brother!" The hammering in his head became unbearable.

On the verge of collapse, his vision began to fade; only his bones kept him aloft. Ending the tumultuous day, he mouthed a single, longing word.

"John . . ."

Then in one blurry motion, his stress-ridden body crumpled to the mattress, out cold.

In his ever sinking consciousness, far removed from his throbbing head and racing pulse, Samuel's mind began drifting, straddling between the rigid confines of the physical realm, and the borderless timeless dimensions of a sleepy dream state.

With an opaque horizon, he was suddenly surrounded by obscure, cloudy images. Nothing was of solid form or substance, there were no points of reference, nowhere could recognizable shapes or colors be found, only a constant blur, a persistent gnawing of nothingness.

Samuel floated freely and dreamily as he cautiously enjoyed his reprieve from the stresses of the world, absent HEdge's blatant corruptness, and free from his dogged fixation with alcohol.

In the midst, he asked, *Where am I?* But no answer came.

The sense of flight and freedom continued, wherever, whenever, it didn't matter. He was free. His sector was gone; HEdge was gone, only peace and serenity remained. And he savored it.

Suddenly, out of the hazy backdrop of the horizon, came a man, gentle and confident, moving towards him. Walking wouldn't be the descriptive word since there was no ground for his feet to travel.

As the person got nearer, Samuel thought he recognized him. With the surrounding murkiness abating, the man finally came into clear view.

You! Samuel tried to shout, but no words came. Surprised, he found himself mute, unable to speak, yet his mind was actively engaged.

It's you! It's you! He was thrilled. It was the man on the elevator, with the same warm smile. Samuel wanted to run to greet him, but found himself strangely unable to move.

"Hi, Samuel," the stranger welcomed.

"How . . . what . . . Who?" Samuel asked, surprised to find his speech again.

"A messenger. Remember?"

"Yes! Of course, I remember! Where did you go? I had questions. So many questions."

"And many answers are to come, Samuel," the stranger interjected. "You'll have to see. You'll have to hear. The answers will come."

Turning away, he motioned for Samuel to follow.

Without hesitation, Samuel obeyed, surprised to find himself mobile again.

"Where are we?" he asked.

The stranger offered a friendly, congenial smile, but provided no answer. It would have to wait.

Following behind, Samuel suddenly found himself on solid ground, the sky above was clear and blue, a brown dirt path was beneath his feet with grassy hills and leafy trees scattered about.

Samuel harkened to his friend, wanting more information.

Without answering, the stranger's eyes took on a tearful, joyous gaze as he directed Samuel's attention forward.

Looking ahead, Samuel saw several men dressed in shepherd's apparel conversing with one another as they walked together along the dirt trail. He glanced to his friend again, seeking an explanation of who these people were. But his friend only continued his sanguine gaze.

Suddenly, the group stopped as the man in the lead walked over to a small tree, a fig tree, Samuel recognized, and reached out, then paused. Seeing there were no fruit on it, the man spoke something, then turned and rejoined his comrades.

Curiously watching the man, Samuel realized there was something special about him, something unique. His mere presence seemed to beckon at him, and yet, he had no idea who the man was.

Samuel's attention was diverted as the group of men began murmuring amongst themselves, all of them staring over to the fig tree, pointing in disbelief. To Samuel's amazement, the tree was writhing away, its branches drying up and cracking under! Samuel watched in horror as the tree decomposed right before his eyes, shriveling back to the ground, a mere twig, decayed and worthless.

Still confounded, the men suddenly noticed their leader had continued up the hill without them. Hurriedly, they ended their discussion and rushed up to him, like lost sheep finding their shepherd.

Likewise, Samuel started after them while glancing back in wonder toward the wilted tree.

Suddenly, everything vanished; the men and the tree. Samuel looked around, startled. Once again, he found himself in a seemingly empty void, no definition, no substance, floating about dreamily. Only his friend, the messenger, remained, keeping his gentle spirited smile.

"Samuel, remember . . ." The stranger spoke in an instructive tone, referring to the vision he had just witnessed.

Just then, before he could appeal for understanding, Samuel once again found himself transplanted to a spot of solid ground with blue skies above. He was standing a short distance from a large stone building, with crowds bustling past in every direction.

A drove of angry men, sneering and scoffing, rushed over to the stone building, tugging a woman behind them. Samuel watched as they practically dragged her to another group of men congregating outside the building. Samuel recognized the person in the center of the crowd. It was the same man who had approached the fig tree!

The woman was frightened, covering her sobbing mouth as she cried, begging for mercy. Ignoring her pleas for compassion, several men were gathering rocks and handing them out to one another.

The individual, who was pulling the woman along, held up his arms, ordering everyone to restrain themselves. Heeding his command, the angry mob held their stones in check.

Shoving the woman into the stony wall, he addressed the man in the center of the group.

"Teacher, this woman was caught in adultery, in the very act! Now, Moses, in the law, commanded us that such should be stoned. But what do you say?"

The man, whom the question was being directed, stooped down and began writing in the sand with his finger, appearing to ignore the mob.

Repeating the question, the angry man asked again for an opinion concerning the woman.

Finally rising, the quiet man spoke, directing his response to the entire crowd, a tone of absolute authority carrying in his voice.

"He who is without sin among you, let him cast the first stone."

After glancing over the many faces in the crowd, he stooped back down and resumed slowly writing in the sand.

Samuel watched in amazement at the crowds' nimble reaction to these few short words. Grumbling amongst themselves, the crowd slowly began dropping their stones, one by one. And with a quiet shame on their faces, began walking away.

Deeply moved by the event, Samuel yearned to meet this man, to talk with him. He needed to understand what it was that made him seem so special.

Just as he was about to rush over, Samuel's friend came up from behind, cupped a small pile of dirt in his hand, and poured it into Samuel's trouser pocket.

Frozen in place, Samuel could only watch as the handful of dirt streamed in.

Once finished, his friend stepped back. Then suddenly everything disappeared again! The crowds, the stone building, everything! In a flash, Samuel found himself back in the dreamy, empty void, no reference points, and no recognizable shapes.

He spun around looking for his friend, and was devastated to see him moving off in the distance, waving solemnly as he spoke.

"Remember, Samuel, remember."

"No!" he pleaded, watching his friend drift away. "No! Don't go!"

"Your time is at hand, Samuel. Do what must be done."

Before Samuel could utter another word, his friend was gone. Strangely he felt himself being pulled back as well, into some invisible, turbulent whirlwind, wrenching and twisting. Everything flashing by, until finally he felt himself abruptly yanked from his dream and thrust back into consciousness.

Awakening, he frantically looked around his room, disoriented and startled. Shaking his head, he couldn't believe how candid the dream was. It felt so real!

Strangely he noticed he wasn't nauseous anymore, or dizzy. In fact, he felt magnificent! No headaches. No body-aches. He felt better than he could remember ever feeling in his life.

Bouncing from his bed with no effort, he felt young and energized. He glanced excitedly around the room, grinning. Not looking for anything in particular, just amazed at it all, as if this were the first time he really noticed any of it.

"Yippee!" Feeling like a kid, he shouted, full of enthusiasm and wonder, leaping into the air.

Landing, he happened to notice some dirt fall to the floor. His pocket, it fell from of his pocket! The dream snapped into his mind . . . the dirt! The man who saved the woman's life!

"No, that was just a dream!" Samuel said to himself, an eerie sensation prickling up his spine.

"Couldn't be."

Standing still, he cautiously placed his hand into his right pocket, almost afraid at what he might find. Reaching down, his fingers grasped a handful of something, and pulled it out. Holding his fist in front of him, he slowly lifted each finger, one at a time, while peering down.

With his jaw hanging open in awe, he watched as a steady stream of sand trickled out of his palm onto the floor. The entire dream flashed into his mind.

With sand still dribbling through his fingers, Samuel finally understood. He had received his answers . . . and much more.

Standing there stunned, he noticed a dim glow from behind his bed. Breaking from his stance, he jumped over the mattress and edged to the side. There, lying open on the floor, was his Bible, a radiant aura surrounding it. He stared at it for a few seconds, feeling it tug at his heart. Eventually, he followed his compulsion and picked it up. Then slowly, reverently, he read the top line on the page it was opened to:

> *"When Jesus spoke again to the people, he said, "I am the light of the world. Whoever follows me will never walk in darkness, but will have the light of life."*

The revelation struck! Samuel now realized for the first time that his brother was right after all! Absolutely, wonderfully right! There is a God! And now, he realized, there is also hope! The hope that he so desperately needed! And the basis of that hope, he knew, was in one person! One person by the name of Jesus Christ!

Falling to his knees, he wept openly, the sins of his past colliding with his present realization. Deeply remorsed, he repented to God, asking forgiveness for his arrogant life of sin.

After several minutes of heart wrenching prayer, an alarming thought dropped into his mind, and right away, he knew what had to be done. And it had to be done fast.

After quickly paging his chauffeur to come and drive him to his private jet, Samuel hastily grabbed a copied disk of the auditorium massacre, then ran out of his suite door. Time was of the essence. He had to fly back to New York from Geneva; and he had to do it now, before it was too late!

Chapter

49

Ted Ferguson, Chief Editor of HRS News, barged into his staff reporter's office, rambling off names. "Prescott! Dumfries! Lewis!"

Halting at the center isle, he was greeted by twenty vacant desks from both sides of the office.

"Just us, boss," Tim Dopler volunteered from his back desk, sitting alongside his partners, Dexter Jones and Chris Lombard.

Squinting in disbelief, Ferguson slapped himself on the forehead.

"You're all I got?" he thundered accusingly. "Where'd everybody go?"

Tim spoke up. "Remember, boss, last day of the quarter. You sent half the office home before they lost their vacation time. The rest are on assignments."

Cheerfully adding her two cents, Chris said, "And that leaves us."

"Oh, no." Ferguson moaned. "Okay, you three," Ted unhappily announced. "Here's a chance to redeem yourselves for that last fiasco." He shook his head, hardly believing what he was about to say.

"We just got word, John Rex is scheduled to go on World Network News in a few hours. Latest scoop from HEdge is, he'll be making a public statement, supposedly denouncing his faith and volunteering to help track down renegade Christians. Lots a' good news!

"It'll be broadcast from HEdge Command and transmitted all over the world. And we're one of the few news agencies offered a seat up front.

"So the job is yours. All right?"

Dexter responded blandly. "Okay, Boss. But do you think we'll actually be able to report this story?"

"Don't try me, Jones. That whole thing could have been a lot worse and you know it."

"No, boss, it couldn't have been any worse. None at all."

Ignoring Dexter's lingering attitude, Ferguson gyrated his index finger toward all three as he bellowed threateningly, "And listen, if I hear so much as a peep about any of you acting up, I swear, a day won't pass that you'll regret ever knowing my name!"

Dexter smirked, but stayed silent.

Ending the discussion, Ferguson hollered, "So what are you waiting for? Get out of here! You have a story to report. Go do it!"

Watching them head to the door, Ted wondered if he was doing the right thing, especially after their last run in with HEdge Forces. But he reconciled that there wasn't anyone else to send anyway. And he wasn't about to miss this story. Not on their lives!

Chapter

50

C'mon, Rex!" the guard ordered as he banged the cell door open. "It's time!"

Sitting on his mattress inside the gloomy cell, John looked up at the six encroaching guards. A beam of hallway-light shined through the bars leaving a vertical shadow across his face.

Grabbing him impatiently by the arm, the guard scolded, "Let's go, Rex. You know the score . . . make it easy on all of us." The five other guards stood by in case a little extra persuasion was needed.

Shrugging off the guard's grip, John got up on his own, quiet and reserved, the darkness under his eyes evidence of his fatigue.

At the cell door, he glanced into the face of each guard, hoping for a signal that one was a Christian. But none came. Most didn't even return his stare.

"Praise Jesus," he uttered under his breath for no apparent reason as he stepped mechanically out of his cell into the hallway.

Not moving quick enough, the lead soldier shoved him in the back. "We don't have all afternoon, Rex! Let's move!"

With all of them in the hallway, the six soldiers split up: two in front, two behind, and one on either side. Surrounded, John was marched down the hall en route to the press briefing room while continuing his silent prayers, crying out to the Lord for his family's deliverance from this nightmare.

Rounding a corner, the sound of anxious reporters echoed from down the hall. The volume peaked as they made their last turn and was confronted with a dozen newsmen and women rushing at them, cameras purring and microphones flinging. Each seeking the same crown jewel: a live interview with the mysterious John Rex.

Halting mid way through the hall, the soldiers debated whether to take another route. Just then, a HEdge public relations man hollered from behind the reporters, "Mr. Rex is not here for interviews, ladies and gentlemen. He is here to make a statement to the world, not to each of you! So please, don't attempt to speak with him or converse in any way. He is a prisoner of the state and will be treated as such."

The reporters gave out a collective sigh as they lowered their gear and turned to face the bearer-of-bad-news.

"Why not?" several challenged. "The world wants to know more about this man; they want to know who he is, where he's from; questions not even HEdge has been able to answer."

Standing absolute, he didn't waiver. "The world has managed this long without knowing everything about Mr. Rex. I'm sure it can wait a little while longer."

Suddenly more than a dozen new soldiers appearing out of nowhere surrounded the reporters, forcing them back into the briefing room.

Once the ruckus was over, the six soldiers resumed their march down the hallway with John Rex safely in their hold.

Outside, a limousine screeched to a halt at the curb. Not waiting for the chauffeur, the passenger swung his door open and leaped out.

Running around the back, Samuel jumped over the curb and rushed across the sidewalk toward the HEdge Command building. Halfway there a tall man wearing a sweatshirt with a hood over his head obstructed him.

"Mr. Treppin?" the hooded man asked.

"Yes, what do you want?"

Removing his hood, the stranger looked Samuel straight in the eyes. "Your brother is in terrible danger, can you help us save him?"

Startled, Samuel dropped back a step, wondering who this was that knew so much about him! Seeing the situation outside, several guards poured out of the HEdge Command building to aid their Sector Chief.

Waving them aside, Samuel regained his composure. "That's okay, I'll be fine. Thank you."

The guards moved back, but only slightly, remaining within reach just in case.

Samuel stared into the man's face, and surprisingly, he recognized him.

"Keeyon? Keeyon Webster!" he spoke quietly.

"Yes, Mr. Treppin," Keeyon acknowledged. "I pray you'll help us save your brother and his family."

Tears found their way to the corner of Samuel's eyes as he thought; *this friend would risk his life to save John's. That's love!* Looking up to the Heavens, he quietly declared, "God, if this is the type of people you mold, I want to meet more of them!"

Wiping a tear off his cheeks, he couldn't help but to hug him.

"You're an answer to my prayers, Keeyon," Samuel spoke softly.

Relieved, Keeyon let out a heavy sigh. He wasn't sure what kind of reaction Samuel would give, but it couldn't have been better than this. Staring closely, he could see Samuel's resemblance to John, especially in his eyes. But more than that, he saw an excited joy in his face, the gleam that accompanies the discovery of hidden treasure. Treasure indeed!

"Praise God," Keeyon espoused quietly. "So you've been touched by God?"

"Oh yes," Samuel nodded. "You wouldn't believe."

Keeyon smiled. He could see God's blessings in the Sector Chief's eyes.

"Are you alone?" Samuel asked.

"No."

"Do you realize what kind of danger you could be in? I'm not sure how much protection even I can offer inside that building."

"My faith is not in you, sir. It's in the Lord."

He grabbed Keeyon's shoulder, and smiled, "We'll do the best we can, my friend. God will have to take over from there."

"That's the plan," Keeyon agreed as he waved twenty of his men over from the side street.

The guards took offensive postures as the men approached, lifting their weapons threateningly.

"It's okay," Samuel assured. "They're my friends. I've invited them."

Cautiously, the guards eased their stance while keeping a watchful eye out. In a moment everyone was culminated on the sidewalk outside the HEdge Command building.

"Follow me," Samuel directed as he swung his arm around Keeyon's shoulder, pulling him through the front doors with him. The twenty men trailed behind, with the guards coming up last.

Inside the front lobby, Samuel waved cheerfully to the guard sitting at the security desk. "They're all with me. Class reunion . . . it's been a long time!"

Following standard operating procedures, the guard politely asked if everyone could fill out the guest-register. "I'm sorry, sir. Everyone without a HEdge Force ID is supposed to sign in, if that's all right with you, sir?"

Frustrated, Samuel understood the soldier's predicament. But he also knew they didn't have much time.

"That's fine, it shouldn't take too long," he finally answered as Keeyon began writing a bogus name and address on the check in sheet, as did the following twenty men.

Chapter

51

Exactly two floors above the press briefing room, Roderick Banchard sat poised on the edge of his leather sofa, his eyes fixed on the large screen monitor built into the wall of his executive suite. He clenched a vintage wine bottle in one hand, and a balled up fist in the other as he eagerly watched the world telecast of John Rex's speech.

On the monitor, he saw six HEdge Force soldiers, all dressed in crisp blue uniforms, escorting John through the press briefing room. A dozen thrilled reporters were analyzing and scrutinizing his every step.

Roderick salivated. "Ooooh, this is good stuff! Good stuff!"

The captured evangelist moved across the screen. His captors marched him to the stage and up to the lectern, then abandoned him as they found their seats off to the side of the platform.

Glancing over his shoulder, Roderick clamored to his secretary, "Michael, what do you make of this? Great stuff, Huh?"

The slim secretary was at Roderick's desk, having just organized some folders before getting hooked on the broadcast himself.

"Yes, sir. Pretty amazing. John Rex on television of all things."

Pointing to the monitor, Roderick gloated, "Yeah, and I'm the one who put him there! It was my idea. My idea! Otherwise, he'd still be on the streets terrorizing the world!"

Not quite as enthused but still fascinated, Michael asked, "Sir, is it true Mr. Rex will be denouncing his bizarre faith and even offering to help capture other fugitive Christians?"

Turning to his secretary, Roderick snickered. "Oh yes, and more," giggling, "much, much more!"

Standing beside the lectern, John gazed over the assemblage of enthralled reporters, watching them as they watched him. Their eyes were locked on his every move, totally enchanted with his presence, yet ready at any moment to trounce like wolves for the slaughter.

Still believing for a miracle, John took his mind off them and continued in quiet prayer; the only course of action he had left. A senior official walked up beside him at the lectern and greeted the reporters, and the world, to this special news broadcast.

Glued to their seats, the press listened with rapt attention, their eyes bouncing between John and the speaker.

Ignoring the opening comments, John glanced down to the TelePrompTer. Visibly shaken, he saw his wife and son strapped in chairs with full body harnesses holding them in place. Two armed guards stood over them, while viewing the world telecast from a monitor in front.

After a brief introduction, the speaker announced to the world, "Mr. Rex would like to share a few words," then stepped aside.

His heart racing, John moved reluctantly to the microphone while keeping his eyes locked on the TelePrompTer with his wife and son. As he stepped into position, his prepared speech began slowly rolling across the screen.

Scanning the first line, he was appalled. "*Citizens of HEdge, the mythological figure known as Jesus Christ is a creation of the mind. Such a person never existed, and I apologize for having any part in spreading this ugly lie . . .*"

Closing his eyes in disbelief, John stood in silence. *How could this be, Lord? How?*

He looked at the TelePrompTer again. He saw Matthew squirming in his seat, nervous and frightened. Melody looked lost.

With watery eyes, he switched his attention from his family, to the cameras. Then, ignoring the scripted text on the screen, and realizing any spoken word would bring certain death to his family, he began forming words with his hands, as he communicated to the world via sign language.

A rustle went up in the seats of reporters as they frantically dictated to the world what was happening.

Smashing his wine bottle to the floor, Roderick screamed at his secretary, "What's he doing! What's he doing?"

Rubbing his chin, Michael took a step back from his boss.

"Sir, he's using sign language."

Screaming, Roderick glared. "Huh?"

"Sir, sign language. You know, communicating with hand gestures."

Dumbfounded that he hadn't considered this in his plans, he fumed, "What's he saying then? Can you understand it!"

Stepping closer, Michael peered into the monitor. "I used to know a lot of sign. I had a friend who was deaf, but haven't used it since he moved."

Cursing vehemently, Roderick threatened, "Tell me what he's saying, you idiot, before I shoot YOUR ears off!"

"Yes, sir," he offered meekly, "I love you."

"What!" Roderick screamed.

"Sir, John Rex is telling his wife and son that he loves them."

"Oh," slightly calmer, "What else!"

"He's signing to the world, sir. He's saying something about his God, about Jesus being the way to salvation."

Kicking his secretary out of the way, Roderick rushed to his videophone. He slammed his fingers over its digits before a picture came on screen.

"What's happening down there?" Roderick screamed to the man on the other end. Without waiting for an answer, he spewed, "You're in the control booth, put a message on Rex's TelePrompTer! Tell him he's got twenty seconds to read his script, or his family dies!"

"Yes, sir," the nervous technician responded as he began keying the message in.

While signing to the world, John's attention was diverted back to the TelePrompTer as a new sentence flashed on the screen.

> **You have twenty seconds to read your speech,**
> **or your family will be electrocuted!**

At that, John stopped his signing and lowered his arms. He took one last look at his family: Melody's eyes were closed tight; Matthew was crying.

Weeping himself, he lowered to his knees. Raising his arms in total surrender, he looked up to the heavens, then earnestly and quietly, prayed.

Just then, the doors of the press briefing room thrust open as Samuel Treppin and twenty other men stormed in.

Every reporter in the room spun around in amazement to see the Sector Chief barge in and strut towards the stage. Even the most experienced newsmen sat open mouthed in amazement, caught up in the sudden excitement of having a Sector Chief in their midst. Some managed to regain their composure long enough to refocus their cameras from John Rex to Samuel.

At the sight of the Sector Chief, every soldier in the room followed military protocol by snapping to attention, ready for orders.

Distracted from his prayers, John looked out in amazement to see his brother, Samuel, charging across the room, love glowing from his face. Elated, he sprang to his feet. Glancing at the TelePrompTer, he saw the seconds ticking down; the number "10" flashed across the screen! He only had seconds to save his family!

Terrified, he pointed to the door against the far wall while leaping off the stage and running to it. Cameramen followed as he reached it and swung the door open.

Startling the two guards inside, John bolted through the doorway and rushed to his family. The guards raised their guns reflexively to shoot, but stopped when they saw Samuel come in. Lowering their weapons, they stood at attention, confused, waiting for the Sector Chief's instructions.

With the help of Keeyon and the other men, John briskly had his family's straps unhitched. Then pulled them free, without a second to spare. As Melody and Matthew rose off their seats, a spark ignited under them as a thousand volts surged through the chairs, only inches from their flesh.

Overwhelmed with joy, John hugged his wife and son as they sank into each other's arms, rivers of tears flowing.

"Dad," Matthew looked up to his father, "I love you, Dad!"

Gazing through tear-drenched eyes, John smiled, "Matty, I love you too, son. I love you too."

Turning to Melody's teary face, he cried, "Honey, I love you so much. I missed you more than you could know." She planted her face into his shoulder and cried. He pulled her even closer, effectively shutting out the rest of the world.

Watching his perverse plan unravel right before his eyes, Roderick screamed virulent curses, meaner and more hateful than ever. Michael left the room, knowing this was not a good, or safe, place to be right now.

Sweeping through his tirade of blatant curses, the videophone suddenly chimed. The urgent signal flashed, surprising Roderick out of his guttural ramblings. Cautiously pressing the connect button, he was shocked to see the anguished faces of two HEdge Council members flaring at him.

"Banchard! What are you doing over there? Treppin is ruining everything! Kill him and Rex; kill them both! Now!"

The screen went dead. The two HEdge Council members disappeared.

Furious, Roderick was beside himself with rage. Before breaking through his door to get to the elevator, he tripped the general quarters alarm, setting off emergency sirens throughout the entire building.

War had just been declared!

Chapter

52

His family in his arms, John glanced around the small room. "Keeyon!" he exclaimed, noticing him standing near the door. Releasing his wife and son, John turned to embrace his dear friend. "Thank you, brother. Thank you for everything."

Returning the hug just as vigorously, Keeyon heralded, "It's great to see you too, John! And Melody and Matthew!"

"This is a miracle, Keeyon!"

"God's hand at work," he agreed.

Looking past him, John noticed Samuel standing back a distance, a contented peace covering his face.

John's heart swelled as he walked over to him. "Thank you, Samuel."

Mimicking a salute, "No problem. You've done well, John Treppin."

"Haven't heard that name in years," John said.

"Sounds good, doesn't it," Samuel chuckled.

"Yeah. Not bad."

Samuel smiled as tears glistened around his eyes.

"You know, John, it should have been different . . ."

"But it wasn't," John interjected softly. "Samuel, everything has a purpose, and I suspect this is exactly how the Lord meant it to be."

With a heavy sigh, Samuel confessed, "Yes, and now I can see why you sacrificed so much to tell others about your God."

"Not my God, Samuel, our God."

A tear fell. There was a quiver in his voice. "Yes, John, thank you."

Samuel received him joyfully as the two came together in a solid, heart-warming embrace. After decades of separation from a world's ungodly dichotomy, the two men were once again united.

Suddenly blaring sirens invaded the amity of the room, plucking everyone from their bliss. With a stirring in his voice, Samuel exclaimed, "You have to go, John. Hurry!"

John quickly offered, "Samuel, you can come with us. Join us."

"No. That's not possible; I've got too much to do here. But I've already joined you in spirit, John. And for that, I'm eternally grateful.

"Now go!" he demanded. "Quickly, before it's too late!"

"Samuel, no, we can't leave you like this. Please. You have to come."

Ignoring him, Samuel shouted over the group of reporters congested in the doorway, "Guards! Over here at once!"

Not having to be told twice, every soldier in the briefing room jumped at his command, forcing their way past the news people.

"I want Mr. John Treppin and his family escorted outside. And then I want them freed."

The soldiers stumbled slightly as a confused glaze covered their faces.

Exasperated, Samuel filled in the blanks. "He's my brother, you dummies. Now take him outside to freedom!"

Looking as if a heavy mallet had just popped them over their heads, the guards sluggishly turned to take John and his family.

"But, Samuel," John fought. "You have to come. What will happen to you?"

With a warmth and tenderness, Samuel took his brother's hand. "I love you, John. And I'm proud of all you've done. But now, there is something I must do." Taking a deep breath, he sighed, "Pray for me, John, just pray for me."

Then, forcing his eyes away, Samuel repeated his orders, "Take them outside, now!" He released John's hand.

Being led out of the room, John strained to look back, desperate to convince his brother to come with them, yet realizing the futility of his efforts. Just before rounding the corner, he shouted, "I love you, Samuel."

Then they were gone, with Keeyon and his men following behind.

Chapter

53

Wiping away tears, Samuel readied himself for what must be done. It was his time and he must not fail.

Ignoring the sirens howling through the building, he stepped past the reporters and climbed the stage. Standing behind the lectern, he gazed over all the news people huddled before him, and said a quiet prayer.

Then, with cameras running and the world watching, Samuel Treppin began to speak.

"Citizens of the world, it's time to wake up!"

Each of the reporters began madly dictating notes into their miniature recorders.

"We've been asleep; asleep for so long we didn't even recognize the enemy was in our camp! But now I'm here to tell you, the enemy has moved in and he's taken over!"

With a blood red face, he pounded the lectern, "I'm talking about Satan!!"

The reporters gasped.

"Life used to be sacred, people, we used to hold God as sacred. Then, in all our human arrogance, we decided God was no longer relevant, we didn't need Him anymore, or so we thought. So we cast Him out of our lives.

"Coincidentally, as we so casually discarded our Creator, we also began losing our own self worth, our own value, until now, we've stooped to the point that instead of life being a testimony to the glory of God, it's become a cheap commodity, easy to destroy and simple to manipulate; a testimony instead to the wretchedness of Satan."

The reporters stopped their note taking and listened in awe to the Sector Chief's blistering speech, hardly believing their ears.

Waving a small plastic disk above his head, Samuel shouted, "This recording is an example of what I've been talking about!"

Inserting the disk into a drive slot on the lectern, he pleaded, "Listen to me, world! We've been lied to. We've been denied the truth that lies waiting in the Word of God, the Bible! Find a Bible! Read it! And let God's Word speak to your hearts!"

Pausing before hitting the 'Play' switch, he glanced over the face of every reporter seated before him. Camera lenses' honed in on him. Lowering his tone to a hard, somber beat, he declared, "This is your warning citizens of HEdge. A warning you must heed.

"Turn back to God. Accept Jesus Christ into your hearts before it's too late! The world is on a one-way path to destruction; a self-destruction that is leading us all into the pits of damnation, an eternal hell. But you don't have to go. You can choose life instead of death."

Pressing the 'Play' switch, he finished with a contented smile, "Though I can't speak for any of you, as for me and my house, we will serve the Lord!"

With that, the recording of the New York State Auditorium massacre began playing on every overhead monitor in the room, and for that matter, in the world.

Sitting in the second row, Tim Dopler was startled. "Do you see that? Dex, that's our recording!"

Dexter's mouth hung open. "I don't believe it."

Chris stared ahead, beaming. "That's the recording?"

"Yeah," Dexter answered as his right hand found itself laying over hers. "That's the one you rescued us from."

Her brown eyes sparkled as she leaned over and kissed his cheek. "And I'm glad I did."

A couple minutes into the recording, the doors of the press briefing room burst open with a flood of armed soldiers whipping through.

Samuel shouted, "Ignore them, and keep your cameras running!"

Charging in behind the horde of soldiers was Roderick Banchard, waving a revolver in the air, screaming, "Turn off your cameras! That's a corrupted disk! It's a fake!"

Trapped between the orders from Banchard and their Sector Chief, the reporters didn't know whom to obey, but with Banchard swinging his weapon around, it didn't take long to decide. They all turned their cameras off. All, that is, except Dexter Jones.

"No! Turn them back on!" Samuel countered, shouting Banchard down.

Roderick aimed his revolver. "I am under orders from the HEdge Council to stop you, sir, by whatever means necessary. So please, remove that disk and come down from the stage."

Samuel shouted defiantly across the room, "The HEdge Council is not your answer, people! Only God can make your life complete! Only God can fill that void we all have! I beg you, heed this warning! Turn to God, before it's too late! Men, rise up! Rise up!"

Roderick snickered, "Have it your way then," and pressed the trigger.

Caught mid sentence, the bullet struck Samuel in the forehead. Toppling backwards, his arms flailed through the air as he plummeted to the stage; crashing with a violent thud, face up. He laid silent and still, blood trickling down the side of his head, a contented expression resting on his face; his purpose complete.

Every reporter in the room froze.

Swinging around, Roderick screamed, "Where's Rex? Where are Rex and his family?"

A reporter sitting in the front row managed to answer. "Mr. Treppin ordered his soldiers to take them outside to be set free."

"Free?" Roderick screamed in disbelief. "Why?" But no one answered.

Turning to his soldiers, he seethed, "A dozen of you stay here, cover the place. The rest of you follow me! We're going to catch Rex, and this time he's going to feel my wrath!"

As Banchard and his men stampeded out the door, Chris Lombard squeezed Dexter's lap. "He killed him! Did you see that! He killed the Sector Chief!"

Dexter pressed his hand over hers, fighting to remain calm.

Reeling in her emotions, she nervously whispered, "Did you get it on tape?"

"You bet," he answered.

"Do you think anyone saw us recording?"

"No. We'd know if they did. But I'm turning it off now."

Tim asked, "So what do you think about all that stuff Treppin was talking about, with God n' all?"

Answering confidently, Dexter said, "I think he's right."

"What are you going to do?" Chris asked.

"Find a Bible and read it."

Chris pressed lovingly closer to him. "I'm with you, Dex."

He winked, "I was counting on that."

Chapter

54

Turning back in the direction of the gunfire, John hesitated, fearing the worst, "Honey, did you hear that?"

Pulling his hand, Melody knew what was going through her husband's mind. "Yes, I did, sweetheart," she despaired, "But we can't stop now, we have to keep going."

A soldier called impatiently from behind, "Who's holding us up?"

Breaking from his pause, John regained his stride with his wife and son. Hugging Matthew, he rejoiced, "You have a mighty uncle in Heaven, young man," wiping tears from his eyes, "and he's dancing with the angels right now." Matthew squeezed up close to his dad, basking in his love.

A raging voice rang out from one of the soldier's transceivers, "This is Roderick Banchard! Who's in charge down there? Do you have Rex?"

Whisking the transceiver from his belt, a soldier answered, "It's Lieutenant Ekstrom, sir. Yes, we have Mr. Rex with us."

"Stop where you are! Don't go any further," Roderick demanded. "I've got your position on my scanner. I'll be right there! I want Rex back!"

"Yes, sir." Flipping off his transceiver, the Lieutenant grumbled, "Does anyone know what's going on around here? First we keep him, then we let him go, now we keep him again!" Visibly upset, he raised his arms to halt the group. "Mr. Banchard wants us to wait here. He's coming for Mr. Rex."

John turned to his wife and son. He knew what had to happen, as did every Christian man present. Without a word passing, they all leaped into action as a major scuffle broke out.

With the element of surprise in their favor, the Christians easily overcame the unsuspecting troops, having them disarmed and defenseless in no time.

Charging to the front, Keeyon shouted, "John, bring your family up here," as the other men strapped nylon cuffs around the soldiers' wrists and ankles. In seconds, every HEdge soldier was laying dormant, completely immobile on the floor.

With no time to spare, Keeyon jerked, "Quick! To the elevators!"

Yanking Matthew by the hand, John trotted down the hall while helping Melody keep pace. In seconds, they were loading into two of the six elevators, beginning their long descent to the ground floor.

The ride down seemed to last forever. Finally at their floor, the elevator stopped and the doors swished open. Ready to jump out and escape, the group was thwarted by a dozen HEdge soldiers staring them down with packed guns and murderous expressions.

"Come out with your hands up," a tough looking soldier ordered, his eyes squinting in meanness.

With no alternative, everyone stepped out, dejected, their hands raised above their heads.

Pivoting his gun to the left, the soldier snarled, "Over there, all of you, against the wall!"

Moving along, John glanced over each soldier's face. They looked callous and weathered. Well trained in the brutal business of snuffing out lives. He noticed a soldier standing off to the side by himself, rugged and intimidating, an icy expression covering his face.

The soldier crinkled his gnarly, unshaven grimace into a discreet smile as he formed the sign of the cross over his heart.

Surprised, John took a second look. He saw the soldier nod toward the doors as he patted the cold steel barrel of his rifle.

Cautiously nudging Keeyon on his way to the wall, John motioned back to the soldier. Glimpsing over, the soldier once again formed a sign of the cross over his heart, making sure the two saw him.

With raised anticipation, they followed the rest of the group to the wall, waiting for the right time to act.

"Mr. Banchard, we have them in our custody," the lead soldier announced over his transceiver.

"Very well. We're on our way down."

At that, the mysterious soldier in the rear moved back a few paces. Then, without warning, raised his gun and fired into the ceiling, sending off sparks as pieces of tile and plaster rained down over the crowd.

He shouted gruffly, "Let them go!"

Without hesitation, one of the HEdge soldiers spun around, his gun leveled. But he was too slow. Before he could get off a round, the renegade soldier fired into his legs. He was down wailing in pain before he knew what had happened.

"Anyone else want to take a chance?" the warrior bellowed daringly.

No offers.

"Drop your guns," he ordered aloud. The soldiers obeyed.

He called over to the Christians. "Hurry, get outside while I hold them in place!"

Taking the soldiers' rifles on their way, Keeyon and his men dashed over to their rescuer. "Thanks, buddy. We'll have to return the favor some day."

"Don't mention it. I came east with Captain Riggins." His gritty voice lowered. "I saw Banchard kill her. Lord help him."

Just then, all six of the elevators wisped opened. Immediately recognizing the dilemma, the HEdge soldiers dodged out into the lobby as they opened fire on the group of Christians. Roderick screamed from the rear, "Kill them! Kill them!"

Spinning around to meet his new challenge, the renegade soldier returned the fire, sending barrages of ammo into the vicious onslaught. But try as he liked, the odds were too overwhelming.

Keeyon was first to go down as bullets penetrated his shoulder and left arm. The renegade soldier followed as gunfire riddled through his chest and lungs. In the middle of the firestorm, John screamed as he leaped back, throwing himself over his wife and son to protect them, landing in a heap near the doors.

With the gunfire ceasing, a handful of Christians stood, arms extended in surrender. The rest were scattered on the floor, bleeding and defeated, their struggle ending in disaster.

Treading over some of his wounded soldiers, Roderick sauntered up to where John was laying protectively atop his family.

"Mr. Rex?" Roderick snickered, not really expecting an answer. "Are you alive?"

Surprisingly, John moved. He turned over and locked his eyes on Roderick's lanky body hovering over him.

Holding Matthew tight in her arms, Melody watched as her husband rose, brazen and angry, ready to meet this hellish beast once and for all.

A burning stare shot from John's eyes into Roderick's, freezing him in place. Roderick wanted to turn away, but couldn't, somehow trapped in a penetrating tug of wills.

"You wouldn't stop." John glared as the words spewed from his mouth, "You wouldn't let me go, you wouldn't let my family go, you've killed and maimed. For what?"

Roderick was confounded. He was supposed to be doing the talking, not this mad zealot!

John edged closer. "Life has become nothing but an endless cycle of hatred for you, Banchard!" His jaw ground, "You've been deceived! You've missed the point entirely: it's not hate, Banchard; it's love! Love through Jesus Christ!"

Finishing, "You picked the wrong side, Banchard. And you're going to lose."

"Shut up!" Roderick screamed, raising his gun to John's chest. "Doesn't look like I'm losing now, does it! Just look at yourself! You don't have the power, you moron! I have it! And evil is the power! Evil! That's the point, Rex! And YOU missed it, not me!"

Undaunted, John returned his screams decibel for decibel, "Do you have any idea where all this is leading you, Banchard? Once you've spent your life inflicting terror, do you know where it's all going to put you? Straight into the bowels of hell, Banchard! Straight to hell!"

Weeping, Melody covered her son's face, afraid for what was about to happen.

Banchard fired back an answer, "To hell is right! Where I'll rule along with the master, forever! In ecstasy! Enjoying his power!"

Unintentionally breaking into laughter, John corrected, "No, Banchard, you don't understand, Satan isn't about joy, can't you see that? Suffering, that's what he's about! Suffering! He doesn't want you to join in his pleasure; he wants you to suffer in his pleasure, through eternal damnation! You'll be in agony, Banchard! Absolute agony! Forever!"

Something deep in the recesses of Roderick's mind clicked. John was striking a nerve somewhere, but it was too deep and too late. Roderick's hunger for evil was stronger.

Fighting back against John's words, Roderick screamed in depravity as he pressed the gun's trigger, "Noooo! You're wrong!"

An explosion filled the air. John lurched back, clutching his chest, expecting the end. But surprisingly, there was no wound, or blood!

Glancing back up, he saw Roderick, his eyes propped open in mad hysteria, a stream of blood flowing from the corner of his mouth.

Mindlessly dropping his gun to the floor, Roderick slowly turned to his right, where he saw Lieutenant Thomas Benson crouching in the corner, mumbling excitedly to himself, "I did it, baby, we've got revenge. Now I can join you and my boy in the flames. Yes, baby, we have revenge."

Slowly, agonizingly, Roderick turned back to face John, his tall, sickly frame tilting loosely, ready to collapse.

"Roderick," John pleaded, "don't die like this. Accept Jesus into your life. Ask His forgiveness."

Suddenly in the spirit realm, a dark sickly veil dripping of evil hovered above Roderick, ready, as he stood on the physical edge of his life, waiting to claim him for eternity.

Peering faintly into John's eyes, Roderick closed the deal as he gasped, "I hate you."

It was complete. The veil closed tight around Roderick, clinging, binding him ever closer, invisibly tearing through his flesh and ripping his spirit mercilessly out while painfully slashing his soul to pieces. The agony was more than he could endure. With silence blanketing the room, he let out a shrill scream while crumpling in excruciating pain to the floor, dead, his eternal misery just beginning.

Back against the wall, the still crouching Lieutenant Benson turned his gun to himself. Without further thought, he fired. He was gone.

In the moment of distraction, Keeyon whisked up a gun lying on the floor and pointed it threateningly to the stunned soldiers. He growled, "Don't move!"

Realizing their oversight, the soldiers glanced past Keeyon and saw several other Christian men likewise aiming loaded weapons at them.

At a complete loss, they surrendered.

Keeyon struggled to get up, his left arm bleeding profusely. Staring at the anxious soldiers, he ordered, "Get back in the elevators!"

Without question, they filed in.

Straining to stand erect, Keeyon shouted loud enough for each of the elevators' sound sensors to hear him. "Sixtieth floor."

A pleasant, animated voice returned from each. "Floor Sixty."

The first set of doors closed, and then the second, and so on, until they were all ascending up the elevator shaft. Then, aiming his gun to the control mechanisms along the wall, Keeyon fired a volley of ammunition into each, shattering them. When he finished, they could hear the elevators come to a screeching halt, trapped between floors. It would take some time before they could work themselves free again.

With blood trailing down his arm and bruises covering his cheeks, Keeyon turned and smiled. "Praise God! Let's get out of here!"

Exhausted, John wearily reached down to his wife and son. "Let's go. We're done here."

With joyous sighs of relief, everyone made their way out the front doors of the HEdge Command building, victorious.

Their losses were apparent as they limped and staggered from the building, carrying two fallen comrades with them, including the daring soldier from Captain Riggins' platoon.

Outside, Keeyon made his way over to John and threw his good arm around him. Returning the hug, John asked affectionately, "So, how are you doing, my friend?"

Lifting his chin in a joyous smile, he exalted, "Blessed by the Best!"

"Amen!" John heartily returned.

Gradually taking on a more somber tone, John asked, "Do you think the world learned something today? Do you think they understood?"

Keeyon nodded questioningly, "I hope so, but it's in the Lord's hands, John. Only He knows. But it's my prayer millions received the Lord into their hearts."

"Yeah. Mine too."

Seeing the blood trickling down Keeyon's arm, Melody tore off some cloth from his sleeve and covered the wound tight, just to hold until they could get some medical attention.

"Are you all right?" she asked with concern.

"Melody, I've never felt better! Thank you, sister."

Feeling the joy of the Spirit in him, John began to chuckle, as did Melody and Keeyon. The burden of the battle was lifted as they dragged their motley group across the sidewalk to the subway entrance on the other side. Escape had finally come, and everyone was relieved for it, if not slightly worn from the experience.

Young Matthew stayed close by his father's side, walking tall for his eleven-year-old frame, tougher and wiser from the experience and more than ever happy to be a child of the Most High God!

Amen!

Epilogue

Though this story is fiction and is set in a future that none but our Lord truly knows, we are implored to open our eyes to the pain and misery Christians across the globe are now enduring on behalf of their faith. Most of us can only imagine the horrors our brothers and sisters in Christ are experiencing because of their strong convictions. Forced to worship in secret underground churches or to live under threat of torture or death for not converting to another religion; these believers are often paying the ultimate price for their faith.

As Edmund Burke (1729-97) proclaimed, "The only thing necessary for the triumph of evil is for good men to do nothing." It is long past time for the silent cries of modern day Christian martyrdom to be heard. Men and women of faith must learn the painful truths of the scourged lives so many of our Church members are living under. We must speak out against these atrocities, bring political capital to their cause, and pray for the Lord to ease their pain and heal their broken hearts.

To learn more about this present day tragedy, please take the time to read one of the following books. Then, before writing your Congressman or your newspaper editor, drop to your knees and pray for your Christian brothers and sisters across the globe.

Their Blood Cries Out by Paul Marshall with Lela Gilbert; Word Publishing

Jesus Freaks, dc Talk and The Voice of the Martyrs; Albury Publishing

The New Foxe's Book of Martyrs, by John Foxe, Rewritten and updated by Harold J. Chadwick, Bridge-Logos Publishers.

About the Author

Published in over twenty issues of the *Washington Times* newspaper, in a trade book and magazine, Jeff Ovall has also been interviewed and quoted in several *Navy Times* newspapers. This is his first novel. He has served in the United States Coast Guard for the past twenty-four years. He and his wife, Debra, have two teenage children and reside outside Washington, D.C.

Printed in the United States
5400